Behind Decorum's Veil

Ukrainian Short Fiction in English

Behind Decorum's Veil

Selected Prose Fiction

by

Ivan Franko

Translslated by Roma Franko
Edited by Sonia Morris

Language Lanterns Publications
2006

Library and Archives Cataloguing in Publication Data

Franko, Ivan, 1856-1914
 Behind Decorum's Veil: selected prose fiction / by Ivan Franko ; translated by Roma Franko ; edited by Sonia Morris

(Ukrainian short fiction in English)
Translation of two short stories: Dlia domashnoho ohnyshcha and Osnovy suspilnosty.
ISBN 0-9683899-9-6

I. Franko, Roma Z. II Morris, Sonia V. III Title. IV. Series

PG3948.F7B44-9-6   891.7'932   C2005-90702-4

All rights reserved. No part of this publication may be reproduced or transmitted in any form or by any means, electronic or mechanical, including photocopy, recording, or any information storage and retrieval system, without permission in writing from the publisher, except for brief passages quoted by a reviewer in a newspaper or magazine.

Series design concept: © Roma Franko and Sonia Morris
Translations: © Roma Franko and Sonia Morris
Editorial and Technical Assistance: Paul Cipywnyk

© 2006 Language Lanterns Publications
website: www.languagelanterns.com

This publication has been funded in part by
Roman W. Franko and Ivan S. Franko, the sons of the translator.

Printed and bound in Canada by
Hignell Printing Ltd., Winnipeg

Contents

Introduction

For the Home Hearth   9

Pillars of Society   169

Glossary   407
    The words in the Glossary are marked by an asterisk the first time they appear in a story

Ivan Franko
(1856-1916)

Ivan Franko, Ukraine's greatest man of letters, was born in the county of Drohobych in *Halychyna, Western Ukraine. The gifted son of a village blacksmith, he studied classical philology and Ukrainian language and literature at the University of Lviv, began work on his doctorate at the University of Chernivtsi in 1891, and completed it with distinction at the University of Vienna in 1893; however, because of his involvement in radical socialist movements for which he was imprisoned three times as a young man, he was denied a tenured appointment to the university in Lviv that now bears his name.

A man of prodigious talents and an indefatigable worker, his literary and scholarly output fills more than fifty volumes. He wrote lyrical and philosophical poetry, short stories, novellas, novels, and dramas; articles devoted to Ukrainian, Slavic, and Western European literary criticism, theory and history; studies pertaining to Ukrainian linguistics, folklore and ethnography; detailed analyses of old and medieval Ukrainian literature; and treatises in which he expounded his philosophical, sociological, political and economic points of view. He served as editor and publisher of Ukrainian literary journals, and of Ukrainian, Polish, and German newspapers. A prolific translator, he worked with numerous ancient and contemporary languages and became known as "the golden bridge" between Ukrainian and world literatures.

In recognition of Franko's invaluable contributions to Ukrainian literature and culture, and of his championing of universal human rights, he has been referred to as the "Ukrainian Moses" who toiled to lead his people to the promised land of freedom envisaged by the renowned Ukrainian poet *Taras Shevchenko.

* * *

Franko attributed his passionate commitment to "stilling the evil of the day" and ameliorating the lot of the common people to his own lowly peasant origins. In his literary works and his scholarly and journalistic articles he expounded the sociopolitical and economic positions that, over a lifetime of study and active involvement in political movements concerned with human rights, evolved from radical socialism to a progressive national democratic position. His intense and self-denying efforts as a writer, scholar, publicist, and political and civic leader were rooted in two personal commandments: a consuming sense of social responsibility and a work ethic of incessant productivity.   .

The themes of the two works in this book reflect the first of these two commandments: the dedication of his talents to the betterment of society. He does not shy away from controversial issues; he views them from multiple perspectives, revels in their rational analysis, and uses the power of language to engage the reader's mind. At the same time, his imaginative storytelling, fuelled by a burning desire to encompass the full spectrum of human existence in his writing, touches the reader's heart. Indeed, his masterful portryal of the frailties of the protagonists in his stories endows even the perpetrators of the most heinous crimes with a modicum of humanness and evokes a measure of understanding, even sympathy, on the part of the reader.

If it were not for the second commandment of unremitting intellectual activity, Franko's literary legacy would be sadly diminished. Unfortunately, however, some of his most powerful and moving stories were written with feverish haste under difficult personal circumstances and often did not enjoy the benefit of editorial scrutiny. A review of the texts prompted the correction of several minor problems of logical flow and the reduction of geographical details to those essential to the plot.

The themes and subject matter of the two novellas in this book are not fictional; they depict real events that are documented in transcriptions of the criminal trials in which they culminated. From 1887 to 1897, the decade during which *For the Home Hearth* and *Pillars of Society* were written, Franko worked as a journalist for the *Lviv Courier* (1883-1926), a liberal Polish daily that supported both Polish and Ukrainian democratic movements in Halychyna. The landmark court cases to which he was assigned stirred his profound sense of social justice and moved him to illuminate the socio-economic backdrop of the crimes and the motivations of their perpetrators.

As Franko explores the social, economic, and philosophical contexts of the protagonists' thoughts and actions, he delineates a realistic, disturbing, and unforgettable panorama of the social strata of the society in which he lived. His sharpest barbs are directed at the moral decadence and insensitivity of the most powerful echelons of that society, a society that Franko strove to change by prodding his readers to rethink the values underlying the systemic social injustice depicted in these two novellas.

Today's readers will readily recognize the persistent social and economic problems around which the stories are constructed. Some may be moved to rethink their views. Others may be moved to action. Franko's passionate cry for human rights, social justice, and democratic reform is as timely now as it was over a century ago. By making his cogent and compelling arguments accessible to the English-reading world Language Lanterns is ensuring that they continue to be heard.

Sonia Morris, Editor

For the Home Hearth

For the Home Hearth
(1892)

In a small, neat, and tastefully decorated salon, two women were engaged in an animated conversation.

They were of the same age and the same height; both were attractive, in the full bloom of their beauty, and both were dressed smartly and tastefully. They were talking intimately, dropping their voices instinctively at times to a secretive whisper, even though there was no one else in the salon, or in the adjoining rooms, or even in the vestibule.

One of them, a voluptuous brunette—with flashing dark eyes, marvellously shaped raspberry-red lips, a youthful, healthy flush on her full, rosy cheeks, and a tiny dimple on her rounded chin that gave her a playfully young and innocent look—was obviously the mistress of the home. Her face and her charming, supple, girlish figure were so youthful, fresh, and artless, that no one could have guessed that she was twenty-eight years old and the mother of two elementary school children.

Attired in a simple, but expensive and stylish housedress, she was busily "putting things in order" in the small salon: removing linen coverings from the soft, plush furniture and the gilded frames of mirrors and paintings, symmetrically lining up figurines and decorative plates on the sideboard, and studiously eyeing how best to position the bouquets of cut flowers that, arranged in delicate filigreed glass vases, were spreading their intense fragrance throughout the room.

After finishing these tasks, she rushed up to a small table inlaid with mother-of-pearl and wound up an old-fashioned brass clock that had drowsed idly for a long time under its crystal cover. In a word, the young mistress was "chasing the emptiness" out of the small salon that apparently had stood closed and unoccupied for some time. The cheerful fire crackling in the fireplace was gradually revivifying and warming the chilly air, as if fine-tuning it to the lively movements, radiant face, and sparkling eyes of the lady of the house.

"My dear Yuliya," she said in a sonorous, strangely penetrating voice, "don't be difficult—take off your coat, sit down for a minute! It's true that I'm busy, but then . . . you know, that's the way I am: I can't waste a single moment. I could do all this after dinner, but I know you won't be offended if I do it now."

"There you go again, my dear Anelya! It's precisely because of that . . ."

"No, no, don't go on, don't say: because of this, because of that!" the hostess interrupted her and, covering her guest's lips with her soft white hand, she firmly manoeuvred her into a chair. "I'm sure there is a reason for your visit. And it's just as well that you have come now," she added, pausing momentarily while her friend took off her hat. "Maryna has gone into town, the children are still in school, and we can talk freely."

"But what about your husband," the other lady said with a troubled look, "he is supposed to come home today, isn't he?"

"Exactly, exactly," Anelya replied briskly, "but not until evening. Antos wrote from *Peremyshl that he had to take care of some formalities there."

"Well, if that's the case, it's all to the good! I thought he might be coming home earlier, on the train that arrived at nine."

"What a thing to say!" Anelya cried in mock indignation. "It's already half past ten. If he had travelled on that train he would have been here long ago. Oh, I know him! He couldn't stay away that long." As she said this, her lips and eyes shone with a smile that was half jocular, half sensual.

"Oh, of course! Without a doubt!" Yuliya said. "You've completely reassured me. And now, turning to the matter that I was going to tell you about," she added, instinctively lowering her voice, "well . . . maybe it's nothing, maybe it's just . . . But you know what I'm like. It can be the most insignificant thing, and yet I instantly fall into such a panic, that God forbid."

Her facial expression, her eyes, and her body language attested to the truthfulness of her words. Everything about her hinted at a permanent state of inner turmoil that was not just a passing phenomenon, but an organic, innate condition that flowed from a lack of balance among the individual strengths of her soul, between her feelings and her will, between her desires and her capacity to realize them.

Even though she was the same age as Anelya, equally attractive, and attired in a modish ensemble, she looked at least ten years older than her friend. It was as if the thick blond braids that she wound around her head were pressing down on her low forehead, already lightly furrowed, and on her pale, fine-featured, and prematurely fading face in which her shining eyes darted anxiously. Her hands incessantly kneaded a perfumed batiste handkerchief, and when she spoke, the corners of her lips quivered nervously.

Anyone who looked at her more closely could not help but notice that she did not let her eyes linger on any one object, that she was in the habit of repeatedly, almost involuntarily, glancing around, as if checking to see if someone was listening in on her, and that she unconsciously adjusted the pleats of her dress just as frequently. Even in those moments when she was laughing, or when words flowed from her lips in a torrential stream—even in those rare moments there was an expression of suffering and anxiety on her face, something mysterious and intriguing, like a riddle, and deep, like a mountain lake.

"Of course, of course!" Anelya smiled, chattering away as she reached into the sideboard for a large silver tray adorned with enamelled angels' heads. "What would happen if, for once, my Yuliya did not have a dreadful foreboding, or was not experiencing a deathly anxiety? Well now, calm down, my dear, and tell me: what foreboding is tormenting you this time?"

"You're joking again, my dear Anelya," Yuliya said sadly. "You're fortunate to be able to joke. I guess you have that kind of a disposition. How I envy you! But oh, as for me . . . This time, however, it is not just a matter of having a foreboding, my dear. I greatly fear that it may be something far worse!"

A light cloud flitted over Anelya's face. Still holding the tray that she intended to place on the table, she halted in the middle of the room and looked intently at her friend.

"You want to upset me," she said. And then she added with a smile: "But I don't know if you'll succeed. Today is my lucky day, you know. After a five-year absence, my husband is coming home from his tour of duty. Well, what is it? Tell me."

"For the love of God, my dear Anelya," Yuliya cried. "How can you say things like that? 'You want to upset me.' Someone would think that I envy you your family, that I want to poison your happiness."

"Who knows?" Anelya said with a laugh. "One can expect anything from lonely old women like you."

And, placing the tray on the table, she took out a sizable box filled with numerous multicoloured visiting cards, greeting cards, invitations, and inquiries, emptied it on the tray, and calmly and systematically began arranging these tangible pieces of evidence of a cordial, active, and widely flung circle of social activity. With a truly feminine charm, she scattered them in such a way that in the disorder it was possible to see a certain main theme, even a certain coquettishness.

Yuliya shook her head sadly. "Shame on you, my dear Anelya, shame on you for thinking such a thing about your friend. No, I do not deserve that!"

"Well, what is it that you want to tell me? What's troubling that beautiful head of yours?" Anelya asked, kissing her friend's face and forehead as she sat down beside her. "There, I've done what I needed to do. Go ahead and talk."

"As I have already said," Yuliya began again, taking Anelya by the hand and lowering her eyes, "it may not mean anything at all. We have been alarmed for no good reason so many times before . . . ever since we started this unfortunate business . . ."

"Oh, it must be Shternberg again!" Anelya cried.

"It goes without saying that it is he, and no one else. You may laugh at me, Anelya, but I have an abiding presentiment that this clever Jew will get us into a great deal of trouble."

"Just laugh it off!" Anelya responded decisively with a hard edge to her voice, the voice of a trader who is confident of his well-thought-out mercantile strategy. "What can he do to us? The stone that he would like to bring down on our heads would smash his skull first, and as for us—well, who knows. But no, no, my dear Yuliya, I feel safe on that account; I fear nothing from that quarter."

"Oh, my dear Anelya," Yuliya responded, "a person can never be that confident! There are times when even the smallest detail, a chance happening, can spoil the best laid plans."

"Ha-ha-ha!" Anelya burst into silvery laughter. "We were aware of that from the very outset, my dear Yuliya! He who fears wolves should stay out of the forest! But thus far God has seen to it that wolves have not devoured us. And now, when we have almost liquidated our business, when all the documents relating to it have been destroyed or archived, and all traces of it have been expunged . . .

"No, my dear Yuliya, look at me! Which one of us took a greater risk? Which one of us had more to lose? You have to admit that it was I. But nevertheless, once I hazarded to enter into our partnership, I adhered boldly to my position, did everything that we thought was necessary, and not once—right?—not once did I hesitate. Well, tell me, is this not true?"

"You're a heroine, my dear Anelya, oh yes, a true heroine. That is why I have admired and loved you from childhood, from our school days. And even now I admire you and envy your steadfastness. But you must admit, sweetheart, that I too have not been an obstacle in this whole endeavour; I too have exposed myself and made myself vulnerable—oh, and how!

"After all, it was I who came up with the entire plan. It was I who selected the partners and agents. It was I who made all the connections. I was the soul of the entire enterprise, isn't that right? And even if I was always afraid, and even if I was always on guard, and even if I occasionally saw danger lurking where there was none, it did not turn out badly for us."

"On the contrary, my dear Yuliya, on the contrary!" Anelya said quickly, kissing her again. "But tell me, my cautious little crane, what fatal portents do you espy on the horizon?"

Instead of replying, Yuliya pulled a telegram out of her pocket and gave it to Anelya.

"A telegram!" Anelya cried in surprise as she hurriedly smoothed out the crumpled piece of paper. "From *Philippopolis! From Shternberg. What's he doing in Philippopolis?"

And then, slowly, almost inaudibly, she read the few words contained in the telegram.

"Komme mit Orient-Expresszug. Schicke weiteres Telegramm aus Budapest. David [Am arriving on the Orient Express. Will send another telegram from Budapest. David].*

Anelya turned pale. She sat motionless, but her fingers contracted spasmodically, and the telegram fell to her knees. Her gaze tautened, and the pupils of her eyes dilated. Staring straight ahead without seeing anything, she searched her mind for something that might help her solve the riddle contained in the brief but clearly ominous telegram. And then, not having found a solution to the riddle, she turned to Yuliya.

"What does it mean?" she asked.

"How am I to know? But I feel that . . ."

"Forget those feelings of yours!" Anelya interrupted her almost angrily. "Why has he left *Constantinople?"

"That's precisely what I would like to know!"

"Why is he travelling on the Orient Express? He must be in a terrible hurry."

"That's precisely what is troubling me!"

"Why is he going to Budapest? Why Budapest?"

"It's an utter mystery."

"Why doesn't he state clearly what is going on?"

"He probably does not feel that it is safe to do so."

"But what could have happened?"

"That's the most important question."

"No, that is not what is most important. If something untoward has happened, it is equally important to know exactly where it happened: in Constantinople, or perhaps in . . . Oh!"

At that instant something completely unexpected and out of the ordinary occurred.

The door to the quiet salon opened with a clattering sound, and an elemental force rushed into it, delved into the remaining pockets of cold air, and blasted the fire in the small fireplace so powerfully that the flaming logs crackled and fiery embers leapt like meteors across the room.

It alarmed both ladies, propelled Anelya into the middle of the salon, and gripped her in a frenzied whirlwind, in a grey frosty cloud in which nothing was visible, and all that could be heard were passionate kisses and cries: "Antos!" "Anelya!" And then, finally, sustained, heartfelt sobbing interrupted by paroxysms of laughter.

II

"Antos! You naughty boy! How could you do this to me? You wrote that you were coming in the evening . . ."

"I got away from them! I got away sooner than I had hoped to. And here I am! I'm here! I'm here!"

And Antos smothered his wife's hands, bosom, and lips with kisses.

"But when did you arrive?"

"At nine."

"And you've come home only now?"

"I had responsibilities, my dear Anelya, duties! I had to take my men to the barracks and report to command headquarters. I'm lucky that I got matters settled as quickly as I did."

"You naughty boy! You great big naughty boy!" Anelya repeated with a pout, playfully slapping Antos's arms that clasped her supple waist and held her tightly against his chest.

That "Antos" or "naughty boy" was a tall, solidly built man of about forty, with thinning, slightly grizzled hair, a reddish-brown moustache, and whiskers of the same hue. He was wearing a military greatcoat and a captain's uniform of the Austrian infantry, and his sword was at his side. His face, even though it reflected great fatigue and bore the marks of the long journey he had just completed, exuded an aura of health. His grey eyes were kind and gentle, but his brisk, assured movements bore witness to the military discipline that had become part and parcel of his very being.

Captain Antin Anharovych had just returned from Bosnia where he had spent five years serving in the army. Assigned to Bosnia with one of the first detachments of the occupying army to be deployed, he took part in all the campaigns and battles that resulted in the occupation and pacification of that country, distinguished himself in the taking of Sarajevo and in skirmishes with bands of rebel soldiers that roamed the countryside, and advanced from the rank of lieutenant to captain.

Then, promised a further promotion and a better wage, he voluntarily stayed on in Bosnia for an additional three years, and it was only now, after a five-year absence, that he had returned to *Lviv, to the bosom of his family.

He was assigned to the Lviv garrison, and in the upcoming May promotions he was to be elevated to the rank of major, with a salary that would more or less suffice to guarantee his family's livelihood and future needs. His boldest and most passionate dreams were about to be realized.

"And now you are mine! Mine! My dearest treasure, my precious, my life! After so many years, so many tribulations, so many dangers!" the captain continued in a voice breaking with emotion as he embraced his wife, who was sobbing and laughing in turn. "Now I am yours; nothing can separate us now."

And with their arms still intertwined around each other, they sat down on the sofa.

It was only now that the captain saw Yuliya who, troubled and embarrassed, was standing ill at ease, obviously wishing that, unheard and unseen, she could take wing and fly out of this blissful nest.

"Halt, regiment!" the captain shouted cheerfully. "Who is this?" he asked, turning to his wife.

"Oh dear, I forgot to introduce you—this is Yuliya Shablinska, a friend from my boarding-school days. My dear Yuliya, this naughty boy with the big ugly moustache—you see?—is the Antos that I rattled on and on to you about."

Yuliya bowed slightly and began to put on her hat.

"*Herstellt* [As you were]!" the captain shouted. "Put down your hat! Over here, on the table! Sit down! Anyone who is my wife's friend is my friend as well. A male friend I would probably challenge to a duel, but a female friend is invited to stay to dinner."

Yuliya, obviously growing even more disconcerted, held on to her hat and appeared to be at a loss as to what to do next.

"Captain," she finally said, "thank you for your kind invitation, but today is such a special day for the two of you that my presence here would not be in order. Truly . . ."

"*Gilt nichts* [Not at all]!" the captain retorted in a jokingly threatening voice. "Today my mood is such that I could embrace and kiss the entire world, even the old Jewess on Zarvanytsi who sells boiled broad beans."

"*Fi donc!* [Fie!] Antos!" Anelya interrupted him with a slap on the shoulder.

"Then your friend should not challenge me to be blunt," the captain responded. "Tell her, explain to her, that there can be no subterfuges where I am concerned, that I do not tolerate any opposition. I have spoken, and there is nothing more to be said. Miss Yuliya will stay for dinner, and that's that."

"Ha-ha-ha! But she is not a miss. You see, her marital status has eluded you."

"She is not a miss? What is she then?"

"It would be some great favour you'd be doing her, if she were to remain an old maid just to please you."

"I do not like old maids. So, she is married. That's all the better. We'll detain her here until her husband sends us a summons."

"You're hoisted once again by your own petard, my old sparrow. Madam Yuliya is a widow."

The look on the captain's face was one of great, comical disappointment.

"A widow? I detest widows. Widows are owls, they are birds that foretell evil. Does the widow wish to go home?" he asked, turning to Yuliya.

"I think, captain, that you . . ." Yuliya began, still debating whether to place her hat on her head or on the table.

"Well, in that case, go with God, go with God," the captain interrupted her.

And, springing up from the sofa, he politely assisted her with her coat and galoshes, found her umbrella and, pressing her tiny hand between his sturdy palms, said with a serious mien: "Forgive me, madam, for my jocular greeting. I deeply regret that you were not kind enough to stay with us, but I must admit that you are right. Today I truly would be insufferable in the company of strangers. You are not angry with me, are you, madam?"

"Really, sir!" Madam Yuliya protested.

"And you will come to see us, madam?"

"Most gladly."

"But soon! Tomorrow!"

"Whenever I have time."

"No 'whenevers'! No 'whenevers'! If you do not come tomorrow, madam, I will take it as an indication that you are angry with me."

"Really, sir! How could you think such a thing?"

As Yuliya bid Anelya farewell, she whispered to her: "If anything happens, I'll drop by to see you this evening."

Anelya kissed her and saw her to the door.

It was only now that the captain took off his greatcoat, removed his sword, and tried to compose himself after his intense emotional outburst. But it was not easy for him to do so. He settled in an armchair and looked around the salon, but he could not focus on the objects surrounding him. They danced before his eyes, blended into a grey mass, veiled themselves in a rosy fog, and emitted a wonderful sound that drummed in his heart and made his blood race faster.

After a few seconds, the captain leapt to his feet and walked around the salon a few times, and the moment that Anelya came back in from the corridor, he seized her in his embrace and began showering kisses on her lips, eyes, forehead, and hair.

"My dear child, you'll choke me to death!" Anelya cried lovingly. "Well, it's plain to see that you've come home from a warmer climate. In the past you weren't nearly so ardent!"

"Are you angry with me?" the captain whispered, ecstatic with happiness. His face was flushed, and he held her by the shoulders, gazing into her wonderful, passionate eyes.

"Of course!" Anelya replied jokingly. She twirled his moustache, and then, tugging at it gently, pushed him down on the soft sofa and, settling herself on his knees, wound her arms around his neck, leaned her head against his shoulder, and said: "Well, tell me, how did things go for you over there? What kind of a life did you lead? What made life hard for you? For you did find it hard at times, didn't you?"

"Oh, very often! There were days . . . But why recall those times now, when I am here at your side, with the children . . ."

And he stopped short.

It was only now that this word flew out of his lips, a word that during the past few minutes he had unconsciously been searching for in his mind—a mind both agitated and enervated by a flood of mixed emotions.

"Anelya, my dear!" he shouted with a look of sheer panic on his face. "What's going on? Where are the children?"

"Ha-ha-ha!" Anelya laughed, enjoying the expression on his face. "That's a father for you! He has been home for half an hour already, but he has completely forgotten that he has children; he has even forgotten to ask where they are and what they're doing! Ha-ha-ha!"

"Anelya, for the love of God!" the captain pleaded. "Don't torture me. Tell me: where are they?"

"Shh! Be quiet!" Anelya whispered, shushing him and placing a finger on her lips.

"Be quiet? But why?"

"Because you'll wake the children. They're sleeping in their cradles in the next room. In fact, they finished sucking on their bottles just before you arrived . . ."

The captain jumped up to rush into the adjacent room, but Anelya's outburst of loud, unrestrained laughter stopped him dead in his tracks.

"Oh, you muddlehead, you muddlehead! Did you really think that your children are still being bottle-fed? That they are still the same as when you left them? Fie, shame on you, you old baby! Your children are in school."

"In school?" the captain shouted, beside himself with happiness. "Since when?"

"Since this autumn."

"And you didn't even write to tell me about it?"

"As if I should have had to! A sensible father would have realized on his own that it was time for his children to be in school, but then a muddlehead like you can enjoy a surprise."

Instead of a response—more embraces, more kisses.

"So, they're both in the first grade!" the captain said joyfully.

"I beg your pardon, but they are in the second grade," Anelya responded sternly. "Tsesya is six already, and Mykhas is going on eight. I didn't want to make them study too soon, but I did teach them the basics myself, and so they were both immediately accepted into the second grade. And they are doing ever so well! The teachers simply cannot stop praising them whenever they see me."

"Oh, my precious! My happiness! My darling mummy!" the captain whispered, pressing her tightly to his chest.

Then he abruptly fell silent, and tears, hot tears of inexpressible joy, burst from his eyes. Flinging himself on the sofa and covering his face with his hands, he sobbed like a little child, while Anelya tried to calm him with fresh caresses.

Her efforts met with little success, but then something unexpected happened that helped him regain his composure.

It seemed to him—through the soft, rosy fog of the joyful swoon into which he had plummeted as precipitously as a darting swallow—that something mysterious, enigmatic, and blurred was flying towards him, and then it suddenly dissolved into sounds, into sweet music that reached his ears not as a melody, but as words.

"Mummy, who's crying?" the words rang out.

The captain raised his head and turned his eyes in the direction from where these words were coming.

Two pairs of eyes—dark and shiny, half-curious and half-astonished—were staring at him. These eyes illuminated and enlivened two little faces—softly rounded, rosy-cheeked, and incredibly beautiful.

There was a moment of silence. The children's hearts, sensing that something out of the ordinary was happening, raced and pounded. The mother embraced both the father and the children with a single loving glance, and as for the father . . . words died on his lips, and he could not breathe. Finally, gaining control of himself, he seized both children in his arms, kissed them, caressed them, wept over them, and between hugs and kisses breathlessly gave voice to his overwrought emotions: "Oh, look! Just look at them! Just look!"

"Children—you see?—this is your daddy!" the mother cried.

When the captain finally released his son from his embrace, the little boy stood before him and, staring intently at his face, asked seriously: "So you're our daddy, are you?"

"Oh, you little doubting *Thomas!" the captain exclaimed. "What's all this about? Don't you believe me? Do I have to prove it to you?"

"But why were you crying?" Mykhas asked.

The captain burst out laughing.

"Because," he replied, "when I got here, I did not find either you or this young lady at home."

"So you were crying because you wanted to see us?" Tsesya asked. Perched on his knees, with her eyes fixed on him, she appeared to be on the verge of tears.

"We would have been waiting for you," Mykhas said judiciously. "My teacher would have let me come home from school if I had known that you were coming."

"What do you mean? Didn't you know that I was coming?"

"Yes, I did."

"Oh, we knew a long time ago," Tsesya picked up on his words. "Mother talked about you every single day."

"Come, we'll show you the little blackboard in our room on which we counted the days till you got here," Mykhas added.

"But Aunt Yuliya confused us."

"I knew she'd fool us. She told us that our daddy wouldn't be coming home until evening. That Aunt Yuliya—she's bad!"

"Who is this aunt?" the captain asked in surprise.

"You saw her just a moment ago," Anelya said.

"Aha, that one . . . your friend! So, she is in our home quite often, is she?"

"Oh, every day!" Tsesya said quickly. "Just wait, we'll show you all the toys she has given us. She gave me a beautiful doll."

"She mostly gives me caramels," Mykhas said. "But I don't like her."

"Why not?" the captain asked seriously.

"Because she tells me lots of things, and then it turns out that none of them are true."

"Well, just you wait, we'll punish her! How dare she try to fool you!" the captain said with comical dignity.

And the conversation proceeded from there—a loving, joyous interchange within a family circle, a discourse about nothing in particular, but nonetheless engaging, refreshing for the soul and the heart, giving the mind a chance to rest, the nerves to experience pleasant, soothing feelings, the eye to feast on beloved faces as it catches every nuance of expression, the most minute movements of loved ones, and the soul to find a fresh, secret source of delight in every little detail.

Suddenly the captain leapt to his feet and, in keeping with his habit of switching abruptly from a cheerful tone to a highly dramatic one, shouted: "I'm done for! I'm so unfortunate! It's all over for me! I'm as good as dead!"

The children turned pale with alarm. Mykhas grabbed his father's hand as if he was trying to protect him from some imminent danger.

"What's wrong?" they asked in chorus.

"I forgot the most important thing!" the captain lamented.

"What's that?"

"You see, I brought you all sorts of gifts from Bosnia."

"Where are they?" Tsesya asked.

"In my valise."

"And where is your valise?"

"Hrytsko has it."

"Who's Hrytsko?"

"My soldier. My servant."

"And where is he?"

"That's what I don't know. Most likely he has vanished, fled, deserted me, and taken my valise with him."

Tsesya wrung her little hands in despair, but Mykhas, still holding his father's hand, peered intently into his face as if trying to determine if his father was joking or speaking the truth.

"That can't be!" he finally said in a decisive voice, and letting go of his father's hand, he ran into the vestibule.

A moment later, his joyful cry resounded: "It's here! Your valise is here!"

And, laughing gleefully, he poked his head through the open door and shouted to his father: "You see! The valise is here! Why did you try to scare us?"

"And is Hrytsko there?" the captain asked.

"No, he isn't."

"What do you mean, he isn't? Take a good look. He must be somewhere near the valise."

Accustomed to obeying, and not noticing the look of amusement on his father's face, the little boy retreated from the doorway and vanished in the vestibule.

The others turned their eyes, brimming with happy but suppressed anticipation, towards the door.

A moment later Mykhas reappeared and, looking disappointed, glanced reproachfully at his father.

"Why are you joking?" he asked. "Hrytsko isn't there."

"He isn't? Well, where do you suppose he could be?"

Mykhas thought about it, but could not come up with an answer.

"Well, wait, we'll try calling him." And walking up to the vestibule, the captain leaned through the doorway and shouted in a powerful voice: "Hrytsko!"

At that moment there was a sharp noise and the thumping of heavy feet. And before the children had time to realize what was happening, the strapping figure of Hrytsko, dressed in a military uniform, appeared in the doorway.

"Humbly reporting, captain, I am here."

"And where were you?"

"Humbly reporting, sir, I was in the kitchen."

"And what were you doing there?"

"Humbly reporting . . ."

"Don't report! Speak plainly. What were you doing?"

"At first, I sat on a bench, then I fetched some water, then I chopped some firewood, then . . . then I sat on a bench."

"And who ordered you to do that?"

"There is a certain Maryna in the kitchen, captain. A very strict military type. Even stricter than our non-commissioned officer Fukhtih."

Madam Anelya sputtered with laughter upon hearing these words, but the captain, with the most serious face in the world, continued his interrogation of Hrytsko.

"So, she is vicious, is she?"

"Like a wasp."

"And did you drink any whiskey?"

"Yes, I did."

"And what did you eat with it?"

"Bread and fried sausage."

"And who gave it to you?"

"She did . . . that Maryna."

"Then she must be a good person, right?"

"Like one's own mother, captain."

"And did you quarrel with her?"

"Yes, I did, Captain."

"And have you made up with her already?"

"Yes, I have."

"Well then, go and ask her if dinner will be ready soon, because we're hungry."

"At your service, Captain." Hrytsko saluted and spun smartly to the left. But before he could make a move to go to the kitchen, the door opposite the salon opened, and Maryna appeared in the doorway to invite the master and mistress to dinner.

Hrytsko turned on his heel, spat, and mumbling: "She's a devil, not a girl!" went into the kitchen.

III

The dinner was a modest one, but it lasted for quite a while. Even though the captain's trip had sharpened his appetite, he could not eat. He was satiated with happiness, with the warm, serene, quiet, and animated family atmosphere that he had dreamed about in mountain bivouacs amidst the Bosnian cliffs, in the rain, the heat, and the discomforts of camp life, and later during the monotonous and a hundred times more boring stint of garrison duty. And his happiness, once so distant and so desired, now seemed to him a hundred times more pleasurable, a hundred times more fascinating than he had envisioned in his dreams. The faces, figures, voices, and words of his children crowned this powerful enchantment.

At the time of his departure, they had been little more than infants—noisy children who cried a lot and caused their parents no end of problems and inconveniences. He remembered that back then there had been times when, in the bottom of his heart, he had been glad to escape from the "children's ward" as he called his apartment. And his children had not played an important role in his dreams; they just wandered through them like pale shadows. He had thought about them abstractly, theoretically, but he had not loved them as one loves living beings dear to one's heart.

But now! The very sight of those two beings in whom he sensed a small part of himself, all of himself—the supple little girl with azure-blue eyes and silky, ash blond hair in whose face he recognized his own features, but incomparably more tender and noble, whose every gesture filled him with wonder; the little boy, so unlike his sister, but so incredibly like his mother, with energy animating his round face and lips, resolute and quick in his movements, and with a hint of childish humour in his words—the very sight of them made his breath catch in his chest and imbued him with boundless, rapturous delight.

This ecstatic joy deepened even more his love and respect for his wife, for that woman who was not only marvellously beautiful, but who also had an iron, steadfast character and a superior intellect, and who, left to her own resources, managed to live on the paltry half of the monthly stipend that he was able to send her, to maintain a home, and to raise his children so splendidly. The children's every gesture and every word attested to the fact that, from their infancy, they had been brought up well, wisely, and in an atmosphere of freedom, without undue constraints on their childish natures, and that their mother had carefully attended to the development of their intelligence, their characters, and their bodies.

All these perceptions, feelings, and observations whirled erratically in the captain's head, overburdening his mind, and it was only gradually, in turn, that they entered his consciousness. Nevertheless, he felt unusually stimulated and excited. He talked, joked, started stories and broke them off, laughed and ate without taking his eyes off his wife and children. It was clear that at this moment he wanted to imbibe and experience everything that he had neglected during those long years of service.

It was only after dinner that he began to feel tired. Nature began to claim its due: his overwrought nerves desired rest and no longer obeyed him.

"Do you want to lie down, Antos? Will you nap for a quarter of an hour?" his wife asked him.

"Oh, as if I needed to! What makes you think that?"

"I can see you're tired. Go ahead; I'll put a pillow on the sofa for you."

"But I don't want to! What can you be thinking? Do you suppose I can fall asleep now?" the captain protested, feeling that it would be shameful to lie down and sleep at such a time.

"Oh, you'll fall asleep, yes you will!" Anelya said softly but firmly. "You're exhausted. Come! Besides, why are we even having this discussion? I am in charge here, and I give the orders. *Allons* [Come], forward march!"

"Well, if it is an order from command headquarters, there is no point arguing!" the captain said and, kissing his children on the forehead and his wife on both hands, he followed her into the bedchamber where a comfortable sofa spread with a white sheet and topped with a pillow awaited him.

"Do not stand on ceremony, my child," his wife said. "Lie down and sleep. I'll close the door so that no one will disturb you. And if you should need anything, just ring the bell."

And she walked out of the room, beautiful and ethereal, like a vision, and her words were so composed, so congruent with the harmony prevailing in her soul, that they, in their own right, were capable of having a refreshing and calming influence on her surroundings.

The captain, still standing, watched her leave and, when she disappeared from view, put his hands together as if in prayer and said: "O God! What have I done to warrant all the good fortune that You are showering on me? It is true that I have suffered more than a little in my life, but others suffer a great deal more. Suffering is not a merit in and of itself . . . But then, it seems that happiness is also not doled out according to merit . . ."

And philosophizing in this manner, he took off his army jacket and stretched out on the sofa. Oh, how pleasant! A feeling of tranquility embraced him, and joy filled his heart. He half closed his eyes and lay there like that for a while, delighting in his sleepy state; at the same time, however, the flame of his consciousness was not extinguished, and it illuminated—at times more brightly and at times more dimly—everything around him. But the circle that it lit was small, ever so small, even though it embraced his whole world—everything that was most precious and dearest to him.

The past few years, right up to and including yesterday, years filled with endless suffering, combat, and discomfort, slid like an avalanche into a dark abyss, without leaving a trace behind. The world beyond that circle vanished, ceased to exist. Only his wife's face shone radiantly over him like the sun, only his children's eyes sparkled like wondrously twinkling stars. The modest apartment, comprised of a salon, three bedchambers, and a kitchen, became inflated in his imagination, grew into an immense sanctuary, the dwelling place of a mysterious force favourably inclined towards him.

Slowly, his sense of time and space dimmed, the rosy flame of his consciousness flickered and vanished imperceptibly, and his dreams dissolved into a peaceful, refreshing sleep. But even in his sleep the blissful feeling did not leave him, and when a flame of consciousness—not the previous one, but a new one—once again flickered on the surface of his soul, the captain saw himself as a little boy playing in the same sanctuary that he had envisioned before he fell asleep . . .

It is so still, so warm in the sanctuary. A golden divinity is looking kindly at him. He feels that under this divinity's protection he can play freely, that he will be safe. What is he playing with? Why, it is the immense diamond that had sparkled like a star on the divinity's forehead. The divinity itself has given him this priceless jewel.

Jumping with joy, he throws it up high like a ball, catches it, and holds it in the sun's rays that beam through the windows of the sanctuary and create a golden pond at the foot of the altar. The diamond refracts the rays and casts an enormous rainbow on the opposite wall, filling the entire sanctuary with a luminous iridescence.

He throws the diamond up high again. Drenched with sunlight and flaming with a wondrously sunny lustre, the gem flies ever so high, to the very ceiling of the sanctuary. Unable to take his eyes off that lustre, he stands transfixed, his eyes turned upwards. But even as he is watching it, the gem plunges downward. It rings out resonantly as it strikes the stone floor, and he can hear it roll away.

He lowers his eyes and searches for the diamond on the floor, but he cannot find it. Where has it rolled? His eyes keep taking in ever-larger circles—the gem is not there. And then, his eyes, deceived by their expectations, begin to lose their focus, to search here and there aimlessly, erratically—the gem is not there.

A dull anxiety gradually awakens in his heart: "What have I done? The jewel is worth an entire fortune! Where is it?" And he bends down to the floor, grasps his knees and, distrusting his own eyes, searches once again in the same spot that he has already run his eyes over. There is no jewel. "But that's impossible! Why, it rang out so close to me; it simply couldn't have rolled that far away! But then, who knows?"

He does not dare to raise his eyes to look at the divinity, for he senses that he would meet its gaze, a gaze filled with severe reproach. The sanctuary grows dark; the golden rays that flowed through the window only a moment before have vanished. Distant thunder can be heard. Panic seizes him. "I must find the gem, I must, I must, I must!" the thought keeps flashing in his head, and the incessant flashes cause him intolerable pain.

He falls to his knees, crawls on all fours, strains his eyes—it is all in vain. He can see that he has searched over an immense area, that the walls of the sanctuary are receding from him. But no, here is one wall, and here is another one—it is some kind of a dark, narrow place. "Where could the jewel have fallen? Perhaps it rolled under this bench?"

He peers under the bench. The gem is not there, but next to the first bench there is another one, and farther on there is a sofa, an armchair, ever so many armchairs, cupboards, sideboards . . . There is furniture everywhere. And he has to peer under all of it; he has to move all that furniture, because the jewel must have rolled under it somewhere. And exerting all his strength, he begins pushing the furniture out of the way, moving it and overturning it. He is out of breath and covered in sweat.

He lugs the ponderous burdens, the dust chokes him, but a mysterious power gives him no peace, egging him on: "Look for the jewel! Look for it! Look for it!"

"But I can't!" he shouts in despair, and tossing about violently—tumbles to the floor.

He awakens with a start. Ah! It was a dream! He is lying in a slick of sweat on the sofa, not on the floor. The distant thunder that he heard in his dream was the clattering of wheels in the street. His fatigued muscles created the painful sensation that he was searching for something but could not find it. Lying there, the captain now smiled at the panic that had tormented him in his sleep.

Recently he had read about the power of suggestion. And what had just happened was very similar to that! Lull to sleep all but one faculty, and then push this one faculty with mechanical or psychic stimuli in a particular direction—and in the sleeping person's mind an idea arises, an impetus that, finding no opposition from spiritual faculties, takes complete control of the person.

As he was thinking, his eyes stared at the ceiling, the walls, and the furniture in the bedroom. How odd! The joy that he had felt before he fell asleep had vanished.

His surroundings seemed strange, unfamiliar. It was true that five years was a long time, and it was possible that he had forgotten the colour, the shape, and the placement of the furniture. But everything that he now saw was quite new, attractive, aesthetically pleasing, and expensive. On the walls hung a large mirror and original paintings in gilded frames. His wife's dressing table with its elliptical mirror seemed like an entity that had lost its way and strayed in from God knows where!

Letting his eyes wander over the bedroom, the captain noticed more and more details and objects that struck him strangely, posing riddles in his mind that were not at all easy to solve. He recalled vividly how modestly, even meagrely, this bedroom had been furnished at the time that he had departed for Bosnia. But what he saw here now must have cost a fortune! Why, except for the beds—the wedding beds as he called them—not a single piece of the old furniture remained. Everything was new; everything was much more beautiful, more elegant than before.

Where had it come from?

The very thought was a scorpion. The captain sat up abruptly on the sofa and began looking around the room once again. Now he no longer looked intently at anything, he did not see anything distinctly; his vision was directed inwards, into the past.

He remembered first of all his momentary surprise a few hours earlier when he had found out from the watchman that his wife no longer lived on the third floor, but on the first. Understandably, the apartment on the third floor, for a number of reasons, was not convenient, but to have one on the first floor! The difference in cost was quite significant! He recalled that at the time he had intended to ask his wife about it, but all that had transpired had pushed everything else out of his mind, everything, including that question.

Then he began to recall the letters that she had written to him in Bosnia. As a rule, she wrote once a week, but at times, if something unusual happened, or if one of the children fell ill, she wrote more frequently. At first she had complained that she could not live on the money that he sent her, that she had to do without even the basic necessities so that she and the children could survive. True, she never fell into despair, did not bemoan her fate, did not blame him for anything, but because of that, her calm, almost stifled anxieties cut even more deeply into his heart. After receiving her letters, he walked around as if he had been poisoned, for he was aware that, except for the promise of a promotion, there was no way that he could help her now, no way that he could cheer her up.

After a few months, however, Anelya stopped complaining. One time she wrote to him that she was looking for some work, but he reacted sceptically to her plans, so she stopped writing to him about them. Later, she had mentioned, in passing, that initially she herself had been to blame, that she had not known how to manage her affairs, that she had wasted money, that the cook had stolen from her, etc. But now, poverty had taught her how to economize, and she was becoming convinced that it was not at all as difficult to make ends meet as it had seemed to her at first. The money that he sent her was entirely sufficient for their needs, and there was even a bit left over.

Still later, she informed him that through a happy coincidence she was giving well-paying piano lessons. From that time on, news about her financial situation became increasingly sporadic, more laconic. "We are getting along very well." "I am not sending you our accounts because I do not want to trouble you with them."

This was what she usually wrote on this theme, and her comments were almost always placed as a postscript at the end of an extensive report about the social scene in Lviv, about military acquaintances, formal balls, lawsuits, accidental deaths, and other matters like that.

In fact, during the past two years she had written very little about domestic matters, about the children, and when he had reproached her about this in his letters, she had replied tersely: "What am I supposed to write? We are healthy; we speak of you very often. Besides, you will be back before too long, and then you will see everything for yourself."

She often added that she did not write about everything in detail so that he would have an even greater surprise when he returned home. She attained this goal so well that the captain could not even remember if she had ever mentioned her friend Yuliya who, as it now appeared, was almost a daily visitor in their home.

For some reason, he had not taken a liking to Yuliya. There was something furtive, troubling, in her face, her eyes, her overall general appearance. Her gestures were affected, her voice was unnatural. Organizing his impressions, the captain concluded that Yuliya looked like a woman who had forgotten how to live in decent society. What a contrast to his wife! But then, contrasts attract one another, and the captain thought too highly of his wife to think, for even a moment, that she would allow an unworthy woman to associate with her and her children.

Nevertheless, even though he tried to explain all this to himself, there remained in his heart a sting of disquiet, of the anxiety that was, perhaps, an echo of the terrifying anxiety that he had experienced in his dream. He was still lying on the sofa, smoking a cigarette and staring at the ceiling, when the door swung open quietly—the door must have been opened before, while he was sleeping—and Anelya entered.

"You're not sleeping?" she asked. "Don't get up! I'll sit down here beside you, and we'll chat."

And with a charming smile she pulled up a chair and sat down. Still lying on the sofa, he took her hand and pressed it to his lips.

"How did you sleep?"

"Oh, wonderfully well! Did I sleep long?"

"Probably for about two hours. It's half past three now," she added, looking at a small, elegant gold watch that she was wearing—a watch that he had not seen before.

The invisible scorpion stirred in the captain's chest. Anelya guessed what he was thinking and, laughing, slapped him on the shoulder.

"Well, why have you turned pale?" she cried without any constraint. "Are you going to be up to your old tricks again? Are you going to be suspicious of me, even if you yourself do not know why? Oh, you incorrigible child!"

The captain's face flushed in shame.

"Forgive me, my angel," he said, "I recall that in your letters you often promised me a number of surprises when I returned home. And I truly have found a lot of them . . . Everything here is so new to me, so unexpected . . ."

"And you instantly thought: my wife must be guilty of something!"

"My dear Anelya!" the captain said, fervently kissing her hand once again. "How can you say things like that? I swear on my honour that such a thought did not even occur to me. Surely you know how much I love you. I love you more than life itself. To suspect you of something dishonourable—that would be like taking an axe to the root of my own life."

"Then why did you turn pale when you saw my watch? Tell me frankly. We have not lived together for many years. That time apart may serve as a point of departure for a fresh, happy life, or it could be a dark, yawning chasm that will separate us forever."

"For the love of God, my dear wife, what are you saying?" the captain shouted, terrified.

"You can see that I am not joking," Anelya replied. "I have had time to get to know life to its very depths, to reflect upon it thoroughly, and I have come to the conclusion that if there are to be any secrets between us, any sources of mutual distrust, then it would be better to go our separate ways immediately, because in such a case our life together would be a torment, not a life."

"But my darling! Where are these words coming from? Why? Surely you know that I have no secrets from you."

"And I do not want to have any from you," Anelya said fervently. "I do not want you to be suspicious of me. If you have any doubts about me—tell me frankly. I feel so pure, so righteous, that I do not fear any forthright accusations."

"O my dearest Anelya, my dearest Anelya!" the captain cried, driven to despair by her words. "As God is my witness, I have not accused you of anything."

"But you turned pale when you saw this watch."

And, unpinning it, she placed the watch in his hand.

"Take a good look at it! Read the inscription engraved on it! You can see that it was my grandfather who gave it to me. He was angry with both of us when I married you, but he finally accepted my apologies."

"So he is the one who has been helping you?" the captain exclaimed in astonishment as his eyes glanced about the room.

"We have more than one thing to thank him for, but you know how harsh he can be. Too great a generosity cannot be attributed to him."

It was only now that the captain recalled his wife's grandfather, a wealthy old widower, the owner of several factories and mansions in *Cracow. The old man played almost no role in the captain's memories. After becoming acquainted with Anelya at the home of distant relatives in Lviv, the captain came up against the determined opposition of old Hurter—that was the grandfather's name.

He had wanted to go to Cracow to meet with him, but Anelya dissuaded him, explaining that his presence there would make matters worse, as her grandfather had a violent dislike of military personnel. She promised to try to overcome his stubborn opposition herself, and had indeed managed to do so. As Anelya had no wealth of her own, he gave her only as much as was needed to pay the legally prescribed *officer's bond for her husband, adding that as she was marrying against his will, he would give her nothing more.

And it was in this vein that he wrote a letter, his first and last letter to the young couple: a congratulatory message on their marriage, with an addendum that from this day forward they should cease to know him, just as he no longer wanted to know or to see them, that they should not venture to write to him, or to count on him for anything, because this would cause him great unpleasantness and he would be forced to return their letters unopened. Finally, notwithstanding how he felt, he wished them much happiness, success, and prosperity.

And that was all that the captain knew about Hurter. Too proud and independent to try to curry his favour with pleas and obsequiousness, he took him at his word and lost all interest in him. His military service and domestic life occupied all his time. It is true that Anelya often mentioned her grandfather gratefully—after all, his gift had provided the foundation for their happiness.

"He is not really an evil man; he is wise and generous, but he is strange and very harsh," Anelya often said. "In Cracow he has fallen under the influence of some pious old women, blind tools in the hands of the Jesuits, who are eyeing his wealth. I am firmly convinced that we have no hope of getting anything more from him."

And they had not hoped for anything. They had lived as best they could until the inevitable separated them for five years. And so it was not at all strange that the captain was both astonished and relieved to find out that the old man had made his peace with Anelya.

"Well, you see, you see!" the captain said with a hint of reproach in his voice. "So why become angry and fall into pathos? It is understandable that I was wondering where such luxury had come our way—a first floor apartment, mirrors, mahogany furniture, bearskin rugs, a gold watch—and only my modest stipend to maintain two homes. I wanted to ask you: what kind of a riddle is this? Is that an offence of some kind? But now your words have dispersed all my doubts."

"Do not be too trusting!" Anelya said, once again assuming the stern mien of an investigating judge. "Do not place too much faith in my word alone! Demand some proof!"

"But Anelya, do you want me to conduct a criminal investigation?"

"It would be better for you to do so now while your vision is clear and your thoughts are not prejudiced."

"Are you of the opinion that I might change?" the captain asked with a bitter edge to his voice.

"Listen, Antos," Anelya said, sitting next to him on the sofa and winding her arms around his neck. "Do not be angry with me for what I am about to say to you. I love you, I love my children—our children, Antos! I love you and them more than life itself, I almost said—more than the salvation of my soul. And it is precisely because my love is so strong that I would not want anything to sully the happiness that love can bring. Surely you want that as well, don't you?"

"Who wouldn't want that?" the captain exclaimed, clasping her to his breast.

"Then listen, my beloved! I know all too well that now that you have arrived, sooner or later you will hear all sorts of gossip and stories. I have no doubt that there will be those who, while fawning upon me, will fling mud at me behind my back, try to debase me in your eyes."

"Anelya! How can you assume for even one moment that I would believe such petty gossip?"

"Do not brag about your strength, my strong one, and do not be too courageous, my courageous one!" Anelya said darkly. "No, my dear one, do not say that! It is not a matter of what I assume or do not assume. A wise person assumes everything and does not assume anything. And so it is better, ahead of time, to prevent the possibility of all such assumptions that could defame me in your eyes."

"What do you mean?"

"I'll explain more clearly to you what this is all about. I have known for some time now that evil tongues are blackening me, implying that I am earning my money in a dishonourable way. I have no idea where this foolish gossip is originating. This past while I have not had a wide range of acquaintances, and I have not been out in society enough to find out. Of your former circle of friends, only a few are still here, and they rarely stop by to see me. And so I do not know what it is that I am being accused of.

"As long as it concerned only me, I cared nothing at all about it. My own conscience and the knowledge of my own innocence were enough for me. But now that you have returned, it is an entirely different matter. Stupid gossip like that can poison your life, create much unpleasantness for you, if you are not armed to refute it. And this is exactly what I am asking of you."

"But if you assure me of your innocence, what other proof do I need?"

"Listen, Antos," Anelya said sadly, "do not say that. A man is not a stone. Some things that are very close to the truth may come to light and be used against me. First, give me your sacred word, swear to me on the love of your children, that you will reveal to me, without holding anything back, without sparing me in any way, everything that you hear about me, and that you will demand an explanation from me."

"Anelya, for God's sake, you're alarming me with your solemn tone!" the captain shouted as he sprang to his feet. "Do you think that it is possible for something so terrible and threatening to come up that it would . . ."

"I do not think anything; I am only asking of you what I have a right to ask. And it seems to me that I have every right to ask for your forthrightness."

"Of course! Of course! The most incontestable right!"

"And will you promise me that you will always be frank and forthright with me?"

"I promise on my honour, on my life!"

"And you will not keep any secrets from me, even if you might surmise that their revelation would be painful to me?"

"I promise! Even though I might surmise that my revealing them to you might debase me in your eyes and make me unworthy of your love."

"Such a thought need not even cross your mind, my dearest!" Anelya said, kissing him on the lips. "And I thank you most sincerely for your promise. You can rest assured that I will not abuse your trust."

"And I . . . I, to tell you the truth, do not understand the need for all these formalities."

"God grant that they prove unnecessary!" Anelya sighed. "But in any event, I hope that they will not harm anyone. Well, good. That was the first matter. And now for the second one."

And, opening a drawer in her dressing table, she pulled out an old book with a grease-stained canvas cover. The captain knew this book well. It was the record book that he had bought the day before he married Anelya, and he had given it to her to keep track of the income and expenditures of their small household.

Anelya had very conscientiously tallied her accounts in it on a daily basis. She now passed this book to him.

"Take it and examine my accounts. And here are the receipts from traders and other people with whom I have had business dealings over the past five years. And here, in this pile, are all the letters that I have received. Please, look through everything, investigate thoroughly every detail, every number, every scrap of paper."

"For God's sake, Anelya! What need is there to do this? I believe you without doing any of it."

"No, I insist!" Anelya replied. "Look into everything very carefully, and then you can either believe me, or not. Give me your word that you will undertake this task."

"Well, if it's absolutely necessary . . ."

"It is. And do it today!"

"Fine, I'll do it."

"Good. Thank you! For me, this will be the best proof of your trust in me."

And, kissing him on the forehead, Anelya walked out of the room, leaving him alone with the account book, the receipts, and a small packet of faded letters.

Astonished, and unable to collect his thoughts, the captain paced the room for some time until he finally concluded that his wife was right, and that this unusual scene attested to her great love for him and, along with it, to her prudence and exceptional intelligence. And having concluded this, he began looking conscientiously at the accounts and papers. In order not to interrupt his work, his wife brought his afternoon tea to the salon and once again left him alone.

IV

After an intimate family supper—Aunt Yuliya, about whom Mykhas kept complaining, as if he knew she would not come, had not put in an appearance—the captain began getting dressed to go out.

"Do you still intend to go out?" Anelya asked. "Where?"

"I should drop by the officers' casino."

"Perhaps it would be better if you did not go . . ?"

"But sweetheart, my friends would be offended if I did not show up. Besides, I too would be happy to see some of my old acquaintances."

"Well, you won't find many of your old acquaintances there. Perhaps Redlikh and . . . I really don't know who else of your former friends might be there."

"Redlikh alone will make up for nine others," the captain said seriously as he fastened his sword.

"Well, at least don't stay away too long," Anelya reminded him. "Today is such a special day for me that I do not want to part with you for even a moment."

"Believe me, my dear Anelya, I too am not all that happy about going, but it can't be helped. I have to. You know that a military rank entails all kinds of obligations."

"Well, go then, go!" Anelya said with a laugh. "Someone is apt to say that I am holding you back from fulfilling your obligations in your old age."

If the captain could have seen his wife's face after his departure, there is no doubt that he would have been greatly astonished. Only a moment ago her face, serene, radiant, and animated, had emitted an aura of health and joy, but now it was pale, like that of a corpse, and it reflected a boundless anxiety. Her lips quivered convulsively, as if they were whispering some inaudible incantations in the captain's wake. She found it difficult to breathe.

Overcome by a strange enervation, she collapsed in a chair and sat for several minutes without moving, a living picture of hopelessness and despair. She was roused from her stupor by the voices and the lively footsteps of her children.

"Mummy! Mummy!" the children cried, as they looked for her. "Where are you, mummy?"

Anelya was in the salon, sitting in the dark.

"I'm here! Over here!" she answered. "What do you want?"

Throwing open the door to the salon and letting in a wide shaft of light, the children entered the room and, nestling at their mother's knees, chattered: "We've learned our lessons for tomorrow! Do you want to quiz us?"

"Tomorrow, my dears! I don't feel all that well today."

"Are you sick, mummy? Are you not feeling well, mummy? Poor mummy!"

Tsesya patted Anelya's face. Mykhas kissed her hand. Anelya turned away so that the children could not see the tears welling in her eyes.

"My poor little children," she whispered, stifling the sobs that choked her throat. After a moment she regained control over her emotions and said: "I'll quiz you tomorrow, but now you should go to sleep."

"We don't want to sleep yet, mummy! Let us go to the kitchen. That soldier is there, and he's really, really big, and really funny! He promised to tell us a fairy tale, a most splendid tale—not one that's scary. May we go, mummy?"

"Well, go ahead, go ahead, but you must not stay up longer than half an hour. In half an hour I'll come to put you to bed."

But the children, without waiting to hear her final words, ran out of the room, clapping their hands in glee.

"What will happen to them? O my God, what will happen to them?" Anelya sighed heavily and once again gave way to her dark thoughts. But then, just a moment later, she straightened up—her customary energy was winning out over her despondency.

"What is to be will be! I will hold my own as long as I can, and when the time comes to pay for my deeds, I will do so."

At that moment there was a hesitant knock on the salon door. Startled, Anelya sprang to her feet and opened it.

"Is it you, my dear Yuliya?"

"Yes, it's me," Yuliya whispered. She was bundled up so tightly in a black kerchief that it was difficult to see who it was. "I heard you talking with the children, and then I heard them run out of the room. I guessed that you were alone, and so I got up the courage to knock. I didn't want to encounter your husband."

"He isn't at home. He went to the officers' casino."

"You shouldn't have let him go there, my dear Anelya," Yuliya said, and a look of alarm crossed her face.

"It was impossible to hold him back. But perhaps God will see to it that nothing comes of it. Well, do you have any news?"

"I came to reassure you, my darling. There has been no further word from Shternberg. If something were wrong, he most certainly would have sent a telegram."

"Thank you, my dear Yuliya. I too, from the very outset, did not see any reason to be alarmed. You are right; if something were not as it should be, he would have sent a telegram. Will you have a cup of tea?"

"No, thank you. I dropped in for just a moment. I must be off at once. I don't want anyone to see me here. Besides, your husband might return and find me here. Good-bye!"

"Good night, my dear Yuliya, but if something new should come up . . ."

"Well, of course, it goes without saying that I'll let you know at once. Good night."

And Yuliya, closing the door softly behind her, slipped away like a shadow.

Anelya went into the kitchen where Hrytsko—not so much for the children's benefit as for Maryna's—was relating an amusing tale about a war between a cat and a bear, a tale that elicited loud and frequent gales of laughter.

When Captain Anharovych arrived at the officers' casino, he truly did not find anyone he knew. There were close to twenty officers present. A few were playing billiards, others were having supper, and over by the table where the newspapers were kept, a group was engaged in a loud conversation interrupted by bursts of laughter and raucous military curses.

The captain approached that table and introduced himself to these comrades-in-arms. They already knew about his transfer from Bosnia to Lviv, and some of them had seen him that morning when he reported to command headquarters. They stood around him in a tight, noisy circle, shook his hand, congratulated him on his new posting, and wished him a speedy promotion.

It was not long before the captain became the focus of a lively conversation. They inquired about his tour of duty in Bosnia and about fellow officers who were serving there, and then a few recalled their own adventures in that country. The captain ordered a flagon of wine in order to drink "to brotherhood" with his new friends.

"I see that Lieutenant Redlikh isn't here. Is he serving somewhere?" Anharovych asked.

"Oh, no, he should be here soon."

And truly, Redlikh walked in before the wine arrived.

"Speak of the devil, and here he is!" a chorus of cheerful voices rang out.

Redlikh, obviously accustomed to the noisy hubbub that reigned in the casino, slowly, methodically, and without looking around, first removed his spectacles—without which he could not see three steps in front of himself, and which, having steamed up when he came in from the cold, were completely opaque—placed them on the table, took off his coat, unfastened his sword, and then, pulling out a handkerchief, wiped his spectacles and settled them on his nose.

"Redlikh! Redlikh!" his friends shouted. "A lady over here is asking about you; she says you've known her very well for quite a long time."

Thunderous laughter accompanied these words.

"I know quite a few ladies," Redlikh responded thoughtfully, drawing out his words, "but not one of them need ask about me here. They all know very well where I can be found without having to ask."

"But that lady is me, my old friend," Anharovych called out, rushing towards Redlikh with outstretched arms. "What's the matter? Don't you recognize me?"

"Antos! You old Bosnian!" Redlikh shouted, and they fell into each other's embrace.

The wine arrived, and the entire company set out for the dining salon. Noise, clamour, laughter, and clinking glasses filled the salon. Toasts were given—at first they were serious, but soon they became humorous—and then they began singing and playing the piano.

Anharovych and Redlikh, walking arm in arm, were engaged in a lively conversation. They were old school chums who had begun their military service at the same time and had written their officers' exams together. They shared many memories. Recalling the happy and sad adventures of their youthful days, they laughed at both the former and the latter.

From time to time, whenever a new speaker wanted to show off with a toast or with a vocal-musical performance, they were called to rejoin the gathering. The wine ordered by Anharovych had long since gone the way of all things past; he wanted to order another flagon, but the officers would not hear of it, declaring their right and their duty to host, in turn, their new friend.

An all-embracing camaraderie—the warm, genuine, heartfelt camaraderie that is so often found in military circles—reigned supreme. Captain Anharovych, touched to the quick, was so fired up and so enthusiastically caught up in it that he forgot all about his wife's order—to come home early. But then, after all, would it have been possible to do so? Would they have let him go? Rocking on the waves of the merriment that encircled him, he felt as happy, contented, and unconstrained as he ever had in his life, and in his heart he blessed this day as the luckiest day of his life, a rare day that, more than any other he had known, was replete with pleasurable impressions.

But then something happened, something that a moment earlier no one would ever have expected, something that everyone in this merry company would have considered to be highly improbable, or even impossible, something that today of all days should not have happened in this company. Something happened? What exactly? Perhaps no one could have explained precisely what had happened.

It was as if an evil demon had swooped over the company with invisible wings . . . as if a tiny, disgusting fly had slipped into this harbour of joy and goodwill and, circling over the heads of the men gathered there, had hovered here and there to buzz ever so softly, barely audibly, but nevertheless in such a way that the buzzing awakened a slumbering echo in the hearts of all those present.

And suddenly the candour and the cordiality vanished. A cold, strained atmosphere spread through the salon; furtive, fragmented whispers interrupted outbursts of laughter; oblique looks were cast, first in one direction and then in the other; there were gestures, insignificant, but not at all ambiguous; clipped words, seemingly innocent, flew from one end of the salon to the other as if they were the signals of an agreement relating to a matter that no one spoke about out loud.

What did it mean? Who had started it? With what purpose in mind? No one talked about that, and perhaps no one could have explained it clearly. But everyone felt that it was something ugly and unpleasant, unpleasant to the nth degree.

At first, the captain did not notice anything. Wine and joy roared in his head. But his nerves, exceptionally taut and sensitive, began to sense a change in the comradely atmosphere that surrounded him. And when this perception reached his consciousness, he looked around with amazement in his eyes.

It was as if the entire company had been transformed. Those who a moment earlier had been warmly shaking his hand and assuring him of their friendship, now either sat closemouthed with a smile frozen on their lips, or walked about the salon looking troubled, as if they would have liked to escape but, held back by a sense of decorum, did not dare to do so in an unseemly precipitous manner.

The younger officers, noisier and already somewhat intoxicated, stood in clusters in the adjoining rooms. From there, snippets of cynical stories interwoven with raucous laughter reached the captain's ears. And what was strangest of all, from those clusters, as well as from groups of older men who sat at the table or walked about the salon, distrustful, furtive glances were being directed at him; his eye caught gestures that were in part disdainful, in part compassionate. And even though no one backed away from him, he felt that when he walked up to a group the men discreetly signalled to one another, and the topic of conversation changed.

Slowly, but with increasing clarity, to the point of physical pain, the certainty arose within him that an empty space was being created around him, that he was surrounded by an unpleasant, stifling, deadly atmosphere. What did it mean? He could not figure it out, but it was causing him great discomfort.

In order to collect his thoughts and take stock of the situation, he sat down on a sofa in a corner. His first thought was: "Perhaps it is just an illusion? Perhaps I have once again created a spectre, only to frighten myself with a figment of my imagination?"

He began to look more closely at the men. Well, they were people just like any other people. They were sitting, walking, conversing, smoking cigars, drinking—there was nothing at all unusual in any of that. It is true that one of them occasionally glanced askance at him. Well, why be surprised by that? After all, he was not well known here, and as today was the first time that he was in their company, they were taking a close look at him. Perhaps it was slightly tactless on their part, but all the same there was nothing terrible about it. They were keeping their distance from him, and no one approached him . . .

But no, Redlikh, who had been engaged in a lively, but oddly hushed conversation with several of the older and younger officers, was coming up to him now.

"Why are you sitting all by yourself, my old friend?" Redlikh asked as warmly as ever.

The ice that had been forming around the captain's heart immediately shattered.

"I feel tired."

"I can see you're tired. Perhaps it is time for us old invalids to go home? Those splendid youngsters over there have no intention of leaving as yet, even though it is eleven already. But I have the morning shift tomorrow, so I have to get my sleep."

"Oh, and my wife ordered me to come home early," the captain suddenly remembered.

"Well then, let's go!"

As they were putting on their coats, a few of the older officers came up to the captain.

"Are you leaving already? It is a pity that you cannot stay any longer. It was a pleasure to meet you."

But it was all said so coldly, and with such forced civility. And not one of them asked him to stay, and not one of them invited him to come and pass the time with them more often. The captain felt that an icy crust was once again forming and beginning to press on his heart. The younger officers, engaged in conversations, jokes, and songs, made no move at all to come up and say good night.

The captain was close to tears as he walked away from the threshold of the officers' casino.

"What does all this mean, my dear Hnat?" he asked Redlikh when they were out in the street.

Redlikh, silent and gloomy, was wrapping the collar of his coat around his neck as he walked beside him, and it seemed that he had not understood the question.

"What does what mean?" he asked the captain.

"What happened to bring about such a sudden change? There was such cheerfulness, candour, friendliness, and then suddenly the atmosphere turned so cold, so formal, and there were whispers and oblique glances . . ."

"What are you dreaming about, Antos?" Redlikh exclaimed. "I didn't notice anything like that."

"You didn't notice a change in their mood? That's strange! But you yourself changed."

"My dear friend, stop imagining things! It's true that there was a slight dampening of our spirits when we found out that our colonel's daughter had died. She was a wonderful girl. All the young officers were in love with her."

"Oh, so that's what it was!" the captain cried. "Well then, you should have said so! I was beginning to think that they were avoiding me because I had offended someone in some way."

"Where would you get that idea? I can assure you that *as far as you are concerned*," Redlikh involuntarily emphasized these words, "everyone is in full agreement that you are an exemplary officer, a true comrade—in short, a chap with a heart of gold."

"Do they really think that?" the captain asked joyfully.

"I give you my word of honour. You can trust me."

"But you know there is one thing that surprises me. When we were leaving, no one invited me to come by more often."

"That's not the way we do things here. It's understood that everyone will come as often as he wants to, whenever he has the desire and the time."

"Well, yes, but it is simple courtesy to ask a pleasant companion to stay longer and to drop in more frequently."

"That's a bagatelle, my brother! I would like to think that you would not let such a trifling matter cause you to draw unfavourable conclusions about your new friends. Moreover, I also think your family life and duties at work, and perhaps even your financial means, will leave you with little time and resources to visit our casino all that frequently."

"That may be," the captain said in a somewhat unhappy tone, "but all the same . . . You know how much I enjoy getting together with friends. And over there, in Bosnia, a fellow got so bored, worked so hard, and suffered so much, that he would like to reinvigorate his soul within a circle of friends."

"I doubt if you will succeed in doing that," Redlikh said. "Except for the two of us, none of our old comrades are here, and as for the new ones . . . You know, I myself associate with them only occasionally."

"But they told me that you are there every evening," the captain observed caustically.

"Well, it must have been some poet prone to exaggeration who made that comment," Redlikh said in a strained voice. "On the contrary, I seldom go the casino. The regulars are mainly petty young lords who bet a lot of money on cards and drink heavily night after night, and how is a poor wretch to keep up to that pace?

"You know, Antos," Redlikh said with unusual fervour as he turned to face his friend, "I advise you from the bottom of my heart to do as I do and visit the casino as infrequently as possible."

The captain halted in the middle of the street and stared at Redlikh who, standing tall and erect, and appearing strangely troubled, was trying to avoid meeting his eyes.

"I do not understand you, my dear Hnat," he said. "A moment ago you assured me that they had all taken a fervent liking to me, and now you are saying that it would be best if I did not go there."

"Because it will cost you too much," Redlikh said, trying to extricate himself. "But then, if you're rich, if you have piles of money to throw around . . ."

There was something in Redlikh's words that struck the captain very unpleasantly.

"Hnat!" he cried. "Who do you take me for? Am I a thief, or a counterfeiter, or an absconding treasurer that I would have money to throw around?"

"Well, if you do not have the money, then why does it matter to you whether or not you were invited to frequent the casino? You will be able to go there only occasionally as it is. Why, even today you spent so much money that your wife . . ."

"Fine, fine, I have had enough of your sermonizing, my old friend! Whatever it is that my wife will say to me, she can manage to say quite well without your help. Well, that's enough chitchat for now. Here we are, at my place. You know what, my dear Hnat, I hope you will do me the honour of coming to visit me in my family nest."

"With the greatest pleasure!" Redlikh said hurriedly. "It is true that up to now I did not visit your wife—I do not have to explain the reasons to you . . ."

"Go on with you, you old sinner! You should be ashamed to even think of something like that!" the captain interrupted him.

"But now that you are home, and you are inviting me . . ."

"There is no need for formalities, no need whatsoever! Come and visit with me whenever you have the time and the desire, like the old friends that we are."

Redlikh shook the captain's hand warmly, saluted, and a few moments later disappeared in the nocturnal darkness.

V

"Ah, my dear Anelya! I see that Baron Reuchlingen's visiting card is here. Tell me, what was the nature of your connection with him?"

The captain and Anelya were chatting in the salon. Anelya, busily engaged in some handiwork, was telling her husband about her life, about the children, and about old Hurter. Her husband, while listening to her stories, was looking through the visiting cards scattered on the silver tray on the table. It was when he read the name: "Waldemar Baron von Reuchlingen" on an elegant, embossed card that he started trembling, as if he had pricked his fingers on a nettle.

"The nature of my connection with him? With Baron von Reuchlingen?" Anelya repeated slowly, as if searching her memory for something as she looked calmly at her husband. "There was no connection."

"None whatsoever?" the captain asked in astonishment. "That can't be! Try your best to remember."

"But what is there to remember?" Anelya responded with even greater astonishment. "After your departure for Bosnia, the Baron paid me one or two visits. Oh yes, I remember now that once, on my name day, he became intoxicated and started a quarrel with the officers. I do not know what it was all about, but suffice it to say that he spoiled our whole evening, and he and everyone else had to go home. I did not see him again, and shortly afterwards I found out that he too had been transferred to Bosnia."

"Hmm, so that's the story? I must admit that from what he told me, I would have guessed that what happened was a much more serious matter."

As he spoke, the captain, who was regaining his composure, watched his wife. And then, to his amazement, he saw that as he uttered his final words, his wife's face turned a cadaverous white, and even her lips paled; her work fell from her hands, and her whole body slumped as if she had wilted or received a unbearably painful blow.

"Anelya, my dearest, what's wrong?" the captain cried as he sprang from his chair.

"Wait, wait a moment, someone is ringing the doorbell!" Anelya whispered, and getting up with difficulty from her chair, she dropped her cloth, embroidery cotton, and needle to the floor and ran into the adjacent room.

After a moment she returned, still pale and trembling, but markedly more composed.

"My dearest Anelya, for the love of God, what's wrong with you?" the captain cried, clasping her ice-cold hands.

She sat down next to him, breathing heavily.

"It's nothing, it's nothing!" she replied. "You know, for some time now . . . dreadful thoughts have been tormenting me. It always seems to me that one of our children—O God!—has been run over by a hansom and is being carried home with broken legs and a cracked skull . . . Oh, it's horrible even to think about it! And just at that moment . . . the same feeling . . . gripped me like a pair of pincers . . . it seemed to me that someone was ringing our doorbell . . ."

"Calm down, there is no one at the door. The children will come home safe and sound," the captain reassured her. "For the love of God, you must not get all worked up like this. Are you ill perhaps? Maybe this is a symptom of a more serious illness?"

"No, no, I'm completely healthy, but there are times when I have these foolish attacks."

"No, my dear Anelya, no, these things cannot be taken lightly. It may be the beginning of a severe nervous ailment. You're so pale! It is imperative that we get a doctor's opinion."

"No, it is not at all necessary! It is not!" Anelya responded quickly. "How will a doctor help me? He will tell me what I already know: that it is necessary to have peace, to avoid undue agitation. Just let him try to attain such a state himself!"

"No, sweetheart, we simply must do something! Look, you still have not regained your composure. Drink some water."

"I drank some already. Thank you, dearest. I feel fine now."

And bending over, she picked up the articles that were scattered on the floor.

"Well, as for me," the captain said a moment later, "I must confess my sin to you. At the moment that you turned pale and started trembling, I thought that what I had just said about Baron Reuchlingen had greatly disturbed you."

"About the Baron?" Anelya said softly with a melancholy smile. "Forgive me, sweetheart, but I have already forgotten what it was that we were saying about him. At the moment when you began telling me something about him, my mind was elsewhere."

"I wanted to write to you about meeting the Baron and about my conversation with him," the captain said, "but the very same evening that I met up with him, I received a letter from you in which you informed me that you were very worried because one of our children had the measles, and then the next day I found out that the Baron was no longer alive."

"No longer alive!" Anelya cried.

"So you did not hear about his death?"

"Not a thing."

"Something very strange happened to him, and it still has not been explained."

"O God!" Anelya whispered, sighing deeply, but in that sigh there was more relief than sorrow. And a moment later she added: "Such a young, handsome, wealthy man, from such a distinguished family, so healthy, so strong—whatever happened to him? Was he ill?"

"No, that's just the point—he wasn't ill. He shot himself."

"Ah! Maybe because of love?"

"I doubt that very much. Listen, let me tell you about our last meeting. It will serve to explain why I asked you what had transpired between you and him."

Anelya lowered her head over her work and listened calmly. Her breast rose and fell regularly, perhaps a trifle more strongly than usually, but that undoubtedly was the result of her recent attack of nerves.

"There's no need to tell you what kind of a man the Baron was," the captain began. "He was a wonderful chap, but completely incapable of handling the practicalities of life. Spoiled by his mother, accustomed from childhood to having his every whim satisfied, and insanely obstinate in trifling matters, he did not have a speck of manly determination and character in situations that mattered most. Anyone who met him for the first time took a great liking to him, but everyone who knew him more intimately turned away from him."

Anelya nodded her head in a melancholy manner to indicate her agreement with his assessment.

"At the time that he was transferred from Vienna to Lviv over some disciplinary offence, his mother was no longer alive. They say she died from worry about his profligate and dissolute ways. His inheritance, once quite a considerable sum, was almost all dissipated. Of course, even then, if he had been economical and prudent in his financial affairs, he could have rescued a sizeable fortune from it—the kind of fortune that would make our children and us happy if God granted us even half of it.

"When he was transferred, the colonel of our regiment and all the officers in our corps received a warning about him and an entreaty to associate with him, to prevent him from squandering what was left of his inheritance, his health, and his honour, and, by accepting him into our close, comradely circles, to try and awaken within him the desire to lead a peaceful and virtuous life dedicated to work and to the fulfillment of his duties. You yourself know that we did everything that we could possibly do in this regard."

"He was not very grateful to you for your efforts," Anelya interjected in an aside, with a hint of bitterness in her voice.

"Well, we were not at all concerned about his gratitude. We were interested mainly in the results. And we could take pride in the fact that the results were better than anyone would have anticipated. After a year of our mentorship, the young fellow changed for the better so greatly that it was hard to believe that he was the same person, and his financial affairs took a turn for the better as well. We even received an official thank you from his family. Then our regiment was dispatched to Bosnia, and the Baron was attached to another regiment that remained here. I have no idea what happened to him after that."

"I only know what I've told you," Anelya said in a dull, deadened voice, without looking up from her work.

"A year ago, I was dispatched for a period of time to Mostar on official business. One winter evening I was returning to my living quarters after a lengthy meeting with my superior. As I walked by a well-lit tavern, I heard shouts, curses, and the sounds of furniture being broken and glass being smashed.

"And then, the door suddenly opened and out of it flew a man wearing an officer's uniform, but without his sword and his plumed military cap. He flew out, propelled violently by a dozen or more hands that instantly withdrew, shutting the door behind them. This man was deathly drunk and would most certainly have toppled into the deep mud in the street if I had not caught him and steadied him on his feet."

"I beg your pardon!" this man said when he saw my officer's uniform, and he made an effort to straighten up without my assistance. "Did I perchance offend you, tread on your toes?"

His hoarse, drunken voice seemed familiar to me. I looked at him more closely, but failed to recognize him right off. He recognized me first.

"Ah, *servus* [at your service], my friend!" he shouted as he slapped me on the shoulder. "Ho-ho-ho, Mr. Anharovych, don't you recognize me?"

"Baron Reuchlingen!" I cried, and I extended my hand to him, but he did not shake it. "What's going on?"

"What's going on? Something good. You see, I'm learning to fly. In fact, I just flew out of that shack. Ha-ha-ha!"

"Have you been here long? I had absolutely no idea that you had been transferred here."

"You had no idea?" the Baron exclaimed. "Your wife didn't write to you about it?"

"Not a word."

"Ho-ho!" the Baron shouted loudly. "You have a wonderful wife! She is an angel, not a woman! Ha-ha-ha! Angels like that use iron pitchforks to ram sinful souls into boiling tar."

"Baron," I said sternly to him, "I am taking into account the fact that you are drunk and do not know what you are saying. Otherwise, I would make you answer dearly for your words."

"For my words?" the Baron shouted with drunken laughter. "For my words? But did I say anything? Come now, my dear friend, don't be angry with me. You yourself just said that I don't know what I'm rambling on about. And your wife, ho-ho, *die ist ein solches Kapitel* [she is such a crafty one] that she should be discussed only by those who are sober."

"You're right," I said. "If you have something to say to me, tell me when you are sober, but now you should go and get some sleep."

"Who, me? I should go and get some sleep?" the Baron yelled. "No, my friend, I'm not accustomed to going to sleep at such an hour. But, but," he said in a voice that was suddenly calmer, "lend me ten *rynski! I've run out of change, and that rogue over there doesn't want to extend me any credit. Lend me the money, and you won't regret it. I'll give it back to you tomorrow and, in addition, I'll tell you a nice story about what happened to one nice young fellow and an even nicer married woman, or rather, a grass widow."

"I do not need to tell you," the captain said to Anelya, "that the blood rushed to my head at the words of this wretched man."

Well, I dug out ten rynski and, handing them to him, said: "I am not joking, Baron, it would be best if you thought about getting some rest."

"Tomorrow, tomorrow!" the Baron said as he grabbed the money. "Thank you, my dear friend. And, you know what, tomorrow at about ten o'clock ask for me here, in this shack. You'll either find me here, or you'll be shown where my living quarters are. And don't worry about the money! Even though my relatives have taken me under their guardianship, I can still look after myself."

And he wheeled around to go back into the tavern. But then he halted abruptly and, turning towards me, said: "Perhaps you'll come with me? Come on, we'll have a chat."

I was so thoroughly disgusted with the wretch and with the dirty, dilapidated shack, that I was startled at his words.

"Thank you, Baron," I replied, "but I have to hurry home. I still have some work to do."

"Oh, spit on all that work! Come with me!"

But I had already begun walking away.

"You don't want to?" the Baron called after me. "The devil take you! I'll do without you. But remember, come tomorrow! You'll hear a nice story about your angel, about your beloved wife! Ha-ha-ha!"

"I fled as if wolves were chasing me, and his coarse, cynical laughter rang in my ears all night long. You can imagine the alarm that beset me, the anxiety that tugged at my heart. What right did that wretched drunkard have to call out your name in such a place and under such circumstances? What story was he talking about? What would he tell me the next day?

"Of course, knowing his unstable character, I immediately surmised that it would be some baseness on his part, or some stupid gossip, but all the same—that is how despicable human nature is—I waited uneasily and impatiently for the next day to arrive.

"Do not impute this as anything untoward on my part, my darling," he added after a moment, squeezing Anelya's hand, "it is not that I wanted to see him so that I could hear something unpleasant about you. Such a thought did not even occur to me. My heart was seething with anger at the Baron. I wanted to see him when he was sober and to demand that he explain what he had said when he was drunk, and eventually, to have him take it all back and never dare to talk about you in that manner again.

"At that moment I felt with my whole being how much I love you, how dear and close you are to my heart, and how painfully I was touched, to the depths of my soul, by anything that could cast even the smallest shadow upon you."

Anelya, without saying a word, seized her husband's hand as he was speaking, raised it, and pressed it to her lips. And as she did so, a heavy scalding tear fell on it.

"My dearest Anelya, what are you doing?" the captain cried. "O God, you're crying. What's wrong?"

He leaned towards her with arms opened wide, and Anelya, weeping bitterly, fell into his embrace.

"My dearest," she said in a voice broken with spasmodic sobbing. "How dearly you love me! How good you are, how noble! What have I done to deserve . . ."

"Calm down, my child!" the captain said, kissing her forehead, face, and eyes. "What reason can there be for tears? It was simply my duty. If I had acted otherwise, I would be a dishonourable man."

It took a few minutes for Anelya to compose herself after this fresh attack of nerves, and then she asked the captain to continue with his story.

"There is not much left for me to say," the captain said as he sat down across from Anelya.

"Early the next day I received your letter, and it pushed the Baron and all his drunken ranting to the back of my mind. I no longer felt any desire to see him and, on sober second thought, I realized to my consternation that if I did go to see him he would most likely think that I had come to demand repayment of the money that I had loaned him.

"I decided, therefore, to wait a few days and, for the time being, only to inquire in the tavern as to the whereabouts of the Baron's living quarters. And so, when I happened to be walking past the tavern on some official business, I stepped in to ask about him."

"Oh, the Baron!" the tavern owner cried. "It's some nice barons they're sending us here! He's not a baron— he's a downright thug! I can't begin to tell you how much trouble and money he's cost me! But yesterday he got what was coming to him! He came in with several Hungarian soldiers, and before long he began insulting and provoking them—and they threw him out of the tavern.

"A moment later he came back in; at first he kept quiet, but then he began taunting those soldiers more aggressively. They attacked him, beat him up terribly, ripped off his coat, his sword, and his jacket, threw him half-dead out into the street, and fled."

"And what happened to him?" I asked in alarm.

"I don't really know," the tavern owner replied. "He groaned and cried out in pain for a long time in the street, but as for me, I feared an even bigger ruckus, and so I locked the doors and windows and refused to let anyone in. Finally, there was nothing more to be heard. He must have dragged himself off to his living quarters."

"Where does he live?"

The tavern owner pointed to a nearby hut that stood all by itself surrounded by a fence, and said that the Baron lived there with a soldier who had been assigned to serve him. And then he added that this soldier had gone off somewhere at dawn and had not yet returned. He assumed that the Baron had sent him to fetch some medicine or some liquor.

I walked over to the hut. It was locked. I tried to look in through the only window—it was draped on the inside with a curtain. I tried knocking on the door, the window, and I called out—but no one answered. Finally, I called the tavern owner, and the two of us, using a pole as a lever, managed to lift the door and push it open.

The Baron, in a torn shirt and muddied trousers and boots, was lying on the floor in the cramped room. At first we thought that he was sleeping, but after we pushed aside the curtain, we realized that it was no ordinary sleep. The Baron's right hand still held a pistol, and on his right temple there was a small wound blocked by a mixture of congealed blood and brains. There was also a large pool of congealed blood on the floor. There were no notes or letters.

"O God!" Anelya whispered in alarm at the end of this sad story to which she had listened with bated breath.

"And that brings to a close my story about the Baron," the captain concluded. "So, as you can see, I did not find out anything from him. If he did have a secret, he took it with him to the grave."

Anelya, agitated and unable to control herself, shielded her eyes with her hands and kept on whispering: "It's horrible! It's horrible! To end one's life like that, to die like that! O God!"

"It truly was a tragic fate!" the captain said with real feeling. "Such a wealthy man, so handsome, so well-placed in society, so many capabilities, and to end up like that."

And, after remaining silent for a moment, he added: "I wanted to write to you about it right away, and then I thought: the poor woman, she is back there all by herself, and she has enough of her own problems—why should I put an additional strain on her nerves by writing to her about this incident. But *a propos* your nerves, my dear Anelya! I swear to God that I am very troubled. We must think of something."

"And what will we think of?" Anelya replied sadly. "I know one thing that could help me, but that is the very thing that you would not be able to do."

"What is it? Tell me! What could there possibly be that would be in my power to do for you, but which I would not do?" the captain cried passionately.

"Maybe it does not lie within your power," Anelya said.

"Well, tell me what it is, tell me!" the captain pleaded.

"You know what, my dear," Anelya said, hugging his neck and pulling his head down to her breast. "For some time now, winter and summer, I have dreamed of leaving the city and settling somewhere in the country. There I would find the peace that I will never have here; and what is even more important, engaging in agricultural pursuits—something that I have loved immeasurably since childhood—would restore my nerves and help me regain my equanimity completely."

"To settle in the country . . . to have one's own estate," the captain said slowly, thoughtfully, "well, that certainly would not be a bad idea, even though I knew nothing about your passion for country living until just now."

"Because you never made any attempt to find out about it," Anelya said hastily.

"Perhaps you're right, sweetheart, perhaps you're right. Oh, I would gladly agree to this. I have also cherished such a dream in my heart for a long time."

"Might it be possible?" Anelya cried joyfully.

"Yes, it might be. I believe that one day we will be able to realize it."

"One day?"

"Well, certainly it can't be today or tomorrow—only after I retire. I do not suppose you would want to part with me now and go live in the country all by yourself."

"Oh, no, no, no! Not for any money!" Anelya cried.

"And furthermore, where would you go?"

"Let's buy a small estate!" Anelya whispered in his ear.

"Let's buy it! *Kupił bym wieś, a pieniądze gdzieś* [I would buy you a village, but there is no money]."

"What do you mean—there is no money? We have the money! What about your caution money, your bond? For that sum we could buy the parcel of land that we need, and there would still be enough left to set up the operation of our estate."

"But my dear Anelya!" the captain interrupted what she was saying. "Why even talk about it? You know very well that I cannot touch that bond while I am in the service."

"Oh yes! I know that very well. And I also know that, as long as you can still drag yourself around, you will not leave the military, and your dream will remain just that—a dream. No, it would be best to stop even thinking about all this," she said, her voice bitter and discouraged. "I knew all along that it was pointless to discuss the matter with you."

Pouting, she turned away, and her hands moved swiftly as she plied her needle.

"You're strange, my darling!" exclaimed the captain, who could not keep up with the rapid leaps of his wife's fantasy. "What is it that you want from me?"

"I do not want anything! Do as you see fit!" Anelya answered angrily.

"You're angry already. But you haven't explained to me exactly what you think we should do!"

"But you can see that I am ill, that my nerves are unstrung!" Anelya said forcefully.

"That's the problem, my dove—they are unstrung!"

"I am telling you once again, that as long as we live here, in Lviv, I will not get any better, I'll just keep getting worse. I sense that it is only in the country, in a secluded spot, that I'll be able to revive, be free, regain my peace of mind."

"That's very possible," the captain said.

"Well, if you think so, and if you love me," Anelya said with unusual fervour, "then I beg you, do it for me. Leave the military service, apply for a pension, take back your bond, and let's buy a small estate somewhere in the mountains in the middle of a forest and leave this place behind us, leave it forever."

"But my dear child!" the captain exclaimed. "Do you suppose that it's so easy to do all that?"

"Everything is possible if the desire is there," Anelya said emphatically.

"Well, as for retiring, it is true that not much time is needed for that—it could be done as soon as tomorrow," the captain said hesitatingly.

"Then do it, do it, my dearest! I am begging you from the bottom of my heart."

"But how much of a pension will I have? Will it suffice for us to live on, to raise our children?"

"Don't worry, it will be enough!" Anelya reassured him. "I have figured everything out, you'll see. But can I tell you still another secret?"

"Well, go on and tell me, my stubborn little nanny goat."

"I have even found a small estate that would be most suitable for us. It is in the mountains, not far from a little town where the children could go to school. The buildings on the estate are in quite good condition, and the wooden cottage is very nice indeed. There are thirty acres of ploughed land, including three acres for a garden, another twenty acres of mountain hayfields, and one hundred and fifty acres of pasture and forest. It's a beautiful estate—it seems to have been made for us. And do you know what the price is?"

The captain, his curiosity piqued, stared at her bemusedly. The extraordinary animation that possessed her perplexed him all the more because from the very outset her plan seemed so fantastic, so inconsistent with her practical nature.

But he did not want to argue with her just then, wisely concluding that later, when she calmed down, she would examine her plan more critically.

"Do you know how much this gem costs? Five thousand rynski! Five thousand! It can be paid without giving it a second thought! And on that amount of land, as many as twenty head of cattle can be kept. And in the summer, a huge mountain meadow can be rented cheaply from the neighbouring landowner, and twenty oxen can be fattened up, and ten ricks of hay can be taken off it. Really, Antos, it's a veritable treasure!"

And when the captain, without responding, continued to look at her thoughtfully, she hurriedly began talking again, trembling with excitement.

"You will leave the military service, and then we'll take back your bond, purchase the estate, and move at once to the country. And we'll take the children away from here. I have relatives in Vadovytsi where they will be well taken care of, and they can go to school there. And we'll get to work on setting up the estate, and when we're better off, we'll be able to put aside some small savings from your pension. Am I right?"

"Yes, yes, you're right, you're right," the captain replied mechanically.

"So, you approve of my plan?"

"Completely."

"You'll go along with it?"

"Wholeheartedly."

"Well, that's good! That's very good! That's wonderful! Oh, I love you so much, my darling! And now that it's all settled, you know what? Go to my bedroom right now; you'll find a pen, paper, and ink on my desk, and you can write your petition to command headquarters."

"A petition? What petition?"

"A petition to let you retire from active military service."

"Right now?" the captain asked in astonishment.

"Well, you did agree to my plan, didn't you?"

"Yes, but there's no fire, there's no need to act so hastily. The estate won't disappear in a few weeks, and then again, who knows if it will appeal to us when we look at it more closely? We must inspect it with someone who knows about these things. And in a few weeks I'll receive my promotion, and then my pension will be higher as well."

"Oh, so that's it!" Anelya said, almost in tears. "So your promotion, a miserable increase in your pension means more to you than my peace of mind, my health, my life. All you men are the same! You're always saying: I love you, I love you! But when the time comes to prove your love in even the smallest way, you at once pull out a thousand queries, reasons, stipulations, and arguments."

"You're being unfair, my dear Anelya," the captain said gravely. "As God is my witness, I am prepared to do anything for you, and if I wanted to wait for my promotion, it was only with the goal of securing a better future for you and the children. But then, if you absolutely want . . ."

"Absolutely, absolutely! Do this for me!"

"Fine, I'll go and write the petition right now."

And with a look of resignation on his face, the captain went into the bedroom, leaving Anelya alone . . .

VI

He had barely walked out when there was a familiar light tapping on the salon door, and almost instantly it opened cautiously, and Madam Yuliya crept quietly into the room.

"Good day, my dear Anelya," she said in a soft, low voice.

Anelya, who had not yet calmed down from the emotional upheaval that she had experienced a short moment ago, was slumped in her chair, exhausted, pale, and almost unconscious.

Hearing Yuliya's voice, she jumped up in alarm and dashed up to her.

"Oh, it's you! Tell me, is there any news?"

"All is lost!" Yuliya said, collapsing weakly into a chair.

"What's happened? Speak up!"

"Oh, I can't! I don't have the strength. Here, read this!"

And she passed Anelya a newspaper page on which a telegraphed news item had been ticked off with a blue pencil:

Budapest, December 10. Today, in response to a request telegraphed by the Lviv police, a certain David Shternberg, who had arrived from Constantinople on the Orient Express, was arrested. Shternberg claims to be a trader who conducts business with countries in the East. The suspicions that led to his arrest are still unknown. Shternberg immediately left for Lviv under police escort.

Anelya perused the telegram for an inordinately long time. It seemed to her that with every word she was swallowing a brick, that she was choking, and that there was no way that she would be able to swallow the next one. And when she had finished reading the whole telegram, it seemed to her that she had not understood a single word, that the words, like startled mice in a cage, had scattered in all directions from their natural order and were so chaotically jumbled that it was impossible to make any sense out of them.

She wanted to read the telegram once again, and then again, to memorize it, and yet, at the same time, disbelief was awakening within her, a feeling that this was a dream, one of those terrible dreams that had tormented her so frequently in the recent past.

"Well, what do you think about it?" Madam Yuliya asked.

"What do I think about it?" Anelya repeated, sounding flustered. "What do I think about it? About this?" she repeated, pointing at the newspaper article and gradually regaining her former confidence. "I think it is of no consequence."

"Of no consequence? That Shternberg has been arrested?"

"Well, Shternberg was involved in many businesses, and he could have got into trouble because of any one of them. There's nothing that's impossible—and so, his arrest is not necessarily connected with our venture."

"It does not have to be," Yuliya said, "that's true. But it seems to me that it is. He must have had a reason for sending me that telegram from Philippopolis."

"And what he did was very foolish, because by sending the telegram he betrayed himself; he alerted the police as to where to look for him."

"That's true! My God, how careless of him!" Yuliya cried.

"But you know," Anelya added hastily, "that same telegram tells me that Shternberg's arrest has nothing to do with our business."

"How is that?"

"Well, just think! The police were looking for Shternberg; that means they suspect him; they have some threads that have led them to the trail of his affairs. If it were connected with our business, then obviously we would already have been paid a visit by the imperial authorities; they would have summoned us to make an official statement."

"O my God!" Yuliya cried, feeling ill at the very thought of an official statement.

"Calm down!" Anelya said. "I am trying to prove to you that your fear is completely unfounded."

"Oh, my dear Anelya!" Yuliya groaned. "I don't know if your arguments are valid or not, but the very thought of those terrible official statements . . . Oh, I can't think straight!"

"That's bad, my dear Yuliya," Anelya said seriously. "No matter how unpleasant the thought may be, you must come to terms with it; you have to prepare yourself for every eventuality. First of all, you must burn all the documents!"

"I don't have any. But, just to be on the safe side, I'll look through all the cupboards and drawers one more time."

"And I'll do the same. Secondly, it is necessary to plan the whole thing carefully. We'll talk more about this matter when my husband isn't at home. But just calm down!"

"You know what," Yuliya said, "I'll go away now for a while, and when your husband goes out, I'll drop by again."

But just as she was preparing to leave, the door opened and the captain walked in.

After his conversation with his wife, it took the captain a long time to compose himself. She was becoming increasingly enigmatic and incomprehensible to him. He could not reconcile her nervous spells with her youthful vigour and her almost girlish appearance.

In her letters, Anelya had never mentioned these attacks, nor uttered a single complaint about them; on the contrary, she had always assured him that she was healthy and that she herself was surprised that she was still thriving. Of course, she could have written this in order not to trouble him, but still, her fear for her children—exacerbated to the point of mania and hysterical attacks—could not have appeared today or yesterday; it had to have come on earlier and gradually grown in intensity, and in that case, it was highly unlikely that there would not have been at least a slight hint of it in her letters.

He found her emphatic insistence that he leave the military odd and puzzling, and her plan to settle in the country and leave her children with relatives in Vadovytsi was in direct contradiction to her excessive concern about them.

All these things, considered together, deeply troubled the captain. After all, the fact that Anelya had nervous attacks was indisputable, and her plan to settle in the country and place her children in the care of strangers attested to a derangement in her thoughts and feelings, to an illness of some kind, to an imbalance in the normal state of her soul.

After entering the bedroom and seating himself at the desk, the captain had begun deliberating all this very calmly and carefully, struggling to understand everything that he had seen and heard, and trying to come up with a sensible plan of action for the future. There could be no doubt that Anelya was ill, even though physically she seemed completely healthy. What could the illness be?

The symptoms that he had observed indicated that the illness had been ongoing for some time now. Every longer illness, especially one of the nervous system, would have caused a greater or lesser derangement in Anelya's organism, would doubtlessly have been reflected in her appetite, her sleeping patterns, her digestion etc. But in this instance, no such indications were visible. That meant that the illness was either of a narrowly psychic nature that had its nucleus in an insignificant centre of the brain and therefore had no influence on her ordinary organic functions—after all, medicine knows of such illnesses—or, perhaps . . .

The captain recalled Anelya's letters, written—especially during the last few years—with the greatest equanimity, coolly, in a tone resembling that of a trader or a reporter, intelligently and clearly; that cool tone took on some warmth, colour, and liveliness only in the paragraphs in which she referred either to the children or to him.

No, a woman who was mentally ill, a woman with a psychic illness would not be capable of writing letters like that, and so correctly and so frequently as well. It might be possible for her to conceal her illness for some time, but sooner or later, despite her will, and without her knowledge, her morbid mental condition would have revealed itself in some word, in a leap of logic, in a sentence, or in the recounting of some incident.

The captain diligently searched his memory, but he could not recall anything in his wife's letters that would so much as hint at an illness, even though he had read and reread them very attentively many times.

He loved Anelya with all his heart, with a youthful ardour, especially now after his return from Bosnia; he felt that a confirmation of her illness would be a great blow to him, but still, as he conscientiously examined his heart, he knew that he would not hide from himself even the smallest observation that would attest to her illness. However, except for her inexplicable nervous fits during his story about Baron Reuchlingen, he had made no such observations.

About the Baron!

An alarming, painful thought flashed through the captain's mind. Was it possible that there was a link between his narration and Anelya's nervous attacks? And if so, what kind of a link? Was it possible that there actually was a story about her and the Baron that was concealed at the bottom of her heart? And if so, what was the story?

But no, that was impossible. Anelya had assured him so candidly, so serenely, without a hint of confusion, and with a childlike innocence, that there was no story, and a contrary supposition would be a crime, a sacrilege, a crime committed against his love, his domestic happiness.

No, no! There was no connection between his story about Reuchlingen and Anelya's illness! If it were otherwise, he would have to assume that she was lying, acting out a role, and doing so with unequalled masterfulness. The very thought filled him with indignation, anxiety, and repugnance, and he pushed it aside with all the power of his love . . .

But then, what kind of a story could it be that at the very mention of it Anelya became alarmed, panic-stricken? The captain's thoughts recoiled in fear from flying into a pit of repulsive conjectures where there would be no hope of latching on to a single concrete fact.

No, no, no! Anelya was ill, dangerously ill, all the more dangerously so because both her illness and the reasons for it were a complete mystery. It was necessary to consult a physician as soon as possible, and in the meantime, to do everything one could to keep her mentally calm, to avoid unnecessary irritations, to keep her amused, to make life pleasant.

First, he had to fulfill her wish and write a petition to command headquarters to relieve him of his duties. She had almost pushed him out of the room so that he would write it. Obviously, her passionate insistence that he leave the service as soon as possible was nothing more than a consequence of her illness, a manifestation of a mania, and he would not necessarily have to leave the service all that quickly. But he could write the petition now. Then if the need arose he could say that the petition had been handed in; for who could be sure that, given her condition, another wish, completely contradictory to this one, would not arise the very next day?

Thinking in this manner, the captain took a sheet of paper, a pen, and the ink out of the drawer, and wrote the petition according to all the prescribed conventions. And it was with this document in hand that he had hurried to his wife, to show it to her as proof that he had fulfilled her wishes.

Seeing Yuliya in the salon—she jumped in fear when he appeared and crouched timidly like a trapped rabbit—he did not really look too closely at her but, grateful for the chance happening that had brought Anelya support in the form of a friend, resolved not to let Yuliya go home too soon.

'Ah, Aunt Yuliya!" he shouted joyfully, approaching her and kissing her extended hand. "How are you, madam? Why were you not gracious enough to visit us last evening, my lady? Here you are Anelya, here is the document that we were discussing. Read it and see if it meets with your approval."

And after giving Anelya the document, he turned once again to Yuliya.

"Why are you not sitting down, my lady?"

"I must go. I just dropped by to see Anelya for a minute."

"Now, now, now! 'I must go.' Do not even consider such a thing, my lady. Take off your coat and hat at once."

"Captain!" Yuliya turned to him as she pleaded. "Please do not insist. I give you my word . . ."

"That's irrelevant!" the captain cried, almost forcibly removing her coat. "I am not listening to anything like that. Attractive young widows have no voice in the matter and must listen to someone else's husband if they do not have one of their own. I am placing you, my good lady, under arrest."

"Well, if that's the way it has to be," Yuliya said resignedly as she removed her hat, "then what is a poor woman like me to do? I'll stay, but no longer than ten minutes."

"What is this? An uprising?" the captain asked good-naturedly. "My lady, you must not, dare not, violate the rules of subordination! Please listen to the announcement of the schedule for the day. You, my lady, will remain at our place to assume the duty of participating in our conversation. We will dine together, drink black coffee, rest a bit, and entertain ourselves by telling happy and amusing stories, and only then will we hoist our sails and sail away—I on the expansive waters of military-social life, and you, my lady, to your peaceful widow's harbour. Halt! No opposition, no protests! Those are the orders, and that is how it must be."

Yuliya listened to the captain's words with unfeigned alarm. Being in his company was most unpleasant and troubling for her. Her crouched and pleading figure evinced a sincere desire to remove herself from this home as soon as possible, to hide from the captain's inquisitive gaze, from his powerful and vibrant voice. In his presence she felt enervated, powerless, and helpless.

She turned to Anelya: "My dear Anelya, sweetheart! Ask the captain . . . Explain to him that it is impossible for me to stay; I give my word of honour that it is simply impossible!"

"Nothing of the sort!" the captain interrupted her. "It is too late. Here comes Maryna now with the news that dinner is ready. Right, Maryna?" the captain asked the servant who had just appeared in the doorway.

"Yes, if you please, sir, dinner is ready," Maryna said.

"Have the children come home?" Anelya asked.

"Yes, if it please your lady. Hrytsko is entertaining them with his stories. He's very amusing."

"That means that there can be no more talk of escaping!" the captain said cheerfully. "Am I not right, Anelya, that we will not give this auntie permission to leave?"

"Oh, my dear Anelya, I beg you, don't do this to me!" Yuliya pleaded. "You know better than anybody how unpleasant all this will be for me."

"Ho-ho-ho! You are afraid, my lady, that we might poison you. And such a suspicion cannot go unpunished. Therefore, I must poison you, my lady, with two thimblefuls of Bosnian wine! *Allons enfants* [Come along, children]! Anelya will take the lead, and the two of us will bring up the rear."

"No, my dear Yuliya. Antos is right," Anelya finally said. "Why rush off? Come, we'll have dinner and chat a while; your household matters aren't likely to run away on you."

"Aha, you see, my lady, how wisely command headquarters has arbitrated the matter!" the captain cried, delighted that his wife, who had clearly wavered at first, had finally spoken and taken his side.

"If you please, my lady!" he said, giving Yuliya his arm. And then, glancing obliquely at her and seeing an expression of dissatisfaction and displeasure on her face, he added: "But my lady, why are you assuming such a pose of disheartened innocence? Do you really find my company so intolerable?"

"Oh, you are joking, my good sir!" Yuliya said as she forced a cheerful smile. "On the contrary! It is just that at home . . ."

"Who cares about what is at home!" the captain said. After all, there are no children crying for you, and as for the cats, dogs, and canaries—they will not die of longing for you."

Yuliya turned her head away as if she was embarrassed. They walked into the dining room, where Anelya was busying herself with the soup. The children, quiet but cheerful, and with smiles sparkling in their eyes, were seated in their places.

"Mykhas!" the captain said as he drew nearer to him with Yuliya. "Is this not the lady you wanted to confront yesterday and make answerable for her misconduct?"

Mykhas rose from his chair, extended his hand to Madam Yuliya and said: "Good day, my lady. I wanted to tell you yesterday, my lady, that you are unkind."

"I am unkind, Mykhas?" Yuliya asked in astonishment.

"Yes, my lady, you are unkind," Mykhas said resolutely. "You convinced us, my lady, that daddy would arrive in the evening, but he came in the morning, and we were in school then, and we didn't go to the train station to meet him."

"But I am not to blame for that, my dear Mykhas," Yuliya said. "That's what your daddy said in his telegram."

"Oh, so what if there was a telegram!" Mykhas responded. "In a letter he said that he would be arriving in the morning. Maybe it was a forged telegram."

"Ha-ha-ha! That's a *kozak for you!" the captain laughed. "He knows how to get his point across!"

"But my dear Mykhas, am I to blame that the telegram was forged?" Yuliya asked.

"You shouldn't have believed it," the boy retorted.

"So you're angry with me?"

"Not today, but yesterday I was a bit angry with you," Mykhas said.

"You're my wonderful little boy!" the captain cried, kissing him on the forehead. "Always be like that. If someone is to blame for something, tell him about it to his face, come right out with what you think. But do not stop liking him. Live that way, and you'll never veer off the straight and narrow path in life."

"Now, now, that's quite enough tutelage! Please eat the bouillon before it gets cold," Anelya said.

A lull in the conversation ensued, and for several minutes there was only the sound of silver spoons clinking on china, and the soft rustling of bouillon being sipped.

The strained and unpleasant atmosphere that had reigned at the outset of the dinner, despite the best efforts of the people seated around the table to mask it, gradually began to lift and clear away.

Like a warm and refreshing breeze, the cheerful chattering of the children chased away the clouds that, crawling out of concealed cracks, continually threatened to darken the horizon of this happy home hearth.

Under the influence of these healthy, innocent childish hearts, Madam Yuliya, even though she was seated next to the captain, laughed and began to feel more at ease.

Only Anelya, who, try as she might, was unable to overcome her recent attack of nerves, kept blanching and glancing at the doorway as if she expected a bearer of ill fortune to appear at any moment. And so, a little while later, when there was a rapid, energetic knock on the door as they were finishing their meal, Anelya almost screamed in alarm, leapt up from her chair and, turning to the window so that the captain could not see her chalk white face, pressed her hands to her breast to slow the pounding of her heart.

In the doorway appeared a man in military uniform, someone who had not crossed this threshold for a long time. It was Redlikh. Enveloped in a cloud of frosty air, he walked into the room and saluted. The captain joyfully rushed to meet him and warmly shook his extended hand.

"Good day to you, captain!" Redlikh said. "Good day to you, ladies and gentlemen!" he added, turning to the group having dinner, even though he could not recognize anyone through his foggy glasses. "I was passing by, and so I stepped in to see you," he said to the captain as he wiped his eyeglasses. "I am going on duty, but I have a few minutes to spare, so we can have a bit of a chat. Or have I interrupted you, ladies and gentlemen?" he asked after putting on his glasses and seeing the remains of the dinner on the table.

"Oh, not at all!" Anelya said. "We are almost done. If you would be so kind, lieutenant, please make yourself comfortable in the salon and wait there a moment for us."

"Ah, my respects, my good lady!" Redlikh said as he bowed to Anelya. "Please forgive me, my lady, for not greeting you in the first instance, but my wretched spectacles . . ."

"Oh, I know, I know!" Anelya said with a smile, trying, with a gesture of her hand, to lead Redlikh into the salon as politely and as quickly as possible.

But Redlikh did not move. He had caught sight of Yuliya who, at the moment that he entered the room, had risen from the table, moved to the window, and tried to assume a stance that would draw the least possible attention to her.

But Redlikh thought he recognized her and, obviously curious, approached her.

A fatal power made her turn to face him.

Convinced now that it truly was Yuliya, Redlikh froze and became confused, incapable of uttering even the most common greeting.

Yuliya bowed her head to greet him.

"Ah, so it is you, my lady?" Redlikh said in a low voice.

"My friend, Yuliya Shablinska," Anelya said. "Or do you already know one another?"

"Oh, no!" Yuliya said hastily.

"Oh, slightly!" Redlikh said at the same time and just as hastily.

The captain watched this scene in astonishment. He was about to burst out laughing and, as was his habit, begin interrogating them, when Redlikh, making a sudden and ostentatious military about-face from Yuliya, came up to him and said hurriedly: "Forgive me, captain, but I must take my leave of you."

"What? What? What?" the captain almost shouted in great consternation and, moving closer to his old friend, tried to look into his eyes.

"I have to go," Redlikh repeated in confusion as he checked his watch. "I miscalculated the time a bit . . . There are still some other matters that I must . . ."

"Redlikh!" the captain said sharply. "I do not understand you. You come to see me, to have a chat; you tell me at the outset that you have some free time, and now you are suddenly rushing off."

"Forgive me, captain, but I swear to God . . . I cannot remain any longer."

"But why? Tell me the truth!"

"Another time. I'll tell you another time, but now I must go!" Redlikh repeated pleadingly, moving closer to the door.

"No, this is ridiculous! Redlikh!" the captain spoke emphatically, and the blood rushed to his head. "You cannot do this to me!"

"Captain," Redlikh said decisively and forcefully, when he saw that the captain was blocking his way. "I give you my word of honour that I cannot remain here even a moment longer."

"What does this mean?" the captain shouted, unable to control himself. "Your tone of voice suggests that your intent is to insult me in my own home."

"Take it any way you wish," Redlikh said. "I give you my word of honour that I have absolutely no intention of insulting you, but I cannot remain here even a moment longer."

Hearing these words, the captain looked stunned. He peered for a few seconds into Redlikh's eyes with the utmost intensity, but Redlikh calmly withstood his questioning gaze. The captain could not read anything in the dark depths of those eyes. And then he seemed to wilt and, like a broken man, stepped aside, leaving the way open for Redlikh to go to the door.

Without bidding farewell to anyone, Redlikh walked out. The captain, dispirited and no longer conscious of what he was doing, collapsed in a chair.

For a few seconds, a deathly menacing silence hung in the room. One could hear the stifled breathing of the children and the alarmed beating of the women's hearts.

At last the captain raised his eyes and, unconsciously letting them wander about the room, said in a whisper: "He is gone."

And then, fixing his eyes on Anelya's face, he asked: "What is the meaning of this?"

"I don't know, my dear!" Anelya replied. "I don't understand Redlikh at all."

And, turning to Yuliya who, confused, pale, and trembling, was still standing near the window, she asked: "My dear Yuliya, perhaps you could explain all this to us? What happened to the lieutenant? Why was he offended?"

"I don't know," Yuliya responded barely audibly.

"But do you know him?"

"No, I don't know him at all," Yuliya said, speaking a bit more boldly.

"But he said that he knew you, my lady!" the captain said.

"I do not know where he got that idea," Yuliya replied, once again lowering her voice and staring at the floor.

"Redlikh never lies, my lady," the captain said severely.

"I too am not in the habit of lying!" Yuliya responded bitingly.

"Then what does this mean? What kind of riddle is this?"

"Perhaps Mr. Redlikh mistook me for someone else, for a woman who has offended him in some way," Yuliya said quite boldly.

"Hmm, that could be," the captain said thoughtfully. "He is nearsighted, and such *quid pro quo* incidents have happened to him more than once. But to lose his self-control and go so far as to insult me in my own home in the presence of a guest—no, I would never have thought it possible."

The dinner was finished in silence. Redlikh's appearance and short stay in the room had abruptly transformed the atmosphere in it. The spontaneity, joy, and informality vanished completely. Disheartened and downcast, they all sat without saying a word. Even the children, saddened and subdued, lost their appetite. The captain did not even taste his favourite dessert, but Anelya ate her portion, and Yuliya, watching her, felt obliged to eat a bit of hers, even though it was obvious that this polite gesture required great effort on her part.

No one wanted any black coffee, and as for the after-dinner conversation that the captain had looked forward to—a conversation that, in order to cheer up Anelya, he had wanted to enliven with amusing and touching stories about his adventures in Bosnia—no thought was given to that now. Their mood was sombre, as if only a moment earlier they had lost someone very dear to them.

Immediately after dinner Yuliya bade a cold farewell to the captain and went home. The captain no longer tried to detain her. As she was leaving, she whispered a few words to Anelya.

The captain entreated his wife to go and rest in the bedroom for a while, and he himself went into the salon, stating that he wanted to lie down on the sofa and doze for a few minutes.

The children went to school.

VII

Leaving the house at about four in the afternoon, the captain was both amazed and alarmed when he reflected on his innermost feelings and pondered the dramatic transformation that they had undergone in one day.

Only yesterday he had returned to his home hearth after a lengthy separation from his wife. Only yesterday this home hearth had seemed like paradise to him, filling him with inexpressible happiness and unveiling before him boundless horizons of even more of the same kind of happiness, pleasure, and love. But today! The captain, with a deep sense of shame, had to admit that he felt relieved when he left the brick building that housed his paradise and his happiness, and walked out into the street.

"I am contemptible, despicable, ungrateful, dishonourable," he reviled himself. "What has happened in my home, what has changed in it that it seems like an oppressive prison to me? Not a single thing has changed, not a single thing has happened! Anelya's nervous disorder—well, that's not a pleasant situation, but it certainly isn't serious. After all, she's like a rose in full bloom, and her appetite is excellent.

"And as for the ridiculous scene that Redlikh staged for my benefit? Well, I'll talk to him and demand an explanation. Maybe he has some accounts to settle with that widow, because it's obvious that she was lying when she assured me that she didn't know him. But how does any of this impinge upon me and my happiness? And yet . . ."

And the captain sighed once again, feeling that his chest was being crushed by something heavy, like the brutal knee of an invisible enemy who had unexpectedly toppled him to the ground and wanted to humiliate him, cruelly and totally.

When he was leaving the apartment, the captain had told his wife that he was going to command headquarters to hand in his petition for retirement. He did not want to lie outright, even though he sensed that Anelya was convinced that he was lying and that, without disabusing her of her conviction, he was lying furtively, lying in his intentions and thoughts.

And so, when he left home, he turned his footsteps almost unconsciously in the other direction, walking upwards along Pekarska Street to the Lychakiv Cemetery. The street was almost empty, with only the occasional passer-by walking along the sidewalk, or servants wading through the snow as they carried buckets of water across the street.

Engrossed in his thoughts, the captain walked on and on without stopping.

Perhaps it was the gloomy sky, overcast with leaden clouds from which snow began sifting down towards evening, or perhaps it was the cold air that forced people to cower, cringe, and seek a warm nook, or perhaps it was the unattractive vista of the long, almost deserted street that ended in a cemetery spreading over a hillock now almost engulfed by the twilight, or perhaps it was the dismal, dreary, and dusky surroundings taken in their entirety that oppressed the captain's thoughts and, instead of bringing him relief and tranquility, pushed him more deeply into an ever darker melancholy.

"I no longer feel as fortunate today as I felt yesterday," the captain ruminated. "I do not know the reason for this, but that's the way it is. I feel that an evil spirit is hovering over our home, that something is poisoning the atmosphere in our home, that there are in it some festering sores, and that if they were touched, even most gently, all the harmony, brightness, openness, and joy would vanish forever.

"What these painful sores are, where they are, what caused them, or how they can be healed—I don't have the faintest idea. They appear at moments when one would least expect them. This uncertainty, this groping in the dark, torments me, torments Anelya, and makes a happy life impossible. And yet, I sense that it is Anelya herself who either does not want to, or is unable to reveal the secret that would explain the entire matter.

"What does this mean? Is there actually a secret that is being hidden from me, or perhaps, am I to blame for the situation because of my own awkwardness? After all, after five years of leading a gypsy-like, almost nomadic existence, one can forget how to interact with people who are more delicate, organized, sensitive and high-strung by nature, people like Anelya.

"And in fact I may have offended her unwittingly more than once, but would that be enough to explain the disharmony, the nervous tension that is creeping in between us? After all, she knows that I love her, I love her ever so dearly! And she loves me, and she loves the children, and for such reciprocal love, much can be forgiven, much can be excused.

"No, it has to be something else! But what? Why would Anelya keep a secret, hide something from me? Is it possible that her nervous attack when I told her about the Baron was actually triggered by her feelings about a disgusting incident that the Baron was in a position to reveal, and that only his suicide prevented him from doing so? That would be horrible!

No, her joy at my arrival, her unrestrained and cheerful mood yesterday—and an awareness of a deed so heinous that even the possibility of it being revealed would cause her to have such nervous spells—these states are incompatible; their coexistence is not even conceivable!"

The captain's train of thought was interrupted by an occurrence that was not the least bit uncommon.

A patch of snow in front of a large gate had been completely trampled down, and the servants carrying their buckets had splashed water on it, with the result that the sidewalk, covered by a layer of tamped snow, was now overspread with a glassy film of ice. It was in this way that a very dangerous sloping surface, known in mechanics as a declivity and in popular usage as a "Lviv break-your-neck," was formed on the smooth road.

It is true that there is an ordinance in Lviv that all such "break-your-necks" must be sprinkled with sand, ashes, or similar substances, but all those ordinances, adhered to quite strictly in the inner city, incrementally lose their regulatory power the farther one goes from the city centre to the outskirts, and on Pekarska Street they are obeyed only after a dozen or more individuals fall victim to such an innocent act of sabotage, and then only if there is one proud and rebellious soul among them who calls in the police, or when one of the victims is so seriously injured that a noisy protest erupts on the street, and the police can no longer ignore the situation.

The captain was just approaching one such treacherously glazed spot in front of a gate. He was still about twenty paces away from it when he noticed an elderly man—hunched over a cane and wearing an old, well-worn fur coat and a lambskin hat with ear flaps that buckled under his chin—coming towards him from the other end of the street.

The man had hardly stepped on the ice when the cane supporting him slipped and, losing his balance, he fell face down on the sidewalk.

"O God!" the unfortunate man shouted and then, falling silent, lay on the ice without moving or speaking.

The captain was at his side in an instant, wanting to help him get to his feet, but the old man did not move. He raised the old man's head: his face, whiskers, and grey beard were sprinkled with blood that was oozing from his nose and a deep gash in his face that had struck a stone wedged in the ice. There was no sign of life in the poor old man, and there was no one else in the street. Seeing that the old man had fainted, the captain laid his head back down on the snow, ran to the gate of a mansion, and tugged sharply at the bell.

At the sound of the bell a watchman ran out, followed by his wife and a few other women, and then a gentleman appeared. The captain set about trying to revive the old man, someone ran to call the police, and the rest of the onlookers stood around the captain and the unconscious man, watching the captain and exclaiming more in surprise than in sympathy.

"Why are you standing there, you blockhead!" the captain shouted at the watchman. "Why don't you at least help me revive this unfortunate fellow who may lose his life because of your negligence?"

"Because of my negligence?" the watchman responded gruffly.

"Yes, yours! It was your responsibility to sprinkle something on the patch of glazed ice where he fell."

The watchman, unwillingly, but motivated by fear, began to assist the captain. Finally, after a few minutes of vigorous rubbing and doing whatever they could to awaken him, the elderly man regained consciousness.

"O God!" he said in a feeble voice. "What's wrong with me? What happened?"

"It's nothing, it's nothing," the captain said. "You fell down on the ice over here."

"Oh, yes, I fell! I hit my head . . . O God!"

"Well, do you think you can stand up?" the captain asked, raising him to his feet. But the elderly man tottered and would have fallen again if a few of the onlookers had not grabbed him under the arms and supported him.

"Oh, I can't. I don't have the strength," he groaned.

At that moment a police officer arrived and, after finding out what had happened, sent a boy to fetch a carriage so that the old man could be taken to the hospital as quickly as possible. He wrote down the name of the negligent watchman, and then, turning to the captain as the main witness, asked him for his name and address.

"Captain Antin Anharovych; I live here, on Pekarska Street, number four," the captain said.

While the police officer was writing in his notebook, the elderly man, upon hearing this name, began to shiver strangely. His head shook like that of a child about to begin bawling, and his lips quivered as if he was trying to say something, but no sound issued from his throat. He tried raising himself a few times, but his efforts were in vain.

None of the onlookers saw his movements; the attention of everyone was fixed on the watchman who, in a tearful voice, was trying to justify himself before the policeman while shouting vile curses at his wife who, it seems, was to blame for everything because she was supposed to look after the sidewalk, but had neglected to do so.

The elderly man was sitting on the sidewalk surrounded by the crowd of people that, having gathered out of curiosity and an eagerness to hear some gossip and witness a scandalous incident, was now ignoring him completely. His face, spattered with blood, pale, and drained by poverty as well as by pain, manifested a desperate desire to do something, to say something—a desire coupled with alarm because of his inability to accomplish what he wanted to do. It was the look of a man who, having fallen into a well in the middle of a deserted field and, realizing that he cannot climb out of it without the assistance of others, is fully aware that all his shouts and pleas are fruitless, of no avail.

And when the captain, looking expectantly down the street while awaiting the arrival of the carriage, happened to draw closer to him, the old man tugged gently at the hem of his coat with a trembling hand. The captain turned around, bent down over him, and was astonished to see a look of profound distress on his aged face.

"What's wrong, my dear fellow, what is it?" he asked, his voice warm with sympathy.

"So . . . you're . . . captain . . . Anha . . ."

"Yes, Anharovych. Do you, by chance, know me?"

The elderly man shook his head, but waved his hand in an agitated manner to indicate that he wanted to say something but could not.

"Where did you hurt yourself?" the police officer asked as he came up to the old man.

"Right here . . . here," the old man groaned, pointing at his face and forehead where a large blue lump was now visible.

"Are you from around here?"

"No, I'm not . . ."

"What is your name?"

"M . . . M . . . Mykhaylo . . ."

But before he could finish what he was saying, he fainted a second time.

"Take him to the hospital immediately," the captain said to the police officer, "so that he doesn't die right here. Obviously he's very weak. And he may be hungry as well. Please, take this, in case you have to buy something for him."

And the captain gave the police officer a *gulden. The onlookers also collected a few *kreutzers among themselves. While they were doing this, the carriage arrived. The police officer had the unconscious old man placed in the carriage, sat down beside him, and ordered the coachman to drive posthaste to the hospital.

This accident—one that is not at all a rarity on the streets of Lviv—pushed the captain's thoughts in another direction. The awareness of having fulfilled his responsibility towards a fellow human being renewed his strength and courage. Even though twilight was quickly descending, in his heart everything seemed to be growing brighter. He even began to reproach himself for having viewed his family relationships in such a dark light only a short while ago, for having suspected that there were riddles and secrets where, more than likely, there were none at all.

"It will all work out somehow, my poor Antos!" he said to himself. "It will all fall into place, perhaps even better than you had hoped. Just go slowly, without any unnecessary hubbub. As the German potter said when his wagon filled with pottery overturned in a ditch: *Nur nicht überstürzen* [Just do not be in too big a hurry]! Just be sure that you do not do anything that you may later regret, and as for the rest, leave it to God!"

Philosophizing and moralizing in this manner, the captain turned off Pekarska Street and made his way into town. He did not really know where he was going and why, but neither did he feel a need or a desire to go home.

He was walking on the streets that were most brightly illuminated and where there were the most people. And, after an hour-long walk spent looking at displays in shop windows, carefully perusing the titles of books on view in antiquarian shops and book stores, and overhearing many insignificant fragments of the conversations of passers-by, the captain, almost without realizing how and when it had happened, found himself in front of the officers' casino.

It was only now that he recalled that he had left home with the express thought of meeting Redlikh here and demanding from him an explanation about the unpleasantness that he had caused in his home earlier in the day.

It was not quite six o'clock yet. There was hardly anyone in the casino except for two young reserve officers in the billiard room who, caught up in a game, were loudly calling out the tally of their caroms. When the captain entered, they saluted him and then returned at once to their game, but now they played less boisterously.

A feeling of abandonment wafted over the captain from the expansive, deserted rooms with their orderly arrangements of chairs, their newspapers neatly laid out on tables like corpses in a large morgue, and their lacquered ceilings, grimy with cigarette smoke. Just before the captain arrived, a casino employee had lit two or three gas lamps, but the far corners of the large room were drowning in semidarkness.

After taking off his coat and sword, the captain sat down at one of the tables and began reading the newspapers, seizing first the Lviv newspapers that he had seen only rarely during the past five years. And even though there was nothing particularly interesting or special in them, he read them from cover to cover, including all the ads. He refreshed his memory of the city, its residents, and their interests and tastes, all the while comparing the present with the recent past.

Every name that he came across in the newspaper reminded him of something familiar: a friend, a schoolmate, a teacher, a doctor, a cobbler's shop where he used to have his boots made, a tailor who had often sewed on credit for him during his student years, a fruit vendor, or a quarrelsome woman neighbour on whom he had played many a trick as a young boy.

The name of every street evoked fresh memories. He smiled at them as at old acquaintances that he was meeting in a crowd of strangers. As he read the inert alphabetic characters, words, and sentences, he did not even try to grasp their logical ties, meaning, and content; instead, he relived, instantaneously, as if he were dreaming or looking into a kaleidoscope, a stream of incidents in his life—incidents that were happy and sad, pleasant and painful.

The casino was slowly filling up with military personnel. They entered with a measured step, *"schneidig* [smartly],*"* stiffly upright in the Prussian manner, jangling their swords and spurs, and greeting one another by saluting and saying curtly: *"Servus! Wie gehts dir* [How are you]?*"*

The largest number gathered in the dining hall, and from there they dispersed either into the billiard room or the long and narrow card room crammed with green tables and chairs. Most of them did not even glance into the reading room. And as the captain was sitting with his back towards the door, the first ones to wander in walked around the table as if looking at the newspapers or searching for something special, glanced at him without any sign of recognition, muttered *"Servus!"* under their noses, quickly took any newspaper at all, and walked out without approaching him.

Later, they did not even do that, and even though upwards of twenty officers gathered in the reading room, not one of them extended his hand, spoke to him, or sat down beside him. The few who picked up newspapers walked into the adjacent room, while others sat down either at tables farther away from him, or in more distant corners.

The captain sat by himself, absorbed in his perusal of the Lviv newspapers.

While he was still alone in the room, he felt unconstrained, and gave way to the somewhat poetic joy awakened within him by these newspapers, or more specifically, by the familiar names from the past that kept popping up at every turn. But upon seeing the officers bustling about the room, jangling their spurs, shuffling newspapers, and even looking directly at him and then fleeing from him in all directions, he quickly disabused himself of any poetic illusions. What did this shunning mean? Was it being done on purpose, or accidentally?

Without lifting his eyes from the newspaper, but seeing nothing that was on the page, the captain tried to convince himself that this was a purely accidental occurrence, that the officers were refined people, and seeing that he was absorbed in his reading, were leaving him alone so as not to disturb him. And yet they were not so considerate when it came to bothering others. Take that lieutenant over there; he too was reading diligently, but a comrade who had just come in put his hand unceremoniously on his shoulder and, starting up a conversation, tore him away from his reading.

"Well, among close friends that's only to be expected, but in actual fact we don't really know each other," the captain thought, glancing obliquely and a bit jealously at the display of close and sincere friendship among the men who were strangers to him. Something seemed to whisper to him: "Come on, put your newspaper aside. Will any of them come up to you then?"

At the same moment, however, he felt a pang of anxiety that no one would come up to him, and then there would definitely be a scandalous incident, and so he did not dare to lift his eyes from the newspaper; he bent over it and held it in his hands like a shield, the way a drowning person hangs on to a board that might save him from perishing.

But to sit like that, bent over a newspaper that did not interest him in the slightest, to pretend to be reading, to remain silent, and to glance furtively at others—all this was very painful for him, and the longer it went on, the more it tormented him. The captain simply could not understand what was happening to him. What had made him lose his nerve? Why could he not get up and casually walk over to the group that had settled in near the fireplace and begun talking with lowered voices?

He recalled almost all their faces from yesterday's gathering. They had all drunk Bruderschaft with him, so they could not rebuff him; besides, what could possibly induce them to rebuff him? Nevertheless, even though he tried to muster his courage several times, calling himself a fool and a coward, he could not force himself to get up and join the group busily engaged in conversation. He felt blood rushing to his head, his eyes were glazing over, and his thoughts were becoming muddled. But his sense of hearing had become unusually acute, and his ears turned into spies listening in on what was being said at the far end of the room.

The conversation was becoming livelier by the minute. Coarse jokes and cynical laughter burst forth from the flood of words that was interspersed with the whispers and prudent admonitions of the older, more circumspect officers. The size of the group near the fireplace gradually grew larger, as almost all of the men in the room abandoned their newspapers and gathered around the fireplace.

The captain felt as if he were sitting on hot coals. It seemed to him that the conversation was about him, that everyone was staring at him, winking scornfully in his direction, pointing fingers at him. The fragments of phrases and sentences that he caught here and there made him feel as if someone were sprinkling glowing embers over his naked body. He was suffering immensely, but try as he might, he could not surmise why, for what reason, he was suffering.

Finally, some of the men who were standing by the fireplace, especially the younger ones, began to raise their voices, and their statements were curt and emphatic.

"That cannot be! We cannot tolerate that!" one of them shouted.

"But it is quite likely that he knows nothing at all about it," a second man said.

"Is he blind and deaf that he does not know what is going on around him?"

"No, we cannot tolerate such a man among us!"

"But first of all we must be convinced that it is true; we must give him a chance to offer an explanation."

There was a general commotion.

The captain's situation became intolerable.

Steeling his will, he put aside his newspaper, got up and, approaching a lieutenant who was standing nearest to him, asked him politely, softly, with a slight quiver in his voice: "Do not be annoyed with me, my friend, but could you tell me about whom they are speaking?"

The lieutenant glanced at the captain with a confused, troubled look and said in a strained voice: "Well . . . it's . . . you see . . ."

"Why beat around the bush, lieutenant?" a heavy-set infantry captain shouted loudly in a deep baritone voice. "He must be told the truth once and for all. You see, Anharovych, you should know that we are talking about you."

If a bolt out of the blue had struck right here beside him, it would not have terrified Anharovych as much as those words. Even though he had felt yesterday that the officers had something against him, in the depths of his soul he had considered it to be an uncertain conjecture, a notion that need not be believed. But there could be no doubt now, and the terrible certainty pierced the captain like a bullet from a musket.

Anharovych turned pale, staggered, and, then, hanging on to the arm of a chair, asked in a broken voice: "And might it be possible to know what it was that you, my comrades, were saying about me?"

"We were debating the question of whether or not we could tolerate having you in our company any longer."

"Me?" Anharovych shouted. "What have I done that you would no longer tolerate having me in your company?"

"Do not be angry, my friend," the infantry captain said. "You know that there are times in a person's life when a misadventure can cast a foul shadow on a man, even though it is possible that he himself has not abetted the misadventure by his actions, or, what is more, even by his thoughts."

"So you are saying that a foul shadow has fallen on me?" the captain asked sharply, now that the certainty and indisputability of a threatening situation had restored his military courage. "Please clarify the matter for me: what is this shadow?"

"We thought that you knew what this is all about."

"Are you saying that, knowing something unworthy about myself, I would have the temerity to show up in your company?" Anharovych shouted.

"Well, my friend, we do not know you all that well," one of the older soldiers said. "And to show up in our company knowing that you have done something improper—that would not be right, but you must admit it would not be impossible."

"For me, it would be absolutely impossible!"

"Ha, that may well be. But then it seems impossible to us that you still do not know with whom and how you are living."

"What? What? What?" the captain yelled in astonishment. "These words are completely incomprehensible to me."

"Well, it is not my obligation to explain them to you," the soldier said haughtily as he turned his back on him.

"But how can this be?" Anharovych shouted as he looked around, scarcely able to contain his anger. "You judge me, shun me as if I were a leper, state that I am unworthy to be in your company, pronounce a death sentence on me and execute it, yet you refuse to tell me what I am guilty of!"

Anger, indignation, a sense of having been wronged, fear that this injustice must have some basis in reality, and a helpless despair at seeing his comrades turn away from him—all these feelings seethed in the captain's soul. He did not know what to do, how to act in this terrible impasse in which he found himself without knowing how or why. Large red spots flashed in his eyes, and from the dark wellsprings of his heart flared a consuming desire to wash away the injustice done to him—the disgrace—in the blood of any one of the proud, robust, men who obviously were so indifferent to his suffering.

"Here comes Redlikh," an officer suddenly said. And turning to the captain he added: "He is sure to want to explain to you what this is all about."

"Yes, yes," a few voices shouted in chorus, "and if he does not want to, then any one of us is ready to be at your service."

"Redlikh!" one of the officers called out to Redlikh who was busily wiping his spectacles. "Anharovych is here, and he wants to have a talk with you. We think that, as his friend, you will want to, and will best know how to, explain the situation to him. But if you do not want to, then send him to any one of us."

"Yes, yes, all of us are ready to be at his service," other officers affirmed as they walked out of the room en masse, leaving the two friends alone.

For a full minute Redlikh stood dumbfounded. He had not expected to find Anharovych here; for some reason he had thought that Anharovych would come to his living quarters and demand an explanation from him for the rude behaviour that he had exhibited that afternoon. He had already formulated in his mind the most sensitive, the most friendly phrases with which he had hoped to assuage the captain's righteous anger. But now! Here!

One glance at the situation that he had walked into and the first words that had flown out of the officers' mouths convinced him that the matter was irreversibly ruined; that there was absolutely no possibility of diluting the truth, of presenting it delicately, or of partially concealing it. There was also absolutely no doubt in Redlikh's mind as to what the consequences would be if he had a conversation with the captain under these circumstances.

The moment that the officers left them alone, Redlikh felt that their comradely arms had placed him on a sheet of red-hot iron. Indescribable pain and grief gripped his soul. Should he wash his hands of the whole affair? Should he send the captain to someone else? Would not a death blow delivered by a friend's hand be a hundred times more painful? But then, looking at it another way, if he stepped back, would not his comrades have the right to look upon him as a coward?

For a few moments a heavy grave-like silence filled the room. The two friends stood facing each other as if they had been sentenced to death—pale, unable to speak, unable to look one another in the face.

Finally Redlikh made the first move and approached the captain; he extended his hand, and the captain shook it. Both their hands were ice-cold.

"What is it that you must say to me?" the captain asked in a dull voice.

"Let's sit down," Redlikh said, almost in a whisper.

They sat down. Redlikh once again remained silent for a moment as he searched for a word, a phrase, with which to begin the fatal conversation.

"You are angry with me," he finally said without raising his eyes to look at his friend. "You feel offended, right? And you have reason to feel that way. I offended you at noon today. And what is even more fatal, I cannot apologize to you, for I acted out of necessity—I could not have behaved otherwise."

The captain recoiled as if bitten by a snake, and overcome with emotion asked in a whisper: "And why is that?"

"I'll explain it to you, I'll make everything clear to you," Redlikh said, "even though, as God is my witness, I would give half my life if only I did not have to explain anything to you, if only everything that I must tell you now was a falsehood, an invention, a phantasm."

"Instead of calling upon God as a witness, just tell me what you have to say!" the captain said with cold resignation.

"As you wish; I shall come right to the point," Redlikh said with a sigh. "The woman I saw in your home belongs to the category of women whose names are never uttered in decent company. You must not think that she is simply a fallen woman. Oh, no! We are all sinful, we all commit sins in our lives, and for fallen women who are often the victims of poverty, gossip, or simply strong passions, we often can even have respect. You know me, and you know that my judgement is not affected by society's prejudices, so that means that you can consider . . ."

"But that woman does not even know you!" the captain cried. "Is it possible that you mistook her for someone else?"

"Unfortunately, no!" Redlikh replied sadly. "I know her all too well, and the majority of the officers also know her, and if you want to see for yourself, we can take you to her residence."

"To her residence? Who is she then?"

"There is no word that could adequately characterize the abominable and base trade in which she is engaged. That trade is all the more revolting because it entails duplicity, concealment from the eyes of the authorities, and is conducted under the innocent title of a boarding school for poor, decent girls."

The captain was petrified with astonishment and alarm.

"O God!" he cried. "And such a person . . . And to think that I was the one who almost forced her to stay for dinner. And such a person . . . my children even call her 'auntie'!"

Hot tears gushed from his eyes, and, hiding his face in his hands, he sobbed like a child.

Redlikh did not say a word.

"Oh, this is terrible, horrible!" the captain repeated, but then suddenly, raising his head and staring at Redlikh with eyes still wet with tears, he said almost cheerfully: "But what of it? So, it was a mistake. After all, until this moment, my wife and I knew nothing about it. And as for this loathsome woman—she is my wife's school friend. So, if that was the shadow that had fallen on us, and because of which the officers wanted to exclude me from their company, then what could be easier than to wash away that stain, to remove that shadow?

"Could you, or anyone else present here assume that, having found out about this, I would tolerate, for even a moment, the presence of this monster in the guise of a woman in my home, or have her name mentioned there? And how could you have allowed the shadow cast by this sin to cause me such grief instead of telling me at once, clearly and frankly, what the problem is! No, my old friend, this was not done in a comradely manner. This is not how friends should behave. But, enough of that! Give me your hand! All of this will be put in order, it will be set aright."

Redlikh listened to the words that poured in an unrestrained stream from the captain's lips. His heart ached as he saw his friend's joy and hope, for he knew that in the very next moment he would have to deal him a death blow; he would have to shove this beautiful, noble soul—full of goodness and faith in people—from its bright heights and cast it into a black pit of hopelessness and despair. But—there was no way out.

"That is where the misfortune lies, my old friend," Redlikh said gloomily, and he did not accept the hand that was offered to him. "Nothing can be set right, and what is corrupted cannot be made good again. What I have told you thus far is only half the problem and, I regret to say, it is the lesser half."

"What? So there is more!" the captain cried.

"There is, and it is something that I would prefer not to talk about, not now and not ever. But, since it has reached the point that I can no longer be silent about it, then you should know that your wife . . ."

"How dare you say anything about my wife?" the captain screamed at the top of his lungs and leapt to his feet.

". . . is fully aware of who that other woman is . . ." Redlikh continued in an even voice.

"You're lying, you're lying!" the captain shouted.

". . . and moreover—we even have irrefutable proof of this—she is her silent partner," Redlikh concluded.

"Liar! Vile slanderer! Shut up, shut up!" the captain roared, rushing at him with his fists. "Only your blood can wash away this abominable, this unprecedented slander that you have hurled at a most decent woman! O God, what is happening to me? Get out of my sight before I tear you to pieces! Get out!"

And the captain, beside himself with anger, grabbed a chair and once again rushed towards Redlikh.

Hearing his shouts, the officers thronged into the room and surrounded the two men.

"Villains! Vile wretches!" the captain shouted, foaming at the mouth and thrashing about wildly. "So that's what you wanted! So this was your conspiracy! You wanted to kill me, to murder me, to torture me to death! But why? What have I ever done to you? And that one—that scorpion who pretended to be my friend—he allowed himself to be used as your weapon. Oh, shame on you! Shame and damnation!"

The officers all remained silent. A few of the stronger ones were holding on to the captain's arms and legs. He thrashed about, cursed, and ground his teeth, longing for revenge, blood, or death.

Redlikh stood to one side, pale as a corpse, waiting for the captain to calm down. Finally, the officers, seeing that the very sight of Redlikh kept sending the captain into new fits of maddened fury, asked him to go into an adjacent room. It was only after half an hour that the captain, completely hoarse, weakened, and exhausted, collapsed lifelessly into a chair and began weeping once again.

It was not until much later that evening that his incensed heart calmed down and he was able to think a bit more clearly about what had to be done. It was then that he expressed a desire to speak to Redlikh.

Redlikh came in, pale but calm, and filled with resignation.

"You told me that you have evidence that speaks against my wife," the captain said. "What is this evidence? Show it to me."

"It is the kind of evidence that I cannot show you, but nevertheless it is reliable. It is the story of the unfortunate Baron Reuchlingen."

"The Baron!" the captain shouted, pierced to the core of his being.

"Yes, the Baron; both women pulled him into their net and ruined him. And it was your wife who had the main role in doing this. Just what kind of role it was . . ."

"Shut up! Shut up!" the captain screamed and, pulling off his glove, flung it into Redlikh's face.

Redlikh accepted the challenge calmly, without any visible agitation.

A half hour later, the matter was settled. The respective seconds, with agreement from both sides, laid down the terms for an honourable settlement of this incident. At eight in the morning there was to be a duel involving the use of pistols. The distance was to be fifteen paces, there would be three exchanges of shots, and if the duellists came out uninjured, there would be a half-hour break, and then the duel would recommence. The captain walked out of the military casino at about eleven.

"And where does that . . . woman live?" he asked as he left.

He was given Yuliya's address, and saluting, but not shaking hands with anyone, he departed.

VIII

After leaving the casino, the captain walked straight ahead, mechanically, like a wound-up automaton, without thinking about where he was going. He avoided passers-by, went from one street to another, and kept walking without knowing or giving any thought to where he was going and why. He felt a need for staying in motion, for darkness and oblivion.

The night was cold, calm, and dark. It was snowing, and icy pellets fell thickly on the captain's face, on his eyes and lips. He felt as if he were being pricked by needles, but at the same time he experienced a certain pleasure in that stinging sensation. He also took pleasure in the clattering of the hansoms that flew by at a furious speed, for the din seemed to deaden the storm that was raging within him—the storm that was destroying, subverting, and rooting out everything in his soul, everything beloved, beautiful, holy.

Trying to find the darkest back streets, he walked for a long time, cutting across familiar streets and squares until he reached

Jesuit Park that was deserted and deathly still in the darkness. The trees in the park were bare, and their smaller branches melted into the darkness, leaving only their thick trunks and larger branches to loom like black pillars against the obscure background. The thickly falling snow blocked the light of the lamps that flickered feebly on street corners. The distant clattering of the hansoms drifted in like a dull, uninterrupted rumbling.

The captain walked without stopping, convulsively clutching the cold hilt of his sword. He was terrified to stop for even an instant, as if there was a monstrous apparition chasing after him, an apparition that could catch up to him at any moment and tear him to pieces.

Finally he gave a startled jump, halted, caught his breath, and tried to focus his distracted mind, his shattered thoughts.

"What is going on with me? What has happened?" he asked himself, striving to find an explanation for the unexpected and bizarre catastrophe that had befallen him. "It was only yesterday that I returned from Bosnia. It was yesterday, only yesterday, that I felt fortunate, more fortunate than ever before in my life. I even asked God why he was granting me so much happiness. What a fool I am! What a fool! I did not sense, I did not surmise that my happiness was a phantasm, a *Fata Morgana, a soap bubble! And now the bubble has burst. And what is next?"

The captain was dressed warmly, more than amply protected from the cold; nevertheless, at that moment he felt that an intense icy coldness was coursing through his body, pressing in on his heart and his brain, and causing him excruciating pain. And, like a wounded animal, at his wit's end, he set out at a fast clip, walking past the regional Parliament Building, and then to the *Church of St. Yura. Gulping for air and breathing heavily, he stopped when he reached the square in front of the church.

And then, once again his mind began to focus. The scene in the casino appeared vividly before him, as if it were happening that very moment.

"What do they want from me? Why are they punishing me? I have done nothing to harm them. Oh, they are vile, vile villains! In order to wound my heart, to kill me, first morally, and then physically—for it is clear that is what they want to do!—they hurl slander at my wife, fling mud at what I hold most sacred.

"They have formed a formal conspiracy against me. 'If you, Redlikh, do not want to take this task upon yourself, any one of us is ready to do so.' Those were their very words! They set a snare for me and attacked me from all sides, knowing full well that I could not escape. They sent that fool, that Redlikh, to my home so that he would offend me, provoke me, chase me into their trap. Oh, you are vile, vile! Judases! But no, you will not devour me that quickly. I'll fight, I'll tear you to pieces—I will not let you triumph over me so easily!"

He straightened up, cast a look full of hatred at the dark, illusory lake of apartment blocks, mansions, flickering lights, and clattering hansoms that spread before him, and in a purely reflexive military movement, pulled his sword out of his scabbard and waved it so energetically that it whistled as it sliced through the air. And then, sliding it back into his scabbard, he set out—with a light step and with his head raised high—back down the street towards the Parliament Building.

But when he was halfway there, he abruptly halted and stood stock-still, stunned. The menacing apparition that had pursued him mercilessly from the time that he left the casino, but which had remained at a distance from him, chose this moment to dig its claws into his chest. It all happened very unexpectedly, without any warning. He was feeling calm. It seemed to him that his resolve—to revenge himself for the officers' conspiracy regarding his death—gave him added strength and confidence. And a thought born of that confidence flashed through his head: "I'll go home."

And it was at this very instant that he felt the apparition dig into him and rip him with its claws; he felt an excruciating pain, he sensed that the cadaverous face of despair was staring him in the eyes.

"Go home? Why? What will I find there?"

These questions rotated in his mind like the pivots on which the door leading to the infernal pit is hung. But as to what might lie hidden behind that door—that is something that cannot be fathomed by any mind, nor conjured up by any imagination. A most horrendous sight—these words do not suffice to convey what lurks there. The underground caverns, where people were once tormented with the cruellest forms of torture—these were more like places of rest and entertainment compared to the yawning void that had opened wide its ugly jaws in the depths of his soul.

After all, his wife was supposedly a monster, a vampire that sucks human blood! After all, this beautiful innocent woman, so full of love, and so dear to him—was supposedly a she-devil, a partner of that female Satan! It was Redlikh who had told him this—Redlikh, a man whom he had never before caught in a lie, a scrupulous man, who did not fling such loathsome rumours into the wind, his old school chum and true friend.

Did that mean that what he had said was true? "Oh, if that is the case, then I curse the day that I was born, and the moment when they said: this is a human being. If that is the case, then there is no greater shame in this world than to be a human being!"

The captain was shaking as if in a fever. He raced through the streets at breakneck speed without knowing where he was heading. But after rushing about aimlessly for half an hour, he found himself on Pekarska Street in front of the brick building that housed his apartment.

There was a light in the bedroom. The captain stood on the sidewalk across the street and stared at that light.

"She is waiting for me!" the thought drifted limply through his mind like a wilted leaf chased by the autumn wind. "And the children, my children, call that woman 'auntie,' that . . ."

He gnashed his teeth. A furious rage surged within him. With a single leap he bounded across the street and ran up to the brick gate. He tugged at the bell to awaken the watchman. He would rush into the bedroom, force her to admit her guilt, and choke her to death, tear her apart, rip her to pieces with his teeth right on the spot—this was his thought.

But before he had even finished thinking it, terror struck his heart and, leaping away from the gate, he fled to the other side of the street like the basest of cowards, hoping that the watchman would not awaken, that he would not see him and shame him into entering the building.

No, at this moment he could not walk into his home for all the money in the world! Given the mood that he was in, he was sure that the next day either Anelya or he would be carried out from the bedroom as a corpse.

Fortunately, either the bell, in the best Lviv tradition, did not ring, or the watchman did not hear the single tug, because no one came to open the gate. After waiting for several minutes in deathly trepidation, the captain, hiding behind the corner of a building, and trembling and glancing around in all directions like a thief, slowly began to calm down, to think a bit more coolly about his relations with Anelya.

"She's probably waiting for me!" a train of jumbled, disordered thoughts swarmed in his head. "She's probably concerned, worried why I'm not coming home. She used to cry when I left her home alone like this until late at night. But by now she must have become accustomed to it. Oh, and she has become accustomed to many other things, as well.

"For everything that Redlikh told me about her is the truth, the utter truth! I feel this with my entire soul, my entire being. And this feeling can make one go mad! Oh, woe is me! Woe is me! And he said that he has proof! So that's what my beloved, my adored, the mother of my children has come to! No, I will not tolerate this! I must, at this very moment, settle accounts with her—once and forever. For come what may, it is not possible for us to live together any longer!"

He once again went up to the gate. But he had hardly reached the middle of the street in front of the brick gate, when he heard the heavy footsteps and the drowsy wheezing of the watchman who was coming to open it.

And at the very same moment he saw the light coming from Anelya's window, the weak, gentle light that, passing through the wavering, heavy veil of snowflakes, took on, in his eyes, a delicate purple sheen, as if it were reflecting a large puddle of blood—and an insane fear gripped his entire being, and without giving it any more thought, without looking back, and clanging his sword against the bricks, he rushed away from the gate, went upwards on Pekarska, and turned into a side street.

A police officer standing on the corner saw a military man who appeared to be in a great hurry and, surmising that something had happened that demanded his intervention, began chasing him. When the captain saw that the police officer was catching up to him, he dashed into a dark side street and began running uphill.

"Sir! Sir! Wait up!" the police officer called in his wake, but then he tripped and realized that he could not catch up to him.

The captain did not hear his call. The police officer whistled, trying to draw the attention of other patrolmen to the mysterious fugitive, but there were no other police close by, and his whistle did not evoke a response.

Meanwhile, the captain reached Kurkova Street. He could hardly breathe. He halted in a dark nook, where no one who was more than ten steps away could see him, and tried to catch his breath; he rested there for quite a while, trying to latch on to his interrupted train of thought.

This time, however, his thoughts went in a completely different direction.

"But she loves me! And she loves the children! It is evident in her every gesture, her every word, her every letter. Is it possible for love and utter depravity to coexist? And have her crimes and her depravity been proven? She warned me not to listen to any gossip. That means that such gossip must have reached her ears. She pleaded with me to leave the army. And I, being the fool that I am, did not understand why she was doing this! But now I understand.

"Oh, now it is clear to me, after the blow has fallen, after it is too late to return. She wanted to pluck me out of this mire, out from among people who are detached from life, accustomed to living off others, depraved people who spread depravity all around themselves. Perhaps she even knew about the conspiracy, about the plot that was woven to destroy me. Her nervous attacks, her fear for the children, her passionate pleading for me to apply for retirement . . .

"Oh, I was blind, blind not to have perceived this at once! She was concerned about me, she wanted me to have happiness and tranquility! But why did she not tell me what it was all about? Why didn't she tell me clearly what was going on and where it was headed? Why?

"Oh, I understand, I understand! She knows my nature all too well—a nature that is stupid, stubborn, replete with prejudgments and vile suspicions. She knew that I would not believe her, that I would suspect her of God knows what. She thought that she could delay the matter, prepare me for the bitter truth. But I, fool that I am, ruined everything. And now I have my just desserts! O God, thank You for using Your hand to push me away from that gate, from the threshold that, had I had crossed it a moment ago, I might well have become a Cain, I would have committed a deed for which I could never have forgiven myself, either in this life, or in the next one."

The storm passed. The whirlwind abated. The captain's love for his wife and family, his faith in her love and goodness, his faith in the nobility of the human soul proved stronger in his heart than the storm, outlasted the dreadful pressure and came out the victor. He calmed down. Of that inner storm there remained only a feeling of being greatly grieved at people—the base, envious, malevolent, people who spatter with the foam of their envy that which stands high above their level of morality.

He was left with a righteous anger, indignation, especially towards Redlikh, towards his friend, whom he had trusted so wholeheartedly, and who had so loathsomely taken advantage of that trust. The captain now felt that, tomorrow, if his opponent did not fell him with his first shot when he stood opposite him face to face, then his hand would certainly not falter, his revenge for the desecrated temple of his home hearth would be decisive, complete, and inevitable.

The chiming of the clocks as they struck the hour interrupted his train of thought.

One o'clock! So late! Anelya was probably waiting for him, worrying about him! A painful feeling stirred in the captain's heart. At that moment he loved her above life itself, above everything in the world, above his own honour. But at the same time he felt that he could not, should not, see her now.

Seven hours still separated him from the moment that would decide whether he was to live or die. The duel with Redlikh was unavoidable. To call it off—that was unthinkable. And to see Anelya now might cause him to waver in his determination.

No, no! Tomorrow he must be calm, strong, prepared for everything, composed in his thoughts and feelings. A meeting with Anelya and the children might unnerve him. If he remained alive, he would see them tomorrow, and he would have spared them hours of anxiety and uncertainty, and if he died, well, they would find out about it soon enough!

A deep pain cramped his heart when he thought that he might die without seeing the ones he loved so dearly, for whose honour and good name he was risking his life.

He did not fear death. On the battlefield he led his detachment boldly, inspiring courage in his soldiers, laughing off the bullets whistling by. But now, knowing that he might die within the four walls of a shooting gallery—with his wife and children nearby but completely unaware of his situation—and sensing his children's pain, their tears, and their difficult fate as orphans after his death, he felt his heart would break.

He chased these depressing thoughts out of his mind and tried to bolster his belief that his opponent either would not take up the challenge or would take back his slanderous remarks before the duel or, barring that, would finally realize the evilness of his deed and purposely miss his target. He considered this duel to be God's tribunal that would judge between him and a clique of villains, who for some unknown reason had taken a vow to destroy him. Surely God, knowing his integrity and innocence, would not allow vileness and intrigue to exalt themselves through their victory.

Lost in his thoughts, he walked slowly along the ramparts that led downwards towards the market. And when he reached the market—where, despite the lateness of the hour and the inclement weather, the figures of guests addicted to inns and taverns could still be seen here and there, either mincing their way alone to some unclear goal, or wandering about in small groups amid loud talk and even louder laughter—he felt hungry and exhausted.

His first thought was to go to the nearest open beer-cellar or restaurant. He was already in the vestibule of a restaurant when he stopped short and hurriedly walked back out into the marketplace. He recalled that in such a place, and at such an hour, the majority of the patrons would be soldiers and officers. To meet up with them, to greet them, to talk with them—he simply could not do that now, not for any money. Moreover, who knows if he might not have to suffer new insults and humiliations that could deprive him once again of the peace of mind that he had attained with such effort. No, no! There was nothing in the world that could force him to go into a restaurant!

And so, carefully avoiding all military personnel who were wandering about in rowdy, boisterous groups, he went to the English Hotel and requested a small room. He ordered supper and a bottle of wine, and asked for a few sheets of paper, a pen, and a bottle of ink. Then, having fortified himself with the food and wine, he sat down to write letters of farewell to his wife and children.

After her husband left, Anelya felt completely calm and strangely elated She was convinced that the captain had gone to command headquarters to hand in his petition for retirement, and she felt easier in her heart and mind that tomorrow or the day after, he would be able to take off the uniform that at one time had made him look so attractive in her eyes, but which she now perceived as threatening, an onerous burden, like shackles. She knew that this uniform imposed various demanding and dangerous obligations on her husband, and it was these obligations that she feared the most.

She also knew that, notwithstanding anything else, it was this very uniform that obligated him to spend time in the company of other military personnel, and just how dangerous this company could be had been revealed very starkly by Redlikh's visit. Just thinking about this visit made Anelya shiver. That stupid fool, that blockhead! Why did he have to insinuate himself into their home? And why couldn't he have found even a crumb of politeness in his cabbage-like head instead of instantly rearing like a wounded bear?

"Oh, I hate him! I hate all of them!" Anelya whispered through clenched teeth as she recalled the ominous gloom that had descended on the dining room after Redlikh's departure, the cold sweat that she had broken into, and the superhuman strength that she had needed to master her agitation and to assume, in front of her husband, the appearance of being untrammelled and naive. But thank the Lord! The fear of being compromised by people such as Redlikh would not be a threat to her much longer. Using the strength of her will and her love for her husband, she would push aside the sword of *Damocles.

Her marvellous eyes burned with a flame of righteous joy at the thought that she and her husband would move far, far away to a village in a God-forsaken corner of the mountains, to their own little estate, their own plot of land, where she could breathe freely, forget all that had happened in the past, root out of her soul the terrifying ordeals that she had to endure here, and devote herself wholeheartedly, unconditionally, to her beloved family, to her home hearth.

Resilient, like all people with full-blooded and energetic natures, Anelya quickly swept out of her heart all the unpleasant and troublesome impressions of the day and began bustling about in a lively manner as she went about her daily household chores. She sorted through the children's clothing, did some patching, sewed on buttons, and ordered the maid to remove a stain. Antos would be home before long; coffee and an afternoon snack had to be prepared, and supper had to be planned.

And then the children came home from school, bringing into the apartment a refreshing wave of cheerful voices, laughter, and chatter. Anelya, talking and laughing with them as if she herself were a child, helped them remove their outer clothing, gave them some lunch, and completed a set of indoor gymnastics with them. And then, after settling them down to do their homework, she went into the kitchen to help Maryna prepare the coffee.

Antos had not yet come home. More than likely, the general, who was very fond of him, had found out about his intention to leave the army and had invited him in to try to knock the idea out of his head by promising him a rapid promotion, a higher pension . . . Well, there was no doubt that a higher pension would not be a bad thing. After all, they could not count themselves among the well-to-do, even though, thanks to her efforts and her initiative, neither could they be considered truly poor. Oh, poverty, privation—for her these were life's most terrible *Furies.

In order to exorcise these Furies and hold them at bay from her home hearth, she had sacrificed so much . . . so much! Antos had no idea how much, and God grant that he should never find out. He loved her ardently, madly—she had seen this at once. He trusted her, saw her love, and was certain that she had not betrayed him. And he was not mistaken in this! She had been faithful to him, and had never betrayed, either in thought or in deed, the faithfulness that she had sworn to him.

But nevertheless, this decent, sentimental Antos . . . If he were ever to find out about everything, who knows what a to-do there would be! Who knows if he would . . .

Anelya shook her head, not wanting to conclude her thought. "So what! I was faithful to him, and this gives me strength. I did not break my marriage vows, and therefore, from that point of view, he cannot accuse me of anything. As for that other . . . the rest of it . . . well, who knows how it will all turn out. This matter can be looked at from many different angles. If only time does not run out on me! If only we can get away from Lviv, away from this social circle, from this environment, the rest will take care of itself."

Six o'clock went by, but Antos did not return. More than likely one of the more high-ranking officers had invited him to join him for tea, and he could not refuse or quickly extricate himself.

She had her coffee with the children and told them that they could play. But the children begged to be allowed to go to the kitchen where Hrytsko, with whom Mykhas had struck up a fast friendship, had made a small carpenter's bench for the little boy, and was now teaching him how to use a hammer and a drill. Tsesya did not want to lag behind, and despite Maryna's efforts to convince her that it was not seemly for young ladies to engage in work of this nature, she got down to business as well, and within an hour the two of them had drilled so many holes in the small board Hrytsko had given them that it looked like a sieve.

While the children were working, Hrytsko, sitting on a bench and smoking a pipe, told them, or rather, told Maryna, about the strange adventures that he and the captain had shared in Bosnia, about mountain brigands and rebels, about Turkish men and women, about mosques and ancient buildings, about the peasants who lived there, about the mountains, and what was grown in that country.

A peasant himself, this was what had interested Hrytsko the most, and on his broad, kind face, adorned with a small black moustache, you could read his sincere inner satisfaction when he saw that Maryna was also interested in such matters, that she asked him, intelligently and with obvious interest, how people over there lived, worked, and conducted themselves.

Meanwhile, Anelya was growing bored in the salon. What could it possibly mean that Antos was not coming home? Naughty Antos! It was only the second evening that he was spending in Lviv, and he was already beginning to neglect her. She racked her brains trying to figure out where he could be, with whom he might be conversing, and about what. She made several conjectures and then dismissed them one by one. There was only one combination of possibilities that her imagination backed away from—that he might be at the casino. She could not say why, but she was firmly convinced that Antos would not go there today.

She picked up some handiwork and sat without thinking about anything, but catching every sound, every noise, every rustle that drifted in from the porch, always hoping that it might be he, and always being disappointed. She was envious of the happy time that her children were having in the kitchen, and several times she was on the verge of joining them, but something always stopped her. What if Antos came!

In her imagination she conjured up his figure standing in the doorway, his movements, his voice, how he would greet her, kiss her, beg her forgiveness, how he would begin to undo the buttons on his coat in his customary manner, and then stop and kiss her hand, and then, shaking the snow off his cap and removing his coat, he would trim the lamp on the table, pace the room and gesticulate rapidly while relating something to her, and then he would once again stand before her, and only then would he remember that he should remove his sword.

A good, dear, honest, man with a heart of gold! The years that he had spent in Bosnia, the hard work and the inconveniences, had scarcely left their mark on him. In fact, he had matured and grown even more handsome; his face was slightly tanned, but otherwise he remained the same as he had always been.

Anelya was sitting at the table with closed eyes, daydreaming, and smiling sweetly in her dreams. A soft knock at the door interrupted these dreams. Startled, she jumped to her feet and glanced all around as if seeking help or a place to hide. But there was no danger of any kind; instead, there was another soft, timid knock at the door.

"Please come in," Anelya said, raising her voice.

An old woman, muffled in a kerchief, hesitantly walked in. Anelya did not recognize her at first glance.

"Glory to Jesus Christ!" the woman said as she bowed.

"Ah, Shymonova!" Anelya cried.

Shymonova was Yuliya's maid, the widow of a servant who had been in the employ of a shoemaker. "What's happened? Why have you come to see me?"

"My lady sent me. I have a letter here for you, my lady," Shymonova said, placing on the table a small visiting card sealed in an envelope.

"Yuliya is writing to me?" Anelya asked in surprise. "What is this all about? Is she ill that she cannot come herself?"

"No, if it please your lady, she is not ill. The explanation is probably in the letter. Be so kind, dear lady, as to read it. My lady asked me to wait for a reply."

Anelya cut open the envelope with a pair of scissors and pulled out a card completely covered with Yuliya's fine, elegant handwriting.

The card contained the following message:

"My dear Anelya! Just this very moment I found out about a matter that is of immense importance to us. You cannot possibly imagine what has happened. It is imperative that we get together to discuss what we should do. I would have run over to see you at once, because I am almost losing my mind, but after the stupid scene during dinner, I am afraid of running into your husband. I respect him greatly, but I fear him even more. Write to me—or better yet, do not write anything, and throw this card into the fire. Just tell Shymonova if and when I can come to see you. Even if it is only for a moment.

Your Yuliya."

Anelya's astonishment reached its zenith. "What is this news that Yuliya is talking about?" she exclaimed without thinking.

"I really can't say, I don't know, may it please your lady," Shymonova replied.

"Who came to see her? Who could have told her something so very important?"

"I don't know, may it please your lady. Various gentlemen come to see us."

"Go home, Shymonova, and tell your lady to come here at once," Anelya said and, giving her a twenty-cent coin, saw her to the door.

She was trembling, gripped by a fever of anxiety. She prayed to God that Antos would be delayed from coming home for another hour or more, so that he would not find Yuliya with her. Glancing at her watch, she saw that it was seven o'clock. She sat down and mentally accompanied Shymonova on her circuitous trip back home.

Right now the old woman was splashing through the muddy streets, going past the booths where the *Boykos sell garden produce, and going on from there to the market, crossing over by the city hall, and then cutting across the market again. Really, how was it that this old woman would never consider taking the short way home? At night, even the smallest cluster of trees filled her with unconquerable fear, and she preferred to go by a roundabout way, even if it made the trip twice as long, so as to avoid going past a stand of trees in a lane.

Anelya cursed Shymonova's strange timidity that went back to the old woman's childhood years. When she was just ten years old, she had been walking through a grove at night with her mother when some villains attacked them and murdered her mother in a most horrendous manner; and she, scared out of her wits, had jumped into a thicket and, after burying herself in a pile of dead branches, had fainted and lain there half-dead for several hours before she was found the next day and pulled out of her hiding spot. From that time on, Shymonova could not walk down a lane or boulevard where even a few trees or bushes grew in a clump.

But she must have arrived home by now. Yuliya would be putting on her coat, walking hurriedly along the more direct route, and at any moment now she would be here to tell her what had happened . . .

Anelya felt her anxiety mounting by the minute. What if Antos came home! What if he found Yuliya here at such a late hour! Late hour? It wasn't even eight yet! In an effort to overcome her vague, irrational fear, Anelya got up and went into the kitchen. "Well, children, it's time to go to bed. You have to get up early tomorrow to go to school."

"We'll work just a little while longer, mummy!" Mykhas cried. "Just look, do you see how straight this groove is? I carved it like that!"

"And I drilled this little circle by making tiny holes; look how nice it is!" Tsesya exclaimed.

"And who taught you to do that?"

"Hrytsko!" the children chorused, pointing at Hrytsko, who was standing bolt upright by the table in front of the captain's wife as if standing at attention before a general, except that he was discretely holding his pipe in the palm of his hand, and a good-natured smile was flooding his broad face.

"Well, that's nice, that's very nice," Anelya said, "but nevertheless, it's time for you to go to sleep."

"Will you go to sleep as well, mummy?" Tsesya asked, putting away her drill and shaking the sawdust off her skirt.

"No, my child, I have to wait up a bit longer until daddy comes home."

"Where did daddy go?"

"He went to see a general," Anelya said without thinking.

"Will he come home soon?"

"I don't know, my child. But I have to wait up for him. He might be hungry when he comes home, and I'll have to give him something to eat."

By talking about their father, Anelya was able to lure the children out of the kitchen. She helped them undress, and put them to bed. She wanted to leave them, but Tsesya, who was lying in bed already, stopped her, seized her hand, and kissed it.

"No, mummy, don't go just yet! Tell us something about daddy."

"What should I tell you about him?"

"How good he is. You know, Hrytsko told us such wonderful stories about him."

And Tsesya half closed her eyes, revelling in her recollection of those stories.

"What kind of stories?" Anelya asked.

"He told us that in one city there was a lot of shooting and slashing with swords—people were slashing other people, mummy!—and there was a fire, and houses were burning . . . it was terrible! And in front of one burning house stood a group of Turks, and our soldiers were attacking them, and they were shooting at our men, and ours kept shooting at them until they finally shot all of them. And when all the Turks had fallen down, and the house was beginning to topple over, our men saw that someone was still shooting out of the windows.

"Our soldiers wanted to shoot back at them, but daddy shouted: 'Stop! They're women!' It was a group of three Turkish women. And our men shouted: 'Let them perish!' And the women shot at our men until they used up all their ammunition. And then they threw their weapons out of the window. And daddy said to Hrytsko: 'Follow me, Hrytsko, because those poor women will die in the fire!'

"They both ran to that house and broke down the door; and those Turkish women thought that they wanted to murder them, and so they attacked them with knives. But daddy grabbed the knife from one of the women, Hrytsko grabbed the knife from the second one, and in the meantime the third one slashed herself with her knife. And they carried two of the women out of the fire, and as soon as they walked out, the ceiling of the room caved in, and the third Turkish woman burned to death."

Mykhas related this story with great excitement, breathing rapidly and quite obviously proud and happy, but Tsesya kept her eyes closed and expressed her admiration with a series of gasps. Anelya could not take her eyes off her children, delighting in them as much as they were delighted by Hrytsko's story about their father's good deed.

"Well, go to sleep already, go to sleep!" she finally said. "Tomorrow daddy will tell you an even better story."

"Ah!" Tsesya whispered, relishing this story ahead of time.

"Oh, he won't be able to tell us a better one," Mykhas said seriously. "Hrytsko told us that this was the best one."

Anelya smiled, kissed the children, and went to the salon. After basking in the warmth of the children's chatter and love, she found herself once again in the grip of chilling feelings of anxiety, uncertainty, and expectation.

Neither her husband nor Yuliya had come. It was almost nine o'clock. What could this possibly mean? Anelya sat down and tried to busy herself with her handiwork again, but her fingers were trembling, her mind could not compose itself, and she could not focus on what she was doing.

Putting her work aside, she sat and listened. The clattering of hansoms, a noisy wave of city night life, some broken cries, fragments of sentences from a street quarrel, the heavy thumping on stairs of feet that seemed to draw nearer but then moved farther away towards the upper floor—all this, as if in a kaleidoscope, flashed through her mind, throwing her, in turn, into a nervous fit, a dull feeling of unrelieved tension, and a melancholy resignation.

Minute after minute went by, a quarter-hour after a quarter-hour. It was half past nine, a quarter to ten. Anelya paced the room, peered out of the window into the street. It was dark. The wave of city life slowly began to ebb, but the greater the silence that settled all around, the more unbearable Anelya's anxiety grew in her heart.

Her fear for her husband and the apprehension evoked by Yuliya's letter intensified by the minute. She could no longer think about these two matters separately, and she flung herself about helplessly like a cat tied up in a sack, and this feeling of powerlessness seared and pained her horribly.

Maryna walked in and inquired if her lady was going to eat supper alone.

"No, I don't feel like eating," Anelya replied. "Have you and Hrytsko had supper yet?"

"Yes, we have, may it please your lady. Hrytsko has gone back to the barracks to sleep."

"Then you go to sleep as well. And put the captain's supper in the warming oven. I'll wait up for him."

Maryna left. Anelya, without really knowing why, pulled out a dresser drawer and began to go through some linens. Just then someone knocked at the door, this time swiftly and emphatically. Startled, Anelya jumped as if someone had caught her, like a thief, in the act of committing a crime. She wanted to say: "Please come in!" but she could not utter a word.

And then the door opened, and without waiting for an invitation Shymonova walked in—no, she ran in, she flew in precipitously. Her face was contorted with terror, her kerchief was thrown askew over her shoulders, her head was uncovered and powdered with snow. The old woman was breathing heavily, clutching at her chest and throat, and making desperate signs with her head and her hands as she tried to produce a sound.

"For the love of God, Shymonova, what's wrong with you?" Anelya exclaimed. After recognizing the old woman, she had quickly calmed down, and now she was staring at her more in amazement than in alarm.

"Oh, oh!" Shymonova groaned, collapsing helplessly in a chair. "I can't . . . My gracious lady . . . I was running . . . as fast as I could . . . down a lane . . ."

"Ha, ha, ha, ha!" Anelya burst out laughing. "So that's why you're so scared! Ah! Shymonova ran down a lane. Ha-ha-ha-ha! O my God! And what prompted you, Shymonova, to take such a terribly rash step? And here I thought that, at the very least, half of Lviv had caved in. But where is Yuliya? Why didn't she come herself?"

Shymonova, who still had not completely recovered from her fear, once again waved her hands in desperation.

"Oh, I can't!" she groaned. "I can't! My gracious lady . . . here . . . I'm choking . . . right here!" she added, pointing at her throat.

"Drink this," Anelya said, handing the old woman a generous glass of wine. "Maybe you'll feel better."

Shymonova took the glass of wine with trembling hands and drained it. The wine clearly made her feel better. She breathed heavily once, and then again, and—began to weep.

"Oh, my lady is no more!" she said, sobbing convulsively. "And our young ladies are no more! There is no one, no one!"

"What are you saying, Shymonova?" Anelya, baffled and confused, asked. "They're all gone? But where did they go?"

"They took them away. They took everybody!"

"Who took them?"

"The police. Just imagine, if you will, my lady: I come home from your place, my lady, and I see about five hansoms in front of the building, policemen at the door, policemen by the windows, policemen on the stairs, and utter ruin inside the apartment. Commissioners, inspectors, shouts, weeping; they're searching through drawers, everything's turned upside down; the young ladies, pale and trembling with fear, are getting dressed. A few gentlemen that the police found at our place are standing around looking embarrassed, not knowing quite what to do.

"And my lady is sitting, pale as a corpse and soaking wet—she must have fainted, and they doused her with water to revive her. As soon as I walked in, a commissioner came up to me and asked who I was, what I was doing there. Oh, my gracious lady, I've never been so scared in my life!"

Anelya listened to these words as if she was half-dead. The news of Yuliya's arrest stunned her, deprived her of the ability to sense and to feel. She felt nothing, neither pain nor fear. It seemed to her that suddenly everything around her was disappearing, reality was dissolving like a mist; people, along with the endless tangle of their relationships, were perishing precipitately; her home, the city, the entire earth was fading, and she herself had been cast lightly, like a poppy seed, into a bottomless pit where, vanishing in the infinite depths, she dissolved into nothing.

There was only one slender thread that was holding her, leaving her dangling between the heavens and the abyss, and this thread was Shymonova's voice—a weak, quivering voice that drifted towards her as if coming from a profound distance.

"I wanted to run away at once," Shymonova said, "but they wouldn't let me go. Then they searched through all my belongings, but didn't find anything. Then they ordered me to help my lady get dressed, and she was as cold as a corpse. And oh, I wept ever so hard over her before I finally got her dressed—it felt as if I was about to lay her out in a coffin. And when she saw my tears, the poor thing came to herself a bit and said to me: 'Don't cry, Shymonova! I have faith in God that this misfortune will pass.'

"And then, at a moment when there was no policeman near us, she whispered in my ear: 'Go at once to Anelya's home, Shymonova. . .' yes, that's exactly what she said, the poor thing. 'Go to Anelya's and tell her everything. Perhaps, with the help of her husband, or of someone else, she can do something for me—and for herself.' That's exactly what she said: '—and for herself.' Yes indeed! I kissed both her hands when they were taking her to the hansom. And they took all the young ladies. Two were sick in bed, but even they had to get dressed and go with the police. But they didn't bother with me. O my God, dear God, what will happen to me now?" And Shymonova began weeping again, occasionally wiping her eyes with her apron.

Anelya was still sitting motionless, with her widely staring eyes focussed on one corner of the room, with slightly parted lips, and with no emotion showing on her face, except for the hint of a strange smile on her lips. Shymonova, involved with her own problems and her lady's misadventure, was not paying particular attention to Anelya, and after having a good cry and wiping away her tears, she finally rose from her chair.

"I'll be on my way now, may it please your gracious lady," she said, bowing to Anelya. "I've done what I was supposed to do, and now I must hurry home. I, may God preserve me, locked everything up, but all the same, I must go. Now I'm all alone. I kiss your hands, my gracious lady! I'm very grateful for the refreshments."

And, after kissing Anelya's hand that was stretched out limply on the table, Shymonova bade the gracious lady good night and left.

Anelya did not get up, she did not stir, nor did she watch the old woman leave. She sat as if carved out of stone. The minutes passed, and then the quarter-hours, and the hours, but she continued to sit without stirring. Only her calm, even breathing indicated that she was not a statue, but a living being.

And if the captain—who, at that moment, had tugged the bell at the gate of the brick building and then engaged in a difficult inner struggle—had entered the salon just then, and taken his sword, sharpened in Bosnia, and sunk it into her bosom, her death would simply have been an insignificant and insensible transition from her present surroundings into an absolute and eternal numbness, a serene and unconscious crossing over from a peaceful harbour into a boundless, unfathomable, tranquil ocean.

It was past one o'clock when Anelya's position changed slightly; her eyelids slowly closed, her head dropped to the table, and her arm, in an unconscious, reflexive movement, shifted to cushion her lowered forehead. She fell asleep.

It was in this position, with the lamp still burning, that an alarmed Maryna found her in the morning.

IX

It was still dark in the hotel room. The captain was sleeping. A heavy knocking on the door awoke him.

"Who's there?" the captain shouted.

"It's me, the porter," a voice said from behind the door.

"What do you want?"

"You wanted to be awakened at seven o'clock, captain."

"Is it really seven already?"

"Yes it is."

"Fine, fine. Thank you."

"Do you need anything, captain?"

"Bring me some coffee in about half an hour. And the bill."

"Glad to be of service, captain."

The captain got up, washed, and began dressing, slowly, calmly. Even though he had slept not quite three hours, he felt that his strength was replenished. Without any particular emotion, he picked up the letters he had written that night and placed them in the side pocket of his army jacket. Then he drank his coffee, smoked a cigar, paid his bill, and left the room.

It was quarter to eight. It was quite dark outside, and the snow was still drifting down. The horizon looked constricted and, like a huge hat shoved down on a forehead, masked and altered the city's physiognomy. Everything looked smaller, insignificant, inconsequential. The traffic on the streets was still quite light. Children hurrying on their way to school formed the main contingent of the passers-by.

"My children are also on their way to school," the captain thought, and suddenly an unbearable pain pierced his heart. The searing pain that seemingly had been silenced yesterday began stirring within him once again. Try as he might to chase away any thoughts about his wife and children, the thoughts, like annoying wasps, flew around him, buzzing and pricking him with their stingers.

"If only I could see them at least one more time, at least from a distance," the captain thought, following a group of passing children with his eyes. "Who knows, it might be for the last time! And yesterday, as I was leaving home, I did not even kiss them. I did not take sufficient delight in them, I did not slake my soul with their sweet chattering. My poor children! What will happen to you if I should die today?"

Tears swirled in the captain's eyes. But, by a supreme effort of will, he chased them away.

The clock began to strike the hour, and he picked up his pace. He had to be at the appointed spot in the shooting gallery within five minutes, and there was still quite a ways to go. The large hall housing the gallery was not used at that hour, so it had been selected as the venue for the duel.

"I'll be a full three minutes late," the captain thought, glancing at his watch. "They're probably waiting already. They'll think I lost my nerve and backed out. Well, let them think whatever they want to. I'll show them that I'm not grist for their mill."

He tried to walk more quickly, but his efforts were in vain. A strange weakness overpowered him. The short stretch of road from the corner of the administration building to the hall seemed endlessly long and difficult to him. He did not feel any fear; he was tranquil, full of a quiet resignation, but nevertheless his feet had grown heavy, as if made of lead.

He pondered where he should aim: at the chest or at the head. He felt that his hand would be sure and would not tremble, and he knew that, if he was not struck down first, he would, without fail, hit his opponent. By aiming at the head, it was easier to miss, but a shot that hit its mark was usually fatal.

The fact that duelling rules stated that one should aim at the chest did not trouble him. To what rules were his enemies, his slanderers adhering? Aiming at the chest made it easier to hit the mark, but it was more difficult to ensure that the shot would be fatal. Should he shoot a little lower, in the area of the stomach, thereby sentencing his opponent to a long, cruel period of suffering before his death?

No, the captain shuddered at the very thought. He would kill Redlikh at once, on the spot—yes! That was the honourable thing to do, and it was demanded by his honour, or rather by the feelings of revenge and indignation that smouldered in the depths of his heart. But to sentence him to a couple of weeks of suffering before he died—no!

After all, he was a man—not an executioner! After all, only yesterday Redlikh was his friend.

In the square in front of the barracks, known by their old name as *Heumarktscaserne* [Barracks by the Hay Market], several infantry companies were performing their regular drills: marching, presenting arms, and shooting without live ammunition. They saluted him as they went past him.

A feeling of anguish stirred in his heart at the sight of those men positioned in two rows, their weary faces reddened by the frosty air, their boots splattered with mud that was mixed with the snow melting under their feet. It reminded him of a Latin expression from his high school lessons: *Morituri te salutant* [Those who are about to die salute you]; and he smiled bitterly when it occurred to him that this time it would have been more fitting to change the saying and say: *Moriturus vos salutat* [The one who is about to die salutes you].

"In half an hour the appearance of this square will change beyond recognition," the captain thought. "You will have a longer *Ruht* [At rest]! my poor fellows. Over there, through that gate, in front of which two officers are strolling, clanging their swords and smoking cigars—I wonder whose seconds these officers are?—one of us will be carried out with a smashed head, or a wounded chest spattered with blood, and with his hands hanging limply. It is quite likely that a few of you will be ordered to carry this burden. And a few others will be ordered to prepare the medical wagon. They will shove the corpse into it so that no one can see it and take it to the morgue at the military hospital.

"And that medical wagon will travel through the city, through streets filled with pedestrians; hundreds of people will pass by it, and not one of them will even suspect that a corpse is being driven past them. My wife, sleepy and angry as she searches for me, will walk by it, and it will not even cross her mind that in that drab yellowish-grey wagon, in that large box, the cold, stiff corpse of her husband, who was shot to death, lies unseen. And it is just as well that it will happen that way!"

Plagued by such darkly tragic thoughts, the captain finally reached the gate that led to the orchard in front of the hall.

The officers who were on patrol there greeted him politely, but coldly.

"Redlikh is here already," one of them said. "The seconds and the doctor are also present."

"And who are you?" the captain asked in surprise.

"We were asked to stay on guard here so that no one would disturb you," the officer said.

"Be so kind as to settle your matter of honour quickly," the other added with a smile. "It's cold out here, and it's time for breakfast."

The captain did not respond to this remark. The officer's smile and his words seemed cynical to him.

"He is in a hurry to have breakfast," he thought bitterly. "But the fact that, in the brief interval between this moment and the time that he has his breakfast, a human heart will burst, a life will be lost, a family will be devastated—he cares nothing at all about that. This is just a matter of honour, and the more quickly, the more radically, that is, the more expeditiously the matter is settled, the better."

The orchard in front of the main building was deserted and lifeless. The denuded chestnut and ash trees lifted their grey branches to a leaden sky. Fresh damp snow was heaped in layers and small mounds on their trunks and thicker limbs. The ground was covered with snow. But between the gate and the main building where the hall was located, the snow had been trampled by several people, and a path was being formed.

The watchman who lived in a side wing, having been informed about what was going to transpire and having received an appropriate sum of money, quietly left his lodgings and went downtown so as not to be a witness to anything. His wife, muttering under her breath, was bustling about in the cramped quarters. She was a very placid and trustworthy woman, not interested a whit in what she did not see, and even if cannons had been fired in the large hall, she would not have heard what was going on, for she was stone deaf.

The captain, walking down the path in a dignified and sober manner, slowly approached the stairs that led to the main entrance of the shooting gallery. In his heart of hearts he imagined how a condemned man feels as he steps up to the gallows.

Such a man counts the steps and examines the boards leading up to the platform, turns his attention to the protruding pole, a poorly hammered in peg—the carpenters had been in a great hurry!—the bald pates of the judges who are standing off to one side, the faces, moustaches, and clothes of the members of the public who, thronging in the cordoned-off area, are wondering if the young man hanging onto the railing of a balcony with his bare hands is feeling the cold, and what thoughts are going through the mind of the lady who is standing behind him with her full breasts positioned conveniently on his back.

The unfortunate condemned man sees all of this, looks closely at it, and hurriedly notes it in his mind, all in an effort not to see, not to observe, and not to take note of what is standing directly in front of him—the terrifying, dreadful, and unavoidable something that is waiting just for him, and which in a few minutes, a minute, a couple of insensate seconds, will seize him in its jaws, choke him, crunch him, grind him with its bloody teeth.

And, imagining the situation of that unfortunate man, the captain felt that his situation at this moment was very similar. He was standing at the door that led into the hall. He glanced backwards once more, trying to capture with his heart's eye the greatest amount of light, of space, but the sparse winter landscape was stingy even in that respect. There was nothing to be captured! Pressing his lips firmly together, the captain calmly opened the door and walked into the hall.

Even before he opened the door, he could hear the loud conversation and cheery laughter of the officers who were already there. They were amusing themselves unrestrainedly, as if they had gathered for a ball and were waiting for the dancing to begin.

But when he appeared in the doorway, they all glanced up at him and suddenly fell silent. It was obvious that the majority wanted to look at him dispassionately and then turn away, but none of them succeeded in doing so. There was something in his stance, in his face, that captured and held their attention.

Upon seeing him, all those present seemed to go into shock. Their eyes, untroubled at first, slowly advanced in their sockets, and their pupils dilated in an expression of fear, as if it was not a living man who had walked into the hall, but a horrifying, unearthly apparition.

"Good day!" the captain said, saluting and looking in bewilderment at those who were gathered there.

No one replied, and for a few seconds they all stood in a silent stupor. Then the doctors, who had been invited to assist in the "matter of honour" and who did not know the captain, cut short this mute scene and began to busy themselves with their instruments and bandages.

"Good day to you, Redlikh!" the captain said, approaching his opponent and extending his hand. "Surely you won't refuse to shake my hand?"

Redlikh silently shook the hand that was extended to him, but at the same time he averted his face, and with his left hand wiped away the tears welling in his eyes.

"After all, until yesterday we were friends, were we not?" the captain said with a melancholy smile. "We can at least greet one another in a friendly manner before we let our pistols do the talking."

"How did you sleep?" Redlikh asked, conquering his emotions.

"So-so," the captain replied. "I slept at a hotel."

"You haven't been home?"

"What for? It's better not to discuss such matters with women. When it's all over, she'll have time enough to find out all about it."

"Well yes, I think you're right," Redlikh responded, and he did not pursue the conversation.

The captain's seconds approached him and extended their hands to him rather ceremoniously, and then one of them took him by the arm and led him into an empty corner of the hall, farther away from the group comprised of the doctors and Redlikh's seconds.

Redlikh was standing by a window, drumming a march on a pane with his fingers.

"In accordance with the wishes of your colleague," the second said to the captain, "we have met with the opposing side and set up the conditions of the duel."

"Namely?" the captain asked.

"We demanded the toughest conditions. Pistols, shooting without a barrier, a distance of ten paces with the right for each side to advance three paces at the time of firing, and the exchange of three rounds."

"And did the opposing side argue about that?"

"The seconds protested, but obviously only in their own names. We stood our ground."

"What about Redlikh?"

"He agreed to our conditions without any hesitation whatsoever."

"That's good," the captain said gloomily. "Well, will we begin soon?"

"This very moment."

The seconds moved away to finish their preparations, and in the meantime, the captain, after taking off his coat and removing his sword, looked around indifferently at a number of lithographs displayed on a nearby wall.

It seemed to him that it was all a dream. He even felt a strange doubling within his inner being and experienced the sensation that the man in the army tunic, the one who was studiously examining the lithographs with his hands in his pockets, was another person, a stranger, a distant and uninteresting person at whom his secret "I" was looking at from the sidelines with faint amazement.

Meanwhile, the seconds, talking softly, were busy making the final arrangements dictated by the traditional code for the conduct of duels. Two of them measured the distance, loudly counting out the steps and marking the floor with chalk, both at the spot where the opponents were to stand, and the one to which they could advance. Two other seconds, one from each side, were loading the pistols, and the doctors were laying out bandages on a little table and placing near them their kits filled with surgical instruments.

Following the captain's example, Redlikh also took off his coat and removed his sword. The others who were present kept their coats on, for it was vexingly cold in the hall.

After loading the pistols, the seconds marked them and then, making the same markings on slips of paper, rolled them up and dropped them in a hat. The opponents silently pulled out these improvised lots—Redlikh was called upon first, and then the captain. They were given the appropriate pistols—large officers' pistols that had already been used many a time in settling matters of honour.

A strange shiver ran through the captain's body when he touched the pistol, as if someone had rubbed a cold piece of ice over his body from his palm to his heart.

"It is a foreboding of death," the thought flashed through his mind. He felt neither fear, nor grief; it was as if all this was happening not to him, but to someone else.

Glancing at his weapon with a wooden stoicism, he walked to the spot indicated to him by his seconds.

"On guard, gentlemen!" one of the seconds said loudly. "Will you permit me to preside?"

"Please do."

"Well then, I remind you, gentlemen, that at the instant that I say 'three,' and no more than five seconds after that, you are to fire. At the time of the firing, each of you has the right to advance three paces closer to your opponent, right up to the horizontal line marked on the floor."

Both duellists stood calmly, at attention, with their pistols pointing downwards.

"One . . . two . . . three!" the second gave the order slowly in a sharp voice.

Two pistols blasted almost simultaneously. Neither of the opponents moved from his spot, either before he shot or afterwards.

The captain felt Redlikh's bullet whistle over his head. Had Redlikh missed on purpose? As for himself, the captain knew that he had no intention of missing.

"Is either of you gentlemen wounded?" the second asked.

"No," the duellists answered in unison.

"Do you insist on a second round, gentlemen?"

"I insist," the captain said. Redlikh did not say anything.

The pistols were cleaned and reloaded once again. The captain clutched the pistol convulsively and bit his lip.

"It's either—or!" The words buzzed noisily in his head.

He tried to renew, fortify, and exacerbate his hatred of Redlikh in his heart. The pungent odour of the gunpowder was stirring a fever in his blood, a fever that was familiar to him from his Bosnian engagements.

"One . . . two . . . three!" The words of the presiding officer resounded.

This time only one shot rang out, only one pistol spewed fire and smoke—from the captain's side. Taking advantage of the conditions that had been set, he had advanced three paces as the order was being given, and had fired as soon as the word "three" was uttered.

In that same instant, Redlikh, as if jerked by the powerful blast of a whirlwind, made a sudden, swift half-turn to the left, dropped his pistol, flung his hands upwards, swung his arms out like a man who is drowning or losing his balance, and then staggered and shouted: "Oh!" and, clutching his chest in the vicinity of his heart with his right hand, toppled to the floor.

The entire duel had not lasted longer than a few seconds.

The doctors and seconds rushed to his side, raised him, and carrying him in their arms, laid him down close to a window. All that was left on the floor was a spreading red stain, round like the bottom of a glass.

The captain stood stock-still and stared at the stain. Finally he walked up to the window to join the group that had closed in around Redlikh, who was not showing any signs of life.

"How is he?" he asked.

"Of what concern is that to you?" one of Redlikh's seconds replied sharply. "You are free to leave; you have done what you set out to do. Do not poison his last few moments—he is dying."

"Are you saying that the wound is fatal?" the captain shrieked, clutching his head and completely forgetting that only a moment earlier that had been his most fervent desire.

"Don't create a scene!" Redlikh's other second said curtly with open scorn and hatred. "You got what you wanted. This is *your second victim*," he added with special emphasis. "I think that's enough. Or do you want yet another one? In that case, I can be of service to you."

"Sir!" the captain shouted painfully, totally broken in spirit, baffled by the glances, the words, and the overall behaviour of the seconds.

"Go, sir! Get away from here!" the second repeated impatiently. "You are not needed here, and our obligations towards you have ended. You proved to us that you know how to shoot, but do not think that it will make even one of us change his opinion of you and of your honourable wife. Adieu!"

The world turned dark in the captain's eyes, and there was a buzzing in his ears. Something struggled within him, trying to break free, urging him to fling himself at this officer as at a rapacious animal, to tear him to pieces, to rekindle his rage with his warm blood. But the better part of his being remained numb, powerless, as if struck by lightning.

Not knowing how and when, he went up to the chair where his sword and coat were lying, got dressed, automatically raised his hand in a salute without really knowing whom he was saluting, for no one in the hall was paying any attention to him, and, with a broken heart and lips grimly shut tight, walked out of the shooting gallery without so much as a backward glance.

X

"And so I have taken a life!" the captain thought. "I have murdered a man, a friend! I am a murderer! I now have a human life on my conscience—yet my life goes on. What is next? What happens now?"

He walked out into the street. The officers on patrol had waited until the shots rang out, and then abandoned their posts and hurried into the hall. Encountering the captain on the porch, they asked him something, but he did not understand what they were saying and brushed past them without responding. When he passed through the gate of the shooting gallery it seemed to him that he had walked out of the sphere of the inhabited world into an endless desert.

He felt that everything that had happened only moments ago, that what he had left behind was *the past*, it was something that was irrevocably gone, that had collapsed behind him like a bridge washed out by water, over which he had crossed onto a new, unknown bank. He could never return to where he had come from, he would never again see what he had left behind. What was about to begin in the next moment would be something completely new and unknown. Would it be bad, or good? He did not know, he was not even interested in knowing. The difference between good and evil was obliterated in his soul, just as there are no sides, either right or left, in a boundless infinity.

"I killed him! I killed a man!" the captain repeated as he slowly walked down the street. He was amazed that it had happened so instantaneously. He was amazed that this fact had not made a greater impression on him, that it had evoked in his heart a feeling of astonishment, a momentary shock, but had not caused him any pain, any moral anguish.

He was well aware that this killing was completely different from those that occurred over there, in Bosnia, amid the cliffs and mountains. There was a war over there, a mutual murdering; there, to kill was an obligation that did not impinge on one's moral being, did not raise the question of individual responsibility. There, one had to kill, and it was with a serene conscience that one issued the command: "*Feuer* [Fire]!" It was with a serene conscience that a few questions were posed to an unfortunate soldier captured with a weapon in his hand, and then the verdict was given: "Shoot him on the spot!" And the order was obeyed instantly—and there was nothing more to it.

But here! Here the value of a human life was completely different, and the question of personal responsibility stood before one's conscience in all its grim grandeur. Nevertheless, he felt composed—as a man who had done what he had to do.

"For truly, could I have acted otherwise? I really did not have a choice. I could either remain dishonoured, put up no protest, and have my name, my honour, my wife's good reputation slandered, or I could wash all that away in human blood—a terrible alternative, but sadly, an unavoidable one."

The two small trickles of blood that had flowed from Redlikh's chest onto the grimy, muddy floor and spread into a circle no bigger than the bottom of a glass suddenly appeared before his eyes.

It seemed to him that he was standing over those trickles, kneeling, lowering his face to the floor and staring at them, putting them under a magnifying glass and analyzing them, trying to find the microbe of that moral illness that so suddenly, in such a mysterious manner, had poisoned his friend's heart. "*Blut ist ein ganz besondrer Saft* [Blood is a unique fluid]," *Goethe's verse buzzed in his head—those ironical, but at the same time, deeply symbolic words of *Mephistopheles.

Do the characteristics of this liquid include the ability to wash out, for example, the stain on someone's honour? Will my good name and that of my wife be protected from all manner of malicious attacks now that it is covered with a purplish circle, no bigger than the bottom of a glass, that was trampled by the feet of the seconds on the grimy floor of the shooting gallery? Now that the two streamlets of blood have been spilled, will our family honour become newly clean and bright, like a freshly polished metal mirror that had been dirty and stained?

The captain's brain, bereft for the moment of the possibility of reacting outwardly, dug and gnawed its way into an impassable thicket of questions and contradictions, taking pleasure in implausible contrasts, and not looking for any answers or appeasement.

What was happening to him now was similar, in a way, to the refraction of light through a prism. Striking against a fact that was hard, smooth, and clear in its essence—"I killed a man!"—his psyche was incapable, for the moment, of mastering and assimilating all the consequences of that fact and, splintering instead into a thousand beams and rays, and transforming itself into myriads of colours, it scintillated like a rainbow and burst like flying foam.

"Human life is a dream. It is all the same as to who awakens me and how. I could be the one lying there, convulsively clutching at my wounded chest with clenched fists. I wonder if they would have rushed up as quickly to save me, or if they would have just let me die like a dog? But Redlikh shot over my head. And because of that, he took a bullet in the chest."

It was only now that the captain felt some unbearably painful pangs in his chest as well.

"Because of that?" he almost shrieked, trying to conquer this new, terrifying feeling. "Because of that? No, no, no! It is because of what he said yesterday. Because of the dishonourable, implausible slander that he would not retract. But why wouldn't he? Because of an innate rancour? Or, maybe, because he couldn't? He couldn't? But why couldn't he? Well, let's see, it could be because what he said was the absolute truth. O God!"

The captain staggered as he shouted these last words. He was slipping into unconsciousness and would have fallen if he had not involuntarily seized a lamppost with both hands. The post was wet from the melting snow, and its cold and slippery surface jolted the captain into full consciousness, but the feeling of pain and alarm did not abate in his heart; on the contrary, it grew stronger with every passing moment.

The terrifying, putrid abyss that had opened at his feet after his conversation with Redlikh and which, during his solitary struggle in front of the gate of his living quarters had almost precipitated a bloody finale, the abyss that he had later filled in and levelled off through a tremendous effort of will and love, the abyss that he had filled in and trampled down forever—or so he had thought—was now once again gaping before him with widely yawning jaws. It was like a monster ravenous for a victim. Redlikh's blood had not satiated it, had not sealed it; on the contrary, it had made it larger, deeper, more terrifying.

What if Redlikh was truly innocent, and what if everything that he had said was the truth? Horrors! After all, Redlikh had not told him this willingly, of his own accord, out of a taste for slander. He had told him because he had to. The fatal meeting with Yuliya at dinnertime, and the disrespect that he had shown because of this had to be justified, and who was to blame if that justification brought out into the open daylight such an abyss of scandal and vileness?

And besides—it was not Redlikh alone who was in possession of that secret. All the other officers obviously knew about it, for they had resolved to exclude him from their company! And each and every one of them had been prepared to tell him the very same thing that Redlikh had told him.

"So, what does that mean? If that is the case, then why did I kill Redlikh? Or better yet, why did he not kill me? Why did he not do me that favour? I would have died with the conviction that I was dying as an innocent victim of a dishonourable intrigue. But now? What am I now?"

Coming up to the nearest bench in the square in front of the viceroyalty building, he sank down, exhausted, and continued with his train of thought. Passers-by who flowed past him in an endless stream peered into his face and, seeing in it the signs of an inner spiritual struggle, shrugged their shoulders or muttered some caustic remarks about him, a man who, in their view had probably had too much to drink the previous night and was now trying to sober up in the fresh winter air. But the captain, preoccupied with the deathly struggle that seethed in the depths of his soul, did not see anything or hear anything.

Among the passers-by there were also soldiers who, on their way to the barracks, saluted him, did a "*links schaut* [dress ranks to the left]" and walked by at attention, stiff as ramrods. The captain, staring blankly with wide-open eyes, did not see them, nor did he respond to their mute greetings. Those swarms of people that wound their way before his eyes seemed so immeasurably distant, foreign, illusory, that any effort on his part to establish a link between them and his inner being would have been futile.

"Is it possible that my wife, my Anelya, was engaged in running a house of ill-repute in partnership with Yuliya? My wife, my Anelya—and a house of ill-repute?"

This thought, that only yesterday he had considered to be ludicrous in its grotesqueness, something so impossible and contrary to all the laws of nature, suddenly seemed to him to be so straightforward, so familiar, so natural . . . Yuliya, her friend, a widow, a practical woman who had no scruples. Anelya—a grass widow, two children, a meagre stipend, no other income, no other means . . . She wrote to him about giving lessons—but it was all a lie! She had played the piano in the past, but not at all competently enough to give lessons.

So—a joint enterprise! An attractive apartment, furniture, a small boarding house for mature girls—and a hunt for hedonistic gadabouts, rich lordlings who desired refined and genteel pleasures. A hunt for golden birds that could be plucked. First of all, for military personnel, officers, and high ranking officials. For aristocracy! And split the earnings. And therein lay the whole secret of her economizing and good housekeeping! And therein lay the nucleus and essence of the story with Baron Reuchlingen!

"Ah, yes! Now I understand! But I warned her about him before I left. He showed a great affection for her, a deep respect, visited our home almost on a daily basis. She kept him at a distance. She never mentioned him in her letters. That seemed suspicious to me, but I did not want to cause her any discomfort by asking her about it in more detail.

"Then, quite unexpectedly, there was the moral ruin of the Baron, the furious rage that flashed in his eyes at the very mention of Anelya. He called her in turn an angel and a devil. Oh, I understand, I understand! She took advantage of his passion without satisfying it. She and her friend sucked him dry, drove him to the point of losing his fortune, his honour, and his mind. How did they achieve this? Alas, is it that hard to figure out?"

With frenzied acuity, with fiendish clarity, the captain immersed himself in that sea of ignominy, dove into it, trying to plumb its depths. What had until now appeared to him to be puzzling, tangled, obscure, and full of contradictions, was suddenly becoming intelligible, clear and lucid, like alphabetic characters that stood a fathom tall.

And he read, hurriedly and with insatiable greed, the terrible book, whose every word he had been willing, only an hour ago, to erase with the blood of his heart. With infinite bitterness he reminded himself that all one had to do was to lose every iota of respect for a person in order to comprehend thoroughly his most secret thoughts and motives.

But all the same, despite his pessimistic outlook, despite the numerous and painful signs that confirmed Anelya's guilt, the captain felt that he had not stopped loving her, that in his wretched, incorrigible heart, the spark of devotion to her had not stopped glowing—and what is more, there was even a spark of senseless, absurd hope that all this might yet prove to be a falsehood, a phantasm, a bizarre dream, that by some magical means, her marvellous eyes, her words, her entire being would annihilate, would chase away these nightmares, disperse the clouds, and begin to shine with a fresh, lovely lustre.

"But the old man! Old Hurter!" he suddenly recalled. "After all, I looked over her accounts, the entries of fairly substantial sums that he sent her at various times. I saw his letters, full of gratitude, fatherly love. Surely this can't be a deception! And that explains everything, everything!

"Of course, I did not verify the sums, or add them up, and I only skimmed the letters. At the time I was hardly in the mood to do otherwise! Rosy clouds of happiness blinded my eyes. I was intoxicated with feelings of bliss.

"But the documents do exist, and in them I have invincible weapons with which I can step forward and belie the slanderers' falsehoods. I will launch a lawsuit and initiate a litigation to redeem my honour, a litigation not just with a single wretched man like Redlikh, but with all of them. Yes, that's the best way! Let that Yuliya be guilty a hundred times over—it is no concern of mine. Anelya may have received her without knowing about her loathsome earnings. But I must clear my name—I must—or else . . ."

The captain rose to his feet and squared his shoulders. He felt reinvigorated. Just as a drowning person clutches at an unsteady reed, so his thoughts, seeking support and succour, found them momentarily by seizing upon Anelya's letters and accounts. And having discovered at least this small patch of firm ground under his feet, he was able to calm down a bit, to think about what he should do next. There could be no doubt that some action, and decisive action at that, had to be taken. Every moment of indecision and uncertainty could bring with it the most catastrophic consequences.

And in that case, the first thing that had to be done was to resign from military service—and to do so as quickly as possible. Not only because every meeting with a military person was now a morally torturous encounter that would in all probability expose him to a host of conflicts similar in nature to the one that had arisen with Redlikh, but also because in an action like the one that he was about to initiate to rehabilitate his home hearth, he had to have complete freedom of movement, freedom to act without constraint to an extent that would not be congruent with his military duties. Finally, the captain was convinced that the matter that would have to be clarified was of a nature not at all befitting a military man, and that if he retired at once, then he could hope that his *ex officio* retirement would be in place when the matter became public.

The resignation that he had hastily written only to appease his wife's strange caprice—or so he had thought at the time—now came in very handy. Without wasting a moment, the captain set out for command headquarters, knocked on the door of the protocol officer, and handed in his resignation, much to the amazement of the functionaries in the office who had seen, only the day before yesterday, how courteously and amicably the general had greeted the captain newly arrived from Bosnia.

After leaving the office, the captain decided to go home. It was ten o'clock. He had to have a conversation with his wife, to speak frankly with her, to tell her everything, to adjure her to tell him the truth. He had to have certitude, to know everything, both good and bad, in order to know what he had to defend himself against.

But he had taken only a few steps when a man on the opposite side of the street spotted him and, taking off his cap, began waving it and contorting his face as he bowed to him. The captain glanced at this odd person but, failing to recognize him and assuming that he was drunk, turned away and continued walking.

The strange fellow, obviously lacking the nerve to shout, raised his coat above his knees, plunged into the muddy street, and ran diagonally across it towards the captain. After catching up to him, he once again took off his cap and, bowing, smiled broadly.

"I kiss your hands in greeting, captain! Obviously, the captain does not recognize me, does he?"

The captain reluctantly glanced at him and replied brusquely: "No, I do not."

"I am Slavinsky. Vitsko Slavinsky. I was the captain's aide-de-camp in Bosnia, captain."

"Ah, Vitsko!" the captain said. He extended his hand, and Vitsko kissed it. "Well, how is life treating you? What are you doing?"

"I'm fine, if it please you, captain. I finished my term in the army and came home. But after I was wounded in Bosnia and received a commendation for my service—you remember, captain, the sticks of dynamite with which I saved our company—I had no way of supporting myself here, and so I was given a position looking after patients in the regional hospital."

The captain smiled when Vitsko reminded him about the dynamite charges. He remembered very well the incident that had resonated throughout the entire garrison stationed in Bosnia.

In its pursuit of Bosnian insurgents, one squad had ventured too far into the mountains. The squad was headed by a corporal, a nice enough fellow, brave and decisive, but not overly intelligent. It was Vitsko who had a monopoly on intelligence in the squad, and he was carrying in his army jacket a dozen or more dynamite charges that the captain had requested from army headquarters for some military purpose.

Not seeing any imminent danger, the soldiers set up camp in a small grove, stacked their muskets in a pyramid, lit a fire, and began roasting a ram that they had caught during their march across the nearby mountain. But while they were peacefully engaged in this work, forgetting all about being on guard, a shot resounded very close to their backs. Terrified, they leapt to their feet, grabbed their muskets, and saw that the grove was surrounded on all sides by insurgents.

"Stop! Don't shoot!" the leader of the insurgents shouted. "We can see all of you, and we've drawn a bead on each and every one of you. If you shoot even once, we'll respond instantly according to our plan. And every one of you will fall, riddled by at least four bullets."

All the soldiers froze in fear, holding their muskets and looking like rams being led to slaughter. And it was only Vitsko, raised in Lviv, who did not lose his presence of mind. Taking in the terrain at a single glance, he observed that the grove was comprised of a rather sparse stand of large oak trees that rose out of a copious growth of thick, short shrubs. He also noted that the insurgents had surrounded the grove on all sides, but had not come in too close, obviously fearing an ambush from the shrubbery. An opportune thought flashed in his head.

"Listen to me, Mykola," he whispered to the corporal. "Do as I tell you, and everything will be fine. Tell us to *Duckt euch* [Squat]!, while you carry on a conversation with that Bosnian. Look as if you want to surrender, but bargain with him as long as you can. And do it boldly; don't show even a twinge of fear!"

"*Duckt euch!*" the corporal shouted, turning to his soldiers, and, following Vitsko's example, they all quickly scrunched down on their heels, and even though they did not disappear completely from the Bosnians' view, they gained a major advantage: the Bosnians could neither count how many of them there were, nor draw a bead on them.

"What are you doing?" the Bosnian leader shouted. He did not understand the command, but he could see that his position was not at all as advantageous as it had been a moment earlier.

"Well, we're not shooting," the corporal replied good-naturedly. "I ordered them to sit down so that none of them would be tempted to shoot. You know, there are moments when a man's fingers get itchy."

"Damned *Swabian!" the Bosnian blurted out, adding his own customary crude word directed at the special saint of those "Swabians," who also spoke good *Rusyn and could converse quite effectively with the Bosnians without the help of an interpreter.

"So what do you want from us?" the corporal asked.

"Surrender!" the Bosnian leader said.

"Hmm, in a word, you're asking a lot," the corporal spoke slowly and in the same tone of voice that he would have used if he were at a market in *Drohobych bargaining over a worthless horse with a gypsy from another village. "But are you aware, my friend, what awaits us from our general if we surrender with weapons in our hands?"

"Of what concern is that to me?" the Bosnian snapped back at him. "If you can't surrender with weapons in your hands, then do the following: put down your arms, and then surrender."

"That's even worse," the corporal said. "In that case we aren't any further ahead."

"What do you mean?"

"Just this, if you don't cut our heads off, then our general will order us shot to death."

"So what are we supposed to do with you?" the leader asked, firmly convinced that the squad could not escape from his clutches.

"I really don't know," the corporal said, scratching his head. "I don't want to do you an injustice, but I also don't wish to lose my head because of you. You know what, my friend, perhaps you would agree to this: take our army jackets and coats, all the money that we have, our stash of gunpowder and cartridges—all of this will come in handy for you, right?—and let us go with our muskets, because we must hurry and rejoin our regiment."

"Is that so? You don't have time?" the Bosnian sneered, and he began to consult with his friends.

At that moment Vitsko crawled up to the corporal on all fours and whispered: "Get behind an oak tree and give the command: fire!"

The corporal instantly jumped behind an oak tree and shouted: "*Feuer* [Fire]!"

The roar of the salvo made the mountains echo. The soldiers, hidden in the bushes and crouching on their heels, could take good aim, and they felled several Bosnians, including the leader. But this alone would not have helped them very much, for there were far too many insurgents, and the small number of "Swabians" had fuelled their courage. But just as they were ready to fire at the soldiers, there was a terrible roar, and the ground shook. One oak tree at the very edge of the grove flew up into the air, roots and all, and with a terrifying cracking sound broke into splinters that fell like hail to the ground and on the heads of the nearest Bosnians.

"Help! The devil is helping the Swabians!" the insurgents screamed.

"Fire a second volley!" the emboldened corporal shouted, and at that moment, at the other end of the grove, a second stick of dynamite exploded, creating the same powerful—and for the Bosnians—puzzling result.

"My God!" they all shrieked. "The Swabians have cannons! It's each man for himself! Let's get out of here! Let's go!"

The explosion of the third stick of dynamite drowned out their screams. Under the cover of these mighty fireworks, the squad was able to extricate itself honourably from a dangerous situation and to rout the enemy without any loss of life.

For his ingenuity Vitsko was awarded the silver medal for bravery and, after his term of military service ended, was assigned to the position of an orderly in the regional hospital.

"I've been looking for you, captain, for an hour already," Vitsko said.

"For me?"

"Yes. I was at the captain's home. The captain's honourable wife told me that the captain was probably at the officers' casino. I went there, and they told me: 'He was here yesterday, but he isn't here now. Maybe he's at the regimental office.' I went there, and they told me that the captain is now on leave and does not come into the office, but perhaps . . ."

The captain, greatly surprised, interrupted this fascinating story. "But what did you need from me so suddenly? Why were you so determined to find me?"

"Well, if you please, captain, I personally do not need anything," Vitsko replied good-naturedly. "But over there, in the hospital . . . you know, captain . . . yesterday an old man was brought in . . . The captain knows him, right?"

"What old man?"

"He said that the captain knew him. Yesterday he fell down on the sidewalk and hurt himself. The fall in itself was nothing too serious, for he had no broken bones. But as it turned out, he had not eaten for two days and was in a weakened condition. In the hospital he fell into a fever. And he kept calling for the captain all night long."

"For me?"

"Yes. It caught my attention. He kept calling—Anharovych, Anharovych! I stayed at his side all night. I asked him a few times: 'What do you want from Anharovych, old fellow?' But of course, he had a fever and couldn't understand anything. But this morning he felt a little better. He called me over and asked me, for the love of God, to find Captain Anharovych and beg him to come to see him as soon as possible. And as I know the captain, and because I had to go into town on some other matters, I promised to do this for him."

"But who is that old man? What is his name?"

"Yesterday he was in such a weakened condition that we couldn't find out anything from him. He couldn't even eat, and we had to feed him like a child. But this morning he told us that his name is Mykhaylo Hurter."

A thunderbolt striking right next to the captain would not have startled him as much as hearing this name under these circumstances. What kind of a riddle was this? Hurter, a millionaire, the owner of several factories—had not eaten anything for two days! He was the indigent old man who had fallen on the sidewalk yesterday before his very eyes, and for whose care he had given a rynski out of the goodness of his heart?

A whirlwind of thoughts, fears, and suspicions that had been slowly abating roared to life once again and swirled in his head. With a single gesture of his hand the captain bade farewell to the obliging Vitsko, jumped into the first hansom he came across, and asked to be taken to the regional hospital.

When the captain walked into the ward, Hurter was sitting up in bed, leaning on a pillow, sipping some broth with the aid of a nurse. His large, powerful, heavy-boned, but extremely emaciated body was wrapped in a coarse hospital gown and a cotton bed jacket. His face, folded in wrinkles like a dried apple, was the colour of old parchment, and it was encircled by a long, unkempt, grey beard. He looked like a church watchman, and it seemed to the captain that he could detect the faint scent of a church censer on him.

Upon seeing the captain, Hurter began to shake and dropped the spoon that he was carrying to his mouth.

"Oh! My dear son! Captain! You've come, after all!" he mumbled in a hesitant, wavering, broken voice. "Oh! I begged God . . . before my death . . . Oh! . . . For I do not have long to live, my son, oh, not long at all! But sit down! Sit down right here, close to me! Do you have a chair? That's good! Give me your hand."

The captain silently took a chair and sat down at the head of Hurter's bed. He felt that something was gripping his heart with iron pincers. He extended his hand to Hurter, and the old man raised it to his lips and flooded it with tears. The captain tried to prevent him from doing this—the old man's tears seared him like drops of boiling oil.

"What are you doing, my dear man? Please don't," he cried, pulling his hand away from the old man's lips.

"No, no! Give me your hand, give it to me . . ." Hurter whispered. "I'm an old fool . . . an old fool . . ." His sobs interrupted his speech. "I owe you . . . this satis . . . oh! oh! . . . faction! God is punishing me . . . and justly so . . . for my prideful ways . . . for my damned pride . . . and my blindness!"

The captain listened with grief and sympathy to these words, even though he could not follow either their order or their causal links. And he did not interrupt Hurter who, while finishing his breakfast with the nurse's help, continued speaking between groans and fits of coughing.

"I was a fool, my son! My pride blinded me . . . oh! You know, whom God wants to destroy . . ." and he coughed helplessly. "I can't talk! I won't last much longer, and there is so much I have to tell you.

"You know, I feel that my heart is frozen within me. It has not died; it is still alive, but it is frozen. It wants to thaw, it shudders occasionally, but it cannot do it by itself . . . Oh, I'm a fool! A fool! I froze it myself, and now I'm dying because of it."

He paused. The nurse made him finish the broth that had already turned cold. Meanwhile, the captain sat with his mind on hold, casting cursory glances at what was happening around him. After the nurse finished feeding Hurter, she replaced the pillow in its usual position, helped the old man lie down, covered him with a blanket and, inclining her head slightly in a farewell gesture to the captain, walked out without saying a single word.

"Well then . . . here is what I was going to tell you," Hurter began speaking again, peering at the captain with dull, deeply sunken eyes that were half-veiled by his shaggy eyebrows. "Thank you, thank you a thousand times for coming to see me. Give me your hand . . . don't worry . . . I only want to place it here, on my heart . . . I know, I know you are a good, honest man! I found that out, but it was too late. Formerly, when I was rich, when I was blind, when I froze my heart and shielded it with steel armour—at that time I did not want to hear or know about you. I hated you with all my heart. I held you in contempt. I cursed Anelya for marrying you. Oh! God has punished me. He has chastened me with two punitive blows, my son, one that is harder to bear than the other. He took away my fortune, and he opened my eyes!"

Dry sobs racked his body and prevented him from speaking. Then he had such a lengthy paroxysm of coughing that the nurse came running to reassure herself that her patient was not in any imminent danger. And after the coughing spell passed, a silence that lasted for several minutes fell on the room until the old man stopped sobbing, regained his breath, and was able to continue speaking.

"Four years ago I lost everything that I had," Hurter said.

"Four years ago!" the captain shouted, unable to control his agitation, and he jumped in his chair as if he had been scalded.

"Yes, yes, my son, four years ago," Hurter repeated, not understanding the captain's reaction. "It is a long story . . . I was duped, cheated—may God never forgive them for what they did! I was left without a crust of bread. They turned me into a church watchman . . . Oh, it was a distressing way to earn a crust of bread, but I had to do it, I had no choice.

"And then I remembered about the two of you, about Anelya, about you. I found out that you were in Bosnia . . . I wrote to Anelya, explained my situation to her, and pleaded for her help. She did not reply . . . A year later I wrote a second time. She still did not reply . . . I became ill . . . I lost my job . . . I was an old man, not suited for any kind of work . . . and no one wants to support a parasite!

"I was forced to go begging, to stretch out my hand for a scrap of bread. But then I thought, after all . . . My God! After all she is my granddaughter! After all, I raised her, I gave her a dowry! Surely she won't throw me out of her house! That's what I thought about Anelya . . . and so I set out for your place. On foot, from Cracow . . . on begged bread . . . hungry and cold . . . Oh, my dear son! I sense that God has punished me justly for my sins. But His punishment has been hard, so hard!"

The captain, listening to these words, felt as if he were being tortured. Every sentence was a nail pounded into his flesh. Every groan the old man emitted twisted his joints like a rack. Every fit of coughing scorched him like a torch. He tried not to look at Hurter in order not to betray the terrible suffering that his words were causing him.

The old man stopped coughing and continued speaking: "She did not write to me. She forgot all about me and did not want to be reminded of me. Perhaps that's justifiable. Perhaps that was what I deserved for forgetting about the two of you back then. But nevertheless, she still should have . . . Oh, my dear son, may God prevent both you and her from tasting what has been my daily fare for the past four years!"

He wiped away the heavy tears that, rolling down from his eyes, lost their way in the deep furrows on his face.

"But as for you, you won't turn me away, will you? You will give me refuge for the remainder of my days, won't you?" Hurter asked in a quivering voice as he turned to the captain.

"But my dear old man!" the captain cried, clasping Hurter's withered hands. "Could you doubt that for even a moment? Just get well enough so that you can leave this place."

"Oh, I'll get better, I'll get better!" Hurter said hastily. "I sense that God has sent you to me. Your very presence brings me additional strength and health. Thank you, my son! Thank you a hundred times over!"

And then, gloomily shaking his head, he added: "But I am afraid of her . . . I am afraid of Anelya. Watch over her, my dear son! She was a good girl, wise, energetic. But I, the cursed and unfortunate man that I am, poisoned her soul! I planted arrogance in her heart, disdain for her inferiors, for the indigent, the disparaged . . . A dread of being in want, of being poor . . . A contempt for the impoverished . . .

"And I fear, my dear son, that those weeds may choke the seeds of mercy in her soul. After all, she did not write to me even once when I confessed to her that I was poor and perishing in indigence. She did not comfort me, or extend a helping hand to me. That, my dear son, is a bad sign, a very bad sign! She used the weapons that I placed in her hands to crush me. Watch her carefully, because these weapons are very dangerous."

The captain, pale and cold as a corpse, stared at Hurter with the eyes of a dead man, and then he rose to his feet and hurriedly bade the old man farewell. He felt that if he stayed another minute, if he listened to Hurter speak any longer, he would lose his mind, go mad. Shrouded in the anxiety that people experience before an apoplectic attack, he was in a hurry to get away, to get some fresh air.

"Are you leaving already, my dear son?" Hurter asked sorrowfully. "Well, go, go! I know you have work to do, you have obligations. But come by to see me whenever you have the time. And then, when I am well again, I adjure you by all that is holy, take me into your home! Give me a small corner in your home and a crust of bread. I will not be around too much longer to trouble you. But do not let me perish from hunger in the street!"

XI

"So she was lying! She was lying in this instance as well!" The captain's brain was whirling. "She has surrounded me on all sides with tangles of lies. O God, how masterfully she played her role. To me she appeared to be pure, saintly, innocent. I would have laid down my head that no evil thought had ever so much as touched her soul.

"And in the meantime she . . . She showed me falsified accounts, knowing that in the excitement of my initial joy, I would not be capable of examining them thoroughly. She showed me forged letters from her grandfather, letters full of gratitude and love, but she did not even deign to answer the real letters from a hungry old man beaten down by poverty. What kind of a nature is this? What kind of a heart? Is she the devil incarnate, or just an actress, a poseur?"

And then he recalled what Hurter had said about poisoning Anelya's soul with pride and disdain for the poor, and he began to think more coolly.

"It is true! Raised in wealth and luxury, in narrow, medieval beliefs, removed from real life and its struggles, removed from people who suffer and are disparaged, how could she learn to have any sympathy for them? Not accustomed to doing any useful work, she was raised in her youthful years to be nothing more than a doll, an ideal, a celestial being, a deity, and a man's plaything—but not a human being, a true citizen.

"She was given a formal religious upbringing, and that means that she was taught her catechism, prayers, and religious practices, but these ethical principles were ruined by the manner in which she was raised, by the life style, the customs, and the traditions both at home and in school. And then, what was bound to happen, happened."

After walking out of the hospital, the captain, looking for the shortest route home, turned off into a narrow, steep alley that was more like a trail leading to Pekarska Street. He was shaking at the very thought that he would soon be facing his wife, that he would have to talk with her, listen to new subterfuges, new lies with new fabricated pieces of evidence, and that, step by step, he would have to untangle the whole vile web.

He felt an overwhelming loathing for her, as for a defiled woman not worthy of bearing his name. How low she had fallen in his eyes in the course of the past twenty-four hours! Lucifer, cast down from the heavenly heights into the bottom of hell had not fallen any lower.

And this was Anelya, the mother of his children! This was the woman who bore his name, the name that she had so unhesitatingly trampled in the mud! So that's what his honour looked like now, the honour for which he had sacrificed the life of his truest friend!

The street was deserted. In order to flee from the thoughts that gnawed at his inner being like voracious mice, the captain forced himself to look closely at the most ordinary objects in his surroundings. He carefully scrutinized the billboard notices, faded and washed by the rain. He counted the posts and the stakes in the picket fences. He stared for a long time at the face of a plaster statue of the Madonna in front of a Catholic monastic institution, trying to find a semblance of Anelya in those sculpted gypsum features.

And then suddenly, for no apparent reason, he picked up his pace, hurrying and almost running to his apartment, as if a fire was raging there and threatening someone's life, or as if a terrible catastrophe was hanging over someone there, a catastrophe that he could avert if he got home in time.

And it was only now, in this moment of frenzied alarm, of absurd agitation, when his heart raced ever more quickly the closer that he came to the familiar green apartment block, that he felt that notwithstanding all the suffering, notwithstanding the shame, not yet effaced, that she had brought down on his name, he still loved her, he loved this beautiful, cheerful, lively woman, her deep, marvellous eyes, her rosy lips, her shiny, luxuriant hair, her supple figure, her voice, her gestures . . .

He did not stop to think what he was going to do now, or how he was going to untangle the damned web in which he was caught. He felt the imminent approach of a catastrophe, the dull rumbling roar of an oncoming storm, but he did not know, nor did he even try to guess, whom the first thunderbolt would strike.

As he drew nearer to the building that housed his cosy home, the captain saw that a rather strange group—comprised of five young women wearing loud, gaudy dresses and hats decorated with feathers, sprigs of artificial flowers, and large bows—was walking on the opposite side of the street, towards the building in which he lived. The gestures and figures of these girls testified at once to the trade in which they were engaged. They cast provocative looks at men, laughed loudly, and in general, tried to attract the attention of all the passers-by. They were being led by a man, a middle-aged fellow, thickset, with a face that was definitely of a Semitic cast, and dressed in civilian attire that was worn and untidy.

As they walked along, the girls ran their eyes over the brick buildings, and finally, stopping directly across from the one where the captain lived, they pointed at it of one accord.

"Here! Here! In this green building."

The man with the Semitic cast of face, dashed across the street to the gate of the building without saying a word, and the girls followed him, giggling and lifting their skirts with exaggerated coquetry.

The captain stopped at the gate and stared in astonishment at this unusual group. The man in the lead came up to the porch and then, noticing the captain, halted and, after a moment's pause, tipped his cap with his right hand and went up to him.

"Excuse me, if you please sir," he said with the saccharine subservience peculiar to waiters and police inspectors, "does the captain live here, in this building?"

"Yes, I do."

"And would the captain be good enough to tell me if there is a captain's wife living here?"

"A captain's wife? A captain's wife, you say?"

"A captain's widow."

"As far as I know, there is no captain's widow living here."

"Well, didn't I tell you?" the man turned around with a triumphant look to the young women who had not gone into the porch and were still standing in front of the gate of the building. "I looked through the whole registry book at the police station. There is no captain's widow living here now, nor has one ever lived here."

"She lived here back then!" one young woman shot back at him and, raising her head high, she glanced provocatively at the captain.

"I would recognize her right away," another one said.

"And so would I! And so would I!" the others chorused.

"What is this all about?" the captain asked.

"Well, may it please the captain, the matter is like this," the man with the Semitic cast of face responded, scratching his head. "I am Hirsh, a police inspector, and these young ladies—well, as the captain knows, they are the kind of ladies . . ."

And he winked knowingly.

"No, I do not know, Mr. Hirsh," the captain replied.

"They are the kind of ladies who have had a certain misfortune . . . well, as the captain knows . . . they have just come back from a distant land. And does the captain know from where? Two came back from Alexandria—the one that's in Egypt—and these three from Constantinople.

"And does the captain know how they got there? They are saying that a captain's wife, that is, the widow of a captain from Lviv—a young, well-dressed lady whose name they do not remember—came to *Stryy or to some other town in search of a maid to serve her in Lviv; she was looking for an attractive, clever girl, preferably an orphan, and she promised her a good livelihood and good pay.

"Well, as the captain knows, there are so many girls like that in Stryy and in all of our little towns that you could gather them up in a ladder-wagon. A dozen or more of them volunteered.

"She picks the one or two that appeal the most to her, and brings them back with her to Lviv. In Lviv she takes such a girl to a hotel, tells her that she herself does not need her right now, but that she'll place her with a friend. That friend keeps her for a few days, doesn't ask her to do anything, feeds her—the poor girl begs to be given something to do, but that woman tells her that she too does not require her services right now, but that a certain acquaintance from *Stanislav asked her to send him a maid. The girl has no money for the fare. The lady gives her a few guldens and travels with her to Stanislav. There she is met by the acquaintance who resembles a rich Armenian lord; he promises the girl a mountain of money and travels with her to *Kolomyya, *Chernivtsi, *Seret.

"The foolish girl does not know what is happening to her and where she is going; she is just surprised that it's all taking so long. The lord thrusts a passport into her hand that she is supposed to show at the Rumanian border, takes her across Rumania to Halats, puts her on a ship, and takes her to Constantinople—and sells her... you know, captain, he sells her like a worthless horse. He sells her to a certain establishment... you know what kind, captain! And those that he cannot sell... he has a warehouse in Halats, and from there he takes them away in gangs... And so, those that he does not sell there, he takes to *Smyrna, to Alexandria, or sends them even farther away, to Bombay, to Rio de Janeiro, and God only knows where else."

"But that's a terrible story!" the captain cried in shock. "It's hard to believe something like that!'

"It is, it is," Hirsh agreed hurriedly, nodding his head. "One does not want to believe it, but still, it is the unvarnished truth. You know, captain, we also didn't want to believe it at first. Two years ago the newspapers wrote that in Constantinople and other Turkish towns there was a completely open trade in girls, and that certain agents were secretly taking large numbers of our girls there from *Halychyna.

"You know, captain, the kinds of things that our newspapers write... perhaps there is a grain of truth in it, but when a reporter gets hold of it, he will make up a pack of lies, confuse the issue, inflate it, so that in the end this kernel of truth becomes unrecognizable even to its own father. And so a policeman reads it and thinks: if this were the truth, then there would be someone who has been wronged, someone who would demand justice, lodge a complaint; well, if that were the case, we could begin investigating this matter. But you know, captain, as it is, *wo kein Klänger, da ist auch kein Richter* [where there is no plaintiff, there is no judge]. The newspapers write whatever they want to, but we keep quiet. Then the newspapers stop writing about it, find something new to write about, and we do nothing."

It was cold and draughty in the porch of the building. Inspector Hirsh who obviously thought it was a great honour that the captain was taking an interest in this matter and listening intently to him, loosened the reins of his talkativeness and, gesticulating all the while, winking, interrupting himself, and then picking up the story again, painted with a broad brush the entire train of events and circumstances of this strange story. Meanwhile, the girls stood on the sidewalk in front of the gate fidgeting, not knowing what to do, and impatiently waiting to hear what the inspector would say to them.

"You know what, Mr. Hirsh," the captain interrupted the endless flow of words, "this story has greatly piqued my interest. I recall that a few years ago a certain military widow did live here—I do not remember if her husband was a captain or a lieutenant. Perhaps I can help you find her."

"I would be very grateful for the captain's help!" the inspector said. "And does the captain know why? This is not a simple matter. It is even a very delicate matter, not a simple theft or even a murder. For if that captain's widow has some acquaintances among the military, or if you happen to hit on the wrong one, then . . . well, as the captain knows, a poor police inspector—he is nothing more than a tiny insect. And it is not difficult to crush it, if one has the power to do so."

"Well, that means that there is a double reason to approach the matter cautiously. I am fairly well-known in military circles here, and I could give you certain information, but I would want to know beforehand where this matter is at. I would invite you in, but my wife is home, our child is ill . . ."

"Oh, no, no!" the inspector exclaimed hastily. "I most certainly do not want to cause the captain and his wife any trouble."

"Perhaps it would be better if we proceeded in the following manner. To begin with, send these young ladies away . . . where do they live?"

"In a hotel, at Hekker's."

"Well, then, let them go to the hotel. And when we find this evil woman, you will call them to confront her. Agreed?"

"I think that would be best," the inspector said, happy to have unexpectedly found such a high-placed partner as the captain, but at the same time wondering why this captain, whom he did not know, was taking this matter to heart so passionately and offering his assistance for no obvious reason.

And then, turning around to the girls and changing his tone to one that was sharp and commanding, he said: "Please go to the hotel and wait for me there. I'll be there soon."

The girls went away, talking loudly among themselves, laughing, and occasionally glancing back.

"And as for us," the captain said to the inspector after the girls had left, "perhaps we could drop in to the nearest restaurant? Have you had dinner?"

"Oh, no! In our job it is impossible to think about dinner at such an early hour."

"That's good. I'm a bit hungry myself. Let's have dinner together and continue our conversation."

The inspector was becoming increasingly suspicious, but he did not let on, all the more so because in addition to the anticipated information, the prospect of having a good dinner in the company of the captain was smiling at him. They went to the Warsaw Hotel.

The captain requested a private room, ordered dinner and a bottle of wine and, sitting at the table next to Hirsh—who, looking a bit troubled, was perched uneasily on the edge of his chair—said in a most carefree tone: "Oh, I forgot to introduce myself, Mr. Hirsh. I am Captain Anharovych. I just returned from Bosnia a few days ago. It seems to me that you eyed me a bit suspiciously when I offered you my assistance in finding that evil woman . . ."

"But captain, sir!" Hirsh yelped as if he had been stung, and leapt from his chair. "Why would I . . ."

"Sit down! Sit down!" the captain said, taking him by the arm and forcing him back into his chair. "There is no reason for you to defend yourself so vigorously. After all, it is part of your profession—to suspect, to guess at various secret ties. I do not hold your suspicions against you, not at all. But first, let's eat!" he added when the waiter brought in the broth and began filling their bowls.

The conversation was interrupted for a few minutes, and all that could be heard was the clinking of tablespoons in the bowls and the sipping of broth. The inspector ate heartily, concentrating on his food, hoping all the while that he was masking his inner anxieties in this unusual situation.

"I will explain everything to you," the captain said after he had emptied his bowl. "There truly is some kind of a link here, something that is urging me to do everything in my power to find this woman. But first of all, finish your story."

Unfortunately, the inspector was far less talkative now than he had been earlier.

"My story?" he asked with a look of surprise on his face. "What else am I to tell the captain?"

"Well, about that . . . woman. What is her name?"

"Oh, if only we knew that!" the inspector exclaimed. "She would be in our clutches by now. Those silly nanny-goats either did not ask her for her name—just kept calling her the captain's wife and the captain's wife!—or if any of them did know it, they have forgotten it."

"And how do they know where she lived?"

"A few of them—namely the ones who were with me today—remembered that after they arrived in Lviv, the captain's widow stopped in for a moment at her living quarters on Pekarska Street. That's all that they remembered. They did not even recall the number of the building, so it was necessary to take them there to have them point it out."

"Well, did that captain's wife have any children?"

"I don't think so. At least, none of the girls mentioned that."

The captain breathed a trifle more easily. "Well, did she recruit a lot of girls in that manner?"

"Who can say? She travelled through all the smaller towns, and her girlfriend went to the places that she did not visit. So far, seventeen girls have come back from Turkey, but they say that there are a lot more who stayed behind. Those that were bought by a wealthy Turk and locked up in his harem are lost forever. And even when it comes to houses of ill-repute . . . well, as the captain knows . . . it is very hard for them to get away. Those who did come back had to overcome great difficulties. Even our embassy had to get involved to make it possible for those unfortunate victims to return to their native land."

"But that's terrible!" the captain said as if speaking to himself. "Plucked from their kin, from their circle of friends, from their native land, thrown into the bottomless mud of depravity, sentenced to eternal servitude, to oblivion, to an early death or what is even worse—to misery in a foreign land. Just the thought of such situations is enough to make one go mad. And that beast—she is not a woman!—took money for this!"

"The embassy investigated the matter as far as it could," Hirsh continued. "For beautiful and innocent young girls the Turks paid as much as one or two hundred *ducats. For others, they paid less, as per their agreement."

"But what about the one who sold them, that agent . . ."

"Oh, we have him already," the inspector said proudly. "Oh, he's a sly fox!"

"He's a Jew, right?"

"Well, that's to be understood," Hirsh mumbled somewhat unwillingly. "Such a business can be ventured upon only by a Jew. I am sure that neither that captain's wife nor her friend would have ever come up with the idea of such a profitable business without him, and that he prevailed upon them to do it, and paid them only a small portion of what he himself earned. That's quite evident in and of itself.

"But now the game is over for him. A few days ago, in response to a request that we telegraphed, he was arrested in Budapest. There are reports from the Budapest police that they found in his possession a lot of documents, accounts, receipts, and a long list of his male and female assistants. That, sir, will be quite the job for us! There will be hunts conducted throughout the country."

The captain shuddered with aversion when he saw on the inspector's face a flash of brutish joy, the joy of a wolf that, seeing a herd of sheep thronging in an enclosure, knows full well that he can choke them, tear them to pieces, and gnaw on them—and not one of them will be able to escape or fight back.

"I understand your joy, Mr. Hirsh," he said after a moment, "but it still seems to me that there would be more to be happy about if you gentlemen had been a little sharper and not allowed so many innocent women to be taken away—right from under your noses—and left to perish in regions unknown."

"Is that my problem?" Hirsh asked completely reasonably as he attacked the roasted meat that had been brought in. "Captain, do I have any authority here? We, the inspectors, commissioners, are like dogs: they show us an animal, let us off the leash—and our duty is to catch it. But as for the rest of it, it is not up to us, but up to those who direct the hunt. We have enough work as it is—oh, there's so much work, so much running around, that a man has hardly any time to breathe.

"Take yesterday evening! Would the captain believe that right here in Lviv, in the very centre of our city, something very similar to the story about the trade in girls was going on for several years? And no one knew about it!"

"What was it?" the captain asked.

"Not far from the Dominican Monastery there lived a certain Mrs. Yuliya Shablinska who called herself a widow, but was, in fact, a divorcee. She is still a young woman, decent-looking, always smartly dressed, well-educated, and accepted in social circles. For several years she had a concession from the government to run a boarding school for girls who had completed their secondary education. She was supposed to prepare them for their matriculation or for some other examinations.

"And just imagine, sir, a few days ago the police discovered that this boarding school is, strictly speaking, a house of the worst kind of debauchery. Only aristocrats, wealthy men, and high-ranking officers were admitted there, but the things that went on there, in such excellent company, are beyond human imagination."

Every word of this narration was a knife that pierced the captain's heart and then twisted and turned in the bloody wound.

Breaking into a cold sweat and scarcely breathing, as if he were being tortured, he found it hard to remain seated, and barely managed to squeeze out a single word: "So?"

"I am just saying this by way of example," Hirsh babbled on after polishing off the roasted meat that had been served for the two of them and dipping into the wine that was gradually loosening his tongue. "It is difficult to imagine that of the gentlemen connected with our senior administration there would not have been at least one who knew something about it. They went there themselves! Around town, the names of some very important fish who were regular visitors there are being openly bandied about. And yet it was all very hush-hush. It was only when a few of the girls in that boarding school became gravely ill, and several died in the hospital, that loud voices of indignation were raised on all sides, and the police had to make a move.

"Yesterday they arrested this lady and the entire school. Well, sir, there was so much shouting there at first, and indignation, and fainting—it was a real farce! Oh my, oh my! And ever so many documents, receipts, and letters were taken away! One will be able to read many a fine story in them! But they won't let any of these stories get out. There are those who will see to it that only those facts that are not damaging to them will ever see the light of day."

"O God, O God!" the captain whispered, feeling something loathsome choking his throat, stifling his chest.

Hirsh saw his reaction as an encouragement to keep on talking and, finishing off a half-bottle of wine, talked on and on, completely without restraint now, verging at times on an outright learned tone.

"And why am I telling the captain all this? In order to explain the politics of the situation. Because it is does not take much to knock down a tree's blossoms, or later to knock down the green budding fruit. But to wait until the little pears ripen, and then to shake the tree and see them tumble down, all ripened, nice and juicy—that's a great joy! There is merit in that! And, if you please, captain, we cannot do it any differently. Because a criminal is not a criminal until he commits a crime. What would be in it for me, for example, if I caught that agent at the moment when he is travelling with a girl from Stanislav to Chernivtsi?"

"You would save the girl!" the captain said.

"Oh, the girl! What's a girl! Only one road lies ahead for the girl!" Hirsh said sharply with a cynical laugh. "If I took her away from one agent today, tomorrow she'd go to the dogs without his help. And there is still the question of whether or not I could rescue her from him. He would tell me that he had hired her to serve, the girl would affirm this, and what means do I have at my disposal to prove otherwise? He could even lay a complaint against me, and after two or three such incidents the poor inspector would be deprived of a crust of bread.

"But now—that's another matter altogether! Now we have proof in our hands: testimonies, confessions, letters; now we can act with confidence; we know what to look for and whom to prosecute. Now, for example, I could go to the captain's home and search it, and the captain could not forbid me to do so."

The captain jumped up like a scalded cat. "My home? Have you gone mad? My home?"

"Ha-ha-ha-ha!" Hirsh guffawed half-drunkenly and half maliciously. "How alarmed the captain is! Ha-ha-ha! Have no fear, my dear sir, I only said it as a joke, as an example, *zum Beispiel* [by way of an example]."

The captain slowly sipped his wine, tasting it drop by drop, in order to appear calm and mask the deathly pallor that—he could feel this quite clearly—was flooding his face. Hirsh looked intently at him with his small beady eyes, and a smile that was half sly and half drunkenly good-natured flitted across his face, opening his thick fleshy lips to reveal behind them large white teeth that seemed ready to rip into and lacerate living flesh.

"So, the captain served a full five years in Bosnia?" he suddenly asked.

"Yes, I did."

"I remember the captain slightly from the old days, when the captain was still a lieutenant. I was a waiter then in a coffee shop; does the captain remember?"

"I do not seem to recall that," the captain responded, assuming an expression as if he was diligently searching in his memory for both the coffee house and the waiter.

"Oh, yes! Mr. Anharovych! I remember very well! All the officers talked about the captain . . . and about the captain's wife who was so young, so beautiful, and so deeply in love with the captain . . ."

"Mr. Hirsh!" the captain cried, deeply offended. "Please, keep those memories to yourself!"

"Oh my, the captain is so touchy!" Hirsh said quickly, without taking leave of his good humour. "I did not say anything offensive. God forbid! I was just wondering how the captain managed to be in Bosnia for such a long time without his wife."

"Well, you know how it is, service, duty," the captain blurted involuntarily.

"Oh, yes, I know that the captain is always mindful of his duties. But for such a sacrifice the captain ought to receive the gold service cross. Ha-ha-ha! Not everyone could do it! To leave a young wife as a grass widow for five years . . ."

The word widow, uttered inadvertently, without any deeper intention, flashed through Hirsh's brain like an electric spark and illuminated a series of impressions, showed him ties between acts that he had earlier suspected rather fuzzily, but which his policeman's mind now saw clearly, as if they were right there on the palm of his hand.

He sat silently for a few minutes, synthesizing everything that he had heard and seen thus far. The longer he thought about it, the more his face radiated with happiness. He moved restlessly in his chair, gesticulated abruptly and jerkily as if the skin on his entire body had begun to itch, and such a joyous transformation was manifested in his whole being that the captain looked at him with both amazement and loathing.

"What is wrong with you, Mr. Hirsh?" he finally asked.

"Oh, nothing! It's nothing. It just happens to me at times," Hirsh replied joyfully, while letting it be known by winking with a comically enigmatic expression that he was hiding a secret in his heart and had to exert the greatest effort not to betray it. But suddenly, with a face that at that moment resembled a Greek satyr, he leaned in closely toward the captain and, winking confidentially, asked almost in a whisper: "If you please, captain, does the captain live there, in the building on Pekarska Street?"

"Well yes, I do," the captain replied, involuntarily averting his head.

"On which floor?"

"On the first."

"And did the captain's wife live there when the captain was away in Bosnia?"

"Yes."

"And is the captain's child truly ill?"

"I don't know. When I left home, my child truly was a bit ill, but may be feeling better now."

An unpleasant feeling of disgust with himself penetrated the captain's heart when he uttered this lie. But he sensed that he could not disentangle himself all at once, and that this cursed, half-drunk Jew was changing from a subservient and troubled little Jew into a man who was assuming the role of a dangerous opponent with whom one should be on guard.

Hirsh smiled half good-naturedly, half maliciously, with that distinctive Jewish smile that, worse than the harshest insult, is so capable of cutting to the quick.

"Oh, certainly, I'm sure the child is better now. Completely well, and gone off to school. Tee-hee-hee!"

The captain ground his teeth and clasped the arms of his chair as hard as he could, forcibly restraining himself from lunging at this loathsome man and smashing his skull.

"Mr. Hirsh!" he barked, breathless from his choked anger.

"It's nothing, it's nothing," Hirsh placated him. "It wasn't my intention to . . . After all, I understand! Oh, I understand everything, everything."

"What do you understand?"

"That's my business. But the captain promised to tell me something, and he hasn't done so."

"What exactly?"

"What do you mean, what exactly? Wasn't the captain supposed to tell me why he is so interested in this sordid affair, this trade in girls?"

The captain's heart grew cold. He sensed that Hirsh was slowly but surely driving a knife into his chest. His head was swimming.

"Oh, that's a long story . . ."

"Why a long one? Why a long one?" Hirsh hissed with his customary smile, continuing to look obliquely at the captain. "If you please, captain, I'll cut to the quick."

And Hirsh placed his arm on the captain's shoulders, and in the course of the conversation even began patting him protectively on the back.

Unfortunately, the gist of what Hirsh said was such that the captain could no longer get up, grab a chair or break off a leg from the table, and with a single blow put an end to Hirsh's smiles, talk, and plans.

"I know that the captain is a good man, a military man, an honourable man. In a word—a noble man. The captain was very humane and courteous towards me and did not scorn my company. And that is why I want to tell the captain something."

And leaning closer, he spoke directly into his ear. "Go home right away, if you please sir, and search carefully through all the drawers, cupboards, chests, and wardrobes of the captain's wife. Take out all the documents, letters, visiting cards—everything to the last scrap! Leave only birth certificates and official documents. As for the rest, the captain should wrap them up in an old newspaper, take them into the kitchen, and throw them into the fire. And this must be done at once!"

The captain sat in a stupor. "What does this mean? What is it that you want?" he asked, speaking as if in a dream.

Hirsh continued patting him on the back. "Come now, if you please sir, the captain is an intelligent man! There is no need to go on about this! Surely the captain understands that I am a police inspector, and that I am capable of doing a bit of thinking. But then, not much intelligence is needed to figure out that the captain's widow who was engaged in recruiting girls is none other than the captain's wife. And who knows if that Madam Shablinska whom we arrested yesterday was not in partnership with her? It is very possible, and the commissars who are going through that lady's papers must have found this out already without my assistance.

"But the captain must hurry! I am going to police headquarters now, and if they have not yet discovered anything, then I'll see to it—and I am doing this out of courtesy for the captain, because I am certain that the captain is completely innocent in this whole sordid affair—that the inspectors will not pay their visit to the captain's home until some time towards evening, or even tomorrow morning. So, my respects, sir."

And, without waiting for the captain's response, Hirsh grabbed his hat and rushed out of the room as fast as he could.

The captain sat for several minutes as if he were petrified, without thinking, without feeling anything. He sensed dully that it was all over now, that there was no way out, that his reason for living and his will to live were destroyed, that a bottomless pit was gaping before him, a yawing emptiness. He sensed that what he had not been able to even think about—an immense, eternal shame that could not be expunged—had fallen on him and crushed him to smithereens under its weight.

He experienced that sensation as if he were a kernel that, furiously swirling in the mouth of a grindstone, all at once falls under that stone and is instantly pulverized into a thousand bits, into dust, into flour, and every one of those particles feels, for a tiny moment, an immeasurable pain caused by its forcible extrication from its natural bonds.

And then he suddenly awakened from his stupor. He was overcome by an insane fear. A single word held his entire being in its grip, tugged at him, threw him into a fever and a fit of shivering.

"The police!"

He rang for the waiter, paid the bill, and raced home. He only had to go a few dozen steps, but it seemed to him that in those few minutes something inexplicably terrible could happen in his absence. The police might come and find a heap of disgusting documents—this was now the most horrible spectre that confronted him. As for the consequences of this fact—he did not dwell on them. Thinking about the moment when the police would enter his apartment—the apartment that only yesterday had been his earthly paradise, but now seemed to him like an inferno—and about the purpose of that visit was a torment that was beyond human power to bear. He had to prepare himself adequately for that moment. He had to do whatever he could!

And, mustering the last vestiges of his strength, the captain ran up the stairs to the first floor, quickly opened the door and walked into the vestibule; not finding anyone there, he kept on going—with the same swiftness, the same nervous haste with which he had walked on the day of his return from Bosnia—opened another door, and entered the salon.

XII

In the salon he found Anelya. She was standing by a table, leaning on it with her left hand, and her eyes were glued to the door. They looked at one another, and an involuntary cry of amazement tore simultaneously from their lips. They could not recognize one another. It seemed to both of them that since yesterday afternoon, from the moment that they had last seen one another, ten years had gone by, and that it was not human beings who were standing face to face, but some kind of spectres that reminded them only faintly of pleasant and happy times in a long ago past.

They looked at one another silently, as if bewitched. They were both spinning in a small circle of their own thoughts and observations; they were both tormented by their own suffering, and neither felt a need to share it with another person.

"Is this the same Anelya," the captain thought, "that I left here yesterday—blooming with health and freshness, lively, vivacious, with shining eyes? Is this the same woman that I see before me now—broken, withered, and looking as if she's been taken down from a cross? Her face has aged by ten years, wrinkles line her temples, her hair has lost its sheen, her eyes have turned glassy! Was it some kind of charms that blinded my eyes yesterday and the day before, charms that prevented me from seeing this devastation, or is it actually possible that a single night—a single day and night—is capable of bringing about such a profound transformation? But what could possibly have been the reason for it?"

"His hair has gone completely grey!" Anelya thought in alarm. "His face has turned yellow, his eyes are sunken, his eyelids are red. It is clear that he has not slept all night. It is clear that he knows everything. It is clear that all is lost. Well, there are no surprises left for me now, but as for him—oh, the poor dear! He must have suffered greatly."

The captain stood by the salon door as if rooted to the spot, not daring to come up closer to his wife. She too could not budge. Finally he dug out of his pocket the receipt for his petition for retirement that he had obtained at command headquarters and, unfolding it, walked up to the table without saying a word and placed it in front of Anelya. She looked carefully at the wrinkled square of paper and then, smiling sadly, nodded.

Still not speaking, the captain took off his coat and threw it on the sofa, removed his sword, and then went into the vestibule and brought in a heavy suitcase that he had not yet unpacked. Placing it on the floor near the ceramic hearth, he knelt down beside it, took a key out of his pocket, and began to undo the straps and unlock the locks.

Anelya, as if in a trance, watched him silently, without moving. After opening the suitcase, the captain suddenly seemed to recall something and, still kneeling and leaning over the suitcase, he turned his head and said calmly to his wife: "Do you have documents of any kind?"

"What kind?" Anelya asked barely audibly.

"Well, any letters from your agents, receipts, accounts, in general, anything that could compromise you."

"I do not have anything."

"Try your best to remember!" the captain said without raising his voice. "And if you do have anything, burn it. There may be a police inspection here at any moment."

"I do not have any such documents," Anelya replied just as calmly, as if she had long been prepared for such a situation.

Seeing that he was searching for something in his suitcase and had no interest in pursuing the conversation, she sat down in a chair facing him and watched his every movement.

After rummaging in the suitcase for a few minutes, the captain removed from it a small, attractive revolver embossed with ivory—a gift that had been given to him in tribute by his comrades upon his departure from Bosnia. A carved inscription was visible on the grip: *Zum Andenken* [In remembrance]. The barrel was masterfully engraved and richly ornamented in the Bosnian folk art style. The captain put this beautiful toy on the floor and then, after searching for a moment in the side pouches of his suitcase, dug out of them a packet of cartridges made for the revolver. Having found what he was looking for, the captain unhurriedly repacked his suitcase, locked it, did up the straps, and carried it back into the vestibule.

Re-entering the salon, he took the revolver and the cartridges, laid them down on the table, and then, turning to Anelya with an expression of cold indifference verging on hatred, said: "And now, please leave this room."

Anelya who only now understood his intent, stayed where she was and asked: "What do you intend to do?"

"Of what concern is that to you? Go to the children!"

"But perhaps it does concern me as well?" Anelya responded in a gentle, hesitant voice.

"There is nothing here that concerns you!" the captain replied gloomily as he cut open the packet and took out the cartridges.

"But I am your wife!" Anelya said even more diffidently. "That means that I have the right . . ."

"You don't have the right, you vile creature!" the captain suddenly shrieked, flinging himself at her with his fists. "You don't have the right, you witch! You've undermined and ruined my life, my honour, the future of my children! Get out of here! Get out and do not tempt me to fall into sin!"

He spat and turned away from her. He was shaking violently. A sudden paroxysm of pain and despair destroyed his feigned calmness, shattered the icy shell with which he had wanted to benumb his heart so that it would not tremble before the completion of his final, decisive act. He collapsed in a chair with his back turned to her, and covered his face with his hands. Tears burst from his eyes. Painful sobs racked his body.

Meanwhile, Anelya rose from her chair ever so quietly, took the revolver and cartridges, and tiptoed like a spectre into the next room.

The captain was still sitting in the same position when he heard the patter of small footsteps, when soft, tender little arms seized both his hands, and his children's beautiful, innocent faces leaned over him, trying to look into his eyes.

The captain leapt up from his chair, and with an expression of utmost hatred he turned to face Anelya, who was standing in her former spot.

"Woman! Satan! Be damned a hundred times over that you did not spare me this pain in the last few minutes of my life! Oh, you are clever, diabolically clever! So that not a single nerve would be left unscarred, not a single muscle would be left unscathed by a fiendish fire! Ancient masters of torture could take lessons from you. May God never forgive you for doing this, just as I do not forgive you in my final hour!"

Anelya stood silently, like a stone statue.

But Tsesya, hearing such terrifying words that she did not fully understand, and seeing her father in such a distraught state, moved away from him, ran up to her mother and, cuddling up to her, began to bawl.

Mykhas stood in a stupor, still holding his father's hand.

"Daddy! What are you saying? Why are you scaring us?" he asked, blocking his way and tugging at his hand.

The captain looked down at his young son, and a wrenching grief gripped his heart. Seizing Mykhas in his arms, he lifted him and, his face flooded with tears, began showering kisses on his head, his face, his neck.

"My children! My poor children!" he groaned. "What will happen to you? What . . . will happen . . . when I am gone?"

"Do you want to leave us again?" Mykhas asked.

At that moment, Anelya flung herself down at her husband's feet. Kneeling, and lowering her head to the floor, she wrapped her arms around his legs and cried from the depths of her despair: "Antos!" Her voice resounded as if it had issued from a deep cavern, and to the captain it seemed distant, foreign.

If Anelya had hoped that bringing in the children would soften his resolve so that she could more easily storm his heart and overcome his hatred, she was badly mistaken. The captain remained unmoved.

"Go away!" he said curtly. "Do not make a scene."

Anelya did not get up.

"Antos! I adjure you with the love of our children that you want to orphan: listen to me! I know that I have earned the sharpest condemnation, and that this condemnation will not pass me by. But I do not want to justify myself. I only want you to understand me. After all, you loved me, Antos!"

"Oh, yes!" the captain said bitterly. "And, trusting in my ardent, blind love, you betrayed me!"

"No. I swear before God, before my soul, before the innocent souls of these children! I was faithful to you! I did not betray you with even a single thought."

"Who will believe you? You have surrounded me on all sides with tangles of lies. You played out your travesty in front of me, feigning joy, while concealing a hell at the bottom of your conscience!"

Anelya, her pale face raised to the captain, was still on her knees, clinging to his legs.

The captain put Mykhas down on the floor and said in a slightly gentler tone: "Well, get up and say what you want to say! Children, go to your room!"

Anelya rose slowly to her feet.

The children stood indecisively, and then Mykhas turned to his father and said: "But you won't beat mummy, will you?"

"No, my son!" the captain said gravely.

The children walked out. Anelya watched them go with a long, emotional look full of boundless love and untold grief. It was evident that she wanted to imprint forever in her mind, to inscribe in her heart, the tiniest feature, every gesture, every expression, every word of those two precious little beings.

It was only when they disappeared into the adjoining room, when the door closed behind them, that the icy mantle encasing her dissolved, her spirit broke and, weeping bitterly, she collapsed, helpless and almost unconscious, into a chair.

The captain sat where he was, cold, immobile, and gloomy, like a dark cloud, feeling no mercy in his heart, nor any sympathy for this woman who had ruined, in such an unconscionable manner, her own happiness and his, had cast such an indelible stain on the heads of their children, covered their name with shame.

In the depths of his heart a thought stirred like a snake: "If only you had died before you started doing all of this! I would have wept over you as an ideal woman and mother! But now it is even too late for you to die."

Anelya stopped crying, wiped away her tears, and turned to look at her husband.

Her face no longer bore the icy expression of stupor or numb pain, nor the humility that had stained it so unbecomingly just a moment ago. A strange fire gradually ignited in her eyes, and her cheeks, that had aged so suddenly and prematurely, were suffused with a rosy flush.

"So you are scorning me now? You are cursing me?" she asked, slowly releasing one word after the other.

The captain just groaned dully instead of replying.

"You wanted to abandon me and the children without a word of farewell?"

"If only I had never seen you!"

"So, does that mean that you never loved me?"

The captain shuddered and writhed in his chair. A frenzied anger was once again stirring in his heart.

"You wretched creature! Shut up! Do not remind me about the love that you are not worthy of, that today has become for me a source of endless suffering!" he shouted.

"So, for the suffering endured for a single day, for a few hours, you are cursing the years of happiness, the whole skein of sacrifices that I made for you?"

"What are all those sacrifices in comparison to the terrible wounds that you have inflicted on me, taking away my honour, the respect that people had for me, taking away my desire to live, the very possibility of a normal existence? You can see very well, can't you, that it is all over for me now?"

Anelya straightened up and looked haughtily at him. "I can see only one thing: you are a coward! A reed that sways with the wind! I can see that, and nothing more. What is it that is all over for you? The fact that the officers do not want to accept you in the casino? Spit on them and do not go there. That it will no longer be possible for you to remain in the military service? Spit on it and leave it. That staying in Lviv will be too painful for you? Spit on Lviv and settle elsewhere, in the country, in the mountains!"

"But the shame! The awareness of the shame that weighs down heavily on you, on me, on our children! The horrible awareness that I must always carry around with me like a snake dangling on my chest. Does that not matter at all?"

"O my dear *Pharisee! What a delicate conscience has suddenly awoken within you! A terrible, unheard-of shame! And exactly in what does this shame lie? In the fact that your wife was in a silent partnership with a woman who kept a house of ill repute, that she recruited girls destined for that house and other houses like it. Oh, how horrible! How shameful! But just tell me, you with your noble and unblemished soul, how many times did you, in your bachelor days—and not just in your bachelor days—extend a helping hand to such a shameful trade by giving a more or less generous profit to such women?

"And as for your noble friends who are so fiercely offended by my shameful trade—are they not reacting this way because they themselves have fallen prey too often to its temptations, have spent far too much money supporting it? Oh, you wretched, vile, lying creatures! Even among those men who ordered the imprisonment of Yuliya yesterday, who will soon be hanging my name on the scaffold of shame with fiendish glee and delivering me up to the scorn of the entire world—almost every one of them knew what was going on at Yuliya's, and some of them were even daily visitors there!

"No, I have minimized their involvement! Some of them were the initiators of this business, protected it with their positions, their patrimonial or official authority. And now, when it is impossible to keep it from view any longer—oh, yes, now let a whole inferno of shame and public condemnation fall on the heads of the women who . . .

"Oh, how I despise you! How I hate you, you Pharisees, you liars and hypocrites! Even the most loathsome deed, the most vile act, means nothing to you. You fear only the condemnation of the mob, the spectre of having to bear responsibility for your acts. A vileness that is well-hidden stops being vile, a secret crime is only proof of daring and cleverness!"

She ran out of breath and fell silent. She was shaking as if she had a fever.

The captain stared at her with an astonished, almost insane look; it seemed to him that she was growing before his eyes, changing into an apparition of menacing fury with a face so fierce that one look could kill a man. He had not expected such a turn in the conversation; he was stunned, disheartened—but he had to admit that there was a lot of truth in what she was saying.

Anelya moved her chair closer to the captain, sat directly across from him and, looking him straight in the face, began talking in a completely different voice, soft and sorrowful.

"And you, Antos! You too are condemning me, cursing me, hating me! You were the first to cast the stone of disdain at me.

You, whom I loved so passionately, so faithfully, for whom I did not hesitate to sacrifice everything, everything in the world!

"It was for you that I abandoned my grandfather and his fortune, and went with you into poverty, into want, the likes of which I had never known. Love built me a golden bridge on that road. Not for a moment did I regret the step I had taken. Not a single reproach crossed my lips. I quietly accepted what my heart would have found alarming if I could ever have imagined what it would be like. I saw that you sensed the position in which I found myself, that you were troubled by it, that you were trying to make things happen so that I would want for nothing, but you did not find a means of doing that.

"The children came along, and our situation became much worse. I secretly wrote a few letters to old Hurter, humbling myself before him, humiliating myself, even degrading myself, and begging him for help. The heartless, blinded old man returned my letters unopened. You were called up to go to Bosnia. I was left alone with the children, on half your stipend. Can you imagine the position in which I found myself? I hinted at it in a few of my letters, but when I saw that these hints troubled your heart and poisoned your peace of mind without doing me any good, I resolved not to say anything, to write only about cheerful matters, and to find a way out on my own. I began looking for tutoring opportunities.

"Do you think that any of your military gentlemen—the ones who are now flaming with righteous indignation, pointing at my shame—do you suppose even one of them offered to help me, or had the slightest inclination to help me? Ah, yes! One did volunteer, one did offer me his help! It was Baron Reuchlingen. But the price of his help was such that the very thought of it filled me with loathing and disgust. I pushed him away, but he did not want to let go; he trailed after me, telling me frankly that by his presence and his inseparability from me he wanted to compromise me in the eyes of the world and then . . . then he hoped that, slandered and condemned by general opinion even before any crime was committed, I would, in the end, fall to the level that he wanted me at.

"What was I to do? I wanted to avoid a scandal, and so, like a drowning man grabbing at a straw, I seized the opportunity that

Yuliya extended to me; I pretended to be favourably inclined to his desires and invited him to visit me, but at the same time I also invited a few resolute girls from Yuliya's boarding school. Keeping myself apart as the mistress of the house, I left him in their hands.

"The results exceeded my expectations. Spoiled to the marrow of his bones, the Baron quickly developed a keener taste for their company than for mine. He drank, threw his money around, made a fool of himself, and tried to make fools of all of us. I accepted his money and gifts, knowing that if I did not take them, he would give them to anyone, even to someone who did not need them. I saw that he was destroying himself, but what business was it of mine to prevent him from going down that slippery slope? And could I have prevented it?

"Finally, Yuliya took him in hand, and with his help her boarding school became what it was until yesterday. He brought in other people, greedy for delights, who were looking for an opportunity to spend some money. And when the Baron finally used up all his funds and fell so low that he was compromising all the officers, they saw to it that he was transferred to Bosnia. You know how it all ended for him!

"That's how my crimes and my downfall began. I know I am not blameless in all of this, but I also know that there were others who were at fault, but they were more clever and were able to hide everything, to conceal their involvement, to take advantage of the evil, but avoid assuming any responsibility for it."

The captain sat with his head lowered, deep in thought. His wife's story dismayed him. It did not awaken any sympathy, nor did it warm his heart; it even infuriated him, for it revealed the brutality, a larger or smaller quantity of which lies in reserve at the bottom of every person's heart, a brutality that everyone tries to conceal to a greater or lesser degree from others and even from oneself—and that, in order to mask it, people invent many decorous and delicate words.

He found the unflinching and calm disclosure of these heinous deeds and motives from the lips of his wife startling and unexpected, and it pained him like a fresh wound. Nevertheless, as he thought about her position, he started to understand her and, as a result, began to condemn her less harshly.

"And what can I say about the other story involving the girls?" Anelya continued speaking. "Having lost respect for people, having learned to play with their feelings and their beliefs, and to see them merely as material to be taken advantage of, I continued going down that path. Do thousands of others not do the same thing, but only in a different form?

"You know, in the cigar store I've often watched poor women—wage earners and beggars—gamble on the lottery. Rivers of these indigent women flow to the cigar store, and every one of them during the course of a week cuts back a penny on the bread she buys, cuts back on potatoes or salt for the children in order to set aside a 'sixpence' by Thursday and stake the money on the lottery. 'Maybe with the help of the Mother of God I will win!' they whisper, and they cross themselves and pray a thousand times. After all, in return for that sixpence, the government promises her hundreds, thousands of guldens, wealth, prosperity, an assured financial future for the entire family, an end to the misery and uncertainty, in a word—an earthly paradise!

"And what comes of her hopes? Week after week, year after year, the indigent stream in a river to the cigar shop, sixpence after sixpence flows into the government coffers and they add up to millions, but the sum total of poverty, of dashed hopes, of crusts of bread, of firewood, and of grains of salt withheld from poor children does not grow any smaller—in fact it grows, grows to immense proportions. And what did I do that was so different when I promised those girls a good position and light work?"

The captain shuddered at this comparison.

"Woman!" he shouted. "It is Satan himself who is talking through your lips. Stop and think what you are saying!"

"It is obvious, my dear, that you never stopped to think about that," Anelya said serenely. "I had plenty of time to think through all of this. Besides, am I the first, the only one engaged in this trade? It has been going on either in the open or covertly for hundreds of years, and our nobility often entered into a partnership with Jews. It is not only in our times that our girls have been going to the markets in Constantinople, Smyrna, and Alexandria, and now there are untold numbers of them in India, Egypt, Turkey, and Brazil. And you know, when I think about the kind of conditions, the kind of poverty, the kind of neglect that more than one of them lived in here, and the humiliation that they experienced, it seems to me that they do not lose very much, and perhaps they even gain something by going there.

"Do you suppose that I had to lie to them, to tell them that I needed them to serve me? There were dozens who told me frankly: 'Even if you sell us on the Turkish market, Madam, we will bless you, because we just want to dig ourselves out of here. There is nothing left for us to do here but jump off a bridge or go down the path of shame, and even that path won't protect us from want, hunger, and servitude.'"

She broke off. A look of anxiety flitted across her face, and she pricked up her ears. The thumping of male footsteps could be heard in the corridor. They drew near the vestibule, and then moved away and went up the stairs. Anelya walked out of the room, locked the vestibule door, and then sat down across from her husband once again.

"But how long am I to go on talking about what has been done and cannot be undone?" she said easily, almost cheerfully. "I wanted to tell you about something else. Give me your hand. Good! And the other one as well. Well, you see how it is. I know that we have to part, perhaps even for a long time. Be a man! Remember that you have children! I . . . I . . . can't . . . any longer . . . them . . ."

Her voice broke, her lips twisted convulsively, and tears once again burst from her eyes. But she overcame her agitation and, without wiping away her tears, and still holding her husband's hands, added hurriedly: "Think of the children, Antos! I raised them as best I could, and I think they're on the right path. And don't do anything foolish with that revolver. You don't have the right to do it! Do you understand that? And as for me . . . if you sometimes . . . think of me . . ."

Unrestrained sobs that she had long held back interrupted her speech. Tears poured in a flood from her eyes. Like a terrified child, she huddled on her husband's chest and whispered in a halting voice: "Antos! Antos! If only you knew! You called me a vile woman . . . without a heart . . . without a conscience . . . you are right, but not completely, as God is my witness, you are not completely right. It is true that I smothered my conscience, but I did not renounce it. Look at me! I saw how alarmed you became at my appearance when you walked into the room. I have suffered so much since yesterday! Not just for you . . . not just for our children . . . but also for all those others! I am sensitive to their fate, their fall, their shame! Oh, believe me, I would gladly offer up my body to the greatest tortures, I would give my blood and my life to give back to them what they lost because of me!"

The captain listened to these words, these broken, hurried words that breathed alternatively with passion, with tender love, and then with despair and genuine sorrow. A gloomy cloud settled on his forehead. Grief tore at his heart. In these words he recognized his former Anelya, his own dear Anelya whom, until this day, he had loved so ardently. But at the same time, an inexorable, invisible hand was pushing him away from her, and a mysterious voice whispered in his heart: "It's too late! It's too late! All is lost!"

At that moment the doorknob in the vestibule rattled, and the very next instant someone rang the bell.

Startled, Anelya jumped up and leapt away from her husband. Tears still trembled on her eyelids.

"Ha! They've come already!" she whispered.

"Who?"

"The police. I have a feeling they're here."

"No, don't be afraid! They won't come so soon. Inspector Hirsh promised me . . ."

"Hirsh? Oh, if he's involved in this matter, then it must be the police. Well, farewell! Think of the children, Antos! And in the presence of the police . . . you know . . . stay neutral, calm! Leave the rest up to me!"

And wrapping her right arm around his neck, she pressed a long, long kiss on his lips.

The bell rang out once again, this time twice as loudly.

"Well, go, go and open the door for them," Anelya said, "because they're about to rip out the wires! Go!"

The captain rose mechanically and went into the vestibule. After sliding back the chain, he opened the door.

On the doorstep he saw the police commissar wearing his uniform and sword; Hirsh and another inspector were standing next to him, and behind them were the girls that he had seen before. The commissar saluted to the captain as he walked into the vestibule. The rest of the group also came in.

"I beg the captain's pardon," the commissar said politely, "but we have to take care of a little official matter."

"Please, how can I be of service to you?" the captain asked.

"Does a Mrs. . . ." he took out his notebook and after leafing through it, continued: ". . . Anelya Anharovych live here?"

"Yes. She is my wife."

"May I see her?"

"For what purpose, if I may ask?"

"For the purpose of confronting her with these young ladies, and eventually, for the purpose of an official hearing."

"Well, that's it, then!" the captain said. "If the commissar has an order like that . . ."

"Oh yes, yes I do! My instructions are clear. Please, have a look for yourself," the commissar said hurriedly, showing the captain the warrant signed by the director of the police.

"In that case, please come in!" the captain said, opening the door to the salon.

At that moment, in the room adjacent to the salon there was a soft popping sound, as if an oak table had been struck by something sharp.

A cry escaped involuntarily from the captain's chest. He recognized the sound, and the meaning of his recent conversation with Anelya stood clearly before him in all its horrifying import. Without paying any attention to his detestable visitors, he sprang to the other room.

The commissar, Hirsh, and all the others in the group rushed in after him.

At first glance they did not see anything all that terrible.

Anelya was sitting serenely on a sofa in the corner. But she did not rise to her feet when the guests walked in. Her head, slightly tipped to one side, was resting on one of the sofa's pillows that was covered in smocked silk the colour of Bordeaux wine. One would have thought that she was drowsing if it were not for her glassy, staring eyes and her half-opened lips on which there remained a cry of fear or despair.

The captain rushed up to her. He lifted her head, and only now saw that blood, mixed with thick, whitish matter, was oozing from a tiny hole in her right temple. The revolver was lying on the sofa, covered by a fold of her dress. There was not the slightest doubt that Anelya's mind had been clear, and that her hand had been steady right up to the very last moment. The shot was accurate, and in a single second it put an end to all her suffering and all her desires.

For a long moment, the captain looked into that face, at peace now, but furrowed with the indelible traces of the inner struggle that she had undergone since yesterday.

The feeling of relief that momentarily flared in his heart was smothered almost instantaneously by inexpressibly bitter feelings of reproach and shame. "She dared to do this! She dared to do what I did not have the nerve to do!"

These words flashed through his mind. But, surprisingly, there was no grief in his heart, just a dull feeling of pain and of an infinite exhaustion.

Forcibly overcoming these feelings, he turned around in a daze and said to the stunned commissar in a soft, even voice: "Commissar, sir, this is my wife!"

The commissar stood as if he had been immersed in water. "Captain," he said after a moment, "I am endlessly grieved that our arrival was the reason for this terrible catastrophe, but it is not my fault. Obviously, in the face of such a fact, our official duties here are over."

"Excuse me, commissar," Hirsh cried, stepping forward. "But we have these ladies here. Verification of the main fact, the one that we are interested in—that can still be done."

The captain threw a look of savage hatred at Hirsh. He could have torn to pieces this odious lizard who, even at this moment, in the face of the majesty of death, did not know how to be anything other than a policeman.

"Well, yes . . . yes, that is true," the commissar said, a little unhappily; he was offended by Hirsh's observation, even though he had to admit that it was justified.

"Girls," he said to the young women who were watching this scene in mute horror and dismay, "come up closer and take a good look at this lady."

The girls drew nearer to Anelya. The captain raised his eyes to them with an expression of pleading despair.

"Tell us now, is this the same lady who recruited you into service?"

"No!" the girls said in one voice.

Hirsh jumped and flushed red with anger.

"That's not true!' he shouted. "That can't be true!"

"Mr. Hirsh," the commissar admonished him. "Please be quiet! Please tell me clearly once again," he continued, turning to the girls, "was it this lady who recruited you to serve, or was it not?"

"No, she was not the one!" the girls replied decisively.

The commissar bowed to the captain. "Captain, my duties here are finished. In the face of the decisive testimony of these girls, all suspicions against your wife are dropped. We have no documents, no testimony that would weigh directly against her, and as for this visit, all the responsibility for it lies with Mr. Hirsh. I do not have any justification for making an inspection of your home. We also do not have the right to investigate more closely what happened at the moment of our arrival. My respects to you, sir."

The captain shook the hand that was extended to him, and bowed to the girls as they walked out.

How noble, almost saintly, these fallen women seemed to him now, these women who had been so terribly wronged by his wife, and who, in this most difficult moment of his life, had found in their hearts the humaneness, and forbearance, and forgiveness to say decisively, with one voice, the single little word that was so important in its consequences: "No!"

This single word reconciled him with human nature, with life, renewed his spirit, and gave him fresh hope. And if those unfortunate, wronged creatures who had been trampled in the mud could forgive his wife, what right did he have to take leave of her with bitter, hateful feelings?

And, weeping profusely, he flung himself on his knees before Anelya's corpse, kissed her cold, stiffening hands, and washed them with his tears . . .

* * *

The sensational court case against Shternberg, Yuliya, and their partners took place much later. Anelya's name was not mentioned even once in the process, and her suicide remained a mystery to outsiders.

After explaining, or rather, after covering up the unfortunate incident, the captain availed himself of an opportunity to revoke his petition to resign from military service. He was persuaded to do so primarily by Redlikh who, after spending several months nursing the wound that he received in the duel, recuperated sufficiently to come and live with Anharovych. His wound made him unfit for military service, and he embraced a new role as governor to Anharovych's children.

And old Hurter, having mourned Anelya's death, left the hospital and settled in the captain's home, blessing his name and watching over his children with infinite love and solicitude.

The captain's career advanced brilliantly.

The children still weep for their mother, honour her memory as the holiest of holies, and the captain, listening to their heart-rending recollections of her, swallows his tears and whispers: "Your poor mother! Your poor mother! She left you without having taken full delight in you!"

* * *

There is no cross on Anelya's grave, not even a tombstone with an epitaph, just a wrought iron railing and a tall cypress tree that, like a candle, reaches ever upwards, lifting high its lush everlasting green boughs—a faithful reflection of the vitality and the staunch resoluteness locked within it.

Pillars of Society

Pillars of Society
A Story of Contemporary Life
(1894)

Part One

I

Lady Olimpiya Torska must have been having a truly horrific dream. Thrashing about violently in her bed, jerking her feet spasmodically like a wounded bird, flailing her arms about wildly like a drowning man and, banging one arm against the wooden bed frame, she yelled out in her sleep: "Help! Help!"

At that moment she woke up and sat bolt upright in bed. Her gaping eyes wandered in the darkness that reigned in her bedchamber. Her heart was pounding at a furious rate. She was breathing rapidly and heavily, and chills ran up and down her spine. One hand convulsively clutched a corner of the night table that stood beside her bed.

Still half asleep, her frantic mind could not instantly comprehend what was happening and, like a bird caught in a hail storm, it scurried here and there, rushing back and forth between an obscure alarm and an indistinct certainty that everything that she had experienced just a moment ago was not reality, but a dream.

"O Lord, save and protect me! In the name of the Father, and the Son, and the Holy Spirit, amen!" she whispered, her hand trembling uncontrollably as she crossed herself. "What a scare I had! O Lord, how terrifying it was! And it was only a dream! But what a dream! I'm still shaking. Tfu! Begone, begone O evil spirit!"

And crossing herself again, she began to whisper a prayer. But the prayer did not soothe her. She tried to pierce the darkness with her staring eyes, to find the window, to look out at the world, where dawn most certainly must have arrived. But the window—the solitary window in her bedchamber—was draped with a tapestry that did not let in even a glimmer of light. Lady Olimpiya cut off her prayer mid-word and muttered angrily: "Oh, there's that tapestry again! O Lord, grant me the patience to put up with that nasty young woman!"

And speaking in a voice that was choked with sleep she tried shouting: "Paraska! Paraska!"

But her voice died in her throat. Perhaps she had been sleeping on her back with her head hanging down, or perhaps the nightmare was still making her blood pound in her head and her breath catch in her chest—whatever the reason, her mute terror intensified.

"No, I can't! I can't wake her up!" the Lady whispered in despair. "Just listen to her snore! What fiends they all are! They will torture me to death with their disobedience!"

And, angrily gritting her teeth, Lady Olimpiya sat in bed for a couple of minutes, pressing on the sides of her chest to increase the rate of her respirations and attentively listening to Paraska's deep, even, and healthy breathing.

Paraska, an eighteen-year-old servant, was Lady Olimpiya's chambermaid. For the past two months, ever since the Lady started being plagued by nightmares and by blood rushing to her head, Paraska had been forced to sleep in the bedchamber with her. During these attacks, the Lady experienced a terrifying fear that made her shout and toss about, and only the presence of another person in the room could calm her.

But Paraska, who was occupied all day with household chores and work in the kitchen, greatly disliked this nocturnal duty of keeping watch over the capricious Lady. The Lady's somnolent yelling frightened her, and she would have much preferred to sleep peacefully in the kitchen or in a closet. Moreover, the Lady was accustomed to awakening very early, and once awake, she immediately roused Paraska.

And so Paraska came up with a plan. Every evening, after the Lady fell asleep, she draped the window with a tapestry and then tucked in rags tightly around it so that the sun's early morning rays could not break into the bedchamber, thinking that if she did this, the Lady might occasionally sleep a little longer, and then she too could get to sleep in a bit. And it was to no avail that Lady Olimpiya grew angry and scolded her. Paraska, with the stubbornness inherent in people with a dull, indolent nature, did not abandon her ritual, and this led the Lady to despair, all the more so because when she did suffer a paroxysm of fear, the tomb-like darkness in the room augmented her terror.

"Paraska!" the Lady called out in a voice that was neither a whisper, nor a shout. "Get up! Undrape the window!"

But Paraska had no intention of getting up. Lying on a straw-filled tick spread on the floor, with rags tucked under her head for a pillow and a coarse heavy blanket for a coverlet, she was fast asleep. Her deep breathing resonated rhythmically; it was clear that her sleep was profound and peaceful, and that even if she had been carried out into a field, she would not have awoken. And it was the girl's sound, undisturbed sleep that gradually restored Lady Olimpiya's composure. She regained her peace of mind, lay down once again, and covered herself with a quilt, even though it was warm in the room, almost stifling.

But she could no longer sleep. Her imagination, agitated by the nightmare, began to thrust all sorts of horrors into her mind. First, a thought flashed into her head: what if a thief had crept stealthily into the entranceway and was even now crawling towards her bedchamber? But no! What could he possibly steal from her? Granted, the door to her room did not close all that securely, and the lock on the outside door was broken. But that did not matter at all! Paraska was lying right in front of the bedroom door, pressing against it like a heavy log; if anyone wanted to get into the room at night, he would inevitably wake up Paraska.

Having chased away the thought about the intrusion of a thief, Lady Olimpiya turned her attention to other sounds that were reaching her from outside. By the church, the watchman shouted: "Be careful with the fire!" And then she even heard him cough as he trudged around the church before lying down once again on a pile of straw by the belfry. In the chicken coop a rooster crowed, and in the distance other roosters responded from the village. In a lane of ancient linden trees that stretched from the orchard to the river, nightingales warbled; one of them even flew right up to her bedroom window and, alighting on a jasmine bush, sang shrilly, as if speaking with a human tongue:

"With a stick, with a stick, with a stick! Whack it! Whack it! Trrr! Come to your wits! Come to your wits!"

Lady Olimpiya felt as if ants were running up and down her spine. The bird was irritating her with its incessant strident shrilling. The harder she tried to hear exactly what the bird was trilling, the more clearly she seemed to hear those strange words—words that evoked the cold terror that gripped her after her dream. And along with that feeling, her dream rose vividly once again in her mind, all those odious scenes that had not stopped tormenting her for the past two months, and that, like vipers, were sucking the living blood out of her heart.

In her dream she is a young girl. Blossoming like a rose and attired in rose-coloured garments, her outlook on life is rosy as well. Everyone and everything—the flowers, the sun, the very air—smiles at her, pampers her, delights in her. Her peers are drawn to her; young lords from the most notable families in the land swarm around her. Youthful faces—round, elongated, suffused with a healthy flush or a romantic pallor, with dark, carefully tended moustaches or without them, with eyes blazing brilliantly with passion or languid with desire—crowd around her like the cherubic angel faces encircling the Sistine Madonna.

And it is no wonder! She is young, beautiful, the daughter of Count Lisovytsky, a nobleman who owns large estates and has extensive assets—and therefore, even though she is not an only child, she is still considered one of the most desirable aristocratic matches in the land.

And she is aware of this, and she walks proudly, coldly, mockingly, among the clouds of faces, under a shower of ardent, enamoured looks, in the midst of whispers of awe and suppressed desires. She finds the torrid atmosphere of wonder, jealousy, and desire pleasant, but she is not attracted to even one of the faces, or to even one of the supple and elegant figures attired in frock coats, top hats, and glossy gloves.

A nightmare pulls her away from the brilliant and fragrant world of salons, balls, and compliments into a rather small, neat, and cozy room in one of the large wings of her father's mansion—wings that extend from the yard deep into the orchard and look like they are hiding under the spreading linden trees. It is the room of Nestor Derevatsky, a young philosophy student and her siblings' tutor. What attracts her there, to this room, to the small parlour in which he has set up an improvised school for the Count's sons and daughters, a room lined with maps and pictures, with a chalkboard for writing, with padded chairs set up in a row to take the place of a school bench in front of a massive oak desk? What draws Miss Olimpiya there? After all, she has completed her education and is no longer compelled, like her younger brothers and sisters, to weary her head with books and notebooks.

She herself cannot say what attracts her there. Nestor, a young man of twenty-eight, cannot be called ugly, but he is rather plain, and there is nothing all that special about him. If judged by his outward appearance, he pales in comparison with the elegant young men who encircle Miss Olimpiya. But his lips, his words, hold powerful charms.

Lady Olimpiya still remembers that she did not pay any attention to the tutor for quite some time. Even though he dined with the Count's family, she never said a word to him; it was as if he were a tiny fly that was free to circle in the rays of her brilliance, but which she did not deign to see.

And then, one day, her brothers took her with them to sit in on one of Mr. Nestor's lessons. At first she listened indifferently, but she became increasingly more interested, and after the lesson was over she engaged in a lengthy conversation with Nestor and discovered in his words a strange mellifluence. From that time on, she started attending the lessons more frequently, telling her mother that, as the older daughter, she wanted to ensure that her younger brothers and sisters were obeying their teacher and studying diligently. But her siblings did not need to be watched, and Miss Olimpiya was watching something else altogether.

How had it come about that she and Nestor had fallen in love? Who had said the first word? Who, and in what way, had first revealed the feelings that had caught fire in the hearts of these two young people? Lady Olimpiya still does not know how it happened, nor did she know back then. She only remembers that for two months she walked around in a daze, as if she were drowning in a rosy mist. Those were the best days of her life. Why had they ended? And if they had to come to an end, why could they not have lasted a little while longer?

It was her youngest brother Staso who overheard her amorous cooing with Nestor and told his mother about it, and the mother told the father. Neither the mother nor the father said a word to Olimpiya, or for that matter, to the tutor, but the next day, when she went to the annex she knew so well, she found the door locked and the room empty. The old gardener Yakiv told her that Mr. Nestor had been dismissed, packed up before dawn, placed in an open carriage, and driven to the railroad station.

Lady Olimpiya still remembers the bitter, heartfelt tears that she had shed as she hid in the thick shrubbery of the park after hearing what had happened. But she, like her parents, never said a word to anyone about her love, nor did she reveal it by ever mentioning him, or by letting so much as a single tear fall in the presence of any of the household members. Mutely and dully she hid her feelings on the bottom of her heart, drenched them with her tears, and sprinkled them with the dust of oblivion. She was still young, but she already knew that this was how it behoved a count's daughter to comport herself if she had the misfortune of falling in love with a plebe.

The nightmare is pulling her away from those scenes to a place where it is cold, dark, damp. It is as if she is entering an endlessly long corridor that is badly lit and has remained unaired for a long, long time. The stuffy air presses on her chest like a stone. Chills run over her body, and her hand touches something cold, slimy, odious . . . Oh, it is the hand of her fiancé, Count *Torsky, who in his youthful days had been her father's friend, and now, having dissipated his strength, his youth, his health, and his wealth in European capitals and resorts, had returned to his native land to save the remnants of his tattered fortune. Upon seeing her, a young, beautiful, and wealthy young lady, the daughter of his old friend, he at once deduced that of all possible financial speculations, this one was probably the best, and he immediately set his plan in motion . . .

The nightmare drags Lady Olimpiya ever farther and farther through the chasms of her cold and unrewarding aristocratic life. Now she is Countess Torska. She is setting out from her paternal home on a honeymoon trip to Italy with her husband. But the two of them get only as far as Monaco, and it is here that her husband loses more than half her dowry. Lady Olimpiya's memories of her honeymoon with the Count hang over her heart like heavy rain clouds. Scenes, tears, despair . . .

They return home, and the Count threatens that he will sell the last village left from his family fortune—the village of Torky in which Lady Olimpiya was fated to live out the rest of her days. And who knows if he would not have carried out his threat, for Monaco beckoned, and he found it more alluring than his young and attractive wife, who wept away her days and nights in an elegant boudoir—hung with tapestries and mirrors, and suffused with fragrances—adjacent to his bedchamber. But things turned out differently from what the Count had planned.

After one particularly tempestuous scene with his creditors, he fell into such a rage that he had an apoplectic fit. His feet and arms were so badly affected that he could not move; he could not even lift a spoon to his lips. And from a licentious gentleman, card shark, drunkard, and tomcat, he suddenly became a helpless child who had to be clothed, fed, wheeled around in a handcart, carried into bed and lifted out again, a child who rewarded all this assistance with curses, cynical jokes, and harsh rebukes.

The nightmare mercilessly draws Lady Olimpiya into that terrible, frigid sea, that abyss of suffering, worry, humiliation, and heartfelt grief in which she had lived from that time on. For her it was the beginning of a life the likes of which she could not have imagined in her wildest dreams.

The ailing Count tyrannized her pitilessly, systematically breaking her tastes and habits, her will and her heart. Through his very weakness, that corpse-like man, enfeebled and helpless, became her fiercest tormentor. If only he had shown her a spark of sympathy, a drop of love, of appreciation, of warmth! But no, there were only cynical jokes, sneers, and reproaches that turned her blood to ice. And the more humbly she bowed before him, and the more diligently she served him, the more capricious and impossible this wasted, aging man of forty-five became, and when he looked at her, ominous sparks of hatred flashed in his eyes. Why did he hate her? What had she done to him? She never asked him about that. Her heart had shut itself off from him in Monaco, and it never opened up to him again.

Over time the Count began to rally. Granted, he never regained the full use of his afflicted arms and legs, but his digestion improved. His helplessness forced him to lead a well-balanced life, to follow a proper diet. He could no longer drink or play cards, and he had to eat what he was given when it was given to him, and this regimen worked in his favour. He regained his appetite, ate heartily and, as never before, slept peacefully and soundly; his cheeks were rosy with a healthy glow, and a downy growth covered his prematurely balding head. The Count regained his youthfulness. He did not think about death, and he thanked God for not allowing him to sell Torky.

When all was said and done, it was a nice little estate with two manors that embraced more than a thousand acres of ploughed land and hayfields, and over two thousand acres covered by an ancient pine forest. And during the years that the Count had lain ill, unable to travel or to gamble and squander his money, the estate, under the capable management of a conscientious administrator, had been cleared of debts, and was now profitable enough that the Count could live in a lordly fashion and still put away some money for a rainy day.

It should be noted that the Countess played no small role in all of this. She looked after the household, supervised the administrator and other officials, set up the budget for the entire estate, and controlled the money. And, after the torments that she was forced to endure day in and day out in her life with the Count, she took pleasure in this work.

The nightmare has a pincer-like grip on Lady Olimpiya's heart, and it evokes in her memory the Count's cynical, heartless gibes and sneers.

"It is wearisome for you, Countess, to fuss with a cripple like me, is it not?"

"Yes, it is," she says, looking away from him.

"You should pray to God to have Him take me from this world as quickly as possible."

"I do."

"And so you should. I would suffer less," he adds with a caustic sneer, "and you would get married, right? Well, tell me in all honesty, do you have a bachelor in mind, someone whom you would marry?"

"Yes, I do!" she says with implacable rancour in her heart as she presses her lips tightly together.

"That's very nice!" the Count hisses ironically. "But here's the rub! Your prayers cannot be all that sincere, because I am beginning to feel better. Would you, my Countess, perchance like to have some children?"

Tears are bursting in sprinkles from her eyes, but she grits her teeth and does not give any sign of the hellish torments that her wedded torturer is inflicting on her. She remains silent, with her head turned away.

And the Count babbles on: "A tiny, rosy, lovely infant—it is simply amazing what a pleasant diversion it would be for you! It would wriggle, laugh, and before long it would begin to crawl. Ah, Countess, why are you not saying anything? Am I not speaking the truth?"

"Yes, you are."

"There you have it. But woe is me, my Countess, I am ill! I am a helpless cripple, unable to fulfill my obligation. Suffer and endure, my Countess, and perhaps God will take pity on you."

Lady Olimpiya understood only too well the bloody mockery of those words. The maidservants who cared for the Count day and night and had to sleep in his bedchamber, all gave birth in turn to children who were sheltered in the manor yard as bastards.

The Countess knew very well whose children they were, and she looked upon them with hatred, but all the same she did not send them away from the manor: it was as if she took a perverse pleasure in feasting her eyes on these tangible reminders of her husband's infidelity, in shoving them around, in treating these children—who had the Count's blood running in their veins—as whelps, as dirt under her feet, and in knowing that a dog's life lay ahead of them, that they were fated to be the dregs of society.

Where, oh where had it gone—that rosy, fragrant aura of naiveté in which she had basked in her father's home!

The nightmare, like an implacable executioner, tugs at her and pulls her ever farther, ever deeper into the abyss, into the impenetrable darkness, vileness, and putrid fumes.

"Have mercy," she pleads. "Have I not had enough of these hellish torments? Have I not suffered enough?"

"No," says a harsh, inexorable voice. "In your heart there still remains a corner that is intact, unwounded, pure, undefiled! Show it to me! Give it to me!"

And once again, new scenes arise. At the very moment when grief was overwhelming her, when she felt that she might go mad at any moment, there appeared something akin to relief, to a glimmer of hope, to a bright glade in a dark impenetrable forest. He appeared—Nestor—the man about whom she had heard nothing and had not been interested in hearing about since the time that she had last seen him in the improvised school in her father's home some twenty years earlier.

What a strange twist of fate!

He appeared in a guise in which she had never dreamed of seeing him. This guise both attracted and repulsed her, simultaneously awakening within her feelings of respect and revulsion. He appeared as a priest, but as a priest who had become a reclusive eccentric—a strange, unsociable person who had spent many years living in the mountains, far removed from civilized society, from spiritual concerns.

Even now, his figure, stooped, hunched over, and bowed down by a premature old age, rises up vividly before her. His eyes, formerly so passionate, so bright and luminous, eyes that reflected a brilliant intelligence and radiated sincerity and kindness, were now extinguished and, deeply sunken, they raced about in their sockets as if they were terrified. The spell formerly cast by his speech had vanished without a trace: during his first visit to the manor he kept stuttering, stumbling over his words, and breaking off his sentences midstream to such a degree that, upon his departure, the Count stated mockingly with his usual cynicism: "What an idiot! He's certainly worthy of my *endorsement!"

Nonetheless, he was a priest. His spiritual position demanded her respect, and she had been raised in an overly pious tradition to deny it to him. But that was not all. Before long she found out from Fr. Nestor the story of his life—well, perhaps she did not so much find it out from him, as she managed to piece it together from his broken and disjointed accounts. And this story made her feel even closer to him. After all, it was because of her that he had become what he was now! It was she who, albeit involuntarily, was the reason for his ruined life, his shattered dreams. Oh, Lady Olimpiya was now able to understand all too well the difficult and sorrowful life of this pitiful, uncouth priest!

After falling in love with her, and then losing all hope of winning her hand, Nestor abandoned his study of philosophy, entered a seminary, and took a vow of celibacy. And it was at that juncture of his life that he heard about her marriage. The spiritual authorities took a liking to him; he was capable, obedient, hardworking. A brilliant career lay before him in the religious hierarchy, but his heart ached and would not allow him to forget his lost happiness.

It was not long before he heard about the Count's illness and the sad fate of his beloved, even though, of course, he could not even begin to imagine the abysmal grief weighing down her heart. He loved her sincerely, and every bit of news about her, be it good or bad, wounded his heart, robbed him of his peace of mind, rendered him incapable of working, of thinking. And he resolved to conquer his feelings.

In order to be farther away from her, to not be reminded about her, he moved to an obscure little town to teach catechism in public schools. But even here his tranquility was disturbed. From time to time he could not help but read about her in the newspapers and hear about her from people passing through the town. And the less frequently this news reached him, the more it fell like a burdensome weight on Fr. Nestor's heart, the longer it tormented him. And he was filled with a desire to flee still farther from the world, to leave behind all vestiges of civilization.

After requesting a parish in one of the most Godforsaken corners of the mountains, he lived there for ten years, caught up in the duties of his position and in a difficult struggle to eke out a meagre subsistence, without ever once leaving it, without reading any newspapers, without corresponding with anyone. The parish was small, impoverished, and what he received as remuneration for his priestly duties was insignificant, and so he had to engage in husbandry, in backbreaking peasant labour.

Fr. Nestor plunged headfirst into a sea of mundane troubles and drudgery: he ploughed and sowed, kept cattle, raised oxen to sell at the market, made hay, sold oats and whey cheese, planted new varieties of potatoes—in short, he became an agriculturalist, a horticulturalist, and an apiarist.

But still, his heart could not find peace. The wound was too deep, and even though it healed on the surface, it left behind deep bitterness, a heavy melancholy, and a perpetual sense of dissatisfaction. Fr. Nestor never stopped feeling that he had wasted his life, that he could have amounted to something. He fulfilled his obligations and did even more than was called for, but he did it all mechanically, ill-humouredly; it was obvious that his deeds were not being done out of love, but out of a contempt for people. And it was not surprising that even though he did not mistreat his parishioners, they did not like him; it was as if they lived in fear of the coldness that had settled in his heart and emanated from him.

After a few years of residing in that mountain nest, Fr. Nestor changed dramatically. He aged before his time, grew stooped, and became unsociable and uncommunicative. He neglected his outward appearance, and his clothing was shabby and rarely cleaned. In the village they spoke of him as being stingy, and his servants complained that he fed them poorly.

On occasion he received a very good price for oxen that he had raised. These larger sums of money that came his way gradually fired up his greed. His heart, not finding any people to whom it could bind itself, became increasingly attached to money. Fr. Nestor did not notice this at first. It seemed to him that he was not going beyond the boundaries of domestic thriftiness, but his heart immersed itself ever more deeply in his new ardour for saving and accumulating money, and his mind, formerly so clear and sharp, began to grow petty and narrow under the influence of that ill-starred passion.

Fr. Nestor became aware of what was happening only after it was too late, when he realized that his new passion had devoured his old memories and his old suffering. After devoting his life to amassing wealth, he forgot about Olimpiya, and even when the thought of her did cross his mind, he did not think about her as he once had. She now appeared to him as a pale, distant shadow that no longer stirred any emotion in his heart.

And so, after many long years, when he happened to notice in the *Eparchial News* that there was a vacancy in the parish of Torky where his former beloved lived, his heart did not respond, but thoughts of a larger income began to dart about in his mind: the number of acres in the parish property, the wealthier parishioners, the proximity of an important shrine for pilgrims. He asked to be assigned to that parish, and his wish was granted.

Even now, chills run up and down Lady Olimpiya's spine when she recalls her first confrontation with the passionate love of her distant youth. She was still religious at the time, and the priestly cassock in and of itself awoke within her a feeling of respect. But this uncouth eccentric, this stammering man of few words who grew confused and could not complete a single sentence, who talked only about grain, potatoes, and cattle—could this possibly be the same Nestor who back then had soared with her in the rosy world of idealism?

Of course, she knew only too well the drastic changes that the hostile world had worked in her, but still she would have wanted him to appear before her as a strong man, clear-minded and full of sympathy. She so badly wanted to, so badly needed to lean on someone, to breathe freely for at least a moment, to forget, for at least a second, about the horrific hell in which her days and nights were passing by. This wretched ruin in a priest's cassock, however, was more likely to evoke feelings of pity, or even disgust, rather than the emotional closeness that she so craved and needed.

But then again, no! A flame still flashed from this ruin. Not a bright flame that illuminates, warms, and spreads contentment, peace, and happiness in radiant waves, but rather the sinister glimmer of an ember smouldering under ashes, an ember that scorches and begets conflagrations, that penetrates and ruins everything it touches. And that ember brushed against her and wounded the last intact corner of her heart.

She rarely saw Fr. Nestor; he was kept busy managing his affairs and taking care of his parish. But one day, as she was walking from the main manor to the smaller one, she met him by chance on a meadow that spread like a green tablecloth between a linden lane in the manor yard and the hills directly opposite it where her fields abutted those belonging to the parish priest.

They met. Fr. Nestor greeted her with a deep bow and then, as if intimidated by the proximity of the Countess, remained silent for some time as he walked along beside her. She initiated the conversation, beginning with small talk about farm matters. She asked Fr. Nestor if he liked his new parish, and what his life had been like in the mountains. He gradually grew more animated. The armour of seclusion with which he had shielded himself in the mountains had already eroded away to some extent. But then the Countess suddenly turned the conversation to a topic that clearly was most distressing to Fr. Nestor.

"Do you remember, Father, the time you spent in Horylisy?"

He grew confused, dropped his cane, and then hurriedly bent over to pick it up.

The Countess halted and looked at him calmly, intently.

"M-m-my m-m-most honourable Countess!" he babbled, turning his eyes away so as not to meet her gaze.

"You have probably even forgotten what my name is," she said serenely, almost as if in jest.

Fr. Nestor's confusion vanished, and he stared at her with faded dark eyes that had lost their former intensity. And in his vapid heart a wound reopened, a wound that he had thought was completely healed and grown over with moss. And he began talking, with difficulty at first, stumbling over his words and stuttering, but gradually speaking more smoothly, with increased confidence.

"M-m-my most honourable Countess! You see f-f-fit to joke at my expense! To m-m-mock me! And that's not right! I haven't forgotten what . . . what I remember. But why go into all that? Do you think that I haven't suffered enough? After all, it was because of you . . . that I abandoned everything. The hope of knowing family happiness . . . and my career . . . and the companionship of people . . . and books . . . Everything! Everything! I buried myself in the mountains among the *Boyko people, among oxen and sheep. And I did it to forget you, to avoid hearing anything about you. Because, you see, the tiniest bit of news about you, every minute detail agitated me to the depths of my soul . . . tortured me as if I were spread-eagled on a rack. Oh, how greatly I suffered! And yet you . . . you feel at liberty to laugh at me!"

And this lonely eccentric, this ruin of a human being, this man of few words, this prematurely old celibate burst into tears. He sobbed like a child, wiping away his tears with the sleeve of his cassock.

After this moment, everything is confused in Lady Olimpiya's mind. Grief and hope, revulsion and pleasure, anxiety and joy—

they all hurtle into her heart, massively, powerfully, turbulently. She tosses about on the bed and flings out her hands as if warding off any more thoughts. She does not wish to recall, she does not want to go over, once again, even in her imagination, the terrible, endless spiral that led her, step by step, to her present condition.

All the agonizing scenes that swept over her head since that time . . . her confession about her life to Fr. Nestor . . . their ensuing conversations and relations . . . the birth of their son . . . the death of her husband . . . the conflagration that burned down the main manor . . . the difficult years that followed, and the vipers that are now creeping up towards her heart—all of these memories congregate around her in a single, confused throng that serves as a leather sack in which she is bound and in which she is gasping, choking, tossing about and shouting, mustering her last bit of strength in near-death terror, in unbridled despair: "Help! Help!"

These dreams, these memories, these thoughts that have been tormenting her now for two months have not grown any less intense; in fact they are increasing in severity with every passing day. How would it all end?

There are times when Lady Olimpiya is truly afraid that she might go mad. During the day it seems to her that her frame of mind is fairly good, but as soon as her head sinks into the pillow at night, a fever begins raging in her blood, and strange, terrible thoughts come alive in her mind. And it is in vain that she tries to chase them away. Like importunate wasps, they keep circling around her, buzzing, and droning, and drilling into her heart with their incessant thrumming.

"Is God putting temptation in my way?" Lady Olimpiya ponders. "Or is it, perhaps, the evil spirit that is making advances on my soul? O Lord, have mercy on me!"

She prays with her eyes opened wide. She is afraid to close her eyes in the darkness, for she knows that as soon as she shuts them, there will instantly arise the same repulsive, cursed scenes—scenes that turn her blood to ice—and the words of the prayer die away on her lips. Finally, with a heroic effort, she gets out of bed, gropes her way to the window, and tears down the tapestry that is covering it.

"Oh, glory to God!" the words burst from her lips. "Dawn has arrived. The sun will appear any moment now."

And she walks up to Paraska, who has rolled off the straw tick and is now sleeping on her back on the floor, nudges the girl's head with her bare foot, and shouts: "Paraska! Hey, Paraska! It's time to get up! Do you hear me? Paraska!"

II

"O you stupid dolt, why do you always cover the window for the night? Haven't I told you that I can't sleep when the window is draped?" Lady Olimpiya scolded Paraska who, having been awakened so abruptly, had jumped to her feet and was now rubbing her eyes with her fists.

"I swear to God, I didn't do it!" Paraska muttered without budging. "It must have been Hadyna. He was putting things in order here last night."

"Hadyna, Hadyna!" the Lady responded angrily. "You always blame someone else! But I am positive that you did it."

"No, may the Lord strike me down, it wasn't me!" Paraska swore vehemently.

"Do not use the Lord's name in vain, you miserable bastard!" the Lady shouted. "I know you, and I know your Hadyna. Both of you are snakes in the grass. Well, why are you standing there? Go and wake the others! No doubt they are all still sleeping, even though the sun is already high in the sky."

"But, if you please, my gracious Lady, today is Sunday."

"Oh sure, you would like it to be Sunday every day! But after all, does one not have to eat on Sunday? Get going and wake up Hadyna; let him run at once to the dairyman for some milk and cream. Don't worry, he is sure to have risen a long time ago and finished milking the cows by now. Maybe he has even left for *Lviv already."

"If he has gone, then he has left some milk and cream for my gracious Lady in the cellar," Paraska reassured her. And obviously not all that concerned about Lady Olimpiya's angry tone, she continued yawning and scratching her head, poking around in her dishevelled, uncombed braids.

"And then go and wake Hapka, and tell her to light the fire in the stove at once. As for old Demenyuk, he is sure to be up already without any help from you. Well, why are you just standing there? Get going, you blockhead!"

Paraska finally began to move, but when Lady Olympia turned away from her, she raised both hands to her face and, crooking her index fingers in the shape of horns, placed them on her forehead, contorted her face into an ugly grimace directed at her mistress, shook her head, and dashed headlong from the bedroom. But in the dark vestibule she almost fell as she stumbled over an old butter churn that had been placed there to prop the outside door shut.

"Tfu! Get the hell out of my way!" Paraska shouted in the entryway, loudly enough for the Lady to hear. "Some she-devil is always jamming this churn against the door, may her arms be wrenched out of their sockets!"

And Paraska kicked the churn so furiously that it rolled with a clattering noise into the depths of the passageway. Paraska knew all too well that it was none other than the Lady who had placed the churn by the door, and so, with this seemingly innocent remark, she wanted to get back at her for interrupting her sleep and berating her first thing in the morning.

But Lady Olimpiya was already going about her morning routine. She washed up and, after combing her still thick grey hair, she donned the plain black dress that she had been wearing for the past couple of years.

She had long since stopped fussing with her attire; first, her material circumstances had worsened considerably after the death of her husband, and secondly, there was no one for whom she needed to fuss. Her family had not so much renounced her as silently forgotten about her; and even when the Count was still alive they did not socialize with the neighbours, so there were almost never any guests at the Torky manor. Having finished dressing, the Countess, mindful of the coolness of the dewy summer morning, threw a black shawl over her shoulders before she walked out of the room.

Coming out of her bedroom that also served as her office and dressing room, Lady Olimpiya glanced about a bit anxiously, almost fearfully. She did not trust any of the people around her;

she knew that they all despised her, that no one liked her or wished her well, and she lived among them as if she were living among wild animals in the forest. From the time of the ghastly catastrophe that had brought about her husband's death and the burning down of the manor, she had not had any peace of mind.

She was obsessed by an alarming thought: what was to stop these people—these wild animals—from attacking her and tearing her to shreds! At the outset, she had thought that she could get on their good side by treating them kindly, but she quickly saw, to her great consternation, that her kindness only emboldened them, made them insolent, and did not incline their hearts towards her.

And so she returned to her old methods: keeping "those brutish beasts" at a distance and making them aware at every turn of her contempt for them. As a consequence, she lived in constant fear. They would rob her, kill her—these were the scenarios that seethed incessantly in her mind.

And so, as she walked out of her bedroom, she cast her eyes over it out of sheer habit, even though she knew that if a robber did enter it in her absence, he would find almost nothing worth taking. It was true that the walnut wardrobe, the inlaid mahogany table for her toiletries, and the chest of drawers for the linens testified to a former opulence. But in the wardrobe there were only a few old gowns that had been set aside a long time ago, the drawer in the table held only a jar of pomade and a couple of ancient combs with missing teeth, and the chest also did not contain any great treasures.

Two or three portraits hung on the walls, and in a corner beside Lady Olimpiya's bed stood her strongbox, a securely locked small oaken trunk bound with iron bands. Unfortunately, however, this safe usually did not have very much in it, and today, except for a few copper coins scattered on the bottom, it was almost completely empty. Nevertheless, Lady Olimpiya did not like to give anyone permission to enter her bedroom, especially during the day, and she always latched the shutters when she left and secured the outside door with a lock.

Lady Olimpiya's bedroom led into a dark, narrow passageway into which light was admitted only through a small transom above the door. At one time there had been thick, frosted glass panes in that window, but they had long since been broken, so while the afternoon sun shone directly into the vestibule, in the morning it was quite dark in there.

At the opposite end of this entranceway stood the "salon," an expansive room that was decorated in a somewhat lordly manner, but which was usually kept shut. It was opened only for "guests": a visiting commissar or a doctor, or even the village reeve—people who felt constrained by politeness to visit the manor. At those times, even though in her heart Lady Olimpiya cursed the brazen interlopers, she nevertheless felt obligated to open up the salon, let in some fresh air, light a fire, and entertain her visitors.

Recently, her son had made her open up the salon more frequently. Indulging in a heady lifestyle in Lviv, he occasionally brought home some of his young friends and acquaintances—a somewhat motley, but consistently boisterous and cheerful crowd. At those times, the salon was filled with the din of youthful voices, laughter, jokes, cigar smoke, and the aroma of various colognes used by these "well brought up" young people—because, of course, it was only with such refined young men that the young Count Adam Torsky kept company. They drank tea until late at night, and played cards or engaged in far-ranging conversations.

Lady Olimpiya was the only woman present at these gatherings, but she felt that she was in her element among them, that she was among equals and, after the unrelenting state of dispiritedness in which her life was flowing by, her heart had a chance to renew itself. It was true that her son's lifestyle was the source of incalculable problems and worries for her, but in the youthful, merry company of his friends she forgot about all that and was grateful to her son for the respite these visits provided.

And it was guests like these that she was expecting today. Yesterday morning, *Adas had come up from the secondary manor and then, right after dinner, he had set out for Lviv with the intention of returning at noon today accompanied by his friends. They would have dinner at his manor—where Adas was in his first year of running a household and taking care of its administration—and afterwards, they would come to the main manor for tea.

Lady Olimpiya wanted to serve these guests coffee, not just the usual clear tea, and so she had ordered a sufficient quantity of cream from the tenant farmer, a Jew who leased the manor yard along with the cattle and sold the milk in Lviv. Knowing full well that she could not rely on either Paraska or Hadyna, she had dressed as quickly as she could and, after locking the outside door of the vestibule, walked out into the yard to take care of everything herself.

"Oh, how wonderful it is out here!" the words escaped involuntarily from her lips, and she breathed deeply, expanding her chest and inhaling avidly. The fresh, clean air was saturated with fragrances emanating from the blossoming linden trees and the flowering jasmine shrubs and vines that wove a covering over mournful ruins—the charred remains of the Count's main brick mansion.

As soon as she stepped out of the vestibule and locked the door behind her, those ruins were the first things that Lady Olimpiya's eyes settled on. Out of habit, no doubt.

For the past fifteen years, ever since the death of her husband, those charred remains of the manor house—remains that were gloomy and uninviting and, just like her memories of Count Torsky, forever present, indestructible—had loomed menacingly before her. As if casting a macabre spell, they lured her eyes to look upon them. There was no other spot on earth that she hated as passionately, as resolutely, as those charred ruins. After all, it was here that the heartless tyrant had tormented and tortured her for so many long years! It was here that her youth had been annihilated, her beauty destroyed, her soul crippled, her heart and thoughts poisoned.

But still, she could not walk across the yard, the street, the orchard, the lane, without casting her eyes at those ruins. And no matter from where she viewed them, they assaulted and stung her heart and, like a mute, mysterious, and terrifying threat, chilled her to the bone.

After the death of Count Torsky, the inhabitants of the village of Torky recounted stories for a long time about how the deceased Count, weeping and groaning loudly, roamed through the charred ruins as if searching for something. The Countess did not believe these stories and grew incensed when they were related to her, but yet she was deathly afraid to go into the yard at night and face the ruins. Was it possible that the stories were true? Was it possible that her tormentor would not give her any peace even after his death?

Lady Olimpiya had made plans more than a dozen times to clean up the site. And there was even one time when workers had actually been hired to do it. But some unexpected incident always interfered with her plans: an exceptionally early harvest, a fierce storm that sent the workers packing, a hailstorm that destroyed the crops and made it necessary to spend elsewhere the money that had been set aside to clear the ruins. It was as if an evil fatality hung over the charred remains, forcing Lady Olimpiya to live under the lingering shadow of the detested site.

"But now, if my plans materialize, the first thing that I will do is have the burned ruins removed and the site cleaned up," the thought flashed through Lady Olimpiya's mind.

She crossed herself and turned around to look towards the opposite end of the yard where there was a smaller wing—a long, low annex that, standing on the boundary across from the larger wing containing her bedroom and salon, stretched out into the orchard. Lining up with the large wing, but standing apart from it, there was a sizeable barn, and farther on, a brick coach-house. These buildings flanked the expansive yard that was dissected diagonally by a tall wooden fence abutting the corner of the coach-house in the east and ending by the annex in the west. And because this long annex extended into the orchard—living quarters consisting of two small rooms had been added on at a later date—the fence stopped about three paces short of it and ended at the pickets that surrounded a small flower garden beneath the annex windows.

As Lady Olimpiya walked through the yard, she looked around intently in all directions.

The servants were quartered in the smaller wing: the lackey Tanasko Hadyna, Hapka the cook, and old Yurko Demenyuk, formerly the farm manager, but relegated now to serving as a beekeeper and a general watchman, as the countess no longer maintained a barnyard and rented her fields to a Jew. The building also contained the kitchen and a room for the dairyman who likewise rented a field from the countess. The remaining farm buildings were located farther away, on the other side of the main road.

A fire had already been lit in the kitchen, and a bluish-pink stream of smoke billowed straight up from the chimney as if trying to rise above the tips of the spreading age-old linden trees whose massive, dark-green heads protruded above the low roof of the annex. And if it were not for that smoke, you would have thought that this entire manor yard, encircled by the ancient linden trees, was fenced off from the world, and that there was not a living soul in it. No human voices could be heard—there was only the shrill trilling of nightingales in the trees.

The dairyman had long since milked the cows and gone to Lviv with the milk, his cowherd had driven the cows to the pasture, old Demenyuk had wandered off somewhere before dawn, and the young servants, thankful that it was holy Sunday, were sleeping in—although, even on ordinary days, they neither rushed out of bed nor worked up a sweat as they went about their chores in the manor yard.

This silence in broad daylight did not please Lady Olimpiya, and she began listening and looking around more intently in an effort to ascertain what her servants were doing. Following a diagonal path that had once been well trodden but was now overgrown with grass, she quietly and slowly approached the windows of the kitchen to take a look inside. She walked near the wall, moving stealthily and making it seem that she was not thinking about anything in particular. The servants were all well aware of this devious habit of hers.

"*Zacznijcie, wargi wasze, chwalić pannę świętą* [May your lips begin to praise the Holy Virgin]!" Hapka's devout rendition of a Polish hymn suddenly rang out in the kitchen.

She was an older woman who had worked from her youth in the manor and, since she had not married, remained there. She used to have a cheerful disposition, ran around with young lords and single men, then spent a couple of years in prison for aborting a child, and upon her return, brought back with her, as the only acquisitions of prison civilization, an invincible bent for piety and for cursing. In her head, Christ and *Belial lived in harmony side by side, and she knew a myriad of pious songs and prayers that she continually whispered or sang in a squeaky, broken voice, and perhaps an even larger quantity of the most profane curses that spewed in all directions from her lips like hail from a black cloud.

Lady Olimpiya gave a startled jump when she heard that voice. "There she goes, singing again!" she muttered. "But let her sing! It is better to have her sing than curse. Although," and a smile flitted over her face as a thought flashed through her mind, "it is likely that the Lord does not pay any more attention to her singing than to her cursing."

Before reaching the kitchen windows, the countess turned off in another direction and walked across the yard to have a look in the barn. The door was wide open, and in its dark depths she could hear rustling sounds mixed with whispers and stifled laughter. She leaned in closely against the wall next to the door, grew very still, and listened.

"Well, come on, you silly thing, Paraska! What are you afraid of?" Hadyna was whispering.

"I don't want to. Leave me alone!" Paraska countered.

"Oh, come on! I swear to God that I won't deceive you! We'll get married in the fall."

"I know the likes of you! When we're married I'll come to you, but as for now, there's no way!"

"Don't be afraid! Come on!"

It was obvious that Hadyna was trying to force himself upon Paraska, but she was the stronger of the two, and she shoved him so hard that he almost flew out the door.

"Oh, what a foolish woman! There's no reasoning with her!" Hadyna said peevishly.

"Then don't!" Paraska replied somewhat reluctantly, as she moved about in the straw.

"But you do want to marry me, don't you?"

"Huh! As if you're doing me such a big favour! If you don't marry me, someone else will."

"But you won't be as well off with someone else as you would be with me."

"That's what you say! As if I don't know how well off you are. I'd probably have to starve along with you."

"You're being foolish, really foolish!" Hadyna whispered hoarsely as he leaned closer to her. "I have already put aside enough money to buy a cottage and a small plot of land, and any day now I'll have even more."

"Maybe you'll buy the whole village of Torky?" Paraska asked in jest.

"I may or may not buy Torky, but I'll have enough to last us and our children until the day we die."

"What are you prattling about, you madman?" Paraska said loudly. "Where will you get that much money?"

"It doesn't matter where I'll get it. That's my business."

"Well, tell me; I want to know."

"Oh, I don't think so; you like to wag your tongue."

"I swear to God I won't tell anyone."

"Don't bother swearing! Why do you need to know? And then again, who knows, maybe nothing will come of it. It's best to wait a while."

"Oh, tell me, tell me, my dear Tanasko!" Paraska coaxed him. "If you tell me, I'll come to you."

"You will?" Hadyna cried out quickly.

"I swear to God, I will."

"Right now?"

"Well, no! Later. This evening."

"Oh, you're teasing me. When you come, then I'll tell you."

"No, tell me right now. If you don't, I won't come to you today, or tomorrow, or ever. I won't even want to know you."

"Well then, listen. Our priest has . . ."

"Which priest?"

"The old one, the one who lives here in the annex. He has money. Lots of money."

"Oh sure, in the savings bank!"

"What he has in the savings bank is another matter. But he has cash on hand. He keeps hiding it in a new place every day. A little pile here, a little pile there. I've been watching him for quite some time now, but he's a wily old bloodsucker. But it's the gardener's dog that's the biggest problem. As soon as I come a little nearer, the dog hears me and startles the old man. But I already got my hands on one little pile."

"Was it a lot?"

"Paraska! Paraska!" Hapka's voice rang out at that very moment from the kitchen. "May God and everyone in the whole world forget about you the same way that you forget about your work! Paraska!"

"Oh, damn!" Paraska cried. "The Plague is bellowing. I was sent for firewood, but I ended up talking with you. Let me go!"

"Stay just a minute longer!" Hadyna pleaded.

"There's no time. All I need is for the old vampire to come and raise a ruckus."

And Paraska tore out of the barn and almost ran headfirst into Lady Olimpiya.

"Oh my Lord!" she screamed, and stood as if petrified.

"What are you doing here?" the Lady asked her sternly. "With whom were you talking in there?"

"With no one," Paraska lied; hearing a soft creak in the barn she knew that Hadyna had leapt into the loft with a single bound and then jumped through a hole in the roof into the orchard. "Hapka sent me to get some firewood."

"So this is where you come for firewood, is it?"

"Well, I thought I'd gather some straw to light the fire."

"But tell me, with whom were you talking?"

"May the Lord strike me down, I wasn't talking with anyone."

"Oh, you damned devil's spawn!" the Lady said angrily. "You dare to lie to my face! Why, I heard you myself. Hey there, Hadyna!" she shouted into the depths of the barn. "Where are you? Come here where I can see you."

"Where in the world did my gracious Lady see Hadyna anywhere around here?" Paraska said, feeling quite emboldened and thinking that the Lady had shown up only after hearing Hapka's shouts. "Please take a look in the barn and see for yourself if there's so much as a living soul in there."

The Lady walked into the barn and began looking around for Hadyna.

In the meantime, Paraska, thankful that she managed to get rid of the Lady so easily, ran to the woodshed that stood next to the coach-house, hurriedly gathered up an armful of firewood, and raced with it to the kitchen before the Lady made her way back out of the barn.

Lady Olimpiya was visibly shaken. The conversation that she had listened in on swept over her like something horrible and odious, something that was entirely out of keeping with the wonderfully clear, deep-blue sky, the fragrance wafting from the linden trees, and the warbling of the nightingales.

Not seeing Hadyna in the barn, she began, in a somewhat perfunctory manner, poking around in the straw in the mangers and peering into the bins and under the troughs to see if he had hidden somewhere. Finally, she stopped and stood still.

"And why, exactly, am I looking for him?" she pondered. "What do I want with him? What would I say to him, and what can I say to her? Filthy, rotten, odious creatures! Begotten in depravity, they were born into it, they are living in it, and they will perish in it. Am I to raise them out of that mire? Am I to turn them away from the road that is so in keeping with their true nature? Oh, no, let the devil take them! Let them continue wading in that muck! After all, they are both his children—the offspring of my tormentor, my tyrant! And both of them, even before they were born, brought derision down upon me, ripped out my heart, destroyed my honour, my good name! Let them continue down the road of infamy and disgrace! I most certainly will not try to stop them."

And she plucked a single straw from a manger and began biting it slowly, spitting out the pieces as she bit them off. And as she did so, her thoughts leapt to other matters.

"But that Hadyna is a real thief! You see, he has begun keeping an eye on the priest. Well, if he has started doing that, he is not about to stop. But what did he mean when he promised her that any day now he would have even more money? Is it possible that he is about to . . .? I better warn the priest. But perhaps it would be even better to . . . what good would it do to warn him? It would be best to keep an eye on him myself. Perhaps Adas might . . . But no! The devil take all of them! We shall see!"

And the Lady, gesturing with her hand as if chasing away an insistent, bothersome fly, walked swiftly out of the barn, out of the semidarkness and the stuffy air heavy with the pungent, pervasive stench of cattle that was prompting oppressive, unpleasant thoughts.

She proceeded to the kitchen to discuss with Hapka the plans for the afternoon tea. She was still in the yard when Hapka's voice reached her through the open kitchen window; and this time it was not being raised in pious singing, even though God and all the saints were being called upon quite frequently.

"Oh, may the merciful Lord smite all of you with thunderbolts! May cholera turn you to dust and wipe you off the face of the earth! And why does the holy earth let you walk upon it? Why doesn't it cave in under your feet and swallow you?"

"But Hapka!" Paraska's voice could be heard. "Why are you picking on me? What have I done?"

"Shut up, you vile creature!" Hapka yelled. "Do you think I didn't see you race right into the barn instead of going to the woodshed? Oh, don't worry—I know you! I saw only too well that he was there, that you were running to meet him."

"What him? Cross yourself and recite the Lord's Prayer," Paraska tried to lie her way out of her predicament.

"Don't worry! I'll recite the Lord's Prayer, and then some!" Hapka rattled on. "Oh, you shameless wench! If you've lost your sense of shame, you should at least fear God! After all, he's your brother! The two of you are berries from a single branch. How can you have anything to do with him? God's thunderbolt will strike you dead! The earth will swallow you alive!"

"May God punish me if I'm involved with him in any way!" Paraska swore. "Why are you picking on me?"

"May you, my fine little fish, be picked on by the one that's boiling in pitch. I'm trying to tell her what's good for her, and this is the thanks I get. Go drown in a lake, for all I care! Do whatever you want to do! As far as I'm concerned, you can go hang yourself, and I won't say a word to stop you!"

"If only that trap of yours turned dumb and was shut once and for all, there's no doubt that things would be better all around!" Paraska blurted out crossly and, slamming down a tin dish that she had been washing, darted from the kitchen.

In the doorway, she bumped into Lady Olimpiya. Obviously not wishing to be in her company just then, Paraska grabbed a couple of wooden buckets and ran to fetch some water, all the while muttering to herself: "The damned Plague!"

Everyone in the manor yard and in the entire village referred to Hapka as "The Plague."

"Tell me, Hapka, why are you carrying on and shouting like that?" Lady Olimpiya asked her as she sat down on a bench near the oven. "It is holy Sunday, the whole earth is rejoicing, but you are filling the yard with your shouting and swearing."

"But you see, my gracious Lady, it's impossible to put up with all these wretched creatures. I don't know if there are any people in the world more disgusting than the lot we have here."

"Well, and what of it?" the Lady responded calmly. "Do you suppose that your shouting and cursing will make them mend their ways? It would be better if you prayed for their souls, so that God would make them come to their senses and abandon their evil ways."

"Do you think I don't pray for them?" Hapka exclaimed, failing to understand the Lady's irony. "Why, I do pray for them, may God strike them down mightily! But my conscience tells me that they're not worthy of my prayers. What belongs to the devil cannot be redeemed from hell at any price."

"Now, now, Hapka," the Lady said, rising to her feet, "let us put an end to this kind of talk. Instead, we would do better to give some thought to today's afternoon tea."

"Well, I've come up with some ideas. I just don't know what my gracious Lady will think of them. I think we could serve some chicken stew with rice."

"If there were any pullets!" the Lady interrupted her.

"Well, I've sent Hadyna into the village. Maybe he'll manage to find some."

"And what will we serve after that?"

"Then some tea, and I'll bake some biscuits."

"But do you have any butter?"

"I have some butter, but it's not very fresh. It couldn't be served at the table, but it's good enough for baking. But there is a problem—there's not enough sugar."

"Well, we'll get some sugar from the Jew."

"He won't give us any on credit," Hapka observed.

"Then we'll have to pay for it. I still have enough money for that. Well, that's fine! That's how it will be. Just be sure to do a good job."

"Will there be a lot of lords?"

"I don't know. Five, perhaps."

"Well, that won't be a problem. But if there are ten, then there might not be enough flour or rice."

"Oh, no. Adas knows that I do not have the means to entertain large numbers of guests. Well, and what will we have for dinner?"

"I thought I'd cook some potato soup . . ."

"The priest does not like it!" the Lady observed.

"Oh, as if I care what the priest likes or doesn't like!" Hapka grumbled angrily. "The devil won't get him if he has some potato soup! And for our second course we'll have cheese pasties."

"There won't be a meat dish?"

"Where's the meat to come from? If we get some pullets, and if the guests don't eat all of them, then my gracious Lady can have some for supper."

"I'm not concerned about myself," Lady Olimpiya responded. "I don't mind having just potato soup. But as for the priest . . ."

"And why is my gracious Lady so worried about that priest?" Hapka said. "He's neither kith nor kin."

"Now, Hapka, you must not talk that way. He has been living in my home for ten years, he pays me for his upkeep, and it would not be nice if he were to start complaining that we are starving him."

"He's paying my gracious Lady!" Hapka cried out, jamming her ladle on the corner of the oven and leaning on it. "That skinflint is paying my Lady! And just how much is he paying? It must be at least ten *rynski a month for room, and board, and laundry, and all the other services!"

"No, Hapka, not ten, but twenty-five. But that is not the point. Regardless of how much he is paying, if I agreed to it, then I must keep my word."

"Twenty-five rynski! Ha, ha, ha!" Hapka roared with laughter. "For that kind of money even potato soup is much too good for him! And yet my gracious Lady keeps stuffing him with as much as she can. There's milk in the morning, then coffee, then dinner, then afternoon tea, and then tea again for supper! No, I can't agree with that. Why, that old miser could pay a hundred rynski per month and it wouldn't make him any poorer."

"No, Hapka," the Lady tried to pacify her. "Just drop the matter! You don't understand. And as for dinner, a meat dish of some kind must be prepared for Fr. Nestor. At least fry a little pullet for him."

"Fry it for him? And not for my gracious Lady?"

"Well, fry it for whoever you want to! Is the coffee ready?"

"Yes, it is."

"Then let me have it. I'll pour it myself. Do you happen to know if Fr. Nestor is up already?"

"No, I don't!" Hapka muttered angrily.

She had no use for Fr. Nestor, and she never ceased to be amazed at how much the Lady fussed over him. Of course, she knew a bit about what had happened between the Lady and Fr. Nestor. But that had been in the past, and in Hapka's way of thinking, what was in the past was over and done with, and should have no bearing on what was happening now. That was how she came to terms with her own unsavoury past, and she applied the same measure to everyone else.

Lady Olimpiya began pouring the coffee. She never entrusted this task to Hapka. She made a special effort to prepare the coffee for Fr. Nestor the way he liked it. She carefully removed the top layer from the cream, placed it in a coffee cup, poured in some choice cream along with a small amount of black coffee, and added far more sugar to it than she took for herself. After filling two coffee cups, she left the rest for Hapka.

"Do we have any white bread?" she asked Hapka.

"There's still a slice. Not much." And Hapka pulled a small piece of home-baked white bread out of the cupboard.

"Well, that's fine. It is enough for Fr. Nestor. And I'll have some rye bread," the Lady said and, placing the coffee intended for the priest on the stove so that it would warm up a bit more, she sat down again on the bench, cut herself a slice of rye bread, and began to sip her coffee while talking to Hapka.

Hapka, with a sour look on her face, glanced into the pots that held what was left of the coffee and the cream, poured them into a single pot, added some scalded milk and a small lump of sugar, placed it on the stove as well, and sat down on the threshold to peel potatoes.

"Why are you not having any breakfast, Hapka?" the Lady asked as she struggled to chew, with the remnants of her teeth, the stale bread that she had dipped in the coffee.

"I still have time," Hapka replied. "I'm not used to having breakfast so early."

Lady Olimpiya knew that Hapka was lying, and that she had prepared the coffee not for herself but for old Demenyuk—for that elderly man of few words, that stern moralist who time and again stung Hapka by bringing up the sins of her youth, who, speaking calmly, as if in a trance, said hurtful things to her that brought her to the verge of tears, things that she would not have tolerated from anyone else, but for whom, despite all that, Hapka still had a soft spot in her deadened heart. She willingly deprived herself of food, drink, and sleep to ensure that old Demenyuk was provided for in the best possible way.

Lady Olimpiya was well aware of Hapka's soft spot, and she felt an urge to goad her about it.

"Where is your Demenyuk?" she asked with a smile.

"My Demenyuk? Why do you call him mine?" Hapka responded curtly.

"But of course he is yours! Do you suppose I do not know that you will not be drinking that coffee, that you are leaving it for him?"

Hapka turned pale, and the potato fell from her hands. Without budging, she slowly raised her eyes and gave Lady Olimpiya such a malevolent look that the Lady felt a chill go up her spine.

"Does that harm my gracious Lady in any way?" she asked in a strained voice.

"God be with you, Hapka!" the Lady placated her. "Am I reproaching you for it? You are glaring at me as if you were about to devour me."

"Then why is my gracious Lady rebuking me with Demenyuk?"

"I am not rebuking you. I was just making a comment. But, you know, you rebuked me with Fr. Nestor, and I did not say anything to you about that. We are both involved in similar situations. Both of us are looking after old men."

"What a thing to say, my Lady!" Hapka cried in a startled voice, forgetting all about the proper forms of address. "How is it possible to compare Demenyuk with that priest?"

"Why is it not possible?"

"It's a sin, my gracious Lady, even to think something like that. Demenyuk is a holy man! Without a grain of malice. A pure soul. If it weren't for him, this manor and the entire village would have caved in long ago, sunk with a gurgle into the lake. It's because of him that the Lord is letting us remain on this earth. But as for that priest—may the Lord forgive me for what I'm about to say! But no, there's no need for me to say anything! My gracious Lady knows better than I what he's like."

"I have not heard anything untoward about him," the Lady replied calmly.

"Really? Well then . . . But then, it's not my place to say anything about him. My gracious Lady can think whatever she wants to."

In the meantime, Lady Olimpiya finished her breakfast and, without responding, picked up the cup of coffee that she had prepared and left on the stove, placed it on a tray along with a couple of sugar cubes and a tin plate with the warmed-up bread, and set out for Fr. Nestor's quarters. As she walked along, she reflected on her relationship with Hapka. This unattractive woman with her pockmarked face, with the prayers and curses that were forever issuing from her lips, with her blemished past, was, nevertheless, the only person in her immediate surroundings with whom she could speak openly, woman to woman, without the rancour that stirred in her heart at the very mention of Paraska, Hadyna, the dairyman, the herdsman, and all the others.

Even old Demenyuk, who according to Hapka was a holy man, seemed to her to be far from holy. Above all, Lady Olimpiya felt that the old man did not like her, that he considered her to be evil and sinful, and that was why she could not relate to him openly and sincerely.

But how was it that she could talk with Hapka, that she could relate to her in a normal manner, even though she had no special liking for her? Lady Olimpiya could not explain the situation to her own satisfaction.

"And, strictly speaking, who is this Hapka?" she thought as, holding the tray, she walked through the yard with slow, careful steps. "She is ugly, and she shouts and quarrels enough for three people, and yet something draws me to her. I doubt that she works wholeheartedly for me. When it comes down to that, they are all the same—they would all drown me a tablespoon of water. But I have tested her in small matters and found her to be honest. She does not steal, for she has no one to steal for. And she truly has gone through a school of hard knocks.

"Poor woman! She came here exactly thirty years ago as a pretty young girl. She was so attractive, so cheerful, so full of jokes and songs! And just look at what serving in the manor has done to her. In those thirty years, she has gone away from here only once—when the gendarmes took her in shackles to a prison in Lviv.

"After serving her time she returned. The Count had already died. She prostrated herself at my feet: 'Don't send me away, my Lady!' And then she sobbed through her tears: 'Take me in, give me a job, or I'll drown myself. There's nowhere else I can go, nowhere at all. After what happened to me I can't go back to my village, to my family—I'd rather die. I lost my youthful years here, my good name, and it is here that I will live and die!'"

Lady Olimpiya remembered that scene very well: Hapka was not agitated, nor did she shout or reproach either her or the late Count; she just rose to her feet and wept silently. And she had taken Hapka in and did not regret having done so.

In prison Hapka had lost her good looks after contracting a severe case of smallpox, but she had learned how to cook. It was true that she had also acquired some bad habits, like bellowing religious songs, sometimes until late into the night, and cursing and swearing no less loudly. She had come out with a very rich lexicon of curses and profanities, and continued to enrich it by drawing on her own fantasy. It was because of these habits that the other servants hated Hapka and never called her anything other than "The Plague."

But Lady Olimpiya instinctively felt that Hapka was the only one among the manor servants who did not hate her and perhaps even sympathized with her, who understood her difficult position, and in her own way, even though she grumbled and cursed, cared about her and the state of her finances. And so, these were the invisible threads that bound the two women, women who were so far apart in terms of their social status, their upbringing, their way of life, and their characters.

After Lady Olimpiya's departure, Hapka also began philosophizing in her own way as she continued peeling potatoes. "The devil only understands our Countess! Is she good, or is she evil? Does she speak truthfully, or does she lie? I can't figure it out. There are times when she talks like a human being, but if you look at her from another side, she's like a witch. I can see how much she hates everyone! Even that beloved son of hers. It is said that a she-wolf's nature is such that at times she's full of caresses, but that at other times she'll attack a human being or even another wolf and rip her prey to pieces with her teeth.

"But as for that ugly old ruin of a man, that skinflint-priest, she fusses over him as if he were her father. What does she hope to get from him? Does she think he'll leave his money to her and her spendthrift son? Oh, if that's what she thinks, she's dead wrong! I'm sure he won't leave her anything; he would sooner burn his money and his bankbooks. And why is she lying that he's paying for his room and board, when I know for a fact that she's been keeping him here free of charge for two years now.

"O Lord! People are so strange! He's such a wealthy man; he could live like a real lord, but he prefers to hang around here like a beggar, in a miserable little room, without any conveniences, relying on the charity of this ruined countess and her son. No, God forgive me for my sinning, but such people deserve to be cursed and to have disaster befall them."

These pious wishes and thoughts that Hapka was expressing loudly, passionately, as if speaking to someone, as if trying to convince a veritable blockhead, were interrupted by the appearance of a rather original-looking figure. He was a peasant of about thirty-five, short, scrawny, dressed in ragged clothing, and with unmistakable signs of alcoholism on his bloated face and in his small, unnaturally shiny, shifty eyes. Even though it was Sunday, he was wearing a shirt that was grimy and tattered. Over this shirt he wore an equally grimy vest, and on his head an old straw hat with a crushed and ragged brim. He walked silently like a cat on his bare feet, and Hapka, not hearing him approach, jumped with a start when his shadow suddenly fell on the ground in front of her.

"What the heck!" she cried, glancing up suddenly. "Oh, it's you, you damn Tsvyakh! Tfu, may you go to the devil! What misfortune brings you here?"

"Oh! Misfortune!" Tsvyakh said grimly, smiling vacantly. "But maybe I have more of a right to be here than you do."

"You have more of a right to be in a swamp, in a deep dark lake, you lazybones, you tomcat!" Hapka scolded him without interrupting her work, but all the while keeping an eye on Tsvyakh who, as the saying goes, was light-fingered—he liked to walk away with anything that was left unattended.

Hapka's chastising did not bother Tsvyakh in the least. Still smiling, he sat down on a bench and looked around with his feline eyes.

"He-he-he! In a swamp! Oh, you're lying, Hapka. This is my rightful place. This is my patrimony! Come on, admit it: who's the true heir of this manor—me or that slobbery young lord, that priest's son, who, for some unknown reason, calls himself Count Torsky? He's Count Torsky like I'm your husband, Hapka! Well? Isn't what I'm saying true?"

As he spoke, a fierce malevolence and an implacable hatred flared momentarily in his eyes. But this blaze quickly subsided, and the vacant smile reappeared on his face.

"Go to the devil's mother with your truth!" Hapka shouted. "What a Solomon he's found to judge what's true. Go and ask your good-for-nothing father if it's true."

"Uh-huh, my father! But he's been done away with! Don't worry, he wouldn't have chased me away like a dog, he wouldn't have turned me into a beggar like this damn witch has! But just wait until I get my hands on her! I'll teach her a thing or two!"

And Tsvyakh leapt up from the bench and began to pace agitatedly, darting about the kitchen like a startled bird that flutters wildly in all directions.

Hapka also rose to her feet. "And why in the devil do you keep coming here, you poor excuse for a human being! Huh?"

"Because I feel like it!" Tsvyakh blurted angrily.

"Well, so you feel like it—then go tell her what's bothering you, not me."

"Tell her? You mean my stepmother? Oh no, I can't do that. I'm scared of her. She's a witch! She'll suck all the blood out of my veins."

"As if she had nothing better to set her sights on than your blood! Probably more than half of it is vile homebrew."

"Heh-heh-heh!" Tsvyakh tittered. "I watched her from a distance, when she left you carrying coffee for her old-time lover! Oh, God has punished both of them, but he'll punish them even more for the injustice they've done me! She was walking along, muttering under her breath. Probably deciding whose heart she'll suck dry tonight. For you know, don't you, Hapka, that she lives by feeding on the blood of others."

"Get away from here, you evil-tongued poor excuse for a man!" Hapka laced into him. "The Lady might come and hear what you're saying . . ."

"And you, you damned bitch, you're afraid to hear the truth! But I won't budge until you give me some of those potatoes."

And Tsvyakh, halting abruptly by the tub of potatoes, began grabbing them and stuffing them down his shirt.

"Oho! I knew your evil eyes were looking around to see what you could steal. Get away from those potatoes, you useless scumbag, get away!"

And she flung herself at Tsvyakh and began tearing the potatoes from his hands and bosom.

"But Hapka, my dear Hapka! For God's sake! I have a wife and children . . . today is Sunday . . . they're crying . . . there is nothing at all to eat . . ."

"Because you've squandered everything on your drinking, you wretched cur!"

"Honest to God, Hapka, we have nothing at all to eat at home!" Tsvyakh kept babbling as he struggled with Hapka and refused to let go of the potatoes stuffed in his shirt. "And yet you have so many!"

"May your life have that many years!" Hapka yelled, but nevertheless, the mention of Tsvyakh's hungry wife and children touched her heart, and she loosened her grip on his hands.

Seizing the moment, Tsvyakh grabbed a few more potatoes and lunged towards the door.

"Fare thee well, you vampire," he shouted at Hapka, "you scrawny bitch, you sooty old log, you crow's throat! Here's hoping that God's grace brings me joy by turning you blind and deaf and dumb by tomorrow."

"Oh, you miserable soul!" Hapka cried as she grabbed a stick of firewood and ran after him.

But Tsvyakh leapt out of the doorway, raced headlong across the yard, flew into the barn that stood across the way, and a moment later bolted out of it, using the same path that Hadyna had used earlier in fleeing from Lady Olimpiya.

"Oh, may God's thunderbolt strike you and maim you, may you melt into a pool of grease!" Hapka cursed him. "He's not a man! He's a monster! And why does our Lord God punish us by letting such beasts live on this earth? Oh, the souls of his father and mother are doomed for raising him the way they did."

Hapka knew full well that Tsvyakh was the illegitimate child of a woman who had looked after the late Count Torsky, and rumour had it that the birth of this child was on the Count's conscience. Hapka knew for a fact that the rumour was true, but even if she had not believed the local gossip, the hatred of the Countess for Tsvyakh and his mother would have convinced her. And yet, she herself did not like Tsvyakh, and she especially hated the reprehensible way he treated his wife—a meek and good soul.

"O Lord!" she thought as she bustled about the kitchen. "To think that our merciful God would condemn any woman to a hell like that, punish her so cruelly by having her live with such a man! Sakes alive! Why, whenever I think of the fate of that poor Marta, that beast's wife, then my own wretched fate seems like paradise to me! Take today, for example! Holy Sunday brings people joy, a chance to rest, but she and her little ones have nothing to eat. Sakes alive! And, more than likely he's run straight to the tavern with the potatoes that he grabbed from me, instead of taking them home."

Obviously, Hapka knew Tsvyakh well.

Still smiling vacantly and mumbling to himself about the "miserable witch" and the "vampire," Tsvyakh was indeed running at a trot to the tavern to beg the Jew to give him at least a shot of whiskey for the potatoes that he had stolen from Hapka and stuffed in his shirt.

It is true that the image of his wife—emaciated, sad, hungry, satiated only with blows and tears—and the picture of his children who for the past few days had survived only because of the mercy of a neighbour, momentarily awoke within his heart an impulse to go home and give them the potatoes for their dinner. But this good impulse did not last any longer in his demoralized soul than water in a sieve and, gesturing dismissively, he laughed.

"Let the devil take them, for all I care! It's not up to me to worry about them! Let them go and find their own means of staying alive, just as I have to. I'm not going to concern myself with them."

And, quieting his conscience in this manner, he dragged himself off to the tavern.

Meanwhile, after heaping an overflowing basket of curses on Tsvyakh's head and resolving to visit Tsvyakh's wife in the afternoon and take her and the children some of the leftovers from the noon meal, Hapka fell into a highly penitential mood and, busying herself by the stove, began singing, in a sepulchral voice, an old, ascetic Polish song:

> Before you, O Lord,
> We lay down our sins
> And we accept
> The punishment
> That we deserve for them.
>
> When you punish us,
> We beg you to have mercy on us,
> And when you show mercy,
> We once again goad you
> Into not indulging us.

III

After walking out of the kitchen with the tray, Lady Olimpiya made her way slowly and carefully to the new annex, the small addition with white walls that thrust itself into the orchard. And as she walked, she looked around intently, as if she wanted to fix even the smallest detail in her memory.

The new annex was a small, shingled, one-storeyed brick building that abutted the outbuilding housing the kitchen. The interior was divided into two halves separated by a small passageway; in each half there was a larger room with two windows that looked out into the orchard, and a smaller room—the kitchen—with a single window that opened out into the yard.

One of the halves was vacant now; it was occupied only once or twice a year.

The other half was where Fr. Nestor lived, and it was on this half that jutted into the orchard that Lady Olimpiya focussed her attention. Just now, the window that admitted light into the kitchen was flashing in the sun's rays. It was shut and shaded by a green wooden blind. But the sash was not completely closed—the bottom latch must have been pulled off.

The fence that separated the yard from the orchard did not quite reach the annex, and so, in front of Fr. Nestor's window, there was a tiny garden plot surrounded by a low picket fence. At one time, flowers had been planted in this small garden, but no one had done anything with the plot for a number of years now. The garden was overgrown with thick grass, and the broad-leaved burdock plants that had taken root next to the fence waved their prickly silvery-pink heads over the pickets. Next to the wall there was a dense growth of plants that had gone wild: spiraea, poppies, and wormwood climbed over one another, peered into the kitchen window, and flaunted their lush foliage in the sun. In one corner of this small garden a huge, solitary sunflower towered over this flowering, fragrant crowd and, fluttering its leaves in the morning breeze, slowly tried to turn its tough thick neck and large showy flower towards the sun floating in the cloudless sky.

The door to the vestibule of the new annex was open. Lady Olimpiya knew that every evening, before he went to sleep, Fr. Nestor made sure that the door was locked. The lock was a new, French one that Fr. Nestor had bought a few years ago in Lviv, and he always kept the key to it on his person. Since the door was unlocked, it meant that Demenyuk had already awakened the priest, or that someone else had come to see him.

As Lady Olimpiya halted for a moment in the vestibule to listen if Fr. Nestor was conversing with anyone, she examined the interior of the passageway just as intently and carefully as she had previously looked at the exterior of this outbuilding. The vestibule was empty except for a bench that stood in one corner; occasionally, when he wanted to sit outdoors to enjoy the cool, fragrant evening air, Fr. Nestor requested that this bench be taken out into the orchard.

The door to the other, vacant half of the annex was locked; the rooms had been aired out a week ago, and the key was still in the lock. Without giving it any thought, Lady Olimpiya mechanically removed the key and put it in her pocket. It was quiet in Fr. Nestor's room; but after a moment she heard the splashing of water—an indication that Fr. Nestor, assisted by Demenyuk, was washing up. Without knocking, she walked into the room.

"Good day to you, Father!" she said loudly, as she knew that Fr. Nestor was hard of hearing.

Fr. Nestor, who was done washing, was standing with a towel covering his face. He was struggling vainly to dry himself, but his hands were shaking, so Demenyuk, putting down the bucket that he was carrying, went up to him and wiped his face, head, and hands for him.

Anyone who saw the frail, hunched, shrunken, and trembling figure of Fr. Nestor for the first time could not help but be reminded of an old mushroom that was shrivelled on the outside and wormy on the inside. It truly seemed that his sallow, wrinkled skin was holding his bones together all by itself, without a shred of flesh or a drop of blood, and that his large head, with its shaven face and thatch of thick grey hair, perched precariously on a long scrawny neck, might topple off at any moment. Frighteningly emaciated hands with long bony fingers, a sunken chest that had once been strong and broad, and skinny bare feet stuck in old, worn-out slippers completed the picture of Fr. Nestor. He was wearing black pants and a black vest over his shirt; his ancient cassock, carefully cleaned by Demenyuk, was hanging on a hook by the door leading into the room.

"Oh, oh, oh!" Fr. Nestor champed his toothless mouth. "It's m-m-my honourable Lady! This is most unseemly . . . But I'm old . . . do not be angry with me . . . you see how things are!"

And trembling violently, he flung himself first in one direction, and then in another, dimly aware that he should be doing something, but not quite sure what.

"Oh, that's fine, Father, it does not matter at all!" Lady Olimpiya tried to reassure him.

But he did not regain his composure; he lurched over to the window, almost overturning the wash basin filled with the soapy water in which he had just been washing, and then he tottered off in the opposite direction towards the large wardrobe, but finding nothing there as well, began clutching at the air with his hands and muttering something that was not actually intended either for himself or for the Lady, who was still standing in the middle of the kitchen with the tray in her hands.

It was old Demenyuk who finally delivered Fr. Nestor from the troubling situation in which he found himself. Calmly, without undue haste, he pulled the cassock off the hook and, holding on to the agitated priest, put it on him. It was only then that Fr. Nestor regained his composure, as if this cassock was like a suit of armour in which he felt completely safe, but without which he felt threatened by certain death.

"I beg . . . I truly beg your pardon that my honourable Lady found me like this!"

"But that's nothing, it doesn't matter at all!" Lady Olimpiya repeated with a smile.

"Oh . . . oh . . . oh . . . My honourable Lady is still standing, still standing! I'm such a gaping fool! Please, do come in."

And with a more confident gait, Fr. Nestor walked up to the door that led into the other room, opened it, and invited Lady Olimpiya to step inside.

"I'll join you in a moment! I'll be at my Lady's service in a moment!" he said, remaining behind in the kitchen to discuss something with Demenyuk who, after pulling up the blind and opening the window, emptied the soapy water into the garden and then proceeded to wipe the basin with an old cloth.

"So what are you saying, Yurko?" Fr. Nester mumbled. "The priest, the parish priest, did not go anywhere yesterday?"

"No, if you please, your Reverence."

'That means he will serve the mass himself?"

"Yes, he will."

"Well, that's fine! Because yesterday, you know . . . he sent someone to me . . . 'I'm going to visit some relatives,' he said —I don't know where those relatives of his live—'and you, Fr. Nestor, will serve High Mass for me.' Well, I promised him that I would, not for his sake, but for the sake of God's holy word. But today I feel so weak for some reason . . . I do not know if I could serve the Divine Liturgy."

"Then perhaps your Reverence will serve the matins?"

"Oh yes, yes . . . I'll serve the matins. Right after I have my breakfast. The service will not be starting all that soon anyway."

"Well, it is almost time to start."

"Well then, go and tell the sexton to ring the bells, and I'll be there shortly . . . I will not tarry too long."

Demenyuk bowed and walked out, and Fr. Nestor went into the adjoining room. Lady Olimpiya had already set the table and placed on it the coffee and the white bread that she had sliced into thin pieces. She was now standing by the window, looking into the depths of the green orchard.

"Oh, my gracious Lady . . . you have gone to all this trouble!" Fr. Nestor babbled, moving anxiously about the room as if trying to tidy up, to reduce the disorder that reigned in every corner. But nothing came of his feeble efforts, and finally, gesturing helplessly, he sat down at the table.

Lady Olimpiya, standing with her back turned to him, was still gazing at the orchard. She wanted to appear calm and composed and, in that way, help him settle down.

It was only after he had seated himself that she slowly turned around and said in a voice brimming with maternal tenderness: "But my dear Father! Do not stand on ceremony. You know that we do everything here in a simple, homey manner. Do not be taken aback by the fact that I brought you your breakfast myself—it just happened . . . And I am not taken aback by anything here. There is no reason at all for us old folk to stand on ceremony with each other," she added with a smile as she gestured reassuringly.

"But whoever heard of such a thing! For my honourable Lady to do this herself!" Fr. Nestor could not overcome his confusion. "Were there no servants?"

"Come now, Father, no more of that! Please help yourself to the coffee before it turns cold."

And as Fr. Nestor stirred his coffee with trembling hands, and broke off morsels of bread and dipped them into the coffee so that he could swallow them, Lady Olimpiya moved a chair closer in, sat down across from him, and continued talking in the same unruffled, kindly tone.

"Well, today is Sunday, Father—bon appetit! It's a wonderful day outside. Nature seems to be flooded with happiness. And it occurred to me that it would be nice to bring some joy to an old hermit like you. But it seems that by coming here I have caused you more trouble than joy."

"But my gracious Lady!" Fr. Nestor cried. "How can you even think that? I swear to God, that it is out of happiness . . . joy . . . that you . . ."

And overcome with that joy, he almost overturned his coffee cup in an effort to catch a soggy piece of bread that he had dropped on the tablecloth.

Lady Olympia helped him set things aright, and then, after begging him to continue eating his breakfast without any constraints, went on to say: "Actually, I should always do this. After all, you are not a common boarder, you are a guest in my home. Even a bit more than that—is that not true, Father?"

She smilingly cast a sly look at Fr. Nestor; and when he once again began to grow agitated, she calmed him with a soothing gesture.

"I did not want to say anything to upset you. Good heavens, do I have the right to reproach you in any way or to cause you any unpleasantness? You are a hundred times more entitled to do that to me."

"But why?" Fr. Nestor quickly interrupted her. "After all, I already have one foot . . . one foot . . ."

He broke off what he was saying, because he did not want to speak about the grave, death, and other things like that, things that he truly feared with an almost frantic, superstitious fear, and then, a moment later, he added with a sigh: "I pray . . . I pray for myself, and for you, and for everyone . . . for everyone . . ."

"You have the soul of a saint, Father!" Lady Olimpiya continued, but the expression on her face spoke volumes about the fact that her thoughts were far removed from holy themes. "Oh, how fervently I pray at times!" she added, turning her eyes reverently upwards, and sighing deeply. "It is prayer alone that gives me strength. If it were not for prayer, there are times when I might be tempted to take my own life."

"May God forbid!" Fr. Nestor cried. "What is my honourable Lady saying? Is it possible to even think thoughts like that?"

"Evidently it is, if such thoughts occur to me. And they enter my mind involuntarily. I know all too well that it is a sin! But how can I help it, if such grief is mine! My grief, like a flood, surrounds me on all sides, threatening to engulf me."

"But what is the cause of this grief?" Fr. Nestor asked with a slight frown as he finished drinking his coffee. He already had an inkling as to where the gracious Lady was heading with her conversation, and he was not at all happy with the turn that it was taking.

"Are you saying that you do not know the cause of my grief? It is always one and the same thing, but it keeps getting worse. Surely you know what it is, do you not?" she added, lowering her voice. "Adas has once again lost one and a half thousand at the card tables."

"One and a half thousand!" Fr. Nestor cried, and he looked as if he was trying to force his imagination to tally up and evaluate the magnitude of such a sum.

"He is making scenes . . . Whereas it is I who should be doing that . . ." Lady Olimpiya said through her tears. "He's saying: 'If I do not pay up within a week, the casino will label me a man without honour, and I will be expelled.'"

"They should have done it long ago! And that would be good for him," Fr. Nestor grumbled. "What is he learning in that casino that is of any use to him? O Lord! I would do away with that casino! It is a nest of dissoluteness, of sodomy! But they, the blind fools, see it as the pillar of their lordly honour."

"Yes, that's how it is, Father," Lady Olimpiya was now speaking with more composure. "Nevertheless, it is not up to us old folks to impose our way of thinking on young people. Young people have to live life to the fullest. Young people require a full range of impressions, emotions . . ."

"That's fine, that's fine! But those impressions and emotions do not have to be so expensive, so costly. After all, a thousand and a half in one evening! And just think how much time, and effort, and work it takes to put aside that much money!"

"Oh, that's true, that's true!" the Lady said. "Do you suppose that I do not tell him that? But what does it help? He still hearkens back to his student days in Vienna. Moreover, the friends that he has chosen . . ."

"That's exactly it! That's the problem!" Fr. Nestor picked up on her words. "It's as the Germans say: *Bő . . . bőse Gesellschaften verderben gute Sitten* [Bad company spoils good habits]! But to make things even worse, Adas's habits never were that good. There was not all that much to spoil."

"No, Father! Do not say that! That is being unfair. Adas has a heart of gold, a noble soul. I know that better than anyone else. He can become and, God willing, he will become a fine, upstanding man."

"May God grant it! May God grant it!" Fr. Nestor said under his breath.

"And the company that he keeps is not all that bad. On the contrary, it is his choice of friends that attests to his character, his refined tastes, and his ability to discriminate among people. They are all children of upper-class parents; they come from good homes, are well educated, and well brought up. It is a true pleasure to converse with them."

"But it is no pleasure to pay for that pleasure!" Fr. Nestor barked angrily.

Lady Olimpiya gave him a long, measured look, a look that clearly manifested the scorn of an aristocratic nature for a plebe and his plebeian logic, a logic that tallies up all spiritual and social pleasures and benefits, and evaluates them in terms of their monetary value. But she refrained from poking fun at Fr. Nestor and continued speaking in a gentle, slightly sorrowful tone of voice.

"It is not just a question of paying. The company in which Adas circulates requires one to make light of money. Nevertheless, all this may prove to be beneficial for Adas's career . . . very beneficial. There is even the hope . . . If only we can keep our heads above water for a little while longer."

Father Nestor was sitting on pins and needles. He was not at all pleased by the theme of this conversation, and it awakened within him unkind, inimical thoughts. Stirred by these turbulent thoughts and feelings, he straightened up and started to look livelier. His voice grew more confident, his movements more brisk and animated, and sparks flashed in his sunken old eyes. He knew from experience how this prelude would end. He had been forced to listen to it many a time in his ten years of residency in the manor. It was played out before him by either Adas or Lady Olimpiya, and it always ended with an appeal to his coffers. Only someone who knew the bottomless depths of his miserliness, as well as the true nature of his relationship to Countess Torska and her son, could fully fathom the difficult and hopeless inner struggle that this unfortunate old man experienced, the agonizing torture that he underwent as a result of these requests.

Up to now, however, the requests of the Torskys had been modest, even though they had been increasing slowly and incrementally. A hundred *guldens, two hundred, five hundred, well, even a thousand—to send Adas to Vienna to the aristocratic *Theresianum Institute. These were still either relatively small donations or ones that could be justified by a need to which even the narrow-minded Fr. Nestor could relate.

But now, apparently, the matter had increased in scope. The introductory remarks about the one and a half thousand that Adas had lost presaged the finale, and the final words of Lady Olimpiya about how—notwithstanding Adas's actions—they would have to keep their heads above water for some time yet, unveiled before his imagination a vast and very unappealing horizon.

"I will not give them anything! Not even a cent!" the thought flashed through his head, and he tightly clamped shut his toothless jaws to harden his resolve.

"You are saying, my Lady," he finally said in a strained voice when Lady Olimpiya, pausing dramatically, looked at him with sweetly melancholic eyes, "that there is some hope? And just what is this hope, if I may inquire."

"Oh, it is a very delicate matter!" Lady Olimpiya said passionately. "A secret matter that I should not be talking about. But when it comes to you, a dear old friend . . ." and consciously evaluating the effect of every carefully chosen word, she stretched her hand across the table, a hand not yet totally devoid of beauty and elasticity, and warmly clasped the bundle of bones bound in wrinkled yellow parchment that constituted the hand of Fr. Nestor.

"You know what a handsome young man Adas has turned out to be, how sociable he is, and how he ingratiates himself with the ladies. Oh, I have been saying for a long time now that the pillars of his good fortune will not be his education, or the extent of his knowledge, or the kind of job he has, but rather his good looks and his social skills. And just think, if you will, a certain young noblewoman—I am not at liberty to divulge her name—has fallen madly in love with him. She is as beautiful as an angel, and as for her wealth . . . Well, there is no need to even talk about that. Suffice it to say that she is the best possible match in the entire country."

"Well, that's good, very good! May God grant him every success!"

"Of course, of course it is good; I too wish Adas every success in this matter from the bottom of my heart. And yet it is this very matter that is causing me no end of grief."

"And why is that?"

"You see, in our station in life, such matters are not settled holus-bolus. In cases like this, both sides are engaged in lengthy negotiations, in discussions and, at times, even in formal espionage. Everything is deliberated, weighed, and calculated. The characters, the inclinations, the likes and dislikes of both young people, their way of life, the level of their education, and everything that they have done in the past—all this is scrupulously analysed on both sides at family councils, and their entire genealogy is put to the test under the severest scrutiny. Well, I have no fears as far as all that is concerned. Our family is not of princely lineage, but nevertheless, in terms of its ancient roots, its traditions, and the brilliance of its service it does not take a back seat to any noble family, and as for Adas's past and his qualities, they too will hold up under any scrutiny."

The malevolent sparks in Fr. Nestor's eyes flashed more animatedly. Lady Olimpiya, feeling his gaze on her face, lowered her eyes and pressed his hand more tightly.

"No, no," she added, as if replying to an unspoken reproach, "do not even think about that! The investigation will not dig into the matter that deeply. But there is something else that is troubling me—the financial side of this matter. It is true that the scrutiny from the other side may not probe all that deeply, but nevertheless . . . It will be necessary to receive guests and to reciprocate their visits—and you know what this single fact means, given the present state of our finances. A great deal of money will have to be invested to bring up to an acceptable level our living quarters, the outbuildings, our wardrobes, our cuisine, and everything else that is required. And that is not all. We will have to show that Adas knows how to manage an estate, that he is capable of looking after property, that he can administer his own wealth and that of others. In fact, he has just begun to build a distillery in his manor yard . . ."

"Yes . . . Yes, I have heard about this fantasy of his!" Fr. Nestor grumbled.

"Why call it a fantasy? After all, a distillery is the only industry that brings honour to a lord and returns a good profit."

"That may well be! But how can he be thinking of building a distillery if he has no money in his pockets, and on top of that, he goes and loses one and a half thousand? Only fools or madmen do things like that."

"Not at all, Father! You must understand his situation! The social circle in which he moves includes the brother of the girl he is courting. That brother plays cards, and he invites Adas to join him—well, Adas can hardly refuse, and then he loses to him. That brother also visits Adas at his manor from time to time—it is likely that he will be there today—and, knowing that Adas has his eye on his sister, he will pay close attention to how the operation is run and will inquire about Adas's plans for the future. What could be more natural than to put forward a plan to build a distillery? You can see now that both the first and the second are closely bound together, they are part of our campaign—if I may call it that. If only we can honourably hold our own for some time yet, to bring the plan to fruition."

"Well, take out a loan."

"That simply cannot be done, Father. No matter what you say—our estate is not large, and in the eyes of outsiders our husbandry owes its good name to one single fact: the interest on the mortgage is always paid promptly. And that's like paying the nicest possible compliment to a young lady. No, I have been thinking about something else—to sell the forest, even though it beautifies our estate and serves in no small measure to impress people. But to sell it now would mean to cast it to the four winds, to give it away for next to nothing. At present there is a lull in the lumber trade, it would be difficult to get a good price, and so, if we sold it now, we could compromise ourselves even more than if we took out a loan. Everyone would say: 'Oho, they must really have been hard pressed if they made such a foolish business decision.' Perhaps the situation will change for the better in the winter, and then, of course, I will sell the forest and be in a position to free myself from all my obligations . . ."

Lady Olimpiya stopped speaking and looked once again at Fr. Nestor with a pleading, melancholy expression. But he acted as if he did not know what she wanted. He slowly moved his lips as if silently whispering something. His head was bent forward, and it was tipped slightly to one side, as if he was straining to hear a distant, secret bit of news.

Just then the large church bell rang out, and immediately after it, came the plaintive ringing of two smaller bells: "Ding-dong, ding-dong, ding-dong! Ding! Ding!"

"Oh! They are ringing the bells for the matins!" Fr. Nestor said joyfully as he rose from his chair. "Forgive me, my gracious Lady—I must be on my way."

"But what about our matter?" Lady Olimpiya said with a disappointed, sharp edge to her voice.

"Our matter? Actually, it is your matter!" Fr. Nestor said hurriedly. "Well, good luck—I wish you every success! I do not want to judge Adas unfairly, and I wish him only the best."

"Oh, I know, I know that!" Lady Olimpiya stated with an affected fervour. "I know that you wish him all the best and that you will not refuse to help him when it comes to attaining it."

"Help him?" Fr. Nestor looked at her in alarm. "In what way can I help him? I am an old man. And I never did know how to dance attendance on young ladies . . ."

"Oh, you are joking, Father!" Lady Olimpiya cried merrily as she rose to her feet and began gathering up the dishes and tablecloth. "But this is a serious matter. We will talk about it again another time, right? After all, I think that our friendship and the length of time that we have known each other give me the right to speak frankly with you! Well, well, good-bye for now! Oh, there is just one more thing—I almost forgot. The young people that I told you about earlier, Adas's friends, will be my guests today. Do you want me to invite you, so that you can meet them and listen to what they have to say?"

"Me?" Fr. Nestor once again cried out in alarm. "Why would I want to be among those young lords? Am I suitable company for them? No, no, thank you ever so kindly."

"Well, as you wish. But you would meet the brother of the young lady that I was talking about."

"Her brother! Of what concern is her brother to me? No, once and for all! I prefer to sit quietly at home or go for a walk in the orchard."

"As you wish! Good-bye, Father!"

And, taking the dishes and tablecloth, Lady Olimpiya walked out of Fr. Nestor's quarters.

The priest, incessantly champing his lips, got ready to leave for church.

IV

Fr. Nestor served the matins very slowly. In matters of ritual and in serving the liturgy, he was a pedant. He read or chanted each and every prayer deliberately, distinctly, without hurrying or swallowing his words; and he demanded that the cantors do the same. The local parish priest, Fr. Nestor's successor, was a young man with a very lively disposition; having arrived at the church half way through the matins, he was waiting impatiently behind the altar. As befits a priest, he had not eaten yet, and before him lay a lengthy liturgy during which he had to deliver a sermon and serve an *akaphist, whereas Fr. Nestor had no duties after completing the matins.

Fr. Kraynyk was not very favourably disposed towards Fr. Nestor, but he acted humbly and submissively in his presence because Fr. Nestor resided in the manor yard and lived under the aegis of the church's patron. It was true that Fr. Kraynyk had not yet required Fr. Nestor's protection, and in his heart he felt that, even if such a need were to arise, the older priest would not be in any great hurry to come to his assistance; nevertheless, he wanted to maintain friendly relations with his predecessor at least for appearance's sake, knowing that the older priest could substitute for him now and again in church, and might even help him in some other way.

It was almost eight o'clock when Fr. Nestor at long last began concluding the matins. Without waiting for him to formally end the service, Fr. Kraynyk put on his chasuble and took his place in front of the holy portal to anoint the parishioners; this function brought in a certain amount of income, and although the sum was quite small, the parish priest did not allow anyone to take his place. Moreover, Fr. Nestor's hands were very shaky, and he was unable to perform this demanding task. As it was, exhausted by standing on his feet at the altar for an hour, he came into the chancel and, still wearing his chasuble and stole, collapsed in a soft leather-bound chair where he coughed and breathed heavily for a long minute while Demenyuk, turning and bending him as if he were an automaton, removed his ecclesiastical garments.

"Yes, yes, there is nothing pleasant about growing old," Fr. Nestor grumbled, heavily nodding his head. "Your feet no longer obey you . . . nor does your chest . . . no, no. But still, the word of God . . . is a holy duty . . . No, no, I will never condone rattling through the service the way our young priests do."

There could be no doubt that this reproach, even though it was stated as a generality, was directed at Fr. Kraynyk who, after completing the anointing, had begun the liturgy, and before Fr. Nestor had even managed to catch his breath was already reading the Gospel.

Fr. Nestor sat in his chair, nodding his head drowsily and occasionally singing the responses in his tremulous old voice along with the cantors; however, as soon as they began hurrying through them, he would stop singing and shake his head disapprovingly.

Instead of giving his sermon after the Gospel reading, Fr. Kraynyk usually gave it at the end of the liturgy, before the akaphist, and therefore Fr. Nestor did not have to wait too long for the divine service to draw to a conclusion. After the cantors had finished singing the hymn "May the word of the Lord be blessed . . ." he rose to his feet with Demenyuk's assistance, adjusted his cassock, crossed himself three times and, picking up his ancient straw hat, walked out of the church by exiting directly from the chancel by means of a side door.

A rather large crowd of men, women, and children had gathered in the cemetery. In accordance with an old, although not very pious practice, before the sermon and the akaphist began, the majority of the faithful walked out of the church for a breath of fresh air, to reinvigorate themselves, to warm themselves in the sun, and to indulge in conversations. Some stood in small groups by the bell tower, others strolled among the graves, reading the inscriptions on the wooden crosses and recalling the deceased, but most of them sat leaning against the church wall in the sun and chatted about the mowing season and the weather, or gossiped about their neighbours.

When Fr. Nestor was still the parish priest in Torky, he often spoke out sharply against this practice and ordered the church doors to be locked so that the people would have to stay and listen to his teachings. Back then, his appearance in the cemetery among these groups of people attired in their holiday finery and happily engaged in benign, if not altogether pious conversations, would have created much consternation and confusion.

But now they no longer feared Fr. Nestor. The new parish priest, executing his official duties in a more perfunctory manner, took an indifferent view of this practice, and Fr. Nestor did not deem it necessary to become involved in his pedagogical methods and herd the people back into the church. And that was why his appearance in the cemetery did not arouse any anxiety. On the contrary, both old and young came up to him, bowed politely, and kissed his hands.

Fr. Nestor was obviously pleased by the marks of respect that the villagers bestowed upon him. His memory was fading: he knew only the older parishioners by name, and he was unable to recognize the younger ones. Nevertheless, he smiled at them benevolently, patted their heads, asked whose children they were, and inquired how their parents were doing; with the older folks he became happily involved in longer conversations. It should be added that Demenyuk, who did not leave his side for a moment, assisted him greatly with his memory, reminding him of names and recounting the more important events in the lives of the people who approached him.

Accompanied in this manner, Fr. Nestor walked through the gate of the church enclosure.

Whether it was by accident or not, he did not go through the gate that led to the manor yard, but through the one that led to the road, on both sides of which, drowning in the thick greenery of willows, linden trees, and fruit orchards, was flung the rather large village of Torky.

On the other side of the road, directly across from the church, stood the local priest's residence—a large new building with a shingled roof, two chimneys, and a veranda with a flower bed in front of it facing the road. The manse was built after the arrival of Fr. Kraynyk, and this was done, of course, at the expense of the parishioners, who complained bitterly about the contributions they had to make towards its construction and ruefully recalled that Fr. Nestor had lived for more than twenty years in the old residence that had a thatched roof and was propped up on all sides with poles.

But Fr. Kraynyk was a young man with a modern education and greater demands; he had a wife and children, received guests, and expected to have suitors come calling on his daughters, and that meant that he could not live in an old house that resembled a peasant's hut.

Even though Fr. Nestor had retired as a parish priest of his own accord because of his advanced years and declining health, he succumbed to a human failing and was happy to see the dissatisfaction of the parishioners with their new priest. He acknowledged their complaints about the burden imposed upon them by the construction of the manse with Jesuit humility, cocked his head, and said: "Well, it cannot be helped! However, now you have a young priest with a wife, with young masters and misses! You thought that your old priest would stay with you forever! No, no, my dears, you must grow accustomed to younger ones."

The parishioners had thought that Fr. Nestor, seeing their insolvency and the steep expenses connected with the new residence, would make a contribution to help cover the costs. They all remembered that when the new church was built during his tenure, he personally donated 3,000 guldens, and then another 2,000 for the icons and the purchase of various church vessels. But this time the parish misreckoned, because Fr. Nestor did not give them anything.

"The House of God—that is an entirely different matter," he said to the delegation that came to him from the parish, "but a residence! . . . I lived in a decrepit old hut, and even now, as you can see, I do not live much better . . . If you want to build your new priest a palace—well, you are free to do so. But I will not be a part of it. Next you will probably be asking me to buy his wife a piano . . ."

Human nature is strange! Even though Fr. Nestor was well aware that remaining celibate had warped his life, pushed him off the path of normal human existence, turned him into a misanthrope, and deadened his spiritual faculties, nevertheless he did not like or respect married priests, visited them only reluctantly, and had never set foot in the new manse, the home of Fr. Kraynyk. Even during the visitation of the Metropolitan, he did not allow himself to be persuaded to cross the threshold of the new residence. It was as if something about it repelled him, as if an alien, repugnant spirit wafted from its veranda overgrown with lush wild grapes, from the wide bright windows with their white, crocheted curtains and vases of flowers on their sills, from the flower bed with its fragrant balsam, gillyflowers, and rows upon rows of mignonettes, tall hollyhocks, and dahlias.

It was from that house that the fresh young voices of Fr. Kraynyk's children often drifted through the air: the silvery laughter of the young misses, the hearty, metallic roars of the student-sons, and along with them, the harmonious chords of a piano—the splashes and waves of the peaceful, but richly eventful and noisy life of a priest, a life that should have been his, but which either an evil or good fate had taken from him.

It could not be said that Fr. Nestor—old, hunched over, and with one foot in the grave—envied the family life that his younger successor enjoyed or that he regretted his own solitary years. His heart had long since withered, and his feelings were much too deadened to feel envy because of such things. The only response that his implacable hostility evoked within him whenever he walked past the new manse was a sarcastic smile accompanied by a censorious shaking of his head and a stubborn unwillingness to cross the threshold of this house that he considered to be profane.

"That's how it is!" he once again grumbled in his usual manner, half to himself and half to Demenyuk, as he trudged down the road. "Daddy is in church serving the Divine Liturgy, but just listen to the merry tune that his daughter is banging away on the piano. She's emancipated! Never fear, she will not set foot in church. That's only for peasants! . . ."

Demenyuk did not respond. Having been raised from childhood in the church and in the company of priests, he was accustomed to honour each and every one of them, and he did not like it when someone voiced disapproval of an ecclesiastic. And in his view, the category of ecclesiastics included not only priests, but also the members of their families.

It was only after they had left the manse behind, and Fr. Nestor had completely regained his peace of mind, that Demenyuk stepped up to walk right beside him and, kissing his hand, said hesitantly: "I would like to ask a favour of the Reverend Father."

"You, Yurko?" Fr. Nestor asked in surprise. "What is it?"

"Well, I don't know . . . Perhaps it won't be right for your Reverence to . . ."

"Oh good God, Yurko! Just say what you want to say!"

"Well, you know, your Reverence . . . my Malanka . . . the one who's a servant at the blacksmith's home . . ."

"So, you say she is your daughter?"

"Why yes, yes, she is my daughter! She is my only daughter! O Lord, that's all the family that I have."

"Well, what about her?"

"It's bad, if it please your Reverence. It's very bad."

"Is she ill?"

"Oh, no, God forbid! Although, to tell the truth, if she were ill, there might be less for me to worry about."

"What is it then? Has she set out on the wrong path in life?"

"Holy, holy, holy! What is your Reverence saying?" Demenyuk stopped short in alarm. "Did I raise my child, and feed her, and love her, and raise her in the fear of God, just to have her go down the wrong path in life? And after all, your Reverence knows her!"

"Yes, I do know her, I do! She is a virtuous girl, generous, hardworking . . ."

"Oh, that's not all! I am her father. I do not want to brag, because it is nothing that I have earned, it is God's mercy. But to tell you the truth: she is not just a girl—she is pure gold.

Obedient, industrious, she likes things to be orderly, she respects me in my old age, and she is like a daughter to the man that employs her . . . No, I'll never have reason to complain about my Malanka."

"Then what exactly is the nature of your concern, Yurko?"

"It's such a concern, if it please your Reverence, that the devil take it! But wait, there is still one other thing that I should tell you about my Malanka . . . You know, your Reverence, that in addition to a good heart and strong working hands, the Lord gave her beauty. I do not know if it was for good or ill. Because beauty in a girl who is just a poor servant rarely brings her good fortune . . . But let us hope that the Merciful Lord will turn things around. You see, the son of the blacksmith in whose house she is serving has taken a liking to her."

"Aha, Maksym, Maksym the blacksmith's son, that Maksym, aha, I remember him."

"That's the one, if it please your Reverence. He is a good lad, kind, generous, and the son of a well-to-do father. He has taken a liking to the girl, and he has told both his father and me about it. Well, all I can do is thank the Lord God for such a happy turn of events—I could not wish for a better son-in-law. And the blacksmith has nothing against it. He is an honest man, and we have known each other since we were young; he isn't concerned about a large dowry, and he has come to know my child and to like her. You see, your Reverence, everything is falling into place, and the ending should be a happy one."

"May God grant it, Yurko! May God grant you and your child all the best. Even if it is with that blacksmith . . ."

"There's only one problem, if it please your Reverence," Demenyuk interrupted him.

"What is that?"

"Well, I don't know how to say this. You see, our young lord, Lord Adas . . . I don't know what has come over him, but for some time now he just will not leave Malanka alone. When there is no one around—in the field, or in the orchard, or in the forest, or in the pasture—he suddenly shows up, right beside her. And he is confusing my child, if it please your Reverence—that is the problem! He tells her all sorts of things: not to marry Maksym, and to come and serve in his house; that he will make a lady out of her, take her with him to Lviv, marry her there, and other nonsense like that. The girl has rejected his advances, begged him to leave her alone, and fled from him, but he just keeps at her. If he were a peasant youth, or a stranger, she would be able to handle him. But he is the son of Lady Olimpiya, I am employed by his mother, and so the poor girl is afraid to cut him off too sharply, you know, so that it will not harm me in any way. Because what is it to him? It is not hard to make life difficult for us poor folk."

As Fr. Nestor listened to what Demenyuk had to say, he lowered his head dejectedly. It was clear that what he was hearing affected him unpleasantly.

"So what do you want from me?" he finally asked.

"I really do not know what I want!" Demenyuk said hopelessly. "I am speaking to your Reverence as to my own father . . ."

"Oh, what has a father got to do with it!" Fr. Nestor retorted sharply; it was evident that this story had touched a raw nerve. "Let your daughter watch her step—what else can one advise in a case like this?"

"That's precisely the problem," Demenyuk said worriedly. "Up to now, even though I knew about the advances of the young Lord, I did not fear anything. But now I am afraid. For a few days now, something has come over the girl. She's not herself. One minute she's so happy that sparks seem to fly from her, and the next minute she's so sad that it's hard to get a word out of her. And it's impossible to figure out what she's thinking, what she wants, and what is going on with her."

"That's a bad sign! A very bad sign," Fr. Nestor said.

"Exactly, exactly! That's what I think, as well," Demenyuk picked up quickly on these words. "And that's why I wanted to ask—but your Reverence must not be angry at my boldness!—if your Reverence might not have a talk with her?"

"By myself?"

"Well, no! Together with me. Perhaps your Reverence will be able to appeal to her heart, perhaps she will reveal what has happened to her."

"Hmm . . . It's possible . . . We'll have a talk with her."

"Oh, thank you, your Reverence, thank you!" Demenyuk said, kissing Fr. Nestor's bony hand. "I know that she respects and loves your Reverence as if she were your Reverence's own child, and she won't hide anything from your Reverence. We're not that far from the blacksmith's house; I'll go and call her out into the orchard, and we'll have a talk with her."

As he said this, Demenyuk's face cleared up and his hunched figure straightened. He involuntarily began to walk more quickly and got ahead of Fr. Nestor, but a moment later he caught himself, stopped in the middle of the road, waited for the elderly priest, and then proceeded to restate his concerns over and over again. Fr. Nestor walked silently, but his lips were mouthing words as if he were conversing with an invisible entity.

Walking along in this manner, they soon reached the outskirts of the village.

The last house belonged to the blacksmith. It stood on the left side of the road and, surrounded by a tall, wooden fence with a wide gate and a small footbridge that led to the road, it resembled a fortress that peered warily into the boundless fields bordering the village to the east and the south. To the north, beyond the small, swampy Torivka River, spreading willows wound their way like a long sinuous snake among the hayfields, and still farther on, beyond the meadows, rose foothills on which, in a wreath of poplars, stood the manor that Master Adas administered, and beyond this manor, completely hemming in the horizon on that side, dreamed a mighty feudal forest.

Immediately across from the fortress-like house, on the right side of the road, stood the village armoury—the blacksmith shop, with a ditch dug around it instead of a fence. Resting on four posts, this small structure with a shingled roof and an overhang in front was always open on working days, and it resounded with the cheerful din of people's voices, the neighing of horses, the banging of hammers, and the sharp metallic clanging of the anvil.

From early morning until late at night, the heavy bellows groaned continuously, flames leapt in the hearth, sparks flew from under the powerful blows of hammers, iron squeaked under abrasive files, a grindstone rotated under its cap, a tumbler of whiskey circulated among the groups of happy workers, and small talk, jokes, and anecdotes alternated with the ongoing intense, vigorous work.

It truly was the armoury of the village. In it were forged all the ploughshares, scythes, sickles, spades, and the teeth for harrows, those forerunners of civilization that would charge into the vast expanses of the fields to dig, crush, overturn, and mow the copious vegetation that was to nourish the people. It was here that wagons, wheelbarrows, and carts were forged, horses were shod, and footwear for humans was reinforced to make it easier to conquer the obstacles that the land itself—those vast expanses—imposes upon people pushing back the frontier.

And as for the trees, forests, rocks, rivers, and even the wind—nothing could withstand the onslaught of that hive of loud, noisy, zealous labour. It was from here that hatchets and axes, sharpened on a whetstone, flashed a deadly threat to the forest that, dreaming like a dark cloud way over there on the slopes, rustled sorrowfully as if it was already grieving over its certain destruction, the seeds of which were being forged in this small village smithy. It was from here that sharp saws, gimlets, and chisels went forth into the world to cut, chip, bore, and gouge the felled trunks of the forest giants, as if gnawing them with teeth of iron for the benefit of people.

From this smithy issued the implements to be used way down there in the valley, beyond the manor, where the Torivka River describes the foothills with a wide arc, to lay down a mighty dam, to create a large pond, to build a mill, and to harness that river—like a second blind *Samson—to have it turn its wheels at no cost. And the wind was also threatened by the smithy, because it was from it, and it alone, that the tools came to erect a long row of powerful windmills on the distant hillocks of the foothills hidden beyond the horizon's edge.

In a word, this small smithy, standing on four posts, like *Baba-Yaha's hut on four chicken legs, was a great and mighty power whose influence spread far and wide, even farther and wider than the west wind could carry the echoes of the hammering and the clanging of the anvil that resounded in it.

And the soul of that armoury, that mighty and productive power, and the heart of the cheerful and hardworking company that gathered there day after day, was the Torsky blacksmith, Ivan *Herder. The strange mixture in his name that struck everyone upon hearing it—a name that combined a *Rusyn first name with the surname of the notable German author—manifested itself in its entirety in the origin, the character, and the views of the Torsky blacksmith.

His great-grandfather, who was also a blacksmith, was a full-blooded German who had been brought in from Saxony by the grandfather of the late Count Torsky in the very first years of the Austrian occupation. The son of that distant Herder married a Rusyn woman, the daughter of a certain affluent Torsky farmer, and today's Ivan, although he knew about his German ancestry, considered himself to be a Rusyn.

It was his grandfather who had left the manor and settled in the village among the serfs, although he himself never became one; and that was why Ivan Herder considered himself to be a peasant through and through, in solidarity with the rest of the peasants, and he stood alongside them, maintaining a position that wavered between distancing himself from the manor and carrying on a quiet feud with it.

He was stocky, strong-limbed, and sturdy. His thick long hair, once a fiery red, had begun to turn grey, and his long moustache, that curled behind his ears, was as white as cream. Nevertheless, Ivan Herder was not yet sixty years old, and his voice, the colour of his face, the swiftness of his movements, revealed a man of unflagging energy, daring, and a love of life. With his large round head, sound teeth and powerful jaws, broad shoulders, hairy arms on which his sleeves were rolled up to the elbow, and hands that were blackened by soot and almost always busily engaged in doing something—he reminded one of the iron rams that were used in ancient times to batter down stone walls.

His outward appearance, so typically German, but with several no less typically Rusyn features, spoke to Herder's character as well. Hesitation, indecisiveness, irresolution, and defeatism were completely alien to his nature. An indefatigable worker, he was, at the same time, highly reliable and unusually conscientious. Any impediments that he encountered, far from discouraging him, only strengthened his resolve to continue with his struggle and his work. Combative by nature, he was, nevertheless, a good neighbour, a cheerful companion who liked to joke and laugh, and it was this talent that enlivened the smithy and made it a popular gathering place.

People went to Herder's smithy as if for holy water: to catch their breath in a fresh, spiritual atmosphere, to fortify themselves, to unburden their souls. The blacksmith had travelled widely in his younger years; he was literate and had an endless store of anecdotes and tales, and he related them with a vivid expressiveness, with a personal touch.

He had a knack of picking just the right story for every occasion, and of drawing such insights and conclusions from it that the people, listening to him in rapt silence, beamed with happiness, smiling and rejoicing wholeheartedly even though they could not say why this was so. Their souls—timid, browbeaten by daily grief, by ignorance, by demoralization—sensed in that man the living stream of his personal thoughts, the strength of his character, and a keen, original poetic artistry that inevitably evokes a joyful, sympathetic response in every living soul, just as a young plant responds to the brightness and warmth of the spring sun.

Fr. Nestor knew Herder very well from the blacksmith's youthful days, but he did not like him. The stale, morbid soul of the old priest was not in tune with the poetry of sturdy, peasant natures. He saw in Herder only a freethinker and a heretic—one that was stubborn, incorrigible, and defiant, and therefore twice as dangerous!

And indeed, the favourite field of Herder's thoughts, reflections, and dreams—and it was also the field on which his combative nature revealed itself most fully—was the one that encompassed religion, the church, and the way in which the priests treated the common people.

Even though his formal education was very limited, Herder had, through his own efforts—by reading books, and by engaging in discussions with a variety of people—elaborated points of view that went far beyond the narrow confines in which it seems to have been prescribed, as if decreed by God Himself, that the brain of the peasant was supposed to remain. He developed his own way of making critical observations—in a manner that was calm and nonconfrontational, but at the same time, not irresolute or deferential.

He did not conceal his heretical views either from the peasants—be it in his own smithy or at the market—or from the priests themselves. Moreover, he held the same critical views about other classes and institutions of society, particularly those that he classified as parasites.

And often, as he pounded the red-hot iron in the smithy with his powerful hammer, Herder, infuriated by the stories people related to him about various injustices and acts of oppression, would begin—calmly, gently, and half ironically at first, but gradually with an ever increasing passion and fervour—to itemize the various rankling wounds of peasant life, the countless maladies inherent in the peasants' way of thinking, and then his voice, growing stronger and more resonant, like sharpened steel, would resound audibly through the din of the hammers, the groaning of the bellows, the sputtering of the sparks, and the rasping of files, and fall deeply, like embers, into human hearts.

Listening to him in the semidarkness of that smithy that had only one door and not a single window, in your mind's eye there arises a picture of an expansive virgin field covered with lush vegetation, burr-bearing shrubs, and nettles. And on that virgin soil a mysterious, invisible hand guides a plough—a simple, ordinary peasant plough with a well-placed ploughshare and a piece of iron in front that, like a crescent moon, sinks into the earth with its sharp horn. And that plough—slowly, heavily, evenly, and without end, creaking at times in the hard ground and scraping its ploughshare on stones and half-rotted stumps—continually presses forward, ever farther and farther, tearing out the vegetation by its roots, breaking the virgin soil, and leaving a thick, even layer of ploughed earth.

It was ploughs like this that issued from Herder's smithy, and they left their mark not only on the rich black earth of the surrounding fields, but also on the overgrown, neglected virgin land of national sentiment, the national psyche.

"You know what, Yurko?" Fr. Nestor said, stopping in front of the gate of the blacksmith's fortress as he doffed his hat and, with a chequered handkerchief, wiped the perspiration that was rolling in heavy droplets down his face, his neck, and the immense bald spot that lit up the crown of his head. "I do not feel comfortable entering the home of that heretic. Not so long ago I censured him and warned him that unless he mended his ways, I would not speak to him, but if I go into his yard, I might meet up with him, and then, obviously, I would have to speak to him. So, might it not be better to do something like this? I'll wait here, out in the street, and you go and call Malanka to come here."

"But no, if it please your Reverence," Demenyuk replied. "The blacksmith is still in church—I saw him there. And after the liturgy he is sure to go to the public meeting. Please, your Reverence, come with me. We'll go into the orchard; there is a bench there, and your Reverence can sit down and wait. And I'll go and call Malanka."

"I really do not want to . . . Well, fine, let it be . . . Because you know what kind of a man that blacksmith is. And how does the holy earth permit such people to walk on it?" Fr. Nestor grumbled as he stepped, most reluctantly, into Herder's yard.

"Well, it just does, if it please your Reverence. Apparently God has need of people like that as well since he keeps them on the earth and, in addition, gives them strength, health, wealth, and children like that Maksym of his."

"Ah . . . Maksym . . . the blacksmith's Maksym . . . He truly is a good child, a fine lad. But it is no credit to the blacksmith that he has a son like that, oh, no! And do not think that God gave him that son because he merited him. No, it is only to test him, to see if he will come to his senses, if he will be penitent before God. Everything that he has will last only so long, Yurko, only so long! And when the time comes . . . I do not want to predict anything, but I can sense it . . . and whoever lives long enough, will see it happen . . . It cannot be that God will not punish a sinner like that."

"To tell the truth, if it please your Reverence, the blacksmith is a good and honourable man," Demenyuk said hesitantly.

"Good and honourable?" Fr. Nestor cried. "And it is you who is saying this, Yurko? How is it possible to be good and honourable if one does not believe in God?"

"He does believe in God, and he prays, I know that for a fact," Demenyuk once again tried to argue, holding Fr. Nestor by the arm as he led him into the orchard, down a narrow path trampled down in the tall grass, to a bench that stood under a huge, spreading pear tree.

"No, no! He does not believe in God!" Fr. Nestor contended. "If he believed, he would listen to what God tells him to do. But he prays haughtily, to show off, like the *Pharisee in the Gospel, so that people will see him."

Demenyuk did not pursue the argument, and after settling Fr. Nestor in a shady spot on the bench, went to the house to call Malanka. Fr. Nestor sat with his head bowed and his hands resting on his cane, all the while silently moving his lips as if continuing his complaints about the blacksmith's godlessness. His eyes were fixed on the arched blade of a flower stem on which a plump green caterpillar, driven by the desire to reach the corolla and its juicy petals, was slowly inching its way upwards to strip it with its covetous teeth.

"That's exactly how fate, and whatever it has in store for us, crawls and creeps up on us!" the thought flashed through Fr. Nestor's mind, and a chill ran over his body.

Perhaps it was the coolness of the orchard, the dampness saturated with the fragrance of flowers and grasses that drifted through the shadows of the age-old trees, but Fr. Nestor felt alarmed. His mind, already upset by the conversation about the blacksmith, was further agitated by this innocent caterpillar. He opened his eyes wide and stared at it.

The caterpillar, as if it were under a microscope, was growing ever larger and more powerful in his eyes, blocking the orchard, the house, and everything in his line of vision with its plump, greenish body, and threatening to eat not only the few petals of the insignificant flower, but also all the thoughts, ideas, and desires of Fr. Nestor himself.

"Yes, that's exactly how fate, and whatever it has in store for us, crawls along and creeps up on us!" he whispered, trembling uncontrollably, and his mind became enveloped in a stifling haze of dreams and spectres, from which he tried to shake himself free, but could not.

Suddenly he jumped with a start. Above his ear echoed a girl's clear, piercing voice, and he heard the words: "What is it that your Reverence would like to say to me?"

It was Malanka. Having walked up swiftly to Fr. Nestor, who was lost in his fantasies, she stood before him, tall, slender, with her upper body flooded by sunlight and her feet drowning in shadows.

Fr. Nestor raised his eyes and peered closely at her.

Her face, flushed like a cranberry, flamed with a healthy glow, her dark eyes burned with a passionate fire, and her rosy lips, that had parted as she uttered these words, gleamed like rubies in the sun. She looked beautiful in her white blouse with embroidery on its sleeves and collar, with an inexpensive string of coral beads on her neck, and with her thick, dark brown braids coiled in a wreath on her head. Her youthful figure exuded an aura of freshness, health, and vitality.

Fr. Nestor looked at her silently for a moment or two, confused as to what he was supposed to say to her, and worried about how he was to begin the conversation. "Uh . . . uh . . . is it you, Malanka? Oh, my, how you have grown . . . so tall and beautiful. I haven't seen you for a long time . . ."

Malanka came up even closer and kissed Fr. Nestor's hand.

"Daddy said that your Reverence has something to say to me?" she was speaking just as she had spoken a moment earlier—clearly and rapidly, and perhaps just a trifle angrily.

"Yes, that is right! I do, I do have something . . . But where is your father? Where has he gone?"

"I gave him a bite to eat," Malanka said. "Because over there, in the manor where you live among the great lords, no one cares about the poor man or if he has had anything to eat."

"Well, Malanka, no one can say that. Your father has never complained to me that he is not given enough to eat."

"What does your Reverence expect? As if my father would ever complain! He would sooner die of hunger than utter even a word of complaint. But you have to know him! I know he's hungry, I could tell just by looking at him, but even so, I could barely force him to have a bite of something. But tell me what it is that you want to say to me, your Reverence. My masters will soon be home from church, and then I won't have any time to talk with you."

"Your father . . . I . . . am not . . . that is, strictly speaking . . ." Fr. Nestor was not prepared for such a sharp, frontal attack.

"My father has probably been telling you things about me!" Malanka interrupted him.

"Your father! About you! Malanka, for the love of God! What are you saying? Do you not know that your father loves you so much that he almost worships you?"

"Yes, he loves me, I know he does!" Malanka said somewhat defensively. "But nevertheless he torments me with his suspicions and admonitions. He gives me no peace about that young Lord of yours. I mentioned to him once that the young Lord was trailing after me and forcing his attentions upon me—that was in the springtime—and ever since then, whenever daddy sees me, all he does is ask me about the young Lord, almost as if he wanted to see me throw myself at him."

"For the love of God, Malanka! How can you say something like that?" Fr. Nestor cried in alarm.

"I told him not so long ago: 'Daddy, if too much salt is added to the borshch, it will be too salty. Do not torment me with that young Lord, for I swear to God that I will never, ever, tell you anything again!'"

"Well, you see, my child," Fr. Nestor said gently. "That is exactly what is troubling your father. He loves you so much, he wants only what is good for you, and he worries and tries to do his best to ensure your happiness. And when you said those things to him, what do you suppose he thought? Well, he must have thought: 'Oh, there must be something going on here, if my Malanka does not want to talk to me about it.'"

"But what am I to tell him? The young Lord has long since stopped thinking about me and does not even look my way."

"What? He has stopped thinking about you? He does not even look at you?" Fr. Nestor shouted, and in his astonished outburst there was an undercurrent of unconcealed joy. "But you aren't lying, are you, Malanka?"

"No, your Reverence, I am not lying!! Why would I lie?" Malanka replied calmly, looking Fr. Nestor straight in the face.

"In that case . . . Why didn't you tell your father, so that he would not be so worried?"

"You think I didn't tell him? I told him a hundred times: 'Daddy, that's enough about the young Lord! He did make advances to me, but I told him off a couple of times, and now he leaves me alone.' But my father, may God forgive me, is like a tick. Once he fastens onto something, he sticks fast and keeps on nattering until he is forcibly removed. He always has to find something to worry about. And in what way am I to blame for that? What can I do about it? That is his nature."

"Well, if what you are saying is true, if the young Lord truly is no longer bothering you . . ."

"But I swear to you, your Reverence, that he is not!" Malanka cried, blushing like the reddest rose.

"Well then, glory be to God! That's good. I'll allay your father's fears."

"Do that, your Reverence! Let him not concern himself about me. I am no longer a child, I will not let myself be deceived, and I will go wherever my heart tells me to go, no matter what!" she added resolutely and, kissing the priest's hand once again, raced off towards the house. "Oh, here come my masters!" she added as she sped along. "Good-bye, your Reverence!"

Her red skirt and embroidered sleeve flashed on the stile—and she vanished from sight; only her ringing, mercurial laughter echoed throughout the orchard, laughter so loud and so close to being spastic, that Fr. Nestor started in alarm and glanced all around. Malanka's laughter did not sound right to him.

"Is she laughing at me? Taunting me that she fooled me, an old man?" he muttered. "Is that it, my poor dear? Let us hope that you are not fooling yourself!"

And, thoroughly dissatisfied with the way the conversation had ended, he rose to his feet with the intention of leaving the orchard without waiting for Demenyuk's return. But it was too late. Herder, who was returning from church with his wife and son, had already seen him. With the all-seeing eye of a householder who instantly spots every stone and every piece of firewood that is out of place, he had caught sight of him as soon as he entered the gate. For a moment he either did not recognize Fr. Nestor, or did not want to believe that it was he.

His wife was the first to comment, whispering to him: "Oh, my goodness! What does this mean? For some reason his Reverence, the old priest, is sitting in our orchard."

"Well, what of it! If he is sitting there, let him sit! It's not likely that he will do us any harm."

"But what brought him to our place?"

"We shall know in a moment."

And all three of them passed through the gate, stepped into the orchard, and made their way down the path that led directly to Fr. Nestor.

The priest, disconcerted by this turn of events, and feeling helpless without Demenyuk at his side, stood for a moment and then sank down once again on the bench.

"Glory to Jesus Christ!" Herder greeted Fr. Nestor and took off his hat while still some distance away.

"Glory forever," Fr. Nestor responded.

The blacksmith's wife and his son Maksym came up closer and kissed the priest's hand. The blacksmith did not follow suit; instead, he smiled pleasantly and spoke in a relaxed manner: "Well, we can see you, but we can hardly believe our eyes! Such a rare, unexpected guest in our yard!"

"Forgive me for being so bold . . . But, strictly speaking, I did not come here by myself; I came with Demenyuk . . . He asked me to have a talk with his daughter . . ."

"With Malanka?"

"Why, yes. You know that old Demenyuk loves her dearly, and worries himself sick over her. And our young Lord . . ."

"Oh, who cares about the young Lord!" Herder said, and an expression of disdain crossed his face as he gestured dismissively. "As long as Malanka is at my place, and as long as she remains virtuous, she has nothing to fear, even if a hundred young lords were pursuing her."

"But, daddy, how can you say something like that?" Maksym intruded into the conversation. "As long as Malanka stays virtuous! You know very well that she is virtuous and that she will not let herself be enticed by anyone."

"We know what she has been like, and that is all we know," Herder said in a stern voice. "But as for what might happen, my dear son, well, when it comes to the female race, no one can know or even guess."

"You're always saying things like that, Ivan!" his wife entered the conversation with a timid reproach. "As if the female race were not part of the human race, but belonged instead to the avian race, fluttering like a bird in all directions, so that you can never tell where it's going to go next."

"Of course they flutter about! And God only knows where they would fly off to if they were not kept in a cage. But as for Malanka, Father, you can rest assured. No harm will come to her at our place."

"Well, I have talked to her already," Fr. Nestor said. "She also assured me that her father is worrying for no reason at all, that the young Lord is not bothering her."

"I had a friendly talk with him the other day," Maksym said. "After all, we know each other, we went to school together. And he gave me his word of honour that he has no evil intentions when it comes to Malanka."

"I too had a talk with him the other day," Herder said. "As for what I actually said to him, that's better left between the two of us, but I think that he will leave Malanka alone."

"Well, if that is the case, I can stop worrying," Fr. Nestor said. "Because I must admit that after my talk with Malanka, I was not at all reassured. Something about her has changed. She is curt, unapproachable, and she seems to be hiding something."

"No, no, Father, you need not be concerned," Herder said.

"Well, that's good. That's very good! Thank you!" Fr. Nestor said, extending his hand and rising to his feet.

The blacksmith did not take the proffered hand, saying instead with a smile: "Stay a while, Father! You're not in any hurry, are you?"

"I must go! I have stayed too long as it is. But where in the world can that Demenyuk be—he has been gone ever so long!"

"Well, where is he?"

"He's at your place, probably talking with his daughter."

"Go up to the house," Herder said to his wife and son. "When Demenyuk finishes what he has to say to Malanka, have him come here."

After his wife and son left, Herder took up a position in front of Fr. Nestor, who was once again sitting on the bench.

"Do not be angry with me, Father," he began, "for not taking the hand you extended to me. I am a forthright man, and I do not want to hide anything. I find it hard to understand you. Not all that long ago you censured me for being a heretic, an unbeliever, a person who was damned, and yet you now offer me your hand—but I did not want to befoul your holiness with the touch of mine." Only a deaf person could have failed to hear the bitter derision in Herder's words.

Fr. Nestor shook his head sorrowfully. "Oh, you are sinning, blacksmith, you are sinning grievously."

"Ha, that may well be," Herder said. "You are an expert in that field, and you can see more clearly than I, but my conscience is untroubled."

"Untroubled? I cannot believe that, blacksmith! How can a man's conscience be untroubled if he does not believe in God and ridicules all that is holy?"

"Ah, your Reverence, your Reverence," Herder said in a voice that was both somewhat placating and somewhat reproachful, "how can you say those words so calmly: he does not believe in God? Who told you that? How do you know that? By what are you judging that?"

"I am judging it by your deeds, blacksmith!"

"That is a very poor measure for something like that," Herder responded calmly. "In Lviv I once saw a murderer who was being hanged for killing four people. Oh, how piously he crossed himself and confessed! How he wept as he kissed the cross! Now surely, there was someone who truly believed in God."

"Who knows, perhaps he will be forgiven by God for his sins sooner than those who stubbornly defend their disbelief, in whom God has deadened even the voice of their conscience," Fr. Nestor stated, and he straightened his back righteously.

"Well, your Reverence, forgive me, but I must tell you that you are mistaken. The voice of my conscience is not deadened. If it sometimes happens—you know, a man is human—that I say something that is not true, or I quarrel with someone, or I wrong someone, then my conscience torments me, doesn't let me sleep until I apologize to that man, or right the wrong that I have done. Does that mean that my conscience is deadened?

"But when someone gets up and says: 'Listen to me! I administer the word of God; I have the authority to bind and unbind,' but I can see that he is a man, just as I am a man, that he usually does not even know what he is binding or unbinding, how then can I believe him, and place my soul, my conscience, in his hands?"

"But he does not do so on his own; it is God's will that does it, and God knows what should be bound and unbound."

"Of course He knows!" the blacksmith picked up on his words. "And He knows that without the help of a priest. And I too can find my way to God without a priest."

"There you go! There you go! You're spouting such heretical words! If God wanted things to be the way that you are saying, He would not have ordained apostles and disciples . . ."

"Oh sure, oh sure! And priests, and deacons, and canons, and suffragans, and mitred priests, and bishops, and cardinals, and popes who wear the holy cross on their slippers—all of this was instituted by God Himself! And He bestowed His authority upon all of them! And He clearly stated: 'From now on you need not know Me or obey Me, you need only to know and obey these consecrated and anointed ones! They will be your church, and your religion, and your God!'"

"You are blaspheming, blacksmith, and offending God by saying things like that!" Fr. Nestor was scarcely able to speak. "Who ever heard of anything like it? It is a sin. A deadly sin!"

"It may well be a sin or two, but the truth must be spoken! Well, tell me, is that not how things are in this world? How many of you consecrated persons truly have God in your heart? Count them on the fingers of your hand! And how many are there who wear greed and pride under their long cassocks?"

"Do not judge others! Do not judge them, blacksmith, so that you yourself may not be judged."

"I am not at all concerned about that," the blacksmith responded. "God will do whatever He wants to do with me, but it is up to me to do what is right. But you, oh yes, you judge me and curse me without getting to know either my heart or my faith, and all the while you hide behind the words of the Gospel: 'Judge not, that ye may not be judged.' Fine, then don't you judge as well! And what will your teachings be like then? And what have they been like up to now? How many years did you spend teaching, and catechizing, and shaming, and prevailing upon people to choose what is right, and yet . . . what is happening in the village today?

"Take a walk through that village, take a look under those thatched roofs, and what will you find there? The fact that there is poverty, despair—that is not what is important. Our people are accustomed to poverty. But as for the drunkenness, the thievery, the quarrels and the cursing, the falsehoods and the injustices in the community—are you aware of all that? Do you not feel— it would seem that your conscience is not deadened—that the responsibility for all the squalor teeming right on your doorstep falls on you?"

"On me?" Fr. Nestor yelped in sincere alarm, as if Herder's words had struck him like a heavy cudgel.

"Yes, on you, Father, and on those like you! How do you go about teaching the people?"

"But even Christ said that some seeds must fall on stones."

"But Christ also said that a worker is worth what he is paid. And how much is a worker worth, if all the seeds that he sows fall on stones?"

"We do what we can . . ."

"Just say that you are incapable of doing anything. And I will tell you why that is so."

"It would be interesting to find out."

"For you it will not be very interesting," Herder said with annoyance. "You lack what causes miracles, what gives life—you are lacking in love! Your speech is like the twanging of a dulcimer, and your teachings are like the trumpeting of brass. A lot of noise, but no substance."

As he listened to these words, Fr. Nestor slumped ever lower and lower, wilting, growing weak, and becoming even more stooped; they were like a sharp-edged knife that pierced his heart.

It was the first time that this blacksmith, this heretic, was talking with him, and it was the first time that he felt as if someone had brusquely, mercilessly, stuck a finger under his heart and used it to agitate fibres that ostensibly had long since been suppressed and deadened.

For truly, what did all the years, the more than thirty years of dutiful holy service amount to? Even though in his heart of hearts he knew that he had never lacked in faith or espoused heresies, what was that worth? Who knows, might that not be simply because he had never pondered matters of faith more deeply?

Even though he conscientiously chanted the liturgy, the matins, and the akaphists without ever omitting even a single word, even though he conscientiously delivered his sermons, held catechism lessons, and instructed the faithful at every opportunity, nevertheless—and he sensed this with extreme bitterness at this moment—he had done it out of a sense of duty, just as a bureaucrat draws up a summons or a decree in matters that do not affect him in any way.

Neither in matters of faith, nor of morality, nor of enlightenment, had he communicated the fervour, the all-consuming passion engendered by a genuine love for an ideal to the impoverished, ignorant, labouring, and heavily burdened people—people who more than once went to church and awaited to hear a truly compassionate word of comfort, of consolation, and then, taking advantage of the long-standing practice, walked out during the sermon to get some fresh air, to warm themselves in the sun, and to talk with their neighbours about the very misery and worries which they had vainly hoped would be attenuated in church.

"But what is the point of even talking about it?" Herder continued after a moment of silence as he bent in closer to Fr. Nestor. "Take even you, your Reverence . . . May God punish me if I mean to judge you, but the truth is the truth. Well, tell me truthfully, what did you care about more in the parish: the souls of your parishioners, or how to accumulate as much money as possible so as not to lose favour with the Countess?"

"Blacksmith! That is enough!" Fr. Nestor cried in agony, as if he were being stabbed.

"But am I telling you anything that you did not know? Does not your conscience tell you the very same thing at least a thousand times a day? Of course, it is true that the parishioners have more respect for you because you skinned them less than either your predecessor or your successor, but is that anything to be proud of? The parishioners respect you for lightening their burden by giving them five thousand rynski for the church, but do you hope to buy God's favour by doing that? To pay off your sin, your heavy sin, the sin of neglecting for so many years to do what you were obligated to do—to love your spiritual flock? Without that love, no work, no sacrifice is worth anything. But when there is love, then everything that is done and all the sacrifices assume an entirely different meaning than when they exist simply *pro forma*."

Herder had not yet had anything to eat that day. At such times his voice became strident, and his words flew out rapidly and hit their mark like shotgun pellets. At those times he did not concern himself about any niceties; he said what he thought without pausing to think if he was offending anyone. And so now he poured out of his heart what had long been brewing in it without the slightest regard as to its effect on Fr. Nestor.

"Oh, blacksmith! Ivan! Have you no fear of God?" a gentle, reproachful voice suddenly sounded behind Herder's back. "How can you say such things? Just look at him!"

It was Demenyuk who, hearing the conversation in the orchard between Fr. Nestor and the blacksmith, had approached very slowly and overheard Herder's last outburst. Cold terror pierced the old churchgoer's heart, and he scarcely dared to look at Fr. Nestor.

The priest was still sitting on the bench, completely slouched over, and with his head hanging low, as if heart-stricken. His hat and cane had long since slipped from his hands, and those hands were now convulsively kneading his chequered percale handkerchief. His lips were moving incessantly, the furrows on his face had grown deeper and merged with the dark circles under his rheumy eyes, and heavy bitter tears, streaming over the ridges of his serpentine wrinkles, fell on his knees. From his chest issued a laboured, child-like sobbing interrupted by a dry hacking cough.

"Your Reverence? Oh, my God!" Demenyuk shouted as he rushed up to Fr. Nestor. "What's wrong? Aren't you feeling well? And I, the fool that I am, got carried away with my talking back there!"

"It's nothing, it's nothing, Yurko," Fr. Nestor whispered almost inaudibly, as he hastily wiped the tears from his face with his handkerchief. "Listen, blacksmith! Give me your hand!" he added as he tried to raise himself from the bench.

Herder was a bit taken aback by the unexpected outburst of feeling on the part of the old priest. He had never seen him like that, and he could never have even imagined such a thing was possible. Nevertheless, seeing Demenyuk's anxiety, and feeling a trifle concerned himself, he began reproaching himself for having been overly harsh with the old man, for having blurted out everything that was in his heart. And so he was happy to hear that the priest was not angry with him.

He quickly extended his hand and said gently: "Let your Reverence not be angry with me for what I said! Perhaps I am not thinking clearly, but I do not like to hide what I am thinking."

"That's fine, that's fine, blacksmith!" Fr. Nestor said with a gasp. "God will reward you for this . . . I am not angry . . . I am grateful to you . . . even though my heart . . . my heart aches when I hear . . . the thanks . . . that I get . . . for my . . ." His voice was quivering, and it kept breaking with every breath.

Demenyuk took him by the arm and began leading him out of the orchard. "Good-bye, blacksmith!" Demenyuk said. "And please forgive us . . ."

"There is nothing to forgive!" Herder responded as he watched them depart. "It is I who should . . ."

"No, no, no! I am grateful to you. I truly am . . ." Fr. Nestor strained to speak more loudly, but a coughing spell broke off what he was trying to say.

The blacksmith sighed heavily as he watched them go, closed the gate of his fortress-like yard, and walked slowly to his house, where his wife and son were waiting dinner for him.

V

"Father Nestor! Father Nestor!" Lady Olimpiya called out from the doorway of her living quarters.

Fr. Nestor, who had just walked down the street past the ruins of the manor house and was entering the yard, jumped with a start and, without saying anything, walked up to her.

"And here I was getting concerned about you. It's time to have dinner, but you were nowhere to be found."

"You . . . you . . . you see . . . I was in the village . . . with the people . . ."

"Well, perhaps you'll come in, and we'll have dinner together. I'm a little early today—you see, I'm expecting guests for afternoon tea."

"But how could I . . . together with my gracious Lady!" Fr. Nestor began saying, but Lady Olimpiya stopped him with an energetic gesture, took him by the arm, and led him to her dining room, explaining that it would be better if he had dinner with her, that there would be no need to feel constrained, that Paraska could serve him better than Demenyuk, and that, in any event, their dinner hour would be abbreviated today.

It was evident that the Lady was in high spirits and that she wanted to put Fr. Nestor into a good mood as well: she talked, told him stories, and even joked. But he remained dejectedly silent and, when he had to respond, he stuttered and grew confused.

Lady Olimpiya finally took notice of this.

"Well, aren't I a fine one!" she said jokingly as she sat down beside him when they had finished their meal, and the table had been cleared. "I'm going on about this and that, about things that perhaps do not interest you at all, and I'm not paying any attention to the fact that you seem sad and a bit downhearted. Well, Father, tell me, what is wrong with you?"

"With me? But I . . . do you suppose that I . . . Well, thank God, there is nothing wrong with me."

"No, do not say that! It is plain to see that there is something wrong. You are worried about something."

"Oh, worried!" Fr. Nestor said uneasily, waving his hand. "Is it so hard to be worried? Is it so rare for us old folks to be worried? It's not worth talking about."

"All the same, tell me!" Lady Olimpiya insisted, happy to have found a theme that caught Fr. Nestor's attention.

"Well you see, my gracious Lady," Fr. Nestor said, abruptly straightening up and beginning to speak in a more confident, almost dignified, tone. "I do have one worry: my death is imminent. I can feel it, and today, as I served the Divine Liturgy, I felt it so sharply, so clearly, as if a voice was whispering to me over my shoulder. Well, that is God's will. But then something else transpired. I was talking with a certain man, and I concluded that I have discharged my duties as a priest in a perfunctory manner, that there is much in my soul that is unfulfilled, neglected. And that worries me."

"Well, Father," Lady Olimpiya began saying a trifle uncertainly, as she had not expected such a turn in the conversation, "you are overstating the matter. Didn't you teach, didn't you . . . accomplish that?"

"Accomplish! What did I accomplish? And how did I accomplish it?" Fr. Nestor cried out painfully. "If I had been replaced by a machine, an au . . . automaton, it would have accomplished just as much . . . I said the liturgy, I performed all sorts of rites, delivered sermons from a book. Can this possibly be called fulfilling my pastoral duties? And in the meantime the people in the village are ignorant, and then there is the moral decay, the poverty, the enmity . . ."

"Oh, Father! There were priests here before you, and there is one here now, and all these sad things are everywhere, wherever there are people, and no one frets about them."

"They have lost their consciences!" Fr. Nestor said, deep in thought. "Oh yes! I see this all too well. And I too did not have one, I did not have one for many long years. And it is only now, before my death, that God has returned it to me . . . perhaps to punish me, but then again, perhaps to have me do some good. After all, my obligations demanded of me much more than the kind of work that I did."

"One man, Fr. Nestor, no matter what he does, will not be able to drive poverty and ignorance out of the village."

"But I should at least have tried. Yes, I should have . . . You know, my Lady, what troubles me the most? The fact that in my heart I purposely, artificially, extinguished my love for people, for everything in the world! And I extinguished it because of you, because of a foolish childish whim!"

"Well, thank you for the compliment!" Lady Olimpiya said with a melancholy smile. "So you are saying that for you I was a foolish whim!"

"Of course you were! Of course! I was just a priest's son, without a pedigree, without any status, and yet I dared to think that you, a Count's daughter, would love me, be mine! Well, was that not sheer madness? And when I did not succeed, instead of committing suicide, instead of hanging myself or drowning myself, I killed my heart, I cut myself off from people, from the world, from everything that constitutes real life. And what came of that? Satan, the enemy of mankind, lies in wait for exactly those kinds of souls. When the living flame was extinguished within me, he replaced it with dust that gives off light when it rots, he replaced it with *mammon, and my dark soul attached itself to it. And having cast a rope around my neck, he led me ever farther and farther into thickets of sin and abomination."

"But Father! What are you saying?" Lady Olimpiya exclaimed. The turn that this conversation had taken and the tone in Fr. Nestor's voice were not at all to her liking. "You must be ill! You must have a fever!"

"Oh, I am ill. Yes, I am ill!" Fr. Nestor said. "But it is not my body that is ill—it is healthy. It is my heart that aches to its very depths; it is quivering like a withered leaf before a storm. Did you never have the feeling, my Lady, that death is drawing near and that it might catch up with you when you are mired up to your neck in sins? But perhaps you do not believe in a life hereafter, in judgment and punishment?"

"Oh, Father! Drop this conversation, I beg you! It is upsetting you, and it can harm your health."

"What do I care about my health?" Fr. Nestor responded irritably. "When death is looking over my shoulder, it is too late to worry about my health. But as for my soul . . . for my soul this conversation can be beneficial . . . I sense that it is making me well. Why, just think where the evil one has led me! Here, right here in this village, souls given into my care are perishing, dying. They long for a tiny ray of light, but they die without it, without a spark of love and mercy—do you know what that means?

"But I cared only about one thing—about amassing money! Savings books, imperial coins, ducats, coupons, lottery tickets, exchange rates . . . Oh, my God! My whole life was taken up with them! And they were thrust upon me by my infernal enemy to take the place of a wife, children, friends, work, and love! But tell me! How am I to die now? How am I to face the Last Judgment of the Righteous Judge?"

"Father, Father!" Lady Olimpiya said, assuming a most heartfelt tone. "Do not speak ill of yourself. After all, you know, in the bottom of your heart you know, and I know, and God knows, that what you have been saying is not true. After all, you did love! And you will not go to the grave without an heir!"

She extended her hand to him and gazed tenderly into his eyes, just as she had done in the past. But he started shaking, his facial muscles and lips quivered spasmodically, and his eyes filled with terror.

"Oh, my Lady!" he whispered, gasping for air and breaking into a fit of coughing. "Do not bring that up! For the love of God, do not bring that up! Do not stir up old memories. It is those memories that are killing me! They are my downfall! Perhaps you do not even realize the full extent of that downfall!"

"A downfall occasioned by love can never be a terrible sin in the eyes of God, who, after all, is the God of love!" the Lady said in a dignified, but somewhat cold tone.

"Do not blaspheme, my Lady! Do not offend God!" Fr. Nestor hastened to say, waving his hands. "After all, you do not know . . . After all, it was adultery . . . After all, it was right here . . . O God, O God! Do not let me die until I atone for at least a thousandth part of my sin! Until I pay for it, until I redeem it with my blood! After all, my Lady, in this instance there was something even more terrible, more heinous than adultery."

"Oh, Father!" Lady Olimpiya said. Then suddenly changing her tone, she stated coldly, sharply, cynically. "What has come over you again? Why are you staging this farce? I understand it very well. And it is not making the slightest impression on me. All those outcries, laments, all that talk about the terrible sin, and so on and so forth—all that is sheer nonsense. Leave that to actors and elderly female pensioners. It does not behove old people like us to act out such a comedy. We are too old for that. We can speak plainly, clearly, calmly, and wisely. After all, you know that Adas is your son, and that your first obligation is to look after him, to ensure his future. If there was a sin or two involved in what happened, that is up to God to decide, but I think that the duty of an honourable man is clear, and no amount of lamenting will let him wriggle out of it."

She said this bitingly, quite emphatically, but without any pathos. Her appearance made it clear, however, that she had summoned up all her will, all her energy, to say what she did. Like a card player who holds only one card, she had placed all her bets on this single round.

Up to now, she had never talked to Fr. Nestor in that tone of voice, but knowing his firm, unyielding, almost obtuse nature, she had always felt that at some point it would be necessary to speak to him in this manner. The opportunity had arisen sooner than she would have liked it to, but that did not matter.

Lady Olimpiya watched carefully to see what effect her words were having on the elderly priest. And without knowing how and when it happened, she rose to her feet and walked up to him in a stiff, tense, and almost threatening guise, the way that a she-wolf, confident in her strength, poises herself to pounce on a lamb and devour it without a struggle.

Fr. Nestor looked petrified. Hunched over in an armchair next to a window shaded by a blind, and leaning his elbows on the arms of the chair, he turned numb with shock and froze in that position. Even his hands and fingers, extended as if to defend himself, stopped trembling and became rigid, as if petrified. He could not breathe. His staring eyes were fixed in mortal terror on Lady Olimpiya's face.

For the first time he sensed in that woman—who had always appeared before him as a lady, as a gentle, tender, higher being—the existence of a beast, a rapacious wild animal that lurks at the bottom of every person's soul, at times moving about in plain view, and at other times hiding so deeply, so painstakingly, that one is misled into believing that it does not even exist. Fr. Nestor had never sensed the presence of that beast in Lady Olimpiya's nature, and so, when he met up with it face to face, his terror was augmented. He felt that he was powerless, helpless against her, and that it was up to her, up to her mercy, her good will, whether she let him go, or tore him to shreds on the spot.

Her calm words, spoken in an even tone, did not deceive him; the cold glint in her eyes, her stiffened lips, the taut muscles that tensed both cheeks, flitting over them, nearing the corners of her mouth and then jumping away from them, and her decisive footsteps all pointed to the fact that it was not good will that ruled this woman's soul.

For a long minute there was a deathly silence in the room. The two people in it faced each other without moving, uncertain of themselves, with fear and hatred in their souls, without taking their eyes off each other, without daring to move.

Then suddenly, they both exhaled. The wild beast in Lady Olimpiya's soul vanished, Fr. Nestor's hands once again began to shake, and the corners of his lips twisted convulsively, as if he was about to cry.

Overcome by emotion and scarcely able to draw a breath, he gasped out the words: "God be with you, my Lady! What . . . what is wrong with you?"

"Nothing!" the Lady muttered dejectedly, and she sat down. A bitter disillusionment, who knows from where and why, was flooding her heart.

"You said: '. . . the duty of an honourable man! You will not be able to wriggle out of it!' But have I not fulfilled my obligations? Did I try to wriggle out of them?"

"Oh, as if you did all that much! Just those few thousand that you gave Adas for his stay in Venice."

"A few thousand! Is that so little? After all, do these thousands grow on trees?"

"With the kind of money that you have, they do not mean anything."

"With the kind of money that I have! But I do not have that kind of money!" Fr. Nestor exclaimed in alarm. For him the topic of how much money he had was even more terrifying than the one about death and the Last Judgment.

"Now, now! You need not play blind-man's bluff with me. I know very well how much money you have, and I am telling you, plainly and clearly, that I consider all of that money, however much of it there may be, to be the rightful property of the son who is yours and mine."

Lady Olimpiya, her nerves strained to the breaking point, spoke these words in a metallic, flat voice, lowering her head as if she did not want to hear or see their effect on Fr. Nestor.

It was the final card in her boldly played game. Having played it, she knew that it was a *fait accompli*: it was win or lose—there was no turning back. And that is why, having spoken her mind, she was almost numb with fear as she waited mutely for Fr. Nestor's response.

"That will never happen!" The words flew out of Fr. Nestor's mouth, not as a premeditated response, but almost involuntarily, as a resonant echo of the feelings that he had harboured for Adas for a long time.

Lady Olimpiya lowered her head even more, as if she had been expecting just such a reply, and then she asked in a scarcely audible voice: "Why?"

"Because . . . because, I do not want to give it to him, and I will not!"

"That is not a good enough reason."

"God would punish me doubly if I gave it to him! First of all, that money . . . it has cost me my soul, my life! It is blood money! It is the blood of thousands of poor people, the sweat of human beings—I amassed this money, and it will blight my soul. No, I do not want that to happen! I will return it all to them, I will return it to the very last penny!"

Lady Olimpiya once again slowly squared her shoulders and said disdainfully, with ill-concealed fury: "What are you going on about? To whom will you return it?"

But Fr. Nestor seemed not to hear her. "And secondly, your Adas . . ."

"He's yours, yours!" Lady Olimpiya shouted.

"Your Adas is not the kind of man into whose hands I could, in all conscience, put all that money."

"So to whom will you give it?"

"I already know! Oh, do not worry! I already know!"

"You will not give it to anyone!" Lady Olimpiya observed firmly and sharply. "You do not have the right to do that! Your son is threatened with bankruptcy, the loss of his estate, and you are going on about some fantastic ideas."

"Oh, my money won't make things go any better for him!" Fr. Nestor exclaimed malevolently.

"You need not fret about that!" Lady Olimpiya cut him off. The beast within her stirred once again and began to growl.

"Permit me to say, my Lady . . . at the moment, you are a trifle . . . a trifle upset . . . or perhaps you did not sleep well . . . or something like that. Perhaps it would be better if we were to put off this conversation for another time?"

And as he said this, Fr. Nestor rose from the armchair and began casting his eyes about in search of his hat and cane in order to leave this room that, with its dark atmosphere and close, warm air, was beginning to choke him, to stifle the breath in his chest, and to fill his heart with an ever greater anxiety.

But at that moment, the rattling of a light carriage and the loud pounding of horses' hooves sounded in the yard.

Lady Olimpiya hurriedly pulled back the blind, glanced out the window, and exclaimed joyfully: "Oh, it's Adas!"

And then, turning to Fr. Nestor, she stated in a stern, commanding tone: "No, wait! You must speak with Adas! You must tell him, straight to his face, what you have against him; this matter must be cleared up. There is no point in having the lad expecting something, if nothing is to come of it."

"But I . . . But is it up to me . . ." Fr. Nestor began to remonstrate; the thought of meeting with Adas was not at all a pleasant one.

Lady Olimpiya manoeuvred him almost forcefully back into the armchair, saying decisively and vehemently: "Do not make a scene!"

And then, going to the door with her arms outstretched, she exclaimed a second time: "Oh, it's Adas! But, what's this? Are you by yourself?"

VI

"Good day, mother!" Adas said, bounding into the room. "Oh, and Fr. Nestor is here as well! Good day, good day!"

Adas extended his hand to Fr. Nestor who remained seated, motionless, pale, and numb. And then, without taking a good look at the priest, he greeted him and, in keeping with lordly conventions, immediately turned his back on him and began a conversation with his mother.

"You know what, mother? Yesterday we played in the casino until three o'clock. I won fifty guldens and, of course, I spent them that night with my friends. It was a great group: Edzo, and Dolko, and *Tadzo were there, and then *Fonso and *Milko came along. We spent the night together having a wonderful time. Today all five will be at my home for dinner, and then we'll come to your place for tea."

"But how is it that you have come here without them? After all, it's almost dinnertime now," Lady Olimpiya observed.

Her face had cleared as soon as she saw her son, and it was evident that she enthusiastically involved herself in his interests.

"They're on their way. But I outstripped them so that I could stop in and see you for a minute. I thought you might need some provisions . . . So I bought a few things—they'll be carried in right away."

"Oh, my good son!" Lady Olimpiya said softly, embracing him and kissing him on the forehead.

"Oh, it's nothing!' Adas said, gently moving away from his mother. "It's not worth talking about. And how are you getting along?"

"Everything is fine, we are surviving one way or another. Fr. Nestor and I were just talking about you."

"About me?" Adas asked in surprise and, swivelling on one foot, he turned and looked down at Fr. Nestor, who had visibly begun to tremble at the mention of his name. "What were you saying about me?"

"We were talking about your future, my dear son. After all, you know that Fr. Nestor is your father."

"Oh, why say such nonsensical things, mother!" Adas fired off impertinently.

"No, my dear son, it is not nonsense! I told you about my sin some time ago, and now I am confessing it here, in his presence. Ask him, if you wish. You can be angry with me if you want to be, but what was done cannot be undone. But now, just imagine this: Fr. Nestor feels that he is close to death, and yet he does not want to fulfill his final obligation with respect to you."

"What obligation is that?"

"He does not want to leave you his fortune."

"Well, Father, that is very inconsiderate of you. If I am your son, who is there closer to you to whom you can leave your fortune? And who is more in need of it?"

And, assuming a comic pose, Adas stood in front of Fr. Nestor. With his diminutive figure, his prematurely thinning hair that was parted in the middle and slickly smoothed down, his sparse, pale, carroty whiskers, his modish suit of clothes, and the ruby pin in his tie, he looked like a doll moulded out of wax. In his grey eyes could be seen fatigue, a surfeit of living, and cynicism. Not a single serious thought had left a trace on his low, smooth forehead, and a carefree smile flitted over his lips.

His mother's statement that Fr. Nestor was his real father had not made any impression on him. He suspected that his mother was putting on an act to convince the dull-witted old man to write a will that would benefit her son, and so, in his own manner, he set about to support the role that she was playing.

"Oh, Father, if you only knew how badly I am in need of money, a lot of money!" he declaimed with false pathos. "Why, just look at me! I am young, handsome, and I want to live, to have a good time . . . When I walk down the street, all the girls smile at me. Good fortune, luxury, and happiness lure me from every window. Music, wine, cards, companions . . . well, why are you scowling like that? Oh, of course, as an old celibate, you do not understand such things. But then again, there is no real danger of that! In your younger days you too tried a thing or two! If you managed to come to an agreement with my mother . . ."

Fr. Nestor lost his patience.

The cynical ramblings of the young Lord confounded his soul and aroused within it a powerfully furious indignation, the kind that only he was capable of. Leaping from his chair, he flung back his shoulders and, striding purposefully, walked up to Adas.

Standing a full head taller than the young man, he shook uncontrollably, like a reed in the wind, and, gasping for air, shouted: "Shut up, you young whippersnapper! Don't you dare talk about what you do not understand! Don't you dare make fun of your mother and . . . and . . ."

But at this point his strength gave way, and his overwrought nerves took their toll. He once again collapsed in his chair and, burrowing his face in his hands, wailed like a child.

Adas just stood there. The cynical smile on his face did not disappear at this outburst from Fr. Nestor, the first one that he had seen in many a long year.

"Oh my, my!" he said mockingly. "My honourable daddy has recalled only now that he has a child, and he wants to treat me like a child. But I must be so bold as to inform my honourable daddy that I came of age some time ago."

"Do not call me daddy!" Fr. Nestor said, conquering his paroxysm.

"Why not? If it is as my mother says it is, then there is nothing to be ashamed of. After all, am I a bad son?"

"You may be the best son that there is, but I do not want to know you."

"Oh, maybe it wouldn't be all that bad!" Adas said. "But then it is your choice. While you are alive, you do not have to know me, I do not insist upon it. But when you are on your deathbed, think of me just once, when you are making your will."

"Well, of course, I'll think of you," Fr. Nestor said curtly.

"And include a couple of words in it."

"Of course I will."

"Well, what will you write?"

"You will read it later."

"No, I want to know now."

"Well, if you do, then listen. I plan to set up a foundation for the indigent with the capital that I have. For various categories of poor people: for peasants ruined by usury, for sinners who are released from prison and have no way of supporting themselves, for the incurably ill. I will direct all my capital towards these goals, and then I will add these words to my testament: 'And if my son Adas Torsky or his heirs find themselves in any one of these categories of the indigent, then they are to have first call for assistance.'"

"You better watch that you do not fall into one of those categories yourself, my dear daddy," Adas shouted. "I hope your hand withers before you write such a testament."

"If I am unable to write it, I will dictate it."

"You will lose your voice before that ever happens."

"I will find a way to do what I want to do. But I am telling you and your mother one thing: do not whet your teeth for an inheritance from me! You will never live to see it."

"We will see how things turn out!" Lady Olimpiya stated. During the entire conversation between Adas and Fr. Nestor, she had remained seated by the window with her back turned to them, but now she turned around to face Fr. Nestor once again.

For a moment there was a gloomy silence. Even Adas sensed that the entire conversation was vile, and he stopped smiling.

The shell of polite behaviour in which these three individuals customarily strove to conceal their true feelings had suddenly, for whatever reason, cracked open and vanished, and the hatred that had been hidden thus far, the avarice, and the cynical longing to live at the expense of others came to the fore.

Fr. Nestor's heart sealed itself off still more tightly from these two people, and for the first time there stirred in his heart the feeling that touches a traveller to the quick when, wandering down a forest path, he suddenly finds himself in the midst of a pack of wolves. And then he gradually became alarmed at his own actions. After all, those brutal words—the ones that had escaped from his breast when he was being pressured by the Lady and her son—did they not echo not only his attachment to that worthless money, to that mammon that was of no use to him, but also his hatred for living people, for those who were close to him, who were bound to him—albeit only with sinful bonds?

Now, after this conversation, these bonds were torn, and his continued peaceful existence in this household was impossible—he could see this clearly, and he once again felt the anxiety of a child that finds itself in the middle of a forest in the dead of night. Where could he go now? To whom could he turn for help? To whom could he entrust himself and the miserable capital that was changing rapidly from being a treasure to being a burden, a source of danger?

Fr. Nestor was so disconcerted and so disturbed, to the very depths of his heart, that he did not have the strength to ponder these questions. He felt only fear, danger, and uncertainty with respect to where he found himself at the moment, and for the second time, trembling and clutching at the air like a helpless child, he rose from his chair and began preparing to leave.

This time neither Lady Olimpiya nor Adas tried to stop him, and they did not utter a word. He stumbled out and, without bowing or saying his farewells, shuffled to his room, where he immediately locked himself in securely, as if fearing that, even though it was broad daylight, someone might sneak up on him at any moment.

Lady Olimpiya and Adas remained silent for another minute. Finally, Adas, looking stricken, turned to his mother. "What, exactly, happened here? Why did he become so angry?"

"I really don't know," the Lady said coldly. "Something got into the old man. He came here and started talking about his imminent death, about his sins, about penance. The devil knows what all that nonsense was about! But I was not interested in all that. He infuriated me by hinting that he wanted to leave all his money to a foundation of some kind. I began to explain to him, as to a sensible man, that he had an obligation to leave it all to you, but oh no—no, he refused to listen."

"But why does he hate me so much?"

"Who can figure him out? I do not think he hates you that much; it is just that he loves his money more, and he is afraid you will spend it foolishly. I have told you more than once, my dear Adas, not to reveal your lordly nature before him, and instead, pretend to be a modest, hardworking, and diligent landowner."

"Oh, as if I'm about to don a mask and put on an act for that old idiot!" Adas shouted with a gesture of revulsion.

"Well, you can see for yourself how things stand. I do not know what will happen now."

"Oh, I'm not worried," Adas said cheerfully. "If he loves his money that much, he certainly will not want to part with it before he dies, and so he won't make a will, and it . . ."

He stopped short. As a former law student he knew that in such a case the money could never legally be his, all the more so because he could never bring himself to claim in court that he was the priest's son, especially since he himself did not really believe it.

"Well, what will happen to it?" the Lady asked.

"Well, according to the law, the money will go to the government treasury, and then maybe a small part of it will go to the parish."

"Oh, who can say as yet what will happen!" the Lady said mysteriously, shrugging her shoulders. "As long as he does not actually make a will without my knowing about it."

"Or as long as he does not want to move out of your home," Adas added. "I have a feeling that he is terrified of you, mother."

"No, do not worry about that! I am not that foolish. I have known how to keep him here thus far, and I know how to make him stay now. In any case, it will not be for too long. But the devil take him! It is time for you to go home. After all, your friends may arrive at any moment."

"You're right! It is time to go. May the devil take the crazy priest! He has ruined my good mood! Tfu! And the way he stared at me—so wildly! It was as if a dead man had arisen from his casket! Well, good-bye for now, mother."

"Good-bye," Lady Olimpiya said. "But hurry back with your friends, do not make me wait too long!"

Adas walked out of his mother's living quarters and, whistling a melody that he had picked up in a nightclub, got into his carriage and drove off.

And a moment after his departure, Hadyna crept out of the Lady's entryway where, hiding in an empty sauerkraut barrel, he had listened in on the entire conversation that the Lady had engaged in with Fr. Nestor and her son. After crawling into the yard, he abruptly stood up and, whistling a song, walked right under the Lady's windows, as if he was just returning home from the village.

Lady Olimpiya caught sight of him.

"Where have you been gadding about, you devil's spawn?" she shouted through the window.

"I was in church," Hadyna replied in a calm and unconcerned tone as he continued on his way.

"Stop! Wait a moment!" the Lady yelled, leaning out the window. "In church? Is this when people come home from church?"

"I spent some time in the village . . . with the fellows."

"In the village? Why in the world would you go to the village?"

"Well, today there's nothing to do in the manor yard, so it's a chance to chat with people!" Hadyna responded curtly.

"Oh, you despicable man!" the Lady said furiously. "To talk with people! What kind of people would want to talk with a beast like you? You were probably in the tavern."

"But did my Lady gave me some money so that I could spend time in the tavern?" Hadyna snapped back sarcastically, and his coal-black eyes flashed at her.

Lady Olimpiya turned white with anger.

"Oh, don't you worry!' she cried. "I know where you're getting your money from."

"Well, from where?" Hadyna snarled sullenly, but firmly.

"The nerve of you to even ask! You wretched man! Just keep this in mind: you'll end up in prison! You hear me?"

"Maybe I will end up in prison but, God willing, I won't be there alone."

"What is that supposed to mean? Speak up!" the Lady shouted.

"My Lady shouldn't shout so loudly, because I also know a thing or two!"

"What? What? What?" Lady Olimpiya screeched. "What do you know? Come on, tell me, what do you know?"

"Oh, there's a lot that I could talk about with my gracious Lady," Hadyna said insolently, knowing full well that he had touched on a sore spot. "But I'm hungry, and they've all probably had their dinner without me."

And, turning his back on the Lady, he went to the kitchen, where the servants, without even thinking of waiting for him, were already eating.

Hapka greeted him with a string of colourful curses, but he just grabbed a spoon and, paying no attention to her, began wolfing down whatever he could get his hands on. It was only after he had caught up a bit to the others that he stopped to catch his breath and glanced around at his fellow diners.

Old Demenyuk was here, and the herdsman and the boy who helped him, and the gardener and his young helper, and Paraska. It was obvious that they were all hungry, because no one was saying anything. They ate in silence, slurping apple soup—made from fallen apples that the gardener had given the cook—from a big bowl, and munching on rye bread. It was only when there was no more soup, and Hapka brought in a huge pot of potatoes, and Paraska followed her in with a bowl of sour milk, that their tongues loosened a bit.

"What happened over there, Tanasko?" Demenyuk asked, turning to Hadyna. "Tell us, why was the Lady yelling at you like that?"

"It seems that she really likes me," Hadyna said with a laugh as he scraped the bowl that had held the soup.

"Well, it seems that you like her even more," the gardener remarked. "We were all listening: you would say a word, and she would respond with ten; you kept lowering your voice, but she kept getting louder."

"Well, of course! I always pay back with interest," Hadyna said none too modestly as he tucked into the potatoes. The potatoes were not peeled, and this fact angered him.

"My dear Hapka, my dear little mother!" he said cordially, turning to Hapka.

"What do you want, you wretched man?" she replied in a gentle voice, assuming the tone that he had used.

"May the good Lord see to it that, after you die, the angels with horns will tear off your skin in the same way that we have to peel these holy potatoes before we eat them."

A roar of laughter from all present was the response to this pious wish.

"Oh, you spawn of the devil!" Hapka shouted. "What have I ever done to you that you're cursing me so harshly?"

"Harshly? I was trying to be as gentle as possible. And I did it because you're serving us potatoes still in their jackets."

"Oh, you useless creature!" And Hapka, swinging a large ladle, rushed at him as if to attack him. "Why, if I let you have it on the nape of your neck, you'd never see God's world again! Do you think that I have nothing better to do than scrape potatoes for you? And just what were you doing this morning? Why didn't you come and scrape them? May your heart and liver be scraped, you vile beast! Just look at him!"

It took a lot of effort on Demenyuk's part to calm Hapka down to the point of finally retiring to a nook where she continued mumbling and reciting a litany of endless moral lessons.

But Hadyna did not pay the slightest attention to her. He was in the most jovial of spirits, and he laughed, made fun of Lady Olimpiya, winked at Paraska, poked the herdsman's helper, and recounted the thrashing that Tsvyakh had been given near the tavern.

And when dinner was over, he pinched Paraska on the arm, winked meaningfully, walked out of the yard, made a few false starts as if going first this way and then that, and after everyone had departed, dashed into the coach-house.

A moment later, Paraska sneaked in there as well.

"Well, what's new?" she asked softly.

"It's wonderful! It's just wonderful!" Hadyna whispered joyfully.

"Well, what is it? Tell me!"

"You know, I listened in on a conversation between the old witch and the priest! I'm telling you—it's wonderful! They've quarrelled for life!"

"Come now! What are you saying?"

"It made even me feel scared. I thought she would fling herself at him and choke him on the spot!"

"For what?"

"I don't know how it all began, because I couldn't hear the first part of their conversation all that well, but I know that the old Lady was insisting that the priest leave all his money to the young Lord. 'He's your son,' she said. But he flatly refused! Then the young Lord came, and the two of them began working on him until the old man lost his temper and shouted—much more loudly than I ever thought he could—at the young Lord."

"How did it all end?" Paraska asked, intrigued by what he was saying.

"The old man wouldn't budge. He kept saying, over and over again: 'I won't leave it to him because God would punish me if I did. I'll give it away to the peasants.'"

"Oh, my goodness! To the peasants. What peasants?"

"How am I to know? Then he said he'd leave it to poor people, but never, no never, to the young Lord."

"Well, what did the old Lady say?"

"The old Lady kept repeating, like a crow: 'You will not leave the money to anyone but us! That money will be ours!'"

"What are you saying?" Paraska cried, slapping her knees in excitement.

"Just what you're hearing."

"What is she planning to do to him?"

"As if I'm supposed to know! But it's clear that they're planning something. After the priest left, they kept on talking for another minute, but they were speaking softly, and I couldn't hear what they were saying."

"Oh my, something bad can come out of this!" Paraska said with a note of fear in her voice.

"No doubt about it. That old witch is capable of anything! But I'm going to keep a close eye on her."

"Yes, do that, do that, and maybe something good will come of it for us!" Paraska said and, like a mouse darting into a hole, she slipped out of the coach house in a twinkling of an eye, just as Hadyna was about to reach out to embrace her.

"Paraska!" he called softly after her, but she was already far away. Annoyed both with her and himself, Hadyna stood for a moment immersed in thought and then crawled up to the hayloft, dug around in the hay, heaped it into a makeshift bed, and lay down to sleep.

After leaving his mother, Adas sped along the outskirts of the village, taking the same road that Fr. Nestor had walked down after his talk with the blacksmith.

The conversation with Fr. Nestor had left a bitter taste in his mouth, but other thoughts quickly dispelled his unpleasant mood. He was by nature a shallow, light-minded person in whom physical impulses outweighed intellectual considerations, and feelings overpowered mental processes. It was not his style to care about the future, to come up with intricate plans; he lived for the moment, without stopping to consider what results that moment would engender, what the consequences would be. He equated life with sensual delights, and therefore the pursuit of these delights constituted the entire essence of his aspirations and endeavours.

When Adas drew up alongside the yard of Herder the blacksmith, he slowed down and snapped his whip loudly three times as he rode by the gate. The cracking sound caused the dogs in the yard to begin barking, but none of the people in the house responded or looked out at the road. Feeling a bit miffed, he rode on.

In front of him spread a wide, endless field, and his eyes flitted over it like swift hawks in search of prey. What was glimmering and fluctuating over there, so crimson and full-blown, amid the tall rye stalks? Could it be a large poppy? No, not likely! It was creeping forward, moving along the boundary and making its way towards the road.

Adas cheered up, snapped his whip gleefully, and whipped the horses; the animals, sensing the aroma of familiar fields and the nearness of the barn, snorted and took off like a shot. They were drawing close to that crimson poppy. It was amply clear now that it was not a poppy, but a girl's head bedecked with flowers and red and green ribbons. From beneath those flowers and ribbons came the sound of a girl's silvery voice, and a song—a mournful but at the same time coquettishly animated dancing tune—poured forth:

> On Thursday, after supper, my mother beat me
> To stop me from gazing into a young lord's eyes.
> Oh, you may beat me, mother, beat me unto death,
> I'll still go out and say: "O my dearest young Lord!

Adas stopped the carriage opposite the boundary along which the girl was walking and shouted joyfully: "Is that you, Malanka?"

"No," Malanka shouted back at him, instantly vanishing in the tall rye. For a full minute she could not be seen, and there was only the sound of rye stalks rustling and swaying as she raced through them.

Dressed in a white blouse and red skirt, and blushing like a crimson flower, she suddenly ran out of the grain field and, like a doe, leapt lightly over the furrow alongside the road and, just as lightly, jumped into the cart.

Adas was sitting up front, driving the horses himself, and Malanka, standing behind him, wound her arms around his neck and covered his face, forehead, eyes, and hair with frenzied, passionate kisses.

"That's enough, enough!" Adas cried helplessly, holding the reins in one hand and the whip in the other.

"O my beloved! My dearest! My handsome one! My flower! My paradise!" Malanka whispered as she kept kissing him. "I had a feeling you would be coming alone; I was hoping that you would come!"

"Come with me to my manor," Adas said, embracing her with one arm and kissing her burning, raspberry red lips.

"Fine!" the girl said happily, but then she instantly grew sombre and added: "But only for a short time."

"But why? After all, it is Sunday."

"Even so, there is a lot of work to be done."

"Oh, spit at that work! They'll manage, they'll get along just fine without you."

"No, my dearest! I am a servant. And to make things even worse—you know what?—they're keeping an eye on me. My father strictly forbade me to see you, and today he even brought the old priest to have a talk with me."

"Aha! So!" Adas cried.

"Well, I pulled the wool over his eyes and told him that I was not even thinking about you, nor you about me. But still, the blacksmith and his son are bound to guess right away where I've gone, even though I got permission to go and see Hapka, the one that works in the manor."

"Don't worry, they won't figure it out!"

They continued driving down the main road for a while and then turned off onto the lane that led to Adas's manor. There was not a soul out in the fields; only the ripening grain rustled gently as it swayed in the light breeze, and here and there a swath of clover filled the air with its honey-sweet fragrance.

"That's far enough!" Malanka suddenly cried as she jumped down lightly and almost soundlessly from the cart. "I won't go any farther. We're quite close to the manor. Someone might see me with you."

"What? You want to go away? To abandon me?" Adas was speaking sadly, softly.

"We'll see each other tomorrow."

"No! Listen, my dear Malanka! Walk along this boundary and go into the orchard—there is a hole in the fence—no one will see you; and then go through the orchard to the bower and wait for me there. I'll only be a moment. I'll just see to the horses and tell the servants what to do. And then I'll come for you and take you to my room."

"Uh-uh, I don't want to! I'm scared."

"Don't be scared, sweetheart! What's there to be afraid of? I'll make sure that no one sees you. We'll have dinner, and then you'll go home."

The thought of spending a few quiet moments with the young gentleman, of dining with him, and talking with him to her heart's content was very tempting to Malanka, and so, after a moment's hesitation, she agreed.

Without saying another word, she dashed into the grain field and disappeared from view, while the young gentleman, whistling happily, drove up to the manor house.

VII

Fr. Nestor was shivering as if he had a fever.

"So that's how things are! So that's what is behind the civility and kindness, the concern about my health, the disinterested helpfulness. Speculation about my wealth! What cynicism! What shameless vulgarity! O my God, my God!"

His trembling hand fumbled for quite some time before he finally managed to fit the key into the lock of the door leading to his living quarters and, after opening the door, he struggled for another long moment before he managed to pull the key out, insert it into the lock on the inside, and double-lock the door.

"I do not feel safe here!" he muttered as he looked around to see if the windows were closed tightly. "No, I don't . . . not for a minute . . . What if they feel that it is too long to wait! What if they . . . O Lord, save me!"

His morbid imagination, aroused by the stressful experience he had just undergone, confounded his entire being, paralysing the last vestiges of his energy. His eyes were open, but he did not see; he tried to recall things, but could not remember; he darted about aimlessly, set about doing first this, and then that, and then something quite different, but he could not organize his thoughts, and he could not accomplish anything.

He could see all too well that the windows did not close tightly, that they lacked catches, that a pane in one of them was broken, and that it would be easy to open it from the outside; at the moment, he saw it all clearly, as he had seen it many a time before—but now he was seeing it even more clearly, he was even more acutely aware of the danger in his situation, and yet, after standing for a moment and staring blankly at the window, he headed off unthinkingly in another direction, because his confused mind had reminded him of something else.

"Everything is out in the open, in drawers, in pockets!" he cried and, breathing rapidly and unevenly, and barely able to move his legs, he tottered into his bedroom and convulsively began opening cupboards, sliding out drawers, and pulling out all manner of old cassocks, trousers, and vests, all the while hurrying, looking for something, and throwing everything into a jumbled heap.

Then, all at once, he stopped dead. The sun was casting a broad shaft of light into his room through the window that looked out to the southwest, and it seemed to him that someone was peering into his room through that window, intently watching his every movement, maliciously mocking his helpless haste, his impotent tugging and tossing. He hurried to the window and glanced outside—there was no one there. He moved away from it, and then suddenly recalled that he had left it open.

"O my God, O my God!" he groaned, fearing that he could not master his anxiety and agitation. But it was precisely now that he needed the greatest serenity and strength in order to think things over, to figure out what his next step should be. Every moment that he tarried threatened him with danger.

Even as it was, who could say how deeply he had already plunged into a trap hole through his carelessness, his negligence—no, through his blind faith in the goodness and probity of that woman. Who could say what nets she had already spread to catch him! Who could say if she had not purposely, calculatedly, exploded today, glared at him, contorted her face like a crazed beast in order to shock him, to paralyse his strength and destroy his peace of mind, to render him helpless and defenceless at the very moment when the greatest danger threatened him!

"O God, dear God!" Fr, Nestor groaned, almost in tears, as he strained, strained to the point of making his head throb, to muster all the powers of his mind, to harness his thoughts in orderly rows, to gain control over his nerves, to restore an equilibrium between his intentions and his deeds.

He sat down by the open window and gazed at the greenness of the trees and the azure blueness of the cloudless sky. The fresh, warm, fragrant air and the expansive, flat, and colourful view of the pastoral plains revived his nerves and inspired a feeling of tranquility. He began to breathe more evenly, more slowly; he stopped shivering, and his head cleared.

"No, I am not a corpse as yet!" he murmured. "I am not yet an *anima vilis* [a dispensable being] on whom you can conduct your experiments! I'll give you the fight of your lives! Perhaps it is all for the better that you revealed your appetite for my wealth so unexpectedly, so cynically, so shamelessly! The evil demon that you serve has made a mockery of you—an abominable joke! You thought that I would cave in, submit immediately, and that you would take control of me and do as you wished with me! But no! No, no, no! I have come to my senses! You stung me to the quick, and I awoke from a deep sleep! It was just what I needed! Thank you, thank you! Now I am no longer asleep; now I can see and hear very well where I am and what is happening to me. Now I will not capitulate! No, I will not! I will lead you on a wild goose chase! I will have an even better joke at your expense than you have had at mine."

And, summoning all his strength, but still feeling a certain amount of dread, he attempted to rise to his feet. He feared his own weakness, but he rejoiced when he saw that this weakness had passed, that it had only been a momentary attack of nerves, and not the onset of a serious illness. He felt light-hearted and at least superficially calm. He felt that he could think and put his plans into action.

Wild, fantastic plans flared in his head like flashes of lightning, but cool deliberation followed on the heels of every such plan, caught it in its flight, tore it apart the way a bird is ripped to pieces by a bullet, and cast it aside in shreds. And in the wake of those wild and fantastic plans that were like the final rockets of his retreating anxiety and agitation, more serious and practical thoughts gradually came to the fore.

"A foundation! I will set up a foundation! Let at least indigent people remember me with a kind word!" He kept repeating these words as if he wanted to confirm them in his memory, to nail them into his mind.

And he started planning how he would travel to Lviv, look up an old acquaintance who was a notary public, and make out his will. And his heart began to feel lighter, lighter and more at ease at the very thought that his money would not be wasted, that it would not pass into the hands of idlers who would just let it slip through their fingers.

But this satisfaction soon began to fade, to evaporate, and out of the dark chaos of his impressions new threats came to the fore. First, he would have to get to Lviv! It was almost two years since he had been there, and it was no easy matter for him, an old man, to make his way to the city! In whose care would he leave his living quarters? After all, his last trip had been made memorable, truly memorable, by the fact that he had been robbed.

Fr. Nestor, like all misers and avaricious money hoarders, was so consumed by the passion of collecting, accumulating, and saving, that he never could reach the point of making a proper accounting of his income and expenditures to have a clear idea as to how much wealth he actually had. On numerous occasions he had firmly resolved that the next day he would draw up an exact account, but a superstitious fear always stopped him from actually doing so. He never went beyond making a list of the numbers of his bankbooks and valuable documents; as for the money that he had on hand—the *chervintsi, *talyary, and other coins that he had tucked away in various nooks and crannies—he never could make himself do a proper job of counting it all up.

And thus it was that during his last trip to Lviv, a robber had broken into his lodgings; it was only because of the broken window pane and the broken lock on the cupboard that Fr. Nestor figured out that a stranger's hand had been at work in his home. What and how much this uninvited guest had taken from his quarters, he never could figure out exactly. It was only through a lot of investigative work and by making countless comparisons that he was able to determine that six bankbooks representing savings in the amount of 6000 guldens were missing—but beyond that, God only knows what had been taken.

Except for Lady Olimpiya, Fr. Nestor did not tell anyone the extent of his loss, and he begged her to keep the matter a secret and not spread the news around.

"The bankbooks will not do the robber any good," he said. "I have the numbers of the books, and I'll telegraph the bank today to notify them that my books were stolen—and that means they will not pay out the money to anyone, and if someone does show up to claim it, he will land in the custody of the police. But as for what else was stolen, well, it's, it's . . ." and Fr. Nestor gestured as if to say: God be with him, with that robber!

"He walked off with some small change," Fr. Nestor added, "it could not have been too much, for how much could he have found at my place! Well, there was also a silver watch—an old piece of junk! It's not worth making a fuss over it. But the most amusing part of the story is that he also took my boots, my new ones, not my old ones. Ha, ha, ha! If only he had known! . . ."

Fr. Nestor did not finish what he had started saying. He was embarrassed to admit that at the time he had a couple thousand ducats hidden in his old, mouldy, torn boots, whereas his new boots had absolutely nothing in them.

Lady Olimpiya truly did keep Fr. Nestor's secret about this robbery, but the matter was eventually divulged through no fault of hers.

And it was the new boots that revealed who the robber was.

One day, when Fr. Nestor least expected it, there was a knock on his door, and when he opened it, he saw a gendarme who had a shackled Tsvyakh in tow. Behind the gendarme stood the reeve and the bailiff, and behind them, a whole mob of people. The bailiff was holding Fr. Nestor's stolen boots. Tsvyakh had tried to sell them to a Jew in the village, but the boots had betrayed him, because Fr. Nestor's name had been stitched with green thread on the inner legging. Tsvyakh, who was illiterate, could not have anticipated the betrayal, but the Jew, realizing in a flash what was going on, turned him in to the gendarme.

Even now Fr. Nestor still got the chills whenever he recalled the scene that transpired in his living quarters at that time. He had been forced to admit in front of everyone that he had been robbed; he had to report the numbers of the stolen bankbooks, state the amount of cash that had been taken—not knowing the exact sum, he had reported a small amount, a few hundred guldens—and provide a description of the watch. He trembled visibly during the entire hearing, and when he spoke, he writhed and faltered to a much greater degree than the thief, who swore that he had not stolen anything other than the boots.

And truly, although a thorough search of Tsvyakh's home did not turn up so much as a shred of evidence of his having taken anything else, his story about how the robbery took place was nevertheless highly fantastic and improbable.

If one were to believe Tsvyakh, he had happened to steal the boots quite by accident, without planning to do so. He did admit to prowling under Fr. Nestor's windows at night, and he had no explanation as to what he had been looking for. But as he was crawling under the windows, he suddenly heard a thump in the room. He cried out in surprise—and at that moment a figure jumped through the open window, saw him in the grass, and threw the boots at him, almost knocking out his eyes with their heels. And Tsvyakh tearfully pointed to a huge, livid bruise under his eye.

But everyone who heard his story, instead of sympathizing with him, just roared with laughter at his account of his misadventure, and the reeve slapped him on the back and said: "Oh, Tsvyakh, Tsvyakh. If you're going to tell lies, you should at least try to come up with something that's a bit more credible!"

Tsvyakh was beaten by the gendarme, who tried to make him confess, but he did not admit to anything. He was taken to Lviv and sentenced to a year and a half in prison. After serving his time, he returned to the village, but his punishment did little to ease Fr. Nestor's mind.

The bankbooks seemed to have disappeared off the face of the earth; it was clear that Tsvyakh did not have any disposable cash, and as for the watch—the police in Lviv found it in the shop of a goldsmith who bought it as an antique from another Jew who, in turn, had bought it from a gentleman who had been passing through *Chernivtsi. The trail ended there, and thus Fr. Nestor, in addition to the financial loss that he sustained, came out of this sad experience with a firm conviction that he had acquired a new enemy in Tsvyakh, a man who had nothing to lose, and who was prepared to take risks and perpetrate the most heinous deeds.

After this incident, and especially after Tsvyakh's return from prison, Fr. Nestor introduced various precautions, kept coming up with new schemes, and implemented many different strategies in an attempt to outsmart and lead astray the thieves that he anticipated.

He continually changed the hiding places for his money, never kept large sums in one spot, made several lists of his valuable documents, and hid every list in a different location— usually where one would least expect such lists to be kept; he instituted a variety of secret procedures with the locks on the cupboards and on the wardrobe drawers—in a word, he initiated a formal, very complicated strategy to thwart imaginary thieves. All this strategizing became the consuming focus of his elderly, impoverished existence, but even though it kept his mind and nerves in a constant state of agitation and tension, it did not always protect his money from the piercing eyes and grasping hands of people the likes of Hadyna.

There were times when either Hadyna or one of the other servants happened to see Fr. Nestor hiding money in one of the secret spots, usually not too large a sum, often just a few guldens, and always less than a hundred guldens. Of course, whenever that happened, Fr. Nestor did not recover his money from that particular cache; however, except for a momentary pang of regret, the loss did not cause him too much grief, and he never raised a ruckus about the pilfered amounts, partly because he feared that people might realize that he had a lot of money, and partly because he feared that the thief, if he were found, would join the ranks of his enemies.

Demenyuk was the only one who, after coming across hiding spots a couple of times in the orchard, would, without saying a word, bring the money he found to Fr. Nestor, and the priest, also saying nothing, would shamefacedly accept it and then hide it in another, safer place.

Fr. Nestor recalled all of this as he, in turn, sat by the open window and then stood up again, while laying a daring plan as to what he should do next to shield himself from an even worse incident, one that—and he felt this with his whole being—threatened him from the people who surrounded him.

"I must do everything that I can! And first of all I must make a detailed account of everything that I have. After all, the money no longer belongs to me. It belongs to the foundation that I am managing, so I must know what I am managing and exactly how much the beneficiaries might expect from me."

No superstitious fear hindered him now from tallying his wealth. Nevertheless, precautions still had to be taken! Fr. Nestor closed the window and drew a linen curtain over it, and then he began taking out wads of paper bills, small packets, bundles, bags, and coins rolled in paper from the cupboard, from pockets in his clothing, from various piles of old papers, from wardrobe drawers, from under the oven, from the oven itself, and from all sorts of likely and unlikely hiding places. He put everything in a heap on the table, and then, tired out and sweaty from all the walking and crawling that this task had involved, collapsed in an armchair by the table, breathing heavily and wiping the perspiration from his forehead.

After catching his breath, he slowly and carefully began untying the packets, unwrapping the rolled coins, sorting and separating into categories the bankbooks, the bonds, the lottery tickets, the shares, the ducats, and all the other coins. The entire table was covered with a mound of paper and metal—a sight that would make many a banker envious of this unassuming, unkempt, shabbily dressed old priest.

Once everything was organized, Fr. Nestor took a piece of paper and began listing—carefully, clearly, and in a definite order—every category of these valuable items. This task took quite a while; two hours elapsed by the time he finished listing everything and figuring out the total value of his fortune.

After slowly counting it all up, he read the final figure silently, barely moving his thin bloodless lips. He read it and then, without taking his eyes off the paper, appeared to turn numb. He read the figure once again, and then tried to read it aloud, as if he could not believe that what he saw was true.

"Two . . . two hundred and f-f-f . . . fifty . . . thousand," he whispered softly, fixing his widely staring eyes at an empty space in front of him. "Two hundred and fifty thousand—a quarter of a million! No, I never would have thought that it amounted to that much! I never would have dreamed it! If someone had told me that, I never would have believed it! But all the same . . . that's what it is. The tally is absolutely accurate—numbers do not lie! So that's how it is! That is what they are whetting their teeth for!"

And suddenly, alarming thoughts once again emerged like black clouds on the horizon of his imagination.

"Oh, she must have some idea, she must know how much money I have! She may not know exactly, but she can guess. That's why she has been ingratiating herself with me all these long years; like a spider spinning a fine web, she has been imperceptibly weaving a mesh around me until she made me her serf, her slave—a helpless, but highly desirable prey!

"O God, O God! Along what byways, along what twisting paths You have led me—in Your righteous anger You have led me—until You forced me to recognize my fall from grace, my calamitous misfortune!"

And he closed his eyes, held his breath, and looked deeply within himself, into his memories, into the past. Somewhere in the depths of his brain there flashed, like two embers, the passionate eyes of the Countess, the young Lady Olimpiya, and the marvellously beautiful features of her face—her lips, her nose, were clearly delineated—and her curly golden hair gave off an aroma, a fragrance that had so captivated his heart back then. But today he shuddered at those memories. That had been the beginning of his misfortune! It had been the sweet potion that, having tasted it once, poisoned his entire life.

From the moment when those shining eyes met his gaze in the wing of the Count's manor that had been transformed into a school, this woman had become the bane of his existence, his ill-fated star that had caused him an untold amount of torment and suffering; like rust eating into iron, it had eroded his youthful feelings and aspirations, paralysed the powers of his soul, destroyed his capabilities, gagged his hopes, gnawed and ravaged everything that made him a real man, covered his soul with spittle, with recollections of sinful desires and sinful deeds—and what was the point of it all?

What was her goal? At first, there probably was no goal, just the powerful fatalism inherent in a woman's nature, and then— oh, and then that fatalism became a conscious demonism! "This woman—she is my evil spirit, she is the devil-temptress that leads a man to his downfall with flattering words only to mock him, to trample him in the mud, to gain power over him!"

Fr. Nestor was still sitting at the table, leaning on it with his elbows and covering his closed eyes with his hands. He was shaking violently as he looked with the eyes of his imagination into the shining eyes of Countess Torska, eyes that now gleamed before him incessantly, stubbornly drilling him to the depths of his soul, just as they had drilled him back then, in the fatal moment of his greatest downfall.

"Demon! Demon! Demon!" the word whirled in his head. "She is no ordinary woman—she truly is a witch. It is no wonder that the people in the village say that she sucks human blood! Has she not sucked out all of mine? Has she not caused me to lose all my powers? Is she not preparing to gobble me up to the very last iota? O Lord, save me from this evil spirit! Help me extricate myself from this abyss, so that I might breathe freely at least once, so that I might right the wrongs perpetrated by my sinful life!"

He leapt to his feet, and with feverish haste and twice his usual strength, began stuffing his money into all sorts of hiding places. He had not finished stashing away even half of it when a loud knocking at his door interrupted the silence and threw him into utter confusion.

He jumped up in fear, looked at the heaps of paper and money on the table and, realizing the impossibility of hiding it all in a single moment, was at a loss as to what he should do.

Should he pretend that he was sleeping and not answer? But what if it was someone who had come to see him with an evil purpose in mind and, not hearing his voice, would grow emboldened and make his way inside? Before he could call out for help, it would be too late. He decided to respond, but first he grabbed a sheet from the cupboard and flung it over the table so that it covered the money, and on top of the sheet he threw a pillow, and then an old cassock.

"I'll say that I'm tidying up my room, and I won't let anyone touch anything . . . I won't let anyone in here, I'll close the door to this room . . . If someone needs something, let him go into the kitchen and talk to me there . . ."

The knocking resounded a second and a third time before Fr. Nestor, having succeeded in hiding the more important traces of what he had been doing, finally got up the courage to go into the kitchen, carefully shutting the door behind him.

"Well, who is it? Who is there?" he called out when the knocking sounded once again, firm, but not overly loud.

"It's me, Father!"

"Me who?"

"It's me, Demenyuk."

"What do you want?"

"Perhaps your Reverence could open the door? Perhaps you need something, and I could . . ."

Fr. Nestor calmed down. Demenyuk's voice, that he had not recognized in his confusion, was like cool water that slaked his thirst. Demenyuk was the only person he did not fear, but he had never betrayed the secret of his wealth even to him.

"Well, you were certainly knocking up a storm, Yurko!" Fr. Nestor said by way of a gentle reproach when Demenyuk came into the kitchen and bowed to him. "I was dozing, and then suddenly I heard a noise, as if canons were booming. I was terrified; I thought that there might be a revolution breaking out in the village."

"Please forgive me, your Reverence," Demenyuk said in a troubled tone. "I didn't mean to do that, I swear I didn't mean to! But—your Reverence knows my nature . . . I can't get that foolish daughter of mine out of my head . . . And these last few days something has been weighing heavily on my heart; I can't rid myself of the foreboding that God will send a great misfortune down upon me."

"Come now, Demenyuk! It is a sin to talk that way!" Fr. Nestor responded, even though he believed in feelings, dreams, and portents no less than Demenyuk. "It is not right that we sinners rush ahead and try to anticipate God's judgments. God will send us whatever He wishes, and we must accept what He sends and endure it."

"I am not saying anything against that, if it please your Reverence. If we are meant to suffer, then there's nothing more to be said—it is His will. But I really do not know what to think about Malanka. The girl has changed completely during these past few weeks."

"Have no fear, Yurko! It only seems that way to you, but nothing has happened to her."

"Oh, your Reverence! I know her! She is not the same as she used to be. There is something seething within her."

"Now, now, Yurko! You are exaggerating your concerns, and it is all for nothing. Malanka spoke to me as if she were in the confessional . . . She has never lied to me . . ."

"But you can't believe her any more! And we can convince ourselves of that right now! I'm just coming from the blacksmith's home. Something made me go there to talk to her again. When I got there—they told me she wasn't there. That she ran off right after dinner, saying that she was going to see the old priest."

"To see me?"

"That's right! She said: 'His Reverence told me to come to see him. He wants to discuss something with me.' And off she went. And so I came here and woke your Reverence to ask . . ."

"But she wasn't here! I haven't laid eyes on her after I talked to her over there, in the blacksmith's orchard."

"Well, you see! You see! Woe is me with that girl, woe is me!" Demenyuk said, not so much speaking, as groaning.

"Now, now, Yurko, it is not such a terrible worry as yet. She may have gone to visit her girlfriends, to spend some time with them, to chat with them . . ."

"I know that, if it please your Reverence!" Demenyuk said hurriedly. "All that may be true! But why is she lying? That is what alarms me. After all, you know how I raised her. She never lied. Whether it was something bad, or something good—she always told me everything; but now, to go out of her way to tell a lie like this—it has never happened before. And there is no need for it now. After all, the blacksmith treats her like his own child. If she wanted to go for a walk or visit with her girlfriends, it is not likely that he would forbid it. Why lie, and drag you into the lie as well?"

Fr. Nestor comforted Demenyuk as best he could, although it was evident that his words were not flowing from his heart, from a true conviction. His lips were mouthing the words, emitting the usual trite phrases, but his mind was dashing off in another direction and, like a drowning man, grabbed at a straw that happened to come along with the current.

And suddenly he changed. No longer calm, drowsy, and phlegmatic, he became animated, started trembling, began gesticulating and rushing about, rapidly blurting out words that did not touch upon either Malanka or Demenyuk, but on his own worries and problems.

"Just imagine, Yurko! I have also lied to you! Yes I have, may the Lord forgive me my transgression—I lied. I said that you had awoken me, but that is not true. There is no way that I can sleep, Yurko! A terrible misfortune is crushing me! A calamity is threatening me—may the Lord prevent it—a real calamity!"

"What is it that your Reverence is imagining?" Demenyuk asked in a gentle voice, as if he were speaking to a capricious, helpless child. "What kind of a calamity?"

"Oh, I am not imagining anything, Yurko, no, I am not! Just listen to what happened to me today. In the morning the Lady herself brought me my coffee. I was surprised, but something in my heart throbbed, as if whispering to me: be on guard. And truly, she sat down and initiated a conversation. She alluded to this and to that, like a cat circling a piece of suet, until she finally came out with the fact that her dear son needs money, and a lot of money at that!"

"Rumour has it that the young Lord is planning to wed a very rich woman."

"That's it, that's it! She also went on and on about that marriage. Well, I don't believe it, Yurko. But then—let him get married if he wants to; I just don't feel like giving him any money. And so at dinner she came right out and said that I was obligated to leave all my money to her and her son."

"She actually said that?"

"Said it?" Fr, Nestor shouted. "No, she did not just say it, she yelled, threatened, attacked me like a wild beast—she and that honourable son of hers. And then they both said to me: 'Your fortune belongs to us and it has to be ours, no matter what you think.'"

"Well, the Countess has long since been spreading the news in the village that in your will you are leaving all your wealth to the young Lord."

"Is that so? Well, I'll show her that she is trumpeting that news too soon. Listen, Yurko! I have decided to set up a foundation with my money, so that the interest that it earns will be used to help indigent people."

"Well, that's fine and good, but who will look after it once you're gone?"

"What do you mean: who? The vice-regency. I will place the money in the government coffers with those instructions."

"Well, may the Lord help you! It certainly would be a memorial . . ."

"But you know what, Yurko? I do not feel safe here. I cannot feel secure here a moment longer. It is obvious that the two of them—you know?" and Fr. Nestor leaned in more closely to Demenyuk and whispered, almost in his ear: "It is obvious that they are lying in wait for my death."

"Oh, no! No, no! May God forbid! That is the worst, the most heinous thing they could do!" Demenyuk cried.

"No it isn't, Yurko!" Fr. Nestor continued whispering. "I fear that it is not the worst! I fear that they are prepared to go even further. You know, until today, I never would have believed it for anything in the world. But now, after I heard what they said, when I saw the wild expression in their eyes, their bestial greed for blood, their shameless equanimity in the face of human suffering—oh, Yurko! May God spare me from seeing anything more! It makes one feel revulsion for human nature! And so now I can expect anything, anything from them."

"O Lord God!" Demenyuk cried, totally disconcerted. But after a moment he added: "No, your Reverence! It can't be. You must be ill. There are a lot of things that can be imputed to the Countess and the young Lord, but to say that they could do something like that—no! I'll never believe it. It simply isn't possible."

"It may or may not be possible, but I do not feel safe here. I am afraid."

"Well, it's unlikely that anything can happen to you in the daytime, and at night, if you wish, I can sleep nearby, here, in the kitchen."

"No, no, no!" Fr. Nestor gestured negatively; despite his fear, it had never once occurred to him to allow another person, even someone like Demenyuk, to spend the night with him in his lodgings. "That is not the point! That will not help. Would you be able to protect me if something were to happen?"

"Well, but still, two people are better than one. Not everyone will dare to attack two people at a time, but when it's only one person, especially someone like you, it's another matter altogether."

"No, Yurko! It won't work that way; that's no good! It would be better if I did something else! Do you know what I am thinking?"

"Well, what is it?"

Fr. Nestor once again leaned in closely to Demenyuk's ear, and even though there was not another living soul nearby and no one could hear them, he whispered very faintly and very secretively: "I am going to flee from here."

"Where to?"

"Anywhere. To any peasant's home, just to spend the night. And then, tomorrow, I'll be on my way! I'll go to Lviv, and once I am there, I'll manage just fine."

Demenyuk shook his head doubtfully. "It won't be easy to do that. And in which peasant's home will you feel safer than you are here? Don't you know what our people are like?"

"What about at Herder's place?"

"What? At Herder's? At the blacksmith's?" Demenyuk cried in astonishment. "You'd want to move to Herder's place?"

"Well, what if I actually did that? What do you think: would he chase me out of his house?"

"The blacksmith? Herder? Oh, God forbid! And if he found out what you're planning to do with your money, he would kiss your hands and feet!"

"There would be no reason to do that, because after all, he was the one who gave me the idea during our conversation today. So, you know what, Yurko? Let's not waste any time. Run over to the blacksmith's place and tell him what I have decided to do. Ask him if he will accept me into his home for a day or two. But maybe he will be scared about what the Countess will say, because she certainly will not thank him for it."

"Have no fear as far as that goes. Herder is not dependent on anyone's favour, and he does not fear anyone's anger. I can tell you that much even without asking him."

"Well, if that is the case, so much the better. Go and ask him. And as soon as he agrees to find me a corner in his house . . ."

"They will find you a private room there, a nice large one, with a separate entrance."

"So much the better! So much the better! If he agrees, find me a horse and wagon at once, or better yet, a couple of horses, so that all my furniture and belongings can be taken to my new living quarters."

Still unable to recover from his astonishment, Demenyuk shuffled off from Fr. Nestor's place. He simply could not believe that Fr. Nestor truly intended to flee from the manor, to abandon Lady Olimpiya; he could not believe that the priest's fear was justified and that either the Countess or her son could have any evil designs on him.

And so, pondering what he had heard, he walked slowly, with such an expression of uncertainty, that any passer-by who saw him would inevitably have thought: what is troubling this man?

Even before she saw Demenyuk, Lady Olimpiya had been wondering what Fr. Nestor would do next.

After his departure she began to have some regrets about her outburst. Like a black, swallow-tailed kite, she watched intently everything that was going on in the yard, keeping her eyes on the door of the annex that led to Fr. Nestor's living quarters. She saw Demenyuk walk up to the door and knock soundly on it for a good minute or so until it was opened, and then she lived through agonies of curiosity and uncertainty until she saw Demenyuk finally come out into the yard again.

She guessed right away that they must have talked about her and conferred about something that she should be aware of. Demenyuk's appearance, the preoccupied expression on his face, and his hesitant gait convinced her of this, and at the same time it gave her reason to hope that it would not be difficult to find out everything from this man if the right approach was used. She was well aware of Demenyuk's good, honest, and forthright nature, and she figured out immediately that it would be easiest to attain her goal by appealing to those qualities.

When Demenyuk was passing by her window, she opened a pane and called out to him.

Demenyuk stopped, but did not draw nearer; he was deliberating, debating in his own mind whether or not he should meet with the Lady.

"Come in, Demenyuk," the Lady said graciously. "I have something I want to tell you."

"Well, you see, I . . . I'll be at your Lady's service right away, but first I have to . . . I have to do a small favour for his Reverence . . ."

"That's fine, that's fine! I won't keep you long, and I'm sure that your matter will wait. Come in, come in! Surely you're not afraid of me!"

"What a thing to say, my gracious Lady!" Demenyuk said in a strained voice and, seeing no way out, he entered Lady Olympia's living quarters.

"Just imagine how worried I am, Demenyuk!" Lady Olimpiya began speaking with a most sincere and anxious look, as if she were a mother talking about an ailing child. "I don't know what has happened to his Reverence. Has he fallen ill, or what? He is convinced that I am determined to get my hands on his fortune, that I want him to leave everything to my son and me, and God only knows what else he has dreamed up! But—as God is my witness—a thought like that has never crossed my mind!

"And I do not even know if Fr. Nestor has any real wealth. I only know that when he was robbed he complained about it to me. Well, as you know, that money was never found, and as to whether he has any more, I swear to God that I do not know. Am I about to covet someone else's wealth? And do I need it? Thank God I have enough of my own, enough to live out my life. And even if God took what I have away from me, I have two brothers, veritable princes, who possess great wealth; they are great lords, and it goes without saying that I could find shelter with one of them. And my sister is also married to a rich lord, and she has asked me more than once to leave Torky, rent it out, and live with her. But I do not want to. I have grown accustomed to living modestly, simply, and within my own means. And I am not from a family that would desire what belongs to someone else.

"And so tell me, Demenyuk, what am I to do? What am I supposed to say to his Reverence to dispel his ill will towards me? I do not know if someone has said things about me to him, or if he had a bad dream, or if it is simply because he is growing old—but I swear to God that I have not given him any reason for thoughts like that. Why, you yourself know, because you have seen it for yourself—do I not look after him, do I not take care of him, do I not treat him like a member of my own family? And this is how he repays me! He is showing his gratitude with all sorts of suspicions!"

Words flowed out of Lady Olimpiya's lips like an unstoppable torrent. She had planned her speech ahead of time, and she mustered her strength to present it, to deliver it according to the rules of the actor's art, to forestall Demenyuk's observations, to stir his nobler feelings, to disarm him completely.

And truly, the old man was left standing in the midst of all those words as if he were caught in a hailstorm, not knowing what to do, not able to come up with a solitary independent thought, and so he let himself be swept away by the turbulent torrent.

And when Lady Olimpiya, looking distressed and troubled to the depths of her soul, uttered her final words and raised a handkerchief to her eyes as if wiping away tears, Demenyuk could have sworn that Fr. Nestor truly had overblown his fear, that he had dreamt up a danger that had no basis in reality, and that he was suffering needlessly because of the machinations of his own sick mind.

"The Countess should not take it all so much to heart," he said, trying to calm her. "His Reverence is very old, and he has many odd quirks. I do not think this will last very long."

"I am not angry, and I am not complaining," Lady Olimpiya said in a tone that conveyed heartfelt good will. "O my Lord! I am not at all concerned about myself, but I am truly concerned that this irrational fear that has taken hold of Fr. Nestor may prompt him to do something rash. After all, you yourself know that he is like a child, helpless, vulnerable, and that anyone who wishes to do so can fool him, rob him, brazenly fleece him in broad daylight.

"While he is at my place, he makes light of anything like that happening to him. But he has no idea how much effort I put into taking care of him, protecting him so that no harm will come to him. Even at the time that he was robbed—and God only knows, was he really robbed? Is he likely to tell anyone how much of anything he actually has? He claimed that his bankbooks were taken, and then he began listing them and looking for them in his hiding spots, and it turned out that he had all of them. But it caused me so much unpleasantness, so much trouble, so much fuss and bother!"

"That's what I told his Reverence as well, that he is scaring himself for no good reason," Demenyuk, moved by the Lady's recounting, began to say slowly. "But he insists that it isn't so. He refuses to listen."

"Yes, that's just how it is! Once he gets something into his head . . ."

"He keeps on repeating the same thing: 'I am afraid of that Lady! I do not feel safe here.'"

"You see! You see! He has lived here safely for ten years, never had a misadventure, and now he suddenly cannot feel safe here! Would a man in his right mind say something like that?"

"Well, it did seem to me that he wasn't all that well. All of a sudden he tells me to go to the blacksmith—you know, my Lady, to Herder, the one who live on the outskirts of the village—and ask him if he would rent him a room."

"So that's how it is!" the Lady cried. "So he has decided to run away from me! And to flee to none other than that heretic, to Herder! Well, my dear Father—you can do whatever you like and say whatever you like, but I will not allow that to happen!"

The Lady said this in a firm, resolute tone—a tone that contrasted so jarringly with the plaintive and gentle sincerity marking her speech to that point that it made Demenyuk shudder. It was only then that he sensed that perhaps Fr. Nestor's fear of this woman was not all that foolish and paranoid, and that under her mask of kindness and generosity, she truly was concealing other plans. But before he could figure out what to do next, Lady Olimpiya almost shoved him out the door, locked up her living quarters, and ran directly to Fr. Nestor's lodgings.

Demenyuk remained standing in the yard as if thunderstruck. He sensed that he had committed a grave error in betraying to the Lady the priest's intention of moving. He felt terribly discomfited and ashamed at having allowed Lady Olimpiya to lead him on like that, and he simply did not know what he should do next: if he should go to the blacksmith's home and convey Fr. Nestor's message to him, or wait and see how the conversation between the priest and Lady Olimpiya would end.

After a long minute, he decided to wait and, hesitating and looking carefully all around, he walked back slowly, with an uncertain gait, towards the annex where Fr. Nestor lived. There was no one in the yard. On the one hand, a powerful force pulled Demenyuk to the door of the wing that led to Fr. Nestor's living quarters, but on the other hand, he felt ashamed to listen in on what was being said in there.

After sending Demenyuk on his way, Fr. Nestor, feeling a trifle calmer, once again got down to the task of stashing his money in secret hiding places. He had almost finished when he heard the door leading from the entranceway to his kitchen being opened. He grew alarmed, and only then recalled that, in his haste to see Demenyuk leave, he had forgotten to lock the door. Stuffing the remaining money and lists in his pocket, he hastened towards the door to see who had come in; the sound of rapid footsteps making their way across the kitchen towards his room frightened him.

But before he knew it, the door to his room opened with a creak, and the figure of Lady Olimpiya appeared in the doorway. Her eyes gleamed even more intensely than they usually did, her face was flushed both from the haste with which she had walked and her inner agitation, and thunderbolts hovered on her authoritative, tightly closed lips.

"Father! Father!" she said without the usual greetings and salutations. "What is this that you are planning to do?"

"Huh? What is this? Is it you, my Lady?" the terrified Fr. Nestor babbled as he seized the arm of a chair and positioned himself so that the chair stood between him and the Lady.

"Oh, so you no longer even recognize me!" Lady Olimpiya said, smiling coldly and, without waiting for an invitation from Fr. Nestor, sat down at the table and began casting her eyes about the room.

"So, you're moving, are you?" she fired off abruptly.

Fr. Nestor shuddered violently, his thin lips turned chalk white, his breath stopped in his throat, and he could not reply.

"Listen, Father!" the Lady spoke sternly and decisively. "Do not act foolishly! Do not go looking for trouble in your old age! Did I spend the last ten years looking after you, caring for you as I would care for a child, a member of my own family, just to have you create a scandal of this nature now? Surely you must know that your flight from me—yes, your flight, because everyone will say that you did not leave my place without reason to move to the home of the heretic-blacksmith—that your flight from me will ruin my reputation! It will be a devastating blow both for my son and for me! It will give evil tongues a reason to come up with all sorts of tales and gossip! Am I truly so odious and despicable that you would prefer to live at some old peasant's house, or to put it more crudely, out in the street, rather than in my home?"

Fr. Nestor shook uncontrollably as he listened to these words and, shrivelled like a withered leaf, could barely hang on to the arm of the chair with his trembling hands to stop himself from collapsing on the floor.

Lady Olimpiya, seeing his confusion, started speaking a little more gently.

"No, your Reverence, it is not nice of you to do that! It is ingratitude! After all, I am not hounding you for your fortune! If you do not want to leave it to Adas—it is up to you. I am not forcing you to do so. Just do not create a scandal! I understand that you might need more amenities, more care than you have here. I truly regret that my financial capabilities do not allow me to provide them for you. But in any event, it is not proper for you to flee from me to a peasant's house, because there you will not have even as much as you have here. If you so desire, then move to Lviv. I do not forbid you to do so. On the contrary, I am prepared to do all that I can, to help you find an apartment, servants . . . There you will have everything that you need. I do not want you to flee, as if from robber's den, from a home that took you in . . . that you formerly . . ."

Lady Olimpiya did not finish what she was saying. Her own words touched her deeply. She sobbed, and began wiping the tears from her eyes with a handkerchief.

"But my gr-gr-gr- gracious . . ." Fr. Nestor, stuttering and barely able to get out his words, began to say, but Lady Olimpiya motioned him sternly to be silent.

"Be quiet!" she shouted through her tears. "You are a wicked man! An ungrateful man! Just because of some whim, to deeply wound a woman's heart, to cause pain and humiliation to a woman who . . . when it comes down to it . . . does not deserve that from you—all that means nothing to you! To flee from me! And where to? To Herder! What is Herder to you? In what way is he closer to you? How has he earned your trust? Well, speak up! Tell me! Perhaps I can learn a thing or two from him."

Stuttering and faltering, Fr. Nestor once more tried to make excuses, to beg her forgiveness.

Lady Olimpiya listened to his babbling for a moment, and then interrupted him again. "Well, that's enough, Fr. Nestor! Enough! Give me your hand! Let's forget about all this! I am not as evil as you think. But you must abandon all thoughts of moving away from my home. Whoever saw the likes of it—to treat me this way, huh?"

Fr. Nestor, extended his hand unwillingly, hesitantly. Lady Olimpiya pressed it warmly and, without releasing it, continued speaking: "So, we have reached an agreement, haven't we? You will stay at my place until such time as I can find you a cozy nook in Lviv . . . Come now, cheer up! Stop frowning! Sit down here beside me!"

And Lady Olimpiya almost forced him to sit down in the armchair beside her, and once again took hold of his hand.

"O Lord, to think that such a fate awaited the two of us! Right, Father? If someone had predicted it back then, when we—you remember—kissed for the first time in that improvised classroom in the wing of my father's manor! Or the time that I hid in the jasmine bushes, and when you came walking down the road deep in thought, I jumped out at you, covered your eyes with my hands, and scared you, and then had to revive you with my kisses! Do you remember all that? It's true that in recalling those golden moments today they seem more like something out of *A Thousand and One Nights*, like something from another world, a brighter, purer, better world."

"Why . . . why is my gracious Lady recalling all that?" Fr. Nestor barely whispered, gently removing his hand from her grip and covering his face. "We both sinned . . . We transgressed natural boundaries with our love . . . And we have paid a heavy penalty for doing so . . ."

"No, no, no! Don't say that!" Lady Olimpiya said fervently. "That can never be! Our love was not sinful. God did not place any natural boundaries between people! As a priest, you should be well aware of that. But I do know one thing: you lead too solitary a life. You require more diversions, more company. No, Father, do not turn away from me! If there is to be harmony between us, then you must do this for me. I will not leave you here alone. My son and his friends are to join me shortly for tea. Come with me! You'll distract yourself, refresh yourself by mingling with young people, and we'll converse for a while!"

Fr. Nestor wanted to object, but Lady Olimpiya did not give him an opportunity to say anything. Her evil and gloomy mood had changed into an animated cheerfulness. She helped Fr. Nestor put on a fresh cassock, and almost forcibly, without taking her hands off him, dragged him away with herself, locking the door to his lodgings and putting the key in his pocket.

Demenyuk, who was waiting by the door, saw them go into the yard together. Seeing the triumphant look on Lady Olimpiya's face and the fresh cassock on Fr. Nestor, he understood that there would be no more talk about a move, and so he shuffled silently into the orchard.

VIII

Lady Olimpiya's parlour was filled with chatter, the clinking of forks and knives on plates, and loud bursts of laughter followed by even louder remarks that, in turn, were interrupted by shouts of agreement or disagreement.

There were more people present than Adas had foreseen. There was Edzo Chapsky—the brother of Adas's fiancée—and three young landowners: *Lord Tadey Rozvadynsky, a friend from his student days at the Vienna Theresianum; *Lord Alfons Dzyerzhykray who had completed his doctorate in Vienna and was preparing for a political career; and *Lord Emil Dolenga who had not finished high school, lived with his wealthy father, and travelled periodically to Lviv to imbibe the urban atmosphere.

In addition, there was Edzo's younger brother who had just graduated from an agricultural school in Dublyany; and a *Lord Kalyasanty—well known in landowning circles under this name that, although not his real name, was supposed to characterize his Armenian roots—a wealthy man, thickset, thirty-five years of age, a connoisseur of horses and equestrian sports, who had suddenly felt a yen for writing and journalism, and who, for more than a year now, had helped to steer opinion in a certain aristocratically-democratic daily newspaper.

Rather surprisingly, to this august noble gathering was added a certain plebe, but one whose presence, it is to be understood, did not embarrass this select company in the slightest. He was one of the more highly regarded lawyers in Lviv, and even though his surname, Vasong, spoke clearly of his peasant origins, his bearing and appearance bespoke a most elegant and proper gentleman, and his convictions—a full-blooded aristocrat.

Lady Olimpiya felt elated and completely at ease in this company. At first, her housewifely heart had experienced a pang of alarm at the sight of the three hansoms in which her guests had arrived: she feared that there would not be enough food to host them properly. But her concerns lasted only a moment. She had a brief conversation with Hapka, and a campaign strategy was laid out.

Now the visit was well underway, and the Lady could see that her guests were fully engaged. This knowledge heightened and increased her joy, an intense, quiet joy that sprang from being with her own kind, from revelling in the impeccably noble nature of the company.

Moreover, her maternal heart delighted in the fact that Adas held his own in this company, treated everybody as his equal and, in a few cases (e.g. with *Dublyanchyk and Dr. Vasong) even assumed the role of someone older and superior, and it was obvious to her that he had everyone's respect and warm affection.

It was only Fr. Nestor who stuck out in this company like a crow among pheasants. After the initial introductions, at which time all of the guests had shaken his hand, a few of them had attempted to exchange a few words with him, but then everyone abandoned him, so he settled into a corner of a sofa and, with his hands folded on his knees and his bloodless lips champing softly and incessantly, he appeared to be either drowsing or thinking deeply about something.

Lady Olimpiya went up to him several times, sat down beside him, talked briefly about this or that. He replied politely, but did not budge or mingle with the company, nor did he participate in the general discussion.

"What am I, an old man, to say!" he said, gesturing helplessly. "What can I say that they . . . that is . . . I beg my gracious Lady not to concern herself about me . . . I'll just . . . listen . . . It's all very interesting . . ."

But it appeared that Lady Olimpiya wanted something more. A short while later, she came up to him with Edzo Chapsky, and it seemed that she had told the young man quite a lot about

Fr. Nestor; but Edzo had no desire to get to know the silent old priest any better and, after uttering a few banal phrases about the attractive countryside and the ancient orchard in the Torsky manor, *polecił się*, i.e. took wing and flew back to his companions.

Nevertheless, the presence of the taciturn and apparently drowsing priest did not spoil the harmony and good humour of the gathering. When they arrived, they had all been in a happy frame of mind, and after drinking a tumbler of whiskey to wash down the dust from the road (even though, coming as they did from Adas's manor where they had already had dinner, not much dust had settled on them) and then a cup of black coffee, they sat in the parlour and rested for a while near the open windows.

It was a hot day, and at three o'clock in the afternoon it was impossible to find adequate shade even in the orchard; in the salon, however, a slight breeze blew in through the open door and windows, and it was cooler. At first the conversation was sluggish. The guests puffed on their cigars, and some of them, resting their elbows on the arms of their chairs, rocked contentedly and exhaled clouds of smoke.

It was only Lady Olimpiya who bustled about here and there, giving orders to the servants, turning Adas's attention to something, adjusting things on the table, or starting up a conversation with this or that lord. She was acquainted with all who were present, except for Dublyanchyk. It is to be understood that she devoted the most attention to Edzo and this young lord, as they were the brothers of the young lady that she—no less than Adas himself—wanted to see her son marry.

Like a virtuoso who seems to let his fingers fall involuntarily on the keyboard, but who always knows how to evoke harmonious sounds from the keys, so she too—as she circulated among the guests and animated the gathering with her movements, her presence—knew how to approach the two Chapsky gentlemen.

She knew how to unobtrusively, and always at the most appropriate moment, provide them—most delicately and, it would appear, most naively and unintentionally, without exactly telling them, without even making allusions—with a representation of both Adas and herself, their dispositions, their tastes, the state of their fortune etc., anything that she thought might serve her purpose and be of greatest interest to them. With Dublyanchyk, the younger brother, she had embarked on a conversation about the local harvest but, noting that he enjoyed hunting, she told him about the abundance of wildlife in her son's forest and related the hunting adventures of her late husband.

The older Chapsky, Edzo, was of a more practical nature. He displayed, according to his parents, a true genius for finances, had graduated from a business institute in Vienna, and now worked in a bank in Lviv—not out of need, but to gain experience in banking matters, all the while pulling down a hefty salary. He was interested in everything: the economic situation of the peasants and neighbouring landlords, the natural wealth of the soil, the cottage industries, and matters of credit. Lady Olimpiya found it quite difficult to carry on a conversation with him, and she kept trying to steer the discussion in another direction by making adroit inquiries about the Chapsky family.

At one time she had known his parents quite well, and had even been on friendly terms with his mother, but she had not had the pleasure of seeing them for many years . . .

"The years have just slipped by, filled with family misadventures . . . the lengthy illness of the late Count . . . the rearing of a son . . . worries related to running the estate," she said with a sigh. "Oh, how happy I would be to see your mother! What a beauty she was! And what a heart of gold she had!" she added in a sincere tone of voice.

Edzo said that his mother and his sister Lyusya were going to be in Lviv any day now, and he suggested that perhaps the Countess might come to see them. Lviv was not far away, and her brief absence would not likely affect the running of the estate.

Lady Olimpiya received this information with great joy and gave her word that she would most certainly come "to warmly greet and kiss" his dear mother Miltsya and her lovely daughter. "Oh, I've heard that the daughter takes after the mother, that she charms everyone with her beauty, that she displays extraordinary capabilities! No, regardless of anything else, I must go to Lviv and renew a friendship that is so dear to me!"

Even though Edzo was an economist and a financier, he was genuinely charmed by the heartfelt sincerity and the depth of the noble feelings that Lady Olimpiya revealed.

Gradually the conversation in the salon grew livelier, louder, and more inclusive. It was the two senior and most respectable men among those who were present (not counting, of course, Dr. Vasong, who never vied for a leading role in such company and who, in large measure, owed his popularity in those aristocratic circles to this modesty) who focussed the conversation on a topic of general interest; gradually, the curiosity of the other guests was piqued, and they occasionally interjected with their observations, until finally, all who were present in the salon had joined the circle. Everyone, of course, except Fr. Nestor, to whom no one paid attention any longer, and who sat tranquilly in his corner, nodding his head and moving his lips as if chewing with his toothless gums.

"I always uphold the national position!" Lord Kalyasanty announced with pathos, but without an exaggerated fervour, as he walked about the salon arm in arm with Lord Alfons Dzyerzhykray. "I consider it to be my sacred obligation to uphold this position. Beyond the national position, there is no salvation for us—certainly not on the grounds of cosmopolitanism. We will disappear, vanish without a trace!"

"That is very admirable on your part," said *Dr. Alfons, "and I think that every thinking man will agree with you on that point. But still, that national position has to be explained more precisely. For otherwise who knows what the ultimate result might be? After all, in 1846, the *Towarystwo Demokratyczne announced that it supported the national position, yet it secretly organized the slaughter of the nobility. The gratuitous mouthing of such broad terms holds within it many dangers, and this is exactly what I see as the shortcoming of the newspaper where you work."

"I dare to assure you, my dear doctor, that you are mistaken. I am prepared to present you tomorrow with as many issues of the newspaper as you desire and to show you articles in them in which it is explained precisely what we understand the national position to be."

"I do not have the temerity to assert that such an explanation has not appeared in your newspaper—God forbid! It must be that I am such an indifferent reader that I never was able to read it there," Dr. Alfons responded, not without a touch of irony.

"I also must confess to such a sin!" Edzo Chapsky added.

His remark touched Lord Kalyasanty to the quick, as if someone had shoved a bunch of nettles into the bosom of his shirt. He jumped up and then, breathing heavily, collapsed into an armchair.

"Well, my lords," he cried emotionally, "that sounds like partiality on your part. Because my newspaper . . ."—in his pathetic fervour he liked to refer to it as "my newspaper," even though he was neither the owner, nor the editor, only an ordinary worker, and his listeners knew that only too well—". . . has a democratic banner line . . ."

"You would do better to say: democracy hanged on a banner!" Edzo said cuttingly.

"A hanged democracy," Dublyanchyk interjected.

"My lords, please!" Lord Kalyasanty cried out seriously and reproachfully. "I have given you no reason to mock me! I beg you most sincerely! This is a serious matter. Because my newspaper has a democratic banner line, you assume that you have the right to view it through partisan spectacles without examining it more closely to find out what, exactly, are its main ideas. I must state frankly—that is irresponsible! It is not how citizens should act. It is not even patriotic, because when you speak negatively against such a newspaper, you stop the advancement of the ideas that it wishes to spread, ideas that I, my lords, as you all well know, accept wholeheartedly as my own."

"Now, that is interesting! Very interesting indeed!" Dr. Alfons cried delightedly as he sat down in a chair directly opposite Kalyasanty. "Since we have among ourselves a man who boldly and openly asserts that he fully espouses the ideas and biases of that newspaper—it means that he can, and certainly will want to familiarize us with those ideas, to make us privy to their significance, since simply reading the printed words and sentences that fill that newspaper day after day does not seem to suffice."

"The doctor still deigns to be ironic," Lord Kalyasanty said somewhat sorrowfully. "I do not wage war with such weapons, I will not respond to irony with irony. I'll come straight to the point. The democracy of my newspaper alarms you . . ."

"But it doesn't alarm us! What have we to fear?"

"Well, generally speaking, it is antipathetic to you. Isn't that so? But how many times have we explained that democracy in our understanding of it is as far removed from demagoguery as the heavens are from the earth! We are democrats, and we understand that at the end of the nineteenth century every intelligent and honourable man must be a democrat."

"Thank you for the compliment!" Dr. Alfons said testily as he bowed to Kalyasanty. "So, in my case, according to you, by proudly proclaiming myself an aristocrat not only by birth, but also by persuasion, I must *ergo* be both unintelligent and dishonourable."

"Have some patience, doctor! Patience! Let us understand one another! Hear me out, and then make your observations. When I mentioned democracy, I immediately stated that it is not to be confused with demagoguery. It would seem unnecessary to define these terms, but it turns out that it is necessary, because in recent times they have been confused far too often. Not long ago, there appeared in Warsaw a populist 'democratic' newspaper that took for its fundamental postulate '*podporządkowanie wszelkich interesów intersom chłopskim* [the subordination of all rights to the rights of the peasantry].'

"This means that the aristocracy, the townspeople, patriotism, literature, science—everything is to be tossed aside! The peasant is coming! Let the peasant sit on the throne! 'I don't know how to read or write, but they want to elect me king of the Poles!' Do you recollect that tale? That was what we called democracy, a true, patent democracy, but in actual fact, it is nothing more than a brutal, simpleminded demagoguery, an oligarchy that, with all its vileness, is dressed up in a metaphysical phrase."

"Well, there is no doubt about it! Lord Kalyasanty expresses himself sharply!" Edzo observed.

"Listen, *Kaytsya," Tadzo, who had been sitting silently, chain-smoking and listening to the various sides of the conversation, was the last to join the group, "I see a clear retrogression in your manners. In the Viennese Jockey Club you spoke differently. You were the perfect gentleman. But now—*fi donc* [shame on you]! You are falling into pathos! You are becoming irritable. You are arguing! No, as I see it, being in the company of newspaper men has made a plebe out of you, and that's that!"

"My friend," Lord Kalyasanty replied, "your criticism is sincere and it flows from the heart, but forgive me if for the moment I do not pay any attention to it. It is understood that a man lives, and therefore he must eat bread from many ovens. There is a time for everything. There was a time for the Jockey Club, for the hippodrome, for horse races, and for casinos, but now the time has come for something different. And the same thing will happen to you."

"Oh, *Tadyk even now is looking for something different!" Emil said. "You know, he is seriously laying the groundwork to run as a candidate for the regional parliament as a representative of the electoral group of the larger estates in the county of N. And his chances look good."

"Ah, congratulations! Congratulations!" voices called out animatedly from all sides.

"That's a bit premature, my friends, a bit premature!" Tadzo stated with a comical seriousness.

"But you know what, Tadyk! I have an idea! Among us here, there are four of your future voters. And in the entire county, there are, I think, only twenty-four voters in all. That means that you have in front of you one-sixth of your voting constituency. Well, what about it? Take advantage of the opportunity! Win us over to your candidacy! Propagate your ideas through us! Lay out before us your political credo! I am sure that you have your campaign speech prepared already, and you must have committed it to memory, at least in outline form."

"Truly, what an idea! That's wonderful!" voices resounded. "Come on, Tadyk, step up with your campaign speech! Present your *profession de foi* [articles of faith]."

Tadzo walked into the middle of the room and threw back his shoulders. "Gentlemen! I do not oppose the idea. But I reserve the right to make some caveats . . . Milko does not understand me; I do not compose campaign speeches, nor do I memorize them *Profession de foi*—fine! But if it is *foi*, then it is *foi*. If it is faith, then it is faith. If you believe in what I believe, then elect me, but if you do not—then do as you wish. But do not wait for arguments from me. Let foolish and limited minds play with arguments. Among intelligent people, they are unnecessary. Scaffolding is not necessary when a building is already built."

"Bravo, Tadyk, bravo! You're becoming a philosopher!" Adas shouted.

"And exactly at the point when he cast out all logic!" Kalyasanty added spitefully.

"My *profession de foi* is brief and clear: I am a nobleman, a landowner, and a Pole. That means that my politics must be noble, agrarian, and Polish. Must I explain what is included in each of those postulates?"

"Do not trouble yourself," Lord Kalyasanty interjected. "All of that was explained back in the eighteenth century by the *Tarhovychany."

"The Tarhovychany!" Tadzo repeated sarcastically. "That is not a gentlemanly manoeuvre, Kaytsya! That name has been shouted over and over again; everyone who hears this word thinks of God knows what kind of evil, treachery, venality, vileness . . . But the true essence of the matter is lost in all those empty words. Did the Tarhovychany want the same things that I want, and did they understand our affairs in the same way that I understand them—neither you nor I can know that, none of us knows that. But with that word you set off alarm bells in your listeners' imaginations without giving their minds anything at all to think about."

"Bravo, Tadyk! Bravissimo!" the young lords shouted.

"There's no doubt that his is a parliamentary talent!"

"Ah, Kaytsya! He has cut you down to size!"

"Oh, how petty our nation has become," Edzo said nasally, imitating the Armenian pronunciation. "When Lord Kalyasanty, the grandfather, drove a team of four horses, he opened the gate with his nose, but Lord Kalyasanty the grandson lets his nose be pulled in his old age!"

"Really, Edzo!" Lord Kalyasanty said a trifle angrily. "You probably think that you said something very new and witty."

"Oh, not at all! But even old witticisms can often do a good job of characterizing our young generation."

"That's enough, that's enough!" voices rang out. "Let Tadzo finish speaking."

"There is nothing for me to finish," Tadzo said as he sat down. "When I say 'aristocratic politics,' I do not understand that to mean that the nobility is to exploit politics for its own benefit.

Let other classes benefit as well, but under one condition: only via the nobility. They must accept from the hands of the nobility all kinds of good decisions, all kinds of abatements, all kinds of benefits. All kinds of proposals in this spirit should originate with the nobility. If a non-noble puts forward a proposal that works for the common good, the nobility must either kill it at its source, throw it out *limine* [at once], or adopt it, take it into its own hands, and send it out into the world under its own auspices. All levels of society should become accustomed to considering the nobility as their guardian, their benefactor, as the one and only politically mature and powerful element, as the only power that is capable of effective, positive, political work."

Bravos resounded once again, but this time neither ironically nor jokingly, and Dr. Alfons warmly shook the hand of his future political ally.

"Listen, Tadzo!" he said. "My compliments! I didn't really know you until now."

"It is my hope that we shall get to know each other better," Tadzo said as he bowed and shook his hand. "And if I am a landowner who wants to implement agrarian politics, what exactly does that mean? Does it mean that we should have no cities at all? No factories? No industry? Quite the contrary! The growth of cities, and industry, and factories is to be desired—it is the preponderance of these elements that is not desirable. I am a landowner, and that means that I am a conservative in political and social matters.

"But being a conservative does not mean being an unthinking supporter of the *status quo*. No, it only means being a supporter of the basic values, of the fundamental principles of an order in which the nobility is truly the nobility; it is the leader, the pillar of society!

"Cities, industry, factories—in our view these are destructive rather than revolutionary forces, and that is why we must keep them confined within boundaries that are strictly defined, we must prune them so that their development parallels our interests . . . but we must not undermine them."

"And in your opinion, my friend," Kalyasanty suddenly interjected, "what will be more difficult: finding the formula for such politics, or squaring a circle?"

"Not at all! It is not all that difficult a task," Tadzo replied calmly. "But one must not be guided by any doctrines, by any theories; one must consider the facts, base one's actions on facts, engage in realistic politics. But anyway, what is there to be discussed? It is exactly that kind, and no other kind of politics that is dictated to us by our third basic principle—our Polish dignity. We must find the formula for such politics, because otherwise our very existence as a nation is threatened. Cities, industry, factories—even though, admittedly, they are under the control of Poles, all the same, they are still cosmopolitan forces. Their nationalism is only a superficial sheen.

"It is not cities, or factories, or offices that give us our Polish dignity—it is our nobility. It is only in the nobility that the Polish spirit is alive and well—a spirit that is free, chivalrous, immutable, and invincible; a spirit that cannot be destroyed by any partitions, by any insurrections, by any theories of demagogues, by any persecution. It is that spirit that gave birth to Polish literature, Polish art, but it revealed itself most potently, most beautifully in Polish politics in the eighteenth century."

"Wonderful! Wonderful!" Lady Olimpiya whispered; she was sitting in an armchair by the window and listening to the speech with great satisfaction.

"Well, Tadyk!" Edzo shouted. "You have our votes. Let your name stand for office, and may God bless you!"

"As for me, I simply can't agree with your deductions," Lord Kalyasanty said.

"Our nation always protests!" Edzo said, once again speaking nasally.

"Ah, I understand! Tadzo interrupted your speech! My poor Kaytsya! But that is not a problem. You can finish it now."

"But perhaps he has forgotten what he was about to say," Milko said.

"I beg your pardon! I never forget anything! And it is just as well that Tadzo interrupted me. It is better for me, because now I can present my views more sharply."

"Are you also running for office with your views?" Dr. Alfons interjected.

"No, definitely not! When I explain my views, it is not with any vested interest in mind, but simply because I hold certain views. To show that I have not lived in vain in this world, that I have thought things through, and that, my lords, is not something that everyone can say about himself."

"Obviously, he is under the impression he is talking to his newspaper friends," Adas observed maliciously. "O my righteous Kaytsya!"

"In my opinion, gentlemen," Lord Kalyasanty began in a scholarly tone, "democracy involves the strengthening, the ennobling of the entire nation. And so, the demos is not only the peasant, not only the worker, not only the water carrier, not only the bureaucrat—it is everyone, the entire nation, except perhaps, for the ruling dynasty. And since we Poles do not have a ruling dynasty of our own, we can boldly assert that we are a completely democratic nation, that we are all democrats."

"*Welche Wendung durch Gottes Fügung* [What an aberration from God's order]!" Dublyanchyk cried in naive astonishment.

But Lord Kalyasanty continued with his deductions without pausing: "The fact that our demos is not a uniform, formless mass, a well-kneaded dough out of which anyone can mould the kind of cookie-cutter figures that he desires, is self-evident. There is a thousand-year history behind us, and it has taught us something. We are not a primitive demos, we are a highly cultured nation with many branches, with differentiated national and social elements.

"Our democracy is progressive, not regressive! It does not demand that we annihilate all the acquisitions of our thousand-year development, pound into a single uniform mass what has differentiated itself appropriately in keeping with various social-political functions. No, our democracy does not tell us to crush within a single mortar the blossoms, and the trunk, and the root of our admirable national tree. A blossom is a blossom, a trunk is a trunk, and a root is a root. Democracy tells us to embrace everything with an equal love, but without predilections, without illusions that we can improve upon the structure of a tree if we rob it of its branches, trample its blossoms, burn off all its leaves."

"It's a botanical democracy!" Edzo said jokingly.

"It is not botany, Lord Chapsky, and what is more, it is not something that should be the butt of jokes," Lord Kalyasanty cut him off. "It is worth thinking about that. Our democracy does not prevent us from seeing the legitimatization of the nobility as a very important, historically necessary, and socially vibrant factor. Even more, our democracy tells us to recognize the nobility as the most important, decisive element in Polish national life, as the pillar of Polish society.

"Because, and I ask you this, what would our Polish nation be today without its nobility? Who in the outside world would know or remember Poland, if the sons of our Polish nobility had not sprinkled half the earth with their blood, if they had not raced up and down through all the countries in Europe, if they had not filled the corners of half the globe with their sorrows, and complaints, and songs, and longings, and hopes? If the Polish nobles had not, time and again, worked feverishly for the rebirth of their fatherland, if they had not conspired, if they had not served as diplomats, if they had not perished in Siberia and on the ramparts, if they had not met their death in uprisings and in thousands of voluntary sacrifices? That is our democracy, the genuine, distinctive Polish democracy!"

"Those are fine words, my dear brother. Very fine indeed!" Tadzo said, slapping Kalyasanty on the back. "But tell us, if you please, are all your fellow democrats of the same mind?"

"Perhaps not all of them, but there are those among them who are."

"That is just the point; it is a far cry from all of them feeling that way, and indeed, it can be said that the vast majority see things quite differently."

"Permit me to dispute that," Lord Kalyasanty rebutted quickly. "Lately, there has been a fundamental reversal in points of view. Not only democrats, but even social-democrats—these people who are completely cosmopolitan and who were hostile at first to Polish patriotism—are now joining the ranks of Polish patriots with an ever-growing decisiveness. And this, gentlemen, is nothing more than a colossal triumph of our idea, of our understanding of democracy. Because, in my opinion, there can be no doubt that once someone becomes a Polish patriot, that person—if one thinks about the matter logically—can no longer be an enemy of the Polish nobility, and having once begun to tolerate it, he will have to arrive swiftly at the point of acknowledging its key, leading, and fundamental status in the Polish nation."

At that moment, the democratic-aristocratic theses of Lord Kalyasanty were interrupted by the appearance of Hapka and Hadyna, who were carrying in large trays with teacups, pitchers of cream, sugar, buns, fresh meat, and all the utensils required for the afternoon tea. Nor had they forgotten the rum and the wine.

Lady Olimpiya hurried over at once to spread the table and put everything in order. Hapka and Hadyna assisted her.

Moreover, the guests themselves did not stand on ceremony and, without waiting to be asked, pulled up chairs, sat down wherever they wanted to, and helped themselves to whatever they liked. This informality had been established quite some time ago: a free and easygoing gathering, without constraints, without any formalities, as if it was meant only for bachelors, and even though a lady was present, she too liked this uninhibited style and felt comfortable with it.

During the tea, the conversation did not die down, but it did become more general, livelier, and noisier, even though it was scattered among several groups. Lady Olimpiya took Fr. Nestor under her wing; she passed him a cup of tea with wine, cut his bun for him, spread it with butter, set everything out on a small walnut table that she had carried over for him, and painstakingly assisted him the whole time.

While fussing over him, she still managed to have a bite to eat herself, and she did it all so adroitly that her care for Fr. Nestor, bordering on the maternal, was not all that evident, all the more so because she carried on a lively half-whispered conversation with him during the entire operation. She asked him if he found Edzo and his brother to his liking, and when Fr. Nestor was noncommittal, she began a lengthy and detailed narration in which she described the brothers' mother, their home, their wealth, and the beauty and the dowry of their sister, the young lady who was to become her daughter-in-law; and she did not neglect to add that, in her opinion, her home and Adas's manor had made a favourable impression on the two young gentlemen.

Fr. Nestor listened implacably, nodded his head, and noisily slurped his tea; it was clear that his thoughts were not focussed on

Lady Olimpiya's words, and the cloud of anxiety that flitted over his forehead from time to time attested to the fact that his mind was circling and flying over his living quarters like a swallow over its nest, and that he was recalling that he had not locked the window that opened out into the orchard and that he had not hidden several valuable documents and some ready cash.

Lady Olimpiya saw that Fr. Nestor appeared troubled, but she was indifferent to his concerns; she wanted to have him there, among the guests, and to attain that goal she was willing to tolerate his clumsiness, his helplessness, and his inattention. Her plan was very simple and natural. She wanted to show her guests a modest and tranquil idyll, a harmonious relationship among a mother, a son, and an elderly priest who had known her husband and was a welcome guest in her home.

All the same, a few of the guests, especially Dr. Vasong, were under the impression that Lady Olimpiya was rather actively engaged in looking after Fr. Nestor, that she helped him invest his capital and keep his accounts; Dr. Vasong had been involved with them in a few such matters, especially in the incident with the stolen bankbooks that had disappeared, and even though he had no way of knowing the exact sum of Fr. Nestor's fortune, he estimated it to be at about ten or fifteen thousand.

Knowing the financial straits of Lady Olimpiya and Adas, he suspected that the Countess was fussing over "the old half-idiot" because she hoped to benefit from his death, but of course, he kept these thoughts to himself, and so, when the young Dublyanchyk, who had noticed the delicate solicitude of the Lady for Fr. Nestor, began a conversation with Dr. Vasong on this theme, the doctor, speaking passionately, proceeded to exalt the generosity, the kindness, and the magnanimity of Lady Olimpiya who, he said, did not begrudge the time and effort required to take care of the old man, mainly because she wished to honour the memory of her husband, who had enjoyed a close friendship with Fr. Nestor.

And when Dublyanchyk inquired about Fr. Nestor's fortune, saying that he had heard something about it, Dr. Vasong, assuming the appearance of a knowledgeable person, told him that it was all a myth, that the entire fortune was worth no more than a few thousand guldens. And then he went on to say that obviously the trifling capital of this poor priest could not hold any appeal to the Countess, or provide any motive for her to care for him with such solicitude, given the fact that she was one of the wealthiest residents in the county and the sister of the Counts Lisovytskys, both of whom were thought to be among the leading magnates in the country. One of these brothers, dating back to the time of the *Constitution, was a marshal of the neighbouring county, a deputy in both the provincial assembly and the state assembly, and a chamberlain of the Tsar, while the other brother—well, he, of course, was the millionaire Count Stanislav Lisovytsky; and the sister of the Countess was married to Lord Krasnobrodsky, who was also a well-to-do landowner. It was only an innate nobility of the soul and an inborn angelic kindness that could inspire such a high degree of self-sacrifice.

"Oh, I have known the Countess for quite some time, and I can tell you that she is an ideal woman—a true model of an old-fashioned Polish matron. Just look at how prudently, how thriftily, she lives! What other ladies in our circles, having her means at their disposal, would reconcile themselves to living in this manner? And to what end? The sole reason is to be found in her love for her son, to whom she wishes to leave his father's fortune in its entirety, intact, preserved unflawed like a precious jewel. O sir, I have the greatest respect for this Lady!"

The young Dublyanchyk welcomed these words joyfully, with a trusting heart. His mother had explicitly charged him to make his own discreet observations, to examine closely the circumstances of Adas and his mother, and Dr. Vasong's account made a great impression on him. Influenced by what he had heard, he slowly began to alter the image that he had formed about Torky based on his first impressions and on a few stories that he had happened to hear, especially from the acerbic tongue of Lord Kalyasanty.

Everything began taking on a rosy hue: the poverty that the young lord, having been raised in opulence, could not help but notice, was now transformed into an intentional prudence and thriftiness, the disorder into unpretentiousness, the comical into ingenuousness and spontaneous cordiality. Even the ugly ruins that remained in the original manor yard—those charred heaps of debris overgrown with nettles and lilac bushes that, resembling the face of a corpse, peered continually through the windows of the salon—now appeared to him like an honoured family reliquary.

After taking his leave of Dr. Vasong, he walked out of the salon into the yard and then went on into the orchard to breathe the fresh, fragrant air in the shade of the trees. As he walked past the barn in which the Lady had overheard the conversation of Hadyna with Paraska that morning, he heard a rustling in the straw and Paraska's sharp cry that was both painful and loving.

His youthful curiosity urged him to glance into the barn, but just at that moment his eyes happened to turn towards the annex across the way in which Fr. Nestor's lodgings were located. The young lord obviously did not know this, and that is why he was even more surprised when he saw Adas's familiar figure flash by in the passageway of this annex and disappear behind the door, which was then quickly closed. This fleeting image cooled his interest in the young woman's cry in the barn and, swinging open a creaking gate and closing the latch with a loud clang, he went slowly and hesitantly into the orchard.

In the salon, the afternoon tea was finished; the table was cleared, some guests were smoking, some were looking through albums, and still others were just sitting and relaxing. The conversation remained unrestrained, varied, and casual, until Lord Kalyasanty, Tadzo, and Dr. Alfons once again turned it to a political theme.

"Everything that you told us is all fine and well, Kaytsya," Tadzo said, carefully enunciating his words as he exhaled clouds of smoke, "if it were not for an error on your part, and a very grave error at that!"

"What error?" Lord Kalyasanty cried.

"Doctrinairism, my dear fellow, doctrinairism. A passion for empty words. Drawing a curtain over practical matters and circumstances with such words. You say: democracy, but you express views that we too do not oppose. What does democracy or any "ism" have to do with any of this? You say: the national point of view, and then you add: progress, the nineteenth century. Why use these phrases?"

"Come now, Tadzo! They are not at all superfluous," Lord Kalyasanty said.

"Not only are they superfluous, they are harmful. They conceal an adulation for certain elements in society that are, frankly speaking, revolutionary elements hostile to us. Because if you go with such words to camps of people who believe in them, you simply turn yourself into a *Wallenrod of sorts, and that means you are demoralizing yourself."

"Well, really, this is too much!"

"But I am in total agreement with Tadzo," Edzo Chapsky said. "I also want to turn your attention to a few contradictions in your views. You talked to us about the progress made in the nineteenth century. Forgive me, my friend, but I am forced to look very sceptically at that progress."

"Well, you can do that, but all the same, you must concede that . . ."

"I do not concede anything!" Edzo cut him off sharply. "What am I to concede? Railroads? Telegraphs? Machines? If we take as the measure of progress what is the highest, the most valuable attainment for man, namely his personal happiness and contentment, then I say that the nineteenth century was not one of progress, but of regress. Never before were the differences and the contrasts between the strong and the weak, the rich and the poor, the well-nourished and the hungry, the enlightened and the ignorant, so excessive and painful. Mainly: painful.

"We have grown soft, become sensitive and nervous, but the age in which we live keeps heaping upon us, from all sides, things that serve only to aggravate our nerves, to sharpen them, but not to temper them. And if someone says that former ages were not any happier, then I say to him that he is gravely mistaken. Perhaps they did not have what we now call happiness—that is true, I concede that. But there was something else: there was a naïve understanding of happiness, and a naive, childlike belief in the possibility, the proximity of that happiness. And that is precisely what we are lacking.

"We have sharpened our minds like razors, and the first thing that we did was to cut off our naivete, our faith. We have shredded, dissected, and chemically analyzed the very concept of happiness to such an extent that there is nothing left of it.

"And then, of course, our intellect came along and said: there is no happiness, and there never can be. And as for the fact that man seeks it? Oh, that is no proof of its reality. I can wish to hide the moon in my pocket—but what is the good of that?

"And so, on the one hand, the desire for happiness is not extinguished, indeed, it is strengthened, refined, but on the other hand, there is that absolute disbelief in the possibility of happiness—and that is the inner rupture that ails all of us. In the first half of this century, *Heine said: '*Der grosse Riss des Jahrhunderts ist durch mein Herz gegangen* [The great rupture of the century has passed through my heart].' Today that rupture has deepened and taken hold of our hearts. Is this a sign of progress, a sign of a bettering of our circumstances? No, I do not believe that!"

"A little less pathos, my dear one, a little less pathos!" Tadey slowly drawled. "Why get all hot and bothered? *Der grosse Riss des Jahrhunderts* [the great rupture of the century] does not prevent you from dining well, from digesting well, from receiving a salary, and enjoying all of God's gifts."

"All of that is only the superficial mask of happiness, but it is not true happiness. And as for the happiness that we do have—what kind of happiness is that? Was it really worth having humanity strive for thousands of years, suffer, spill its blood, and endure hardships to attain that kind of happiness! Thank you for the favour!" Edzo assumed a resigned and haughty mien. Then he became animated and began speaking again, but this time more calmly.

"Or take our peasant! What has he benefited from all the glorified, civilizing efforts of the nineteenth century: liberalism, the abolition of serfdom, equality, the constitution, and all those foolish newfangled notions? Has he actually derived any benefit from all that? I do not think that anyone will contradict me when I say that not only did he not benefit from them, he almost ended up on the brink of disaster. A peasant is a conservative element—not out of a predilection, nor out of ignorance, but out of necessity. He has to be conservative or he will stop being true to himself. This is demanded by the nature of his occupation, his social function.

"And so? Even the most determined liberal and socialist sees today that it was only under the conditions of feudalism that the peasant truly was who he was destined to be. By uprooting him from that position, forcefully pushing him out from under the paternal care of the lord, and shoving him into the cosmopolitan crush of competing economic interests and revolutionary ideas, the lords who espouse liberalism have pushed him beyond the boundaries of his nature. They diverted a river from its natural bed, and then they are surprised that part of it floods fields, another part fills swamps and marshes, and yet a third part washes away roads, but there is nothing left to run the mills and carry the ships.

"They wanted to turn the peasant into a progressive man, a civilized man, to give him equality, and now they look on in terror when they see that he is turning into a proletariat, a petty bourgeois, a usurer, or a red revolutionary, that he is losing the pillars of religion in his heart, abandoning the faith of his fathers, casting off his age-old apparel, renouncing his native language, songs, rituals and customs, and, joining with others to form locust-like masses, he dashes forth to race to the sea, to Russia, to the ends of the world. But these are the direct consequences of liberal husbandry, liberal ideas, and one has to be born blind and unobservant like the liberal and democratic lords of all shades," and he stressed the words *all shades*, "not to see this."

Lord Kalyasanty felt the barb.

"Then what do you suggest?" he asked. "What does our peasant need? Should we turn him back into the blessed harbour of serfdom with all of its kind favours and benefits?"

"You see, the newspaper mentality has taken possession of your mind completely, my dear Kaytsya!" Edzo said. "If I cannot assume the mask of liberalism, then, according to you, I want to reinstate serfdom. But that is not logical! Of course, it would be better for our peasant to go back under the wing of his natural guardian, and even from the national point of view it would be better for him not to lose his intrinsic age-old attributes in favour of new, civilized acquisitions that are often of dubious value.

"But what is the use of even thinking about that! I know that the wheels of history cannot be turned back, even though at the same time I also know that these misguided peasants often end up in an aberrant circumambulation and that, after wandering about for a long time, they return to the same place from which they started. Therefore, in my opinion, they are now rolling along in just such an aberrant circumambulation, and it is up to us, up to thinking people, politicians, and lawgivers, to correct the evil committed from the *year of 1848 up to now, and partially even before that date, by foolish doctrinaires, and even by elements that are hostile to us. After all, even without reinstating serfdom, a lawgiver has thousands of ways to return to the nobility a right that belongs to it both innately and traditionally—its natural guardianship over the peasants!"

"Well, I have nothing against that," Lord Kalyasanty said. "And I think that this is exactly the main pillar, the leading idea of our autonomous jurisprudence, insofar as the tight framework of our jurisprudence will allow that thought to be implemented. And that is why you can be sure, that we, the national democrats, welcome and will continue to welcome every step taken along that path with the greatest joy, and we will always be ready to assist in its implementation."

"Well, I confess that as much as your declaration cheers me, I am equally saddened by the fact that up to now I have come across very few democrats who would share that point of view, or even deign to try to understand it better."

"To me it is amply clear," Dr. Alfons said. "And it is not only clear, it is especially gratifying. For what is the difference between a democrat and a conservative? It almost always amounts to this: a conservative is a practical man, close to nature, a representative of certain clearly defined interests, while a democrat is a doctrinaire, an ideologue, *Prinzipienreiter, who instead of knowing about things from experience, espouses ideas seized at random from books, instead of deliberation—fervour, instead of general interests—broad phrases. And that is exactly what comforts me, because when such a man—if he is sincere and intelligent—engages in practical work, sooner or later he will be cured of democratic phraseology and will turn to us. And it is precisely the existence of such democrats and their metamorphoses that in my view is the best proof of the tenuousness of democracy among us in the European meaning of that word."

"And the necessity of democracy in the meaning that I put forward," Lord Kalyasanty cried triumphantly.

"If you say so!" Dr. Alfons agreed laughingly.

The aristocrat and the democrat shook hands. A general ovation resounded at the sight of this agreement. And, witnessing such a happy ending to this verbal joust, they all began talking cheerfully as they walked about the salon. Even Dr. Vasong, who was modest and sceptical at heart, caught fire and asked to be heard.

They all fell silent, and most of those present gathered around the speaker.

"I would not speak up," he said seriously, "because I have nothing very new to add to the essence of the matter that has been discussed here, but I am prevailed upon to do so by something else. I do not recall how we stumbled upon this political theme today, but I am very happy that such a sensitive and important theme was discussed here so calmly, carefully, and maturely.

"And who did the talking? Was it old men with silvery hair, tempered by the burdensome experiences of life? No, it was young people, representatives of the enlightened and noble youth, who are only now preparing to enter upon the field of practical endeavours. I say this without flattery, my Lords, without compliments, but my heart swells when I listen to your speeches, when I penetrate your thoughts. The stratum of society that produces such young people has not outlived its time, has not finished acting out its role. And fortunate is the nation whose leadership that youth must, in time, embrace.

"Believe me, my Lords, believe me when I say that I come into contact with various strata of society and that, because of the nature of my profession, I must penetrate the most secret hiding places and wellsprings of their actions, their efforts and interests! Believe me when I tell you that of all the levels in our society, it is in our nobility that I find the greatest amount of honesty, intelligence, talent, and a noble and often inspired way of thinking. I do not idealize our nobility, I see its faults, but who is there in this world without fault? But when I compare the sum of its good qualities with the sum of its faults, I see in it a great preponderance of the first over the other. I compare the sum of its good qualities with the sum of those qualities in other levels, and I see in it an even greater preponderance.

"It has been said here, and I, the son of a peasant, want to repeat that idea, elevate it, and sustain it with all my heart: it is the nobility that is the pillar of our society, it is its powerful trunk, the elegant crown, the fragrant blossoms, and the ripe fruit. Without our nobility, our society would not exist; we would be the powerless victims of an invasion. Our peasants and petty bourgeoisie—they are only the roots, a very necessary and useful part of a plant, but by virtue of this fact, it is only in the depths of the earth, in silence and obscurity, that they can fulfill their appointed function in society.

"When someone other than the nobility rises or tries to rise above the peasant station—he is either like the bark of a tree that serves to conceal its noble heart and protect it from the hostile influences of external conditions, or quite simply, a parasite. And let whoever wants to talk about the enervation, the ruin, the decline, the degeneration of the nobility, from my own experience I can assure you: it is not true! It cannot be true! Even though hostile circumstances, hostile influences of the newfangled liberalism and capitalism have made painful notches and cracks in that national jewel of ours, they have not touched its soul, its essence, its inner being. It is healthy and strong and—let us hope!—it will soon be able to heal, to recover from the injuries that it has suffered.

"And most importantly: the nobility knows, it ought to know and must know, must sense with all its being, that it is the pillar of society, that the future of the Polish nation lies in its hands, on its shoulders, and this knowledge must endow it with the strength, the stamina, and the courage to act."

This speech of the talented lawyer evoked genuine enthusiasm among those present. Lady Olimpiya was the first to press his hand warmly, while the others exchanged kisses with him, although, it is to be understood, not without a certain degree of condescension that Dr. Vasong pretended not to notice.

But suddenly this joyful, noisy scene was interrupted in quite an unexpected, although, it seemed, in quite a natural manner. Fr. Nestor, about whom everyone seemed to have forgotten, began looking about nervously and anxiously, searching for something on the sofa, and emitting dull nasal sounds; then he stood up and, whispering silently, hurried towards the door.

"Where are you going, your Reverence?" Lady Olimpiya asked kindly, coming up to him and taking him by the arm.

"I'm ju . . . just . . . Please don't trouble yourself . . . I'll only be a moment . . ." And, mustering all his strength, as if propelled by an inner force, he walked out of the salon.

All the guests felt very uncomfortable. They felt embarrassed for the hostess, and she was embarrassed for them. Everyone accepted this exit of the old priest as a mark of coarseness, of a dulled sense of delicacy, and a lack of proper upbringing. Lady Olimpiya glanced at the guests with a pleading look, as if asking them to forgive the feeble old man for his lapse of good manners. After a momentary silence she began speaking, and she linked what she was saying to her silent plea.

"The poor old man! There is nothing one can do about it; one has to put up with much from him. But nevertheless, he has a heart of gold! Just imagine, gentlemen: he has a bit of capital, and he plans to set up a foundation for the indigent. Of course, I support this idea of his, and I hope that it will all come to pass. It is not an easy thing to do. You know, he is an old man, and it is not seemly to tell him directly that he should make his last will and testament. But, I am not losing hope."

"You see, gentlemen, this is another example of what I was talking about," Dr. Vasong continued. "It is only a close acquaintance of the Countess, like I am, who can tell you how much actual abnegation, motherly sorrow, generosity, and true civic foresight is present under this roof; it is revealed in this touching image of an old, helpless priest and a lady who, respecting his friendship with her deceased husband, assumes the burden—completely selflessly—to put herself out, to look after and take care of him. And, if you please, gentlemen, this image, besides having a human significance, has another one of political import.

"After all, this old, helpless, infantile Rusyn priest—is he not a true representation of the Rusyn question that is festering like a large wound in our national psyche? Despite its infantile mind, its capriciousness, its lack of upbringing and manners, *Rus does, nonetheless, have good, noble potentialities within it; with the right inducement, patience, and systematic leadership, it can be used to further the good of society.

"And so, gentlemen, you should learn, from the example set by our honourable hostess, how to approach the resolution of this aggravating question. Let the Rusyns be capricious, let them rush about, let them shout about equality, raise a ruckus about being the victims of so-called injustices! Let us be wiser than they are, let us do their thinking for them, let us look after them, keep them in our care, never stop doing good things for them, and most certainly . . ."

He did not finish what he was saying.

The door to the salon burst open with a bang, and Fr. Nestor—pale as a sheet, trembling, and looking frightened out of his wits—appeared in the doorway. He was opening and closing his mouth and wildly waving his hands—it was evident that he wanted to shout, to communicate something terrible, but he could not make a sound.

Lady Olimpiya who had been uneasy during his absence—walking out into the vestibule, peering through the window, and talking in whispers with Adas who, all out of breath, had just darted in from the orchard—jumped with a start and rushed up to Fr. Nestor with her arms raised as if she was prepared to cover his mouth with her hand in the event that he managed to say something.

"For God's sake, Father!" she said with genuine alarm. "What's wrong? What's happened? Sit down over here. O Lord, you're not yourself at all! Here, have a drink of water."

Fr. Nestor waved his hands impatiently, but he did sit down and drink some water. His fright had abated somewhat, and he refrained from shouting; instead, he spoke in almost a whisper to Lady Olimpiya, who sat down beside him in such a way that she shielded him from the guests and prevented them from listening in on their conversation.

From her demeanour it seemed that Lady Olimpiya was no less upset and distressed than Fr. Nestor.

"Oh, my Lady," Fr. Nestor groaned. "It's a misfortune! I . . . lost . . . somewhere . . ."

"What? What did you lose?"

"The key! The key!"

"What key?"

"To my lodgings."

"The key to your lodgings? But when you came here, didn't you lock your room and take the key with you?"

"That's just it! I thought I had, and I was quite at ease. But then I checked my pocket: the key wasn't there. I felt a jolt, as if someone had poked me. I went to my living quarters . . ."

"But Father!" Lady Olimpiya interrupted him. Although deathly pale, she remained calm as she listened to his whispered account. "You're making things up! Look over there—your key is by the cushion in the corner of the sofa."

"What? My key?" Fr. Nestor shouted. "It can't be! I looked for it very carefully before I left."

Instead of replying, Lady Olimpiya picked up the key from the corner of the sofa and, saying that it must have fallen out of Fr. Nestor's pocket when he was sitting there, handed it to the distraught priest

He reached for it with a trembling hand and stared at it as if he could not believe his eyes. "It can't be! It can't be!" he whispered. "I looked very carefully, and moreover I saw . . ."

But Lady Olimpiya was no longer listening attentively to what he was saying about what he had seen. A hubbub had arisen in the salon. Adas had reminded the guests that it was time to go to his manor, where supper was awaiting them, and they had all risen to their feet and begun taking leave of their hostess.

"As for me, Adas, I thank you for inviting me for supper," Dr. Vasong said. "But I don't have time—I have matters to attend to! I must go directly to Lviv from here."

"Well, I do not feel that I have the right to detain an eminent lawyer; I know that your time is valuable," Adas said with delicate resignation.

"Perhaps some of the lords would like to return with me?" Dr. Vasong asked as he turned to face the gathering.

The two Chapsky brothers volunteered to be his travelling companions.

"That's wonderful!" Dr. Vasong said. "We'll all go in one carriage."

"Oh, there is no need to cramp yourselves!" Adas cried. Earlier on he had asked both Chapskys to stay for supper, but they had made their apologies, saying that their mother was to arrive in Lviv that evening, and it would not be very pleasant for her if she did not find them at home. "You can take two hansoms, my Lords. And as for the lords who are staying behind, perhaps some of them would like to take a walk to my manor through the fields. It is not too far, it has cooled off outside, and there is a breeze wafting in from the forest—it is truly delightful out in the fields just now."

"Oh, we'll all go! We'll all go!" the guests called out.

"And after supper, I'll give everyone a ride back to Lviv in my coach," Adas added.

The matter was settled. The guests leaving for Lviv said their good-byes and left.

Adas kissed his mother's hand, whispered a few quick words into her ear, and then bolted headlong out the door to lead his remaining guests through the yard and into the orchard; from there a path wound through a meadow, onto a lane in the fields, across a little bridge, and then rose upwards quite steeply, winding like a sinuous snake through a lush field of wheat, across a potato field, and on to the manor.

Dr. Vasong stayed behind in the salon; he walked around as if he had lost something, kept his eyes on Lady Olimpiya, and furtively tried to catch her attention.

"My Lords," he said to the Chapsky brothers who were waiting in the doorway, "please get ready to leave, and I'll join you in a moment. There's something I still want to say . . ."

The lords, without waiting to hear the rest of his sentence, went to the hansoms that were standing near the gate and, without unhitching the horses, let them graze on the grass.

Left alone in the salon with Lady Olimpiya, Dr. Vasong walked up to her and began talking in a whisper: "If it please my gracious Lady, I wanted . . ."

"Shh . . . Excuse me!" she whispered, and she looked around as if searching for someone. She was obviously looking for Fr. Nestor, but he was no longer in the salon.

"Oh dear!" she said in a somewhat impatient tone, and then, turning to Dr. Vasong, asked him: "Well, my dear sir, what can I do for you?"

"I beg your pardon. Perhaps it is indelicate on my part . . . but I have an order, a direct order from the board of the nobles' casino to present to my gracious Lady a matter pertaining to Count Adam. Even though he is of age, all the same . . . the board, taking into consideration his name, his notable family, did not want to proceed rashly . . . My gracious Lady knows how unpleasant this story is . . ."

The eminent lawyer was clearly uncomfortable, but Lady Olimpiya was listening to him quite impatiently; her mind was obviously occupied with another matter.

"I do not know, my dear sir, if I understand you: what is this all about?" she asked, masking her impatience with a smile.

"I think that Count Adam has told the gracious Countess about his debt of honour, about the three thousand guldens that he is in arrears. The deadline for paying off the designated debt has passed. According to the rules, the board should display his name on the tablet of dishonour, but I—knowing how unpleasant this would be for my gracious Countess . . . and for others as well—pleaded with the board, and even guaranteed . . ."

"Thank you, my dear sir, thank you very much!" the Lady said, shaking Dr. Vasong's hand. "I appreciate your frankness and your kindness. And as for the debt, there is no need for you to worry. I think Adas will pay it off tomorrow."

"Tomorrow?" Dr. Vasong asked in surprise. He was well aware of the financial problems of the Countess and Adas; only today, as they had been travelling, Adas, unaware of Dr. Vasong's delicate mission, had complained to him that he had no money for the harvest.

"Yes, tomorrow!" the Countess said curtly and firmly. "Adieu, my dear sir! Have a safe trip!"

"Where do they plan to get hold of such a large sum of money by tomorrow?" Dr. Vasong wondered, as he got into the hansom. "Because it is highly unlikely that the old skinflint would suddenly become that generous if she asked him for that amount. Well, we'll see, we'll see!"

The guests who were walking had not yet disappeared completely from view, the racket they were making still resounded from the orchard, and the hansoms were still being readied for the trip to Lviv, when Lady Olimpiya rushed off and flew directly to the annex where Fr. Nestor lived.

As soon as she turned away from the last guest, a dramatic change came over her. Her majestic tranquility vanished, and so did her easygoing manner and her cheerfulness. Her face turned pale, her thin lips parted and trembled nervously, and cold chills raced over her body. She was driven by a dreadful impatience, a deathly anxiety: she hoped that the looming storm would not catch up with her departing guests, that the pleasant visit would not end in a scandal.

She ran directly to the door of the annex. And she was in luck. Another moment, and it would have been too late. In the entranceway of the annex she bumped into Fr. Nestor, almost slamming into him with her forehead.

The old man appeared to have gone mad; he was squealing, shouting, wringing his hands, and groaning heavily.

"O my God! Fr. Nestor! What's wrong with you? What's happened?" Lady Olimpiya cried and, trying to make it seem unintentional, she firmly and resolutely blocked the doorway to prevent him from going out into the yard.

"I am ruined! Ruined!" Fr. Nestor groaned. "I've been robbed!"

"Who? How? When?" asked the Lady, shaking violently.

"Let me go! Let me shout for help! I want the people to know, to come and see! How could this have happened? Why, just a few moments ago . . . In broad daylight . . . It's unheard of . . ."

Fr. Nestor gasped for air, swallowed his words, and was so near to fainting because of this terrible turn of events that he could barely stay on his feet.

Although ostensibly alarmed and perturbed by the news to the core of her being, Lady Olimpiya, took him by the arm and gently led him back into the room, sat him down on the sofa, and seated herself across from him. It was only then that she started to talk—soothingly, softly, wisely, and calmly, as if rocking to sleep a child that had been frightened by a nightmare.

"For God's sake, Father! Don't create a scandal! Things will work out better for you if you don't. Tell me exactly what happened. We'll think about it together, discuss it, and then decide what we should do. Don't be afraid! It isn't possible that this could happen in my home in the middle of the day . . ."

"But as you see, it is possible!" Fr. Nestor interrupted her. "And I just do not understand how it could have happened. While I was still sitting in your salon, I recalled that I had left a window unlocked. It was closed from the inside, but not latched. It was as if something was nagging at me. And so I thought, I better go and latch it. God takes care of those who take care of themselves. I came up to the annex—the door, this one here, the door of the vestibule, was latched from the inside. O Lord, what could that mean?

"I glanced at the window in my vestibule—it was shut, and the curtain was drawn. But I remembered very well that when the two of us were leaving, the curtain was open. My legs almost gave way under me. I hurried as fast as I could to the gate, went into the orchard, and ran around the annex to look in through this window over here, but when I rounded the corner, I heard a thump in my room, the rattling of a lock. I went up to the window—it was also latched from the inside and draped with my cassock. I hurried back as fast as I could, tried the door again—it was shut. I tried opening it—it was unlocked.

"I walked into the vestibule, went up to the door of my room—it was locked. I reached into my pocket for the key—it wasn't there. Then, feeling as if I had lost my mind, I went back to the salon where you gave me the key. What am I to think about all that, huh? Was it a miracle of some kind, or plain thievery? And who could have done it?"

"O my dear Father! Do not be in too big a hurry to blame someone," Lady Olimpiya said, trembling all the while as she listened to the story. "I do not know anything except that after you came back, I saw the key on the sofa. But, go on, what happened next?"

"After getting the key from you, I hurried right back here. At first glance, everything seemed in order; the locks were not broken, everything was where it should be, but here, in this drawer—the money was gone."

"Are you sure that you left it there?"

"I counted it and wrote down the sum on a card just before the guests arrived. I wanted to hide the money, but you walked in, and I left it here."

"Was there a lot of money?"

"F . . . f . . ."

"Fifty rynski?"

"No, no!" Fr. Nestor cried. "F . . . f . . ."

It was as if his lips could not state the amount.

"Five hundred?"

"No, five thousand! Look! Here is the card! He left the card, the valuable documents, and took only the cash."

"No one else but Tsvyakh could have done this!" Lady Olimpiya said calmly and decisively after thinking about it for a moment.

"Tsvyakh?"

Fr. Nestor mechanically repeated the name while staring blankly at the Lady with his faded eyes.

"It had to be him! Hapka told me this morning that he was here very early, and he was swaggering, telling her that he would settle accounts with you."

"But why didn't my L . . . L . . . Lady tell me this?"

"I did not want to frighten you. Besides, I told Hadyna to watch over you. But who can guard against such a thief? He must have noticed that the window to your room wasn't latched, and he took advantage of the opportunity."

"But how could he have locked the door to the vestibule from the inside?"

"Well really, Father! That must have been an illusion. The door was only latched—it just seemed to you that it was locked from the inside: in your fright, you could not open it right away, and after that you probably didn't try again."

Fr. Nestor once again stared at her with a long, childishly helpless, and trusting look. It seemed that he was ready to believe what Lady Olimpiya was saying.

"But the window? If Tsvyakh crawled in through it, why would he lock it from the inside?"

"And when you came in now, was it locked on the inside?"

"I don't know. Please have a look."

Lady Olimpiya went up to the window. It actually was draped with an old cassock and latched from the inside.

But Lady Olimpiya unlocked it with a deft movement and opened it half way.

"There, you see!" she said. "That's what I thought! It's open. It's all clear now. The thief crawled in through the window, locked it and draped it, so that no one could see from the outside what he was doing in your room, and after he was finished, he crawled out again through the window and, understandably, he couldn't lock it."

"But why were locks rattling and keys squeaking at the exact moment when I was standing by the window?"

"It could have been a figment of your imagination. Or perhaps the thief had another key. But that's not very likely. Well, in any case, listen to my advice. I am advising you, like your own sister. Be quiet about this. Do not raise a ruckus. In the meantime I'll notify the reeve, the gendarmes, and tonight, this very evening, they will search Tsvyakh's house. You can be sure that by tomorrow your money will be found."

"Oh! My gr . . . gr . . . gracious Lady! How kind you are! How good you are! May God r . . r . . repay you for . . ."

"That's enough, that's enough!" Lady Olimpiya said humbly. "But just stay calm! I am going now, and I'll attend at once to everything that needs to be done. Five thousand—that's quite a sum! That's a lot of money. It must not be lost! Well, good-bye, Father! O Lord, how it pains me that you met up with such a misfortune in my home."

And she walked out. In the doorway of the vestibule she ran into Hadyna, who might have been listening in on her conversation with the priest or, perhaps, just cleaning up the yard across from the door. Lady Olimpiya gave him a fierce look, as if he had slaughtered her favourite child and then, opening the door to Fr. Nestor's room and raising her voice so that Hadyna could hear her, she called out: "Lock yourself in securely, Father! Be on guard! Good night, good night!"

IX

Evening was falling. A rosy radiance flooded the western sky. Silence reigned. After the departure of the guests, it was as deserted, hushed, and still in the Torsky yard as in a tomb. The shadow of the annex slowly crept over the yard. Now and again, crows called out to each other from the tops of the linden trees.

Lady Olimpiya was walking in the orchard. Her heart was perturbed, and she sought out the densest corners, the darkest shadows, in order to be alone. But her disquiet followed her even there, preventing her from sitting or standing in a single spot, and driving her ever onward.

The gardener, sitting in his straw hut under a spreading apple tree and puffing on his pipe, watched her closely as she floated like a spectre here and there in the thickets, meandered among the raspberry bushes and the young cherry trees that struck her in the face and grabbed at her hair with their slender branches, and then, as if assiduously searching for something, went to the beehives—formerly they had constituted the famous Torsky apiary, but now there were no bees in them—peered under their wattle covers and poked around in them, staring vacantly all the while as if she was not fully aware of what she was doing, what she was looking for.

And as he followed her with his eyes, he crossed himself, spat, and whispered to himself: "She's roaming around again, like a maniac!"

For some time now he had taken notice of the Lady's "roaming," and it frightened him, all the more so as the Lady walked past him a few times and looked at his hut, but seemed to be either unaware of him, or deemed him to be an inanimate log, for she never said a word to him. The gardener also found it strange that this roaming took hold of the Lady only in the evening, and that during the day she was completely tranquil, rational, and talkative.

"There has to be something more to this!" the gardener said thoughtfully as he watched the Lady who, like a black cloud in her black dress, flitted soundlessly here and there among the trees, appearing and disappearing in the twilight.

"Is she looking for something, or does she have some kind of illness? If she was looking for something, she would have found it by now, or told someone else to look for it. No, it must be a spell that comes over her. They do say that there are people like that . . . If such a spell comes over a man, he'll leave everything, forget about his wife and children, and go off into the world, without knowing where he's going or why. But it's strange that it's always in this orchard that the spell comes over her. It must be a spell cast by an evil spirit."

In the meantime, the Lady walked out of the young orchard. The dew was falling. Her satin shoes, the same ones that she had worn while hosting her guests, were soaked. The hem of her dress was also wet and flapped damply and coolly against her legs, but she did not seem to feel it or be aware of it. Continually looking around, glancing here and there, and listening intently, she wandered into the depths of the orchard, among the old trees, to the place where the orchard, protruding towards the north, spread over a flat-topped ridge that sloped gently towards the hay meadows.

The nightingales began to spin out their trills in the treetops. An owl hooted in the hollow of an old linden tree. A light breeze stirring the branches sounded like the last sigh of the dying day.

Lady Olimpiya shuddered and stopped for a moment.

What was she thinking about? If someone had appeared before her just then and asked her that question, more than likely she would have stared at him in astonishment and would not have been able to come up with an answer.

She was not thinking about anything, but nevertheless her brain was churning, her nerves refused to calm down. When the armature in a clock is broken, its spring unwinds unhampered, its inner workings begin to rattle, its hammers beat more rapidly, its bells ring, its wheels turn, and its weighted levers noisily descend lower until the energy of the mechanism is all used up—and something akin to this was happening in her mind during those solitary evening walks in the orchard.

The armature of her will, strong and firm during the day, seemed suddenly to turn into clay, lose its power, vanish completely, and in her head there swished and swirled, in a kaleidoscopic jumble, a thousand impressions and thoughts: images of her feverish imagination, phantoms born of her passionate, unfulfilled desires and of the dashed hopes of her life. They flowed in a turbulent, motley current, leaving nothing behind except for an ache in her head and a quickened beating of her heart.

It was in vain that her mind forced itself to capture this image or that one in its flight, to look more closely at it, to examine its links with the others. New incoming waves of that current swiftly bore those images away, drowned them, and in their place dozens of new ones—sad, happy, odious, insipid images—pushed their way forward, filled the entire horizon, crammed the entire space, only to be transformed again in the very next moment, to be blotted out and replaced by still more new ones.

It truly was an illness of sorts. At first Lady Olimpiya did not pay any attention to it, all the more so as at first its symptoms were almost imperceptible. But now the attacks were growing stronger and lasting longer.

The onset always began with a mysterious anxiety; there was a lack of air in her chest, and her breathing quickened. When that happened, the Lady could not bear to remain in her room; she could not sit or stand in one spot. Usually she went into the orchard, and even though the twilight and the coolness did not calm her, it was here that she felt most at ease and, unseen by anyone, could overcome her nervous helplessness by walking, or "roaming" as the gardener called it, for an hour or two among the trees.

Now she has stopped for an instant in a small clearing. She knows that she will not stay longer than a moment, that she will have to keep on moving. She glances up: through the thick mesh of boughs and branches a swath of the bright pink sky is visible. Here and there, stars peek through. A long, filmy, slender cloud, like a smoothly combed strand of softly spun yarn, is suspended directly above her head. She glances down: under the spreading trees, twilight stands like a gloomy wall, and fireflies are darting about in it like golden sparks.

But no! Right over here, in the darkest spot, there is a faint glow. A light, ever so pale, is spreading. It is not a light—it is the figure of a tall woman; dressed all in white, with her dark hair cascading loosely over her shoulders, she is walking slowly, with a measured gait, with her eyes closed, with her right hand extended in front of her. In her left hand she is holding a candle—no, it is a small lamp that flickers with a gentle green light. It is deathly still. There is the sound of loud, steady, sleepy breathing.

Ah! It is *Modzrejewska in the role of Lady Macbeth. Now she is squatting, gathering the dew from the grass, washing her hands . . .

"Out, damned spot! Out, I say!"

Lady Olimpiya hears those somnolent whispers distinctly, very distinctly. Right here, close by, next to her ear, or perhaps even inside her ear. She is not afraid, nor is she amazed. She knows that it is Modzrejewska whom she saw in this role not so long ago on a stage in Lviv—but as to what she is doing in the Torsky orchard, and how she got there, there is no time to think about that.

"To sleep! To sleep! To sleep!" the tall figure whispers as it dissolves into nothingness.

And at that very moment, Lady Olimpiya, taking a few steps forward, sees a bedroom in front of her: a humble bed, a meagre old coverlet, and from under it protrudes a grey-haired old head with parted bluish lips, a nose hanging over the upper, hairless lip, and deeply sunken eyes. It is Fr. Nestor—Lady Olimpiya knows this; she is not at all afraid or astonished. She keeps on walking—the image vanishes.

"I feel so sorry for him! In his sleep he looked so much like my father!"

Who said this? Where was it said? This is not the time to think about that. The mill by the river. A huge wheel turns slowly, noiselessly; the water falls, splashes, and disintegrates into millions of pearls, but without the slightest sound. Down below, past the dam, there is a large pond—still, bright, and deep, ever so deep. The bottom of the pond is visible, the moon and the stars can be seen in the water, and among the stars crawl black crawfish, and a huge, lazy fish is striking the moon with its tail. And above those depths, on a board with one end hammered into the dam, someone is sitting and rocking: a woman . . . a girl . . . a mermaid? This is not the time to think about that. She is rocking . . . wringing her hands . . . tearing at her hair . . . her face is familiar, but who is it? She is just about to recognize her, just another moment, another quick look! But no, the image dissolves, fades, vanishes . . .

There is the sound of footsteps. The dark figure of a woman walks down the linden alley. Suddenly it stops, shudders, crosses itself, and begins to sing a Polish hymn in a tremulous, but piercing voice:

> "O star of the sea,
> You nourished our Lord with your milk,
> You destroyed the tree of death
> That Adam grafted in paradise."

Lady Olimpiya stands not far from her, hidden in the shadows, holding her breath. It is Hapka—is she real, or a phantom? This is not the time to think about that. The figure strides purposefully, heads towards the manor yard, disappears. She must have been in the village, at Tsvyakh's place, at Herder's, at Malanka's.

And Lady Olimpiya's imagination paints new images for her: Tsvyakh . . . and his wife, who cries from hunger with her children; then Tsvyakh in his youthful years, when he was here, in the manor yard, not quite a servant, not quite a foster child, a lord's page, until the terrible disaster that changed everything.

And before the Lady's eyes the old manor house arises clearly, the expansive master bedroom, the imposing bed, and on it, lying on elegant pillows, a living corpse, as helpless as an infant, but as malicious as the devil—her late husband, Count Torsky. And on a stool by the bed, this very same Tsvyakh—no, not this one—a young, active boy with clever, thievish eyes, in courtly livery, is passing the Count some medicine.

She also sees herself—right over there, in the opposite corner, behind the dividing curtain, in bed; she hears her own sleepy breathing, but she is aware that she is not asleep, that she is diligently catching every rustle, every whisper in the room, that in her heart she sees every movement that this young Tsvyakh makes, every gesture, every change of expression, however slight, on her husband's face.

"I think she's sleeping already!" the Count whispers.

"Yes, she is," Tsvyakh responds in a whisper.

"Well, tell me, what did you see?"

"They were kissing."

"Who started it?"

"She did."

"What did they talk about?"

"They were plotting."

"Against whom?"

"Against you . . . She's trying to persuade him. 'When he falls asleep' she said, 'come to me; we'll each press a pillow down on his face, and in a couple of minutes, he'll be gone!'"

"Th . . .that's what she said? He'll be gone?"

"Those very words!" Tsvyakh lies with brazen daring.

"Well, and what happened next?"

"He didn't want to. 'Why should I?' And then she began to cry: 'You don't love me! He has poisoned my life.'"

"Poisoned, she said?"

"Yes. And he said: 'Forgive him! Let him settle his accounts with God. Do this for our son!'"

"For our son, he said?"

"Yes! For our son."

"And then what?"

"She started up about the pillows again. 'Don't be afraid of anything! No one will know! We'll say that he had a heart attack, an apoplectic fit!'"

"That's clever!" the Count whispers.

"He didn't want any part of it. 'It will come out,' he said. 'He doesn't have long to live as it is. That's what the doctor said.'"

"The doctor said that?"

"That's what he said: 'The doctor said that. I purposely asked the doctor, and he said that the slightest agitation—and that could be the end of him.'"

"So, that's how it is!" the Count whispers barely audibly, tossing about on the bed.

Then it grows quiet.

Tsvyakh is still whispering something. And then he leans over the Count and says in a barely audible voice: "Well, that's that! He's done for, once and for all! I never thought it would be over so quickly!"

Even now, after all those years, a deathly fear seizes her at these words. She heard everything, she had not been sleeping; she understood instantly that something terrible had happened. Her fear left her bereft of her strength, her ability to think. She did not know what to do: should she get up, run to her husband, call for help, or should she just lie there and wait for morning? Wait? To sleep—no, to lie sleepless all night right here, in the presence of a corpse! No, that is terrifying, she cannot endure that! But to jump out of bed and shout—that would mean that she would reveal the fact that she had heard the entire conversation, she would reveal that to Tsvyakh!

But what is happening now? Tsvyakh is fussing with the corpse, jangling keys, opening the safe! Terror presses on her chest like a stone mountain. She wants to get up, to shout, to seize the thief, but she is unable to move. And now Tsvyakh has closed the safe, put the keys under the dead man's pillow, and tiptoed out of the room. It is a good thing that he did not put out the light.

But what is this? The light sputters. Smoke chokes her. Flames crackle and roar. O God! The Lady jumps to her feet— her husband's bed is engulfed in flames

Amid the smoke and the flames, as if on a hellish bed in an infernal nest, lies his corpse—calm, smiling wickedly, its lips slightly parted, as if saying: "So that's how it is!"

Shouts! Cries! Bedlam! Feet thunder, windows shatter, bells clang. Confusion, desperation. And the fire soars and blazes. It breaks out from the room through the windows and doors, into the vestibule, up into the attic, to the roof. The infernal nest grows, spreads, and it no longer crackles and hums, it roars, wails, scatters sparks to the heavens, licks the darkness of the night with fiery tongues. There is screaming everywhere, the entire village has gathered, people are trying to save things, gossiping, getting in the way.

And amid all the clamour, smoke, shouting, over there, in the very middle of the inferno, at the bottom of it, in the core of the conflagration, she still seems to see the corpse—untouched by the flames, calm, with its partly open and maliciously twisted lips. He is no longer alive—she can feel that, but his eyes are open, and they blaze with a sharp, hellish lustre, they burn with an immortal, insatiable malice, and they are fixed on her, they follow her about. No matter where she moves, where she turns, she always sees them before her, senses their searing glare upon her, feels, in the depths of her soul, their piercing stare. And with those eyes, the corpse continues to talk to her, to harrow her, to torment her.

"Aha, so that's what you're like, my Countess! You were ready to suffocate me! With pillows, like *Peter III was suffocated. So you learned this from *Catherine II, did you? You wanted to be free of me? Oh, no! You wanted to free yourself from a living person, and here's what you get for it!

"You get a corpse, a dead man from whom you will never be able to free yourself! You will never be able to shake him off, to tear yourself away from him, to suffocate him, to poison him, because he is inside you, in your inner being, in your soul! I wish you a pleasant time with your friend and your son! Tee-hee-hee! It will be my pleasure to look at you always, everywhere, with these eyes—the eyes that charm you so greatly, right Countess? The eyes that cast such a magical spell on you—tee-hee-hee! The eyes that sharpen your appetite, fire up your blood—or how would you put it, my gracious Countess, huh?"

Was someone talking at this very moment? Were those horrific eyes still staring at her out of the darkness, the ones that so very, very long ago had almost driven her mad for so many long years? It was only now that Lady Olimpiya felt a numbing coldness coursing through her body, a deathly fear surging in her heart and, hiding her face in her hands, she screamed like a frightened child and began to flee like a maniac.

Not knowing where she was going, she tore out of the darkness of the orchard in a few bounds, and then, coming upon a gate, opened it and leapt into an open field, trembling and breathing heavily, just like on that night, when, almost fainting, she had fled from the fire that had buried within itself the corpse of her husband.

"O God, it's mother!" she heard a voice right beside her. "What's wrong, mother? What made you scream like that? Did something frighten you?"

She just stood there, without speaking, without thinking, breathing heavily, weakened, looking shattered.

Before her stood Adas, staring at her in amazement. And when he saw that she recognized him, he came up to her and took her by the hand.

"Mother, you're completely chilled! You have a fever!" he said, with a hint of reproach in his voice.

"It's nothing, sonny, it's nothing!" Lady Olimpiya whispered as she nestled against him. "But what are you up to? Why have you come here on foot? Why are you out of breath? Did you run all the way here?"

"That's neither here nor there! Let's go inside, and I'll tell you everything."

And slowly, stealing ever so quietly through the orchard, they arrived at the linden alley and, a moment later, vanished in its darkness.

High above them, the evening star was fading in the heavens. The deep croaking of frogs drifted in from the river. Black bats swooped about silently among the trees, and nightingales, concealed by the darkness, tirelessly poured forth their songs.

X

Hadyna had been lying on the straw in the barn for a good hour already. He wanted to fall asleep, but could not. He was waiting for Paraska, but she did not appear. He had begun to curse her, but then he stopped, because he realized that he really did not feel like seeing her just then.

Something seemed to be gnawing at him, troubling him, and he felt a strange emptiness that he did not know how to fill. He could go into the village, to the tavern, talk to the young men, joke around with the girls—but no! The very thought of having people around him was unpleasant, odious. It was as if something was binding him to this manor yard, as if he was waiting for something, hoping for something, even though he did not know what that something was. He simply could not bring himself to leave this place. Sprawled on the straw in the barn, he peered through a crack in the wall at the yard and at the annex across the way that housed the kitchen, the guest room, and Fr. Nestor's living quarters.

His thoughts circled around those lodgings like crows around the tip of a hollow tree. The leisurely life in the manor had given him the opportunity to taste pleasures that life did not offer up to ordinary peasants; it had ignited within him a desire for wealth, but it had not given him the knowledge required to attain it with honest labour, nor had it developed within him the moral strength to withstand temptations.

To acquire a fortune in an easy manner, to take advantage of what belonged to others, to seize what he had not toiled to earn—that was his ideal. And Fr. Nestor, the feeble old priest, who possessed—what was, in Hadyna's opinion—a large fortune from which he neither knew how, nor wanted to benefit, was such a natural, even a deserving victim, who could be used to satisfy his appetite that, in his view, it was stupid, even sinful not to fleece him, not to tear his wealth away from him for the benefit of someone else.

But Hadyna was not very brave by nature. His natural bent and his upbringing had made him more of a petty pickpocket than a robber on a grander scale. To pilfer furtively, to spy on someone, to sneak into a place, to run off with something—he was a master of all that, but his imagination did not dare to go beyond such petty acts of thievery.

He had, however, succeeded a couple of times in catching sight of Fr. Nestor as the priest hid a few, or even a few dozen guldens in the hollow of a tree, among the beehives, or in a crack under a thatched roof, and he had stolen that money.

Understandably, this did not satisfy him; it only whetted his appetite, fanned his desires, and now, for the past few days he had comforted himself with the fantastic hope that he would succeed in secretly catching Fr. Nestor in the act of leaving his room and forgetting his key in the lock. To be able, in such an event, to dash into the room of that damned priest for at least a moment, seemed to him to be the height of good fortune.

Fr. Nestor always locked his room so carefully, was so compulsively cautious about letting any of the servants into his room, that all Hadyna could think about was how, once he got in there, he would scoop up money with both hands, for he imagined that there must be money lying on top of the table, in drawers, and perhaps even on the floor. The manorial culture had completely corrupted his heart, but it had done nothing at all to sharpen his intellect, to broaden it.

Evening arrived. It was completely dark in the barn, and the yard, flooded with the shadows of trees, was only faintly lit by the dying lustre of the evening sky. There was not a sound to be heard. Hadyna felt uneasy lying by himself in the barn. It was even a bit scary.

He got up and quickly walked out into the yard. Something urged him to poke around Fr. Nestor's living quarters that from the outside appeared to be utterly deserted. There was not a sound, nor any sign of a living being, and the locked door and the windows that were shut and draped with curtains lured him to them like an enigma, like an unsolved mystery. Walking on tiptoe, even though there was absolutely no one in sight, Hadyna came up to the gate that led into the orchard and slowly opened it, being extra careful to ensure that the latch did not clank, and that the gate did not creak on its rusty old hinges.

But as he stole into the orchard, he almost collided with the gardener, who also knew how to prowl around stealthily, and who seemed to be waiting expressly for him by the gate.

"Oh!" Hadyna cried, startled by the unexpected appearance of the gardener, but then, instantly recognizing him, said: "Is that you, gardener?"

"Yes, it's me."

"What is it—is there someone in the orchard, perhaps?"

"No, it's nothing like that. I'm looking for a hammer. Have you seen it?"

"What hammer?"

"My hammer. I had my hammer here—in case I had to fix the fence or something like that. I had it at noon today; it was lying right here on the beehive. But now, when I came to get it—it was gone."

"I didn't see it. But you're here all day long, so you would have seen the person who took it."

"Well, who was here? I didn't see anyone. Just a little while back, the Lady was here. But it's unlikely that she would have been tempted to take my hammer. Moreover . . . it seems to me that when she was walking around, it was no longer here. It couldn't have been here! Because I was sitting in my hut and looking right over here. If my hammer had been lying here, I would have seen it."

"Well, Tsvyakh was roaming around here this morning—did you see him?"

"No, I didn't. But in the morning I still had my hammer."

"Oh, who knows, perhaps he was here later on as well?"

"Well, unless it happened while I was gone for dinner."

"Do you suppose that he couldn't have come here? He darts about everywhere, like the devil himself. He takes root no matter where he's planted."

"But why would he need my hammer?"

"Oh, don't you know what a thief is like? He'll take it to the tavern: even if he gets just a shot of whiskey for it—that's good enough for him."

"And yet it's a loss to me! May the Lord smite him! But then—why am I cursing him? Maybe it wasn't him?"

And the gardener, a devout man, crossed himself and, mumbling a prayer, went off to his hut, leaving Hadyna alone.

Hadyna was no longer thinking about the gardener. His eyes and his thoughts had turned once again to the living quarters of Fr. Nestor. He got a sudden urge to sneak quietly around the corner and glance inside through the window that opened out into the orchard, not from the vestibule, but from Fr. Nestor's inner room.

He had already hunched himself over and crouched down in order to creep through the raspberry bushes that grew up against the wall in that spot, when he heard a sharp, familiar voice behind him.

"Oh, you fiendish thief, where do you think you're going, huh? Do you want to make trouble for the poor gardener? May your hands be bent and twisted! May your tongue turn into a stake in your mouth the moment you taste the stolen cherries! Have you not stolen enough of them already? Isn't that enough for you? Oh, I hope you get good and bloated and burst!'"

Hadyna stood up and, waving his hands, tried in vain to calm down Hapka. Finally he almost shouted in order to stem the irrepressible flow of her oratory.

"O you clattering windmill! Stop! Why are you rattling on like that? Why would I be prowling around at night, like an owl or a cat, to steal cherries? Whew, the woman has completely lost her mind! I was just talking with the gardener, and he asked me to go around this side of the orchard to see if some wretched rogue might have sneaked in and hidden here."

"Oh, you're lying, Hadyna, you're lying! You're lying so outrageously that your nose is smoking," Hapka said, but her voice was a bit gentler.

"If you don't believe me, go and ask the gardener!" Hadyna said boldly.

"As if it's any of my business!" Hapka said indignantly. "If the gardener wants to partner with you, that's up to him. If he wants to spare his dog, and hires a wolf to look after the sheep— he's free to do so! It's not my millet, they're not my sparrows, and I'm not about to chase them out. Well, go on, go on where you were set on going, and break your neck! I have faith in God that you won't avoid the branch on which you are bound to be hanged. You'll jump up on it yourself! You'll put your head in the noose voluntarily."

And with that prediction, so replete with brotherly love, Hapka bade farewell to Hadyna and stalked through the gate into the yard.

"God grant you the same! God grant you the very same thing that you wish for others!" Hadyna called out after her, watching through a crack in the fence to see where she was going.

Hapka had set out at first for the kitchen, but seeing that it was dark and deserted, she hurried over to Lady Olimpiya's quarters. Hadyna knew that if she did not find the Lady in her rooms, she would sit down on the threshold and wait for her; he had heard from the gardener that the Lady had been in the orchard a short while ago; that meant that she must have gone through the orchard, into the field, then to the hay meadows, where she often liked to walk around until late at night. That meant—this was a good time. It was unlikely that anyone would get in his way now.

For Hadyna really wanted to at least hear what was going on in Fr. Nestor's room, even if he could not see into it. Was the old man sleeping, or was he pacing his room, or sitting and counting his money? And so, doubling over, he stole past the bushes and the tall grass to the corner of the annex, then, slinking along the wall to the other corner, he went around it, and quietly, ever so quietly, like a cat inching its way along a chicken roost, crept up to the window.

Even though the window was shut and draped, he could see through the curtain that there was a light on in the room. That meant that Fr. Nestor was not sleeping.

Hadyna's curiosity doubled in intensity. What was the priest doing? For a long minute he could not hear anything. It seemed that there was not a living soul in the room. But then there came the sound of paper being flipped, and a dull thud on the table. A sigh, and a hushed muttering. Then a rustling once again. The scraping sound of a chair being pushed away—and suddenly, like thunder shattering the silence of the night, a loud thumping on the door of the vestibule.

Fr. Nestor cried out in alarm: "O my Lord! What's that?"

The thumping was repeated, more loudly this time. Then a voice said: "If you please, your Reverence! If you please, your Reverence!"

Fr. Nestor rose to his feet and took a few steps. Hadyna could tell by the sound of his footsteps that he was still wearing his boots, and that meant that he had not yet undressed.

"Who . . . who's there?" Fr. Nestor asked, obviously finding it difficult to find his voice.

"It's me, Demenyuk. Please open the door. I'll be just a moment."

Fr. Nestor went to open the door. It must have been dark in the vestibule, for in a moment Fr. Nestor came back into the room with Demenyuk.

"What's happened to you, Yurko? You seem frightened."

"I'm afraid, your Reverence, that something terrible may have happened."

"Like what?"

"Malanka's disappeared."

"What do you mean, disappeared?"

"She talked with you at noon, and then she walked out of the house and hasn't been seen since."

"Come now, Yurko, what are you saying? Where could she have disappeared? She must be somewhere in the village, at the home of one of her friends."

"She's not there, your Reverence. I tore through almost half the village, and Maksym has also been racing around all evening—no one in the village has seen her."

"Well then, perhaps she went into town—after all, at times she probably does go into town on Sunday."

"Yes, but she always tells me: 'I'm going here and there, and I'll be back at such and such a time.' But today, she didn't say anything to anyone: she just up and left."

"Did she get all dressed up?"

"Well, she really didn't dress up at all. She left in what she was wearing in the house. The blacksmith's wife says that from the house she went into the garden, and from the garden over the stile onto the path. There are two paths leading from their place: one goes into the village, and the other goes into the field. So, there is no way of knowing which path she took. But no one in the village has seen her."

"Hmm . . . maybe she's walking around in the fields?"

"But what would she be doing in the fields all day long? Why wouldn't she have come back by now? And there's one more thing, your Reverence! Today is Sunday, people are wandering around all over the fields, so someone should have seen her."

"Now, now, Yurko, there's no reason yet to be so alarmed. After all, she isn't among wolves! Perhaps she has overstayed in the forest gathering berries. It's not all that late, as yet. Who knows, perhaps she has come home this very minute."

"May the Lord be speaking through his Reverence!" Demenyuk said, feeling a little better. "But all the same, I'm afraid. I'm afraid of one thing . . ."

"What's that, Yurko?"

"That she has gone to the other manor."

"To the other manor? Why would that be so terrible?"

"Oh, your Reverence! I fear our young Lord! I would prefer to see my child dead today—even though she is my only child, and you know how much I love her—than to have that young Lord have a laugh at her expense."

"Come now, Yurko! God be with you! After all, Malanka isn't a child!"

"Oh but she is a child, your Reverence! She has a good heart, she doesn't know how wicked people can be, and it would be easy to deceive her. But Heaven help the young Lord or anyone else who does her an injustice!"

Demenyuk's voice was controlled, but Hadyna felt chills run up and down his spine when he heard these threatening words. He had never heard Demenyuk say anything like that.

"For God's sake, Yurko! What are you saying? How can you, of all people, say something like that? You have nothing to fear—God is compassionate. Nothing will happen to your Malanka."

"May God grant it! But I feel as if pincers are squeezing my heart. I'm going straight to the blacksmith's house, and if Malanka is not there, I'll run over to the other manor."

"To the other manor?" Fr. Nestor asked in surprise. "I don't think there's any reason for you to run over there."

"No reason? If she isn't home by now, then it's certain that she's there."

"It's not at all certain, Yurko! It would be better if you stayed here and spent the night with me."

"With your Reverence?" Yurko asked in astonishment.

"You know, Yurko," Fr. Nestor said a little more softly, "I've decided that tomorrow I'm moving from here."

"To Herder's place?"

"Maybe even to Herder's place. I won't stay here any longer for anything in the world. You know," and he lowered his voice still more, so that Hadyna could scarcely hear him, "today I was robbed again."

"Robbed!" Demenyuk shouted, and his body jerked back in horror.

"Hush, Yurko! The Lady forced me to go to her quarters, to be with the guests, and while I was there, a thief went about his work here."

"And did he take a lot?"

"He did not take any documents, but he took all the ready cash that he could find. He grabbed about five thousand."

"Five thousand! O my Lord!" Demenyuk shouted, unable to control himself.

"Almost all the cash that I had on hand," Fr. Nestor said in a somewhat tearful, plaintive voice.

"But how did he get in here?" Demenyuk asked. "You must have left the door unlocked, right?"

"No, Yurko! I locked the door. I had the key."

"So, did the thief break the lock?"

"No, when I came back, the door was locked. I reached for the key in my pocket—it wasn't there. I went back to the salon, and the key had fallen out of my pocket and was lying on the sofa, half-hidden in a corner. Then I unlocked my room and saw that the money was gone."

"Maybe he came in through the window?"

"That's what the Lady said. But just think, Yurko: through which window? He could not crawl in through the one facing the orchard, because it has grates on it."

"Oh, those are some grates! A small man, someone like Hadyna, could crawl through them."

"But it seems to me that the window was latched from the inside. It is true that the Lady said that it was unlatched, but I think that she unlatched it. And no one can crawl in through the window facing the yard."

"Well, what did the Lady say?"

"She immediately put the blame on Tsvyakh, from the very first moment."

"On Tsvyakh?"

"Yes. She said that Tsvyakh did it, and no one else."

"When could this have happened?"

"Sometime between six and seven."

"Well, your Reverence, in that case I can assure you that Tsvyakh did not do it."

"He didn't? But how do you know that?"

"I talked to the bailiff. Tsvyakh spent the entire afternoon in the tavern; he got dead drunk, started a fight, and the bailiff had him put in jail for twenty-four hours. He's probably still there. No, Tsvyakh most certainly did not do this."

Fr. Nestor stood silently for a moment, struggling to solve this twisted riddle that rose before him like a dark cloud. Then he sighed heavily, as if sensing his helplessness, and said: "Well, whoever did it, did it, but I'm afraid . . ."

"Oh, now your Reverence can feel safe!" Demenyuk said. "Whoever did it won't dare to hurry back here a second time."

"Do you really think so?"

"I'm sure of it. Lock yourself in securely and don't be afraid of anything. I'll run over to Herder's home for a minute to find out if Malanka is there. If she is, I'll come right back."

"That's good, Yurko, that's good! Do come back, because it is ever so terrifying, so scary for me to be here by myself . . ."

"No, no, you can feel safe!" Demenyuk said hurriedly as he walked out of the room.

Fr. Nestor followed him to the door. Hadyna heard him turn the key twice in the lock, and then go back in.

Hadyna stood another minute under the window and listened as Fr. Nestor, sighing heavily once again, began to undress. After listening to the conversation, Hadyna's heart ached. Something akin to a heavy disappointment and a foreboding of misfortune stirred in his soul. Fr. Nestor had been robbed! Someone more clever than he was had grabbed all the cash. Yes, that's what he had done—he had grabbed it! Five thousand! What a huge amount! And what was even worse, now there was nothing left for him. Fr. Nestor was leaving the manor tomorrow, and that meant there was no hope left for the future. Damn it all to hell! There went all the shining prospects that he had bragged about to Paraska!

But that was not the end of his problems. That damned Demenyuk, for no good reason, had cast suspicion on him. And if the real robber was not found, they would start picking on him. Hadyna was truly scared, and shivers ran up and down his spine. Even though he was innocent of today's robbery, he felt guilty enough with respect to Fr. Nestor that if he was asked about it, he would not be able to speak calmly—he was sure about that.

From an early age, the sight of a gendarme had filled him with indescribable terror, and even now he did not know what he would do if a gendarme were to come up to him with a shiny feather on his cap, with a carbine and a bayonet, or if he were to put handcuffs on him and wanted "to have a talk with him" face to face, which really meant that he would cuff his ears once or twice or twist his hands in the shackles so tightly that they would bleed.

Hadyna was very sensitive to pain, had a terrible fear of physical altercations, and was well aware that, under the threat of a beating, he would disclose everything that he knew and even what he did not know.

Thinking these heavy and cheerless thoughts, he crawled once again into the bushes in the orchard, made his way to the gate, and went into the yard. But here he once again almost bumped his forehead into something soft, and just as he was about to scream in fear, that soft something moved and turned to face him. It was Lady Olimpiya, who had been standing huddled against the fence with her back to the gate.

"Who is it?" the Lady asked softly but firmly.

"It's me," Hadyna barely whispered.

"Me who?"

"Hadyna."

"Why are you roaming around here? Why don't you go to sleep?" the Lady was speaking sternly, but not too loudly. "And yet when it is time to go to work tomorrow, it will be next to impossible to wake you."

"I'm going, I'm going," Hadyna grumbled and set out for the kitchen.

"And remember," the Lady said as he left, "tomorrow morning, when you get up, cut down all these weeds in front of the window and around the raspberry patch! How many times do I have to tell you to do it?"

Hadyna was tempted to tell her that until this minute she had never told him to do it, but he remained silent. The Lady's order, taken together with what he had heard while crouching under Fr. Nestor's window, cut him to the quick. Why had this suddenly occurred to the Lady? Why were the weeds to be mown down the very next day? If it was for the good of the raspberries, mowing the weeds now would not help them at all, because they had almost stopped bearing; moreover, there were no raspberries right under Fr. Nestor's window.

Hadyna, unable to fall asleep, tossed and turned for a long time on his cot in the kitchen passageway. He listened intently to every faint nocturnal noise, but he could not discern any sounds other than the singing of the nightingales, the hooting of an owl, and the strident, intermittent, and unintelligible prattling of Hapka, who was talking in her sleep under the window in the kitchen. Paraska was sleeping in the Lady's quarters.

It was hot in the passageway, like in a sauna. Hadyna could not fall asleep, and he kept tossing from side to side. He was not thinking about anything, and he was no longer trying to hear what was going on; he was drowsing, but he was still turning from time to time on his hard bed. The impressions of the outside world still reached him, but his half-sleeping mind could no longer connect them to a certain spot, to keep them in order.

The boundary between dreams and reality gradually grew more and more tenuous. His powers of observation were fast asleep, but his consciousness, working independently, was still mechanically registering new impressions. A key clanged gently as it turned in a lock, a door creaked faintly—one door, a second door, it seemed, and a third, and a fourth. There was the sound of footsteps that were soft, ever so soft, as if they were cautiously walking barefoot, or in soft slippers on a floor. Swish-swish-

swish—and then silence. Then once again: swish-swish-swish—and that was it.

Where was this happening? Was it above him, or under him, or next to him? Something flashed in his head: someone must be spending the night in the guest room that adjoined the passageway to the kitchen, but his mind was unable to determine if this was truly the case. Swish-swish-swish—and silence. Shoo-shoo-shoo, hoo-hoo-hoo . . . Some whispers, a scarcely audible noise. And then somewhere deep below the earth, a long, prolonged, plaintive groaning: O-o-o-h! O-o-oh! O-o-o-h! Then silence once again. More groaning, then a dull thud from somewhere far, far away, as if someone had fallen from the loft to the threshing floor. And then, once again: swish-swish-swish. Then silence again.

Then a long piercing whistle from somewhere far, far away. Fiiiii! Or was it a train that was approaching? The railway was far from here; it could not be heard from here. Fiiiiii!

That was the final, half-perceived impression that Hadyna could recall a few days later. After the whistle that went on and on for what seemed to him as an inordinately long time, evenly, shrilly, like a copper wire—that impression of a shiny, straight, endlessly long copper wire that hung in the air, remained with him after the whistle—he fell soundly asleep and did not hear anything more.

XI

Adas's manor was alive with activity.

In the kitchen a fire was crackling in the stove, food was being boiled and fried, menservants and maids were on the run getting firewood, fetching water, going to the granary, to the cellar. The salon was brightly lit, filled with the hum of male voices. It was there that the guests sat as they waited for supper. After returning from the afternoon tea at the Countess's home, they had toured the manor yard while it was still light outside, wandered into the forest, and delighted in watching the setting sun from the high ridge; and now, after coming back to the house, they were smoking cigars and sipping wine.

Their conversation centred on topics quite unlike those that had occupied them at the Countess's home. The gathering was comprised of unmarried, like-minded young men who basically had little interest in public affairs and used them only as convenient stepping-stones that would lead them to honours, influence, patronage appointments, and distinction. And so, in this close circle, they did not need to put on an act and drape themselves in the togas of public tribunes—here everyone freely revealed his feelings and opinions.

Understandably, Lord Kalyasanty was the hero of their conversation. During their walk, he had shaken out before them whole bagfuls of knowledge—everything he knew about different breeds of horses, about the art of selling forests to be felled for lumber, about how to treat peasants in order to keep them obedient and dependent—and now he was winding down his weighty pronouncements on this topic.

"Because, in actual fact what does it all come down to? Civilization is a flower bed. The peasants are the manure, expedient only for making it possible for us—the exquisite flowers, the representatives of civilization—to grow on their backs by drawing nourishment from them. If they object to their destiny and get the notion of becoming flowers themselves—*O pardon*—in that case, not only will there not be enough soil for us, but the entire country will turn into a desert."

"They themselves know that, Kaytsya," Lord Emil said. "They have a saying that goes like this: if everyone gets the notion of becoming a lord, who will herd the swine?"

In the adjoining room, Tadzo, walking arm in arm with Adas, was talking to him in a hushed voice.

"Adas, is something wrong? Are you feeling out of sorts?"

"Me?" Adas responded in a tone that sounded half-surprised and half-alarmed. "Not at all."

"Don't fib! You can't hide your feelings from me. I've been watching you all afternoon. Come on, tell me, are you short of cash? Don't worry, it happens to all of us. On that point, you have my complete sympathy."

"Sympathy?"

Adas once again stared at Tadzo and was about to say that he did not need any money, but on second thought he added, trying to speak in a calm voice: "Oh, it's nothing! I'm a trifle short at the moment, but I . . . Today I'll travel to Lviv with you, and once I'm there, well . . . But actually, you know, I'm not the one who needs it, it's my mother."

"And what about your debt at the casino?"

"Oh, the devil take them and their casino! I'll pay it, what else can I do?"

"Well, how much do you need? You know, it just so happens that I have a bit of money now—and that's a rarity for me. But I'm afraid that if it stays in my pocket it will soon be gone, and so I could lend you some for a short time."

"Oh, thank you!" Adas said fervently as he clasped his friend's hand. "About two hundred gulden would do me nicely for the present. And in a week or two . . . When will you need the money?"

"In about two weeks, I think . . . not any sooner."

"Well, that's fine. In two weeks I'll give it back to you."

Tadzo removed two hundred guldens in tens from his pocketbook, gave them to Adas, and returned to the gathering.

Adas went out into the passageway, glanced into the kitchen, yelled at the servants to hurry with supper, and then walked around the yard where his coach and a single hansom from Lviv stood ready for the trip. The horses were still in the stable, munching on wilted clover.

Adas returned to his guests. They were growing bored. Lord Kalyasanty was trying his best to amuse them, demonstrating how to cheat while shuffling cards and relating various gambling incidents, but the gathering did not find his narrations overly engaging.

Tadzo was pacing the room with a frown on his face, Dr. Alfons sat in an armchair and chain-smoked cigars, and Lord Emil was examining Adas's rifles and pistols.

Supper was finally served, and the mood of the young lords immediately went up a whole octave. Their conversation became animated; they began joking and laughing, and even Adas seemed to cheer up, even though he kept looking around every minute, as if he expected an unpleasant bit of news.

After supper, a whole array of bottles was brought in, and Adas, after asking Tadzo to assume the role of host for a few minutes, begged the guests to excuse him, because he had to attend to an urgent matter. The guests did not pay any attention to his departure.

The young lords drank and amused themselves. The wine bubbled in their heads, their singing resounded loudly, and their conversations grew livelier by the minute. The smoke from their cigars hung in a blue cloud beneath the ceiling, and two of Adas's lackeys were kept busy uncorking bottles and pouring wine into goblets.

"How do you live here, in this wilderness?" Lord Kalyasanty asked one of the lackeys. "You're quite a ways from the village, all the serving maids here are old—how do you manage without any young women?"

"We get along as best we can, if it please your gracious Lordship," the lackey replied, grinning broadly.

"Well, how do you get along? Come on, tell us!"

"It's like this! Alongside the farmstead, there's a path leading into the forest where there are mushrooms and berries . . ."

"Aha, and you stand on guard and collect a toll from the girls going by."

"I can see that your gracious Lordship understands how these things work."

"Ha-ha-ha!" Lord Kalyasanty laughed uproariously. "Why wouldn't I understand, little brother! Ho-ho! But wait a minute—here's an empty goblet. Pour yourself some wine and drink it. Right now!"

The lackey did not wait to be asked twice.

"And what about your young Lord, Lord Adas," Kalyasanty inquired further, "does he like to go . . . after the girls?"

"I don't know, if it please your gracious Lordship. It's none of my business."

"Ho-ho, little brother! You won't get out of answering that easily. It's none of your business? And what if Lord Adas says: 'Matzko'—or what is your name?"

"Antin."

"If he says: 'Antin, I want this or that girl to come to me tonight?'"

"Things aren't done that way here, if it please your gracious Lordship. They're not that kind of people."

"So that's how it is! You say that they're not good people? That they don't obey?"

"No, they don't."

"Oh, that's bad. But I can't, I don't believe that Lord Adas doesn't . . ."

"Come on, Kaytsya," Tadzo interrupted the interrogation, "that's enough. I'm taking the place of the host, and I won't allow you to compromise his servants behind his back."

"But Tadyk!" Lord Kalyasanty, who was quite tipsy already, continued speaking. "How am I compromising them? All this is perfectly human! After all, I'm sure that our dear, beloved, righteous Adas does not live here like a monk, any more that he does in Lviv, and these old servants only serve to add to my suspicions. And that's why I, like the practical, experienced fellow that I am, would be happy to know how he manages."

"Knowing that won't benefit you in any way," Dr. Alfons said phlegmatically.

"Who knows! I'm assuming that even now he's gone off to a rendezvous with some *Daphne or *Chloe."

"That may well be," Dr. Alfons said thoughtfully. "To be sure, he's a very determined fellow. He left us without even saying why and where he was going."

"I admire that!" Lord Kalyasanty exclaimed, almost shouting. "In matters like that one must be resolute. In the military fashion, or the aristocratic manner. Slam-bam, and it's over. In the meantime, let's drink to Adas's health! *Niech żyje nam* [Long may he live]!"

They all rose to their feet, raised their goblets, and sang in tipsy voices: "*Niech żyje nam* [Long may he live]!"

But their singing broke off in the middle of a bar. In the adjoining room that served as Adas's bedroom, something moved, there was a rustling noise, a mumbling as if someone had awoken from a deep sleep, and then the sound of footsteps and a loud knocking on the door.

"What's this?" all the guests cried in chorus.

The knocking was repeated. The lackeys stood, either amazed or afraid, and neither of them moved. Lord Emil was the first to run to the door that was being knocked on from the other side. The door was locked, and the key had been removed.

"Where's the key to the door?" Emil asked one of the lackeys.

"I do not know, if it please your Lordship."

"What does that mean: I do not know? Get a move on, find it, and stop talking nonsense."

The lackeys rushed about and brought a few keys; one of them fit the lock.

"It will be interesting to see who is hidden in there!" Dr. Alfons said, staring at the door from the table.

In the open doorway of the bedroom appeared the tall, slim figure of a village girl. Obviously not quite understanding where she was, she fixed her sleepy, astonished eyes on the lords who, startled and curious, stepped up quickly to look at her.

"Heh-heh-heh!" Lord Kalyasanty cried cheerfully. "So that's the nymph that's guarding Adas's *penates."

"So that's the kind of monk our honourable host is!" Lord Emil observed with a smile.

"You must admit one thing, gentlemen, that his taste is not bad, and that this beauty is truly worthy of our protection," Dr. Alfons said judiciously.

The girl, still standing in the doorway of the bedroom, was looking around vacantly and not saying a word.

Tadzo turned to one of the lackeys.

"Listen," he said softly, "do you know who this girl is?"

"Yes, I do, if it please your gracious Lordship."

"Who is she?"

"She's from here, from the village, and her name is Malanka. She serves at . . ."

"Ah, she's a servant! And is the young Lord, is he, uh, you know . . . with her?"

"No, if it please your gracious Lordship. I have never seen her here before."

"You have never seen her here? And today?"

"And I did not see her today—when and how she got here."

"Do you mean to say you did not know that she was here?"

"No, I did not."

"So that's how it is! But how can that be? How then did she get here?"

"I do not know, if it please your gracious Lordship."

Tadzo walked up to Malanka and took her by the hand.

She did not protest; she just stared blankly at him with fiery dark eyes that were filled with an impotent anxiety, as if her mind, somehow rendered powerless, was trying desperately to bestir itself and make some sense out of what she was seeing around her.

"Listen, my girl," Tadzo said, "tell us, what are you doing here? How did you get here?"

Malanka just continued staring at the young lord. But the touch of his hand was like a shock that jolted her mind into functioning normally. She started to come to her senses and to understand where she was. And this realization was not a pleasant one for her.

Finding herself in the young Lord's salon, in the glare of burning lamps, and in the midst of a group of curious, drunken lords, she panicked

She understood that it was evening now, that she had slept away the entire day, and that she would be late getting home; however, there was something that she did not understand: how was it possible that, after having dinner and drinking the glass of wine that Adas had given her, she could have fallen asleep so soundly, and why did her head ache so terribly, and why did she have such a foul taste in her mouth, and how was it that instead of Adas being there, she had ended up in the company of these lords, and Adas was nowhere in sight.

"O, my God!" she cried as she tore her hand out of Tadzo's grasp. "What have I done? I should have been home long ago."

And she took a step as if she wanted to make her way through the group of lords to get to the door.

"Oh, no, sweetheart, you can't do that," Tadzo cried. "You must tell us what you are doing here."

"I? Nothing . . . I was sleeping," Malanka said.

"You were sleeping, sleeping. But how did you get here? How did you get in without any of the servants seeing you?"

"I was with the young Lord . . . I certainly would not come here on my own . . ."

"Ah, so you were with the young Lord!" Lord Kalyasanty exclaimed. "Did he bring you here, or did you come of your own free will?"

Malanka stared at him and at the others, as they chimed in.

"Well, tell us, do you love him very much, huh? Or did you just come to see him, to visit him?"

"Do you often come here like this?"

"And since the young Lord is not here, perhaps you would like to visit with us? You are such a beautiful girl—we would find that very pleasant."

"Truly, Malanka!" Tadzo said. "Until your young Lord comes back, sit down and have some wine with us! Hey, you over there, let's have a goblet with some wine over here."

"For all of us! For all of us!" Lord Kalyasanty called out. "We shall all drink to the health of our beautiful Malanka—is that really your name, huh? It's a pretty name!"

"Here you are, Malanka, do not be afraid of us!" Lord Emil said soothingly, passing her the goblet of wine. "The young Lord will be here soon, and we are his guests. Well, why are you just standing there? Here, take this and drink it!"

"Let me go!" Malanka shouted, and she sprang forward, shoving aside the lascivious lords with her strong, firm hands.

Lord Emil staggered and spilled the wine on the floor, and Lord Kalyasanty was jostled so violently that he bounced against the wall and sloshed wine all over himself, not only from his glass, but also from the bottle in his left hand.

"Oh, you uncouth cow!" he exclaimed, slipping instantly from a sentimentally tearful tone into a coarsely vulgar one. "What do you think you're doing? We're treating you nicely, and you're knocking us around? Do you think that you're out in a pasture with your peasant boys?"

And without pausing to think what he was doing, he took a swing at her and slapped her face.

Malanka, who had been stopped in her flight by the two lackeys, shrieked and lunged forward again in an attempt to escape.

"Hold her!" the enraged Lord Kalyasanty yelled. "She's probably a thief who has stolen something from the young Lord's bedroom."

"You're a thief yourself!" Malanka shouted back at him, and her face flamed with anger. "Let me go! What do you want from me? O dear God! Help me in my hour of need!"

And, summoning up all her strength, she shoved one of the lackeys so hard against the wall that he toppled to the floor, while she dragged the other one after her as she dashed to the door. But Lord Kalyasanty, Tadzo, and Emil blocked her path.

"No, wait! Now you won't get away," Tadzo said gently but firmly. "We can't let you go until the young Lord returns. The servants say that they did not see you come in here, but they saw the young Lord. That means that it cannot be true that you came here with him."

"Let me go! Let me go!" Malanka begged; she was breathing heavily, and tears were welling in her eyes.

At that moment, the lackey who had fallen to the floor leapt to his feet, bounded up to her, and angrily slammed his fist into the nape of her neck.

"You wretched woman!" he cried. "You think you can get away from me? Just you wait, we'll tie you up and hand you over to the gendarmes. They'll show you what's what. You'll be singing a different tune then."

For Malanka, this threat was like the blow of a cudgel on her head. From childhood she had greatly feared the gendarmes, and even now she could not look at them without feeling scared. And so, hearing that they wanted to turn her over to the gendarmes, she recalled all the horrible stories that she had heard about them. Through her head flashed shackles, chains, carbines with bayonets stuck in them; and she saw herself being led in shackles through the village, with everyone running up to look at her, with everyone laughing at her, with mothers pointing her out to their children, and the children whispering, talking, and then shouting, screaming after her: thief, thief!

And she lost her ability to think, to reason, to act prudently. An uncontrollable panic almost drove her out of her mind. She flung herself about, trying desperately to get away, and repeating all the while: "Let me go! Let me go! I'm not a thief."

A short but frenzied struggle ensued. For a few minutes, five men (because Dr. Alfons looked on silently, with philosophical tranquility, at the scene) wrestled with one girl. She struck one of the lackeys in the face so hard that blood spurted from his nose, then she punched the aristocratic Lord Kalyasanty in the chest, tore Tadzo's sleeve off his jacket, and kicked Lord Emil so vigorously that he yelped and collapsed in a chair. But in the end, they overpowered her. One of the lackeys grabbed her right hand and twisted it behind her back so forcefully that the bone cracked, and Malanka shrieked and fell to her knees.

"You viper! You dissolute tramp!" Lord Kalyasanty shouted as he grabbed her by the hair and shoved her head downwards. "Just you wait, we'll show you how to fight with us! Come on, fellows, tie her hands!"

The lackeys instantly tied her hands behind her back.

"Take her in there!" the preacher of aristocratic democracy then commanded, pointing at the bedroom door.

The lackeys shoved Malanka into the bedroom that was completely dark except for a shaft of light that entered it from the adjoining room.

"Search her to see if she has stolen anything," he ordered, and, after lighting a candle in the bedroom, he shut the door.

A moment later Malanka's loud scream rang out—so loud and desperate that the lords who remained in the salon shuddered.

"Kaytsya, don't do anything foolish!" Dr. Alfons shouted without budging from his chair.

"Well, what would you say about a witch like that?" Tadzo said angrily as he examined his torn sleeve. "She really deserves to be taught a lesson."

Lord Emil was still sitting in the armchair, holding his stomach and gnawing his lips in pain. "Oh, I could tear her to pieces! I could . . . She's some kind of beast, not a girl!"

The shouting died down in the bedroom, and all that could be heard were dull whispers, Lord Kalyasanty's hushed curses, and Malanka's heavy breathing.

The lords in the salon fell silent and listened; their anger gradually abated, to be replaced by a more sober deliberation, and in their hearts they all felt a growing uneasiness that escalated into disgust and abhorrence.

They felt that, before their very eyes, with their help and participation, something so savage and absurd, so abominable and loathsome had happened that it could fall as a heavy, indelible blot on their lives and shatter their hopes and plans; that they, who just a moment earlier had been a cheerful and carefree group of revellers, had unexpectedly and inconceivably just gone through one of the most decisive, fatal, and horrifying moments of their lives.

How had it happened? How had it started? Why, for what reason, had it turned out the way it had? The fatal moment had been so brief, so unusual, so irrational, so unmotivated, that in the first instance, the mind could not process the impressions that assailed it or make sense of what had happened.

They all sat gloomy and depressed, and even Dr. Alfons lost his philosophical serenity and, throwing his half-finished cigar into a corner, turned towards the bedroom door and shouted loudly: "Kaytsya! I am telling you decisively that you are a beast of the worst possible kind!"

At that moment the door that led into the vestibule opened with a loud clatter, and in the doorway appeared the figure of an old, grey-headed man, without a hat, with long, windblown hair, barefoot, in a short felt vest. His face was the picture of terror and alarm. It was old Demenyuk.

"My child! My daughter! Where is my daughter?" he shouted as he barged into the room. "Where is she? I heard her screaming while I was still out there, beyond the garden; I heard her shouting: 'Daddy! Daddy! Save me!' Tell me, gentlemen, where is she? Where have you hidden her?"

At that moment a groan resounded from the bedroom, a terrible, penetrating groan, as if someone, dying in horrible agony, is gagged and cannot shout.

Demenyuk lunged at the bedroom door like a wounded animal, threw it open and, seeing what was happening there, roared as if he had gone mad, and it seemed to the lords that the entire manor yard was rocked to its very foundation by that inhuman cry.

Then there was a loud thump, as if someone had thrown a sack of grain from a loft to the ground, and the dull yelp of Lord Kalyasanty—then a long, long silence, broken only by muffled sounds, agitated whispers, and heavy sobs. The lords sat silently, without moving. Only Dr. Alfons tiptoed unobserved out of the room and ordered that the horses be harnessed as quickly as possible.

Then the bedroom door opened, and old Demenyuk walked through it, supporting Malanka. She was deathly pale, her exquisite head hung weakly on her father's shoulder, her arms were wound around her father's neck.

Silently, the two of them walked out of the room, and a moment later were beyond the boundary of the manor yard; like two incorporeal shadows, they sank into the darkness of the warm, still, summer night.

A couple more minutes went by, and the guests, without waiting for Adas, got into the hansom and Adas's coach, and ordered the coachmen to drive off as quickly as they could.

The lights were still on in the room where such horrific scenes had transpired just moments ago, and the lackeys were tidying up after the melee, when Adas burst into the room without saying a word. He was out of breath, wet from the dew, and as white as a sheet. But the lackeys did not pay attention to that, for they too were upset and shaking at the very thought of the matter in which they had assisted.

"What happened here?" Adas asked as he looked around.

"N . . . n . . . nothing, if it please your gracious Lordship," one of the lackeys mumbled.

"Have they gone?"

"Yes."

"Why didn't they wait for me? What does this mean? Why is there such a mess in here? Oh my God!"

Adas shouted the last words as if he had inadvertently stepped with a bare foot on a shard of broken glass that drove itself deeply into his flesh. And there was a reason for this shout: the door to his bedroom was open, the bed was in disarray, a candle was lit, and a chair was overturned.

"What happened here? Speak up! What happened?"

"Well . . . well . . . well nothing . . . What could have . . ."

Adas leapt up to one of them in a fit of rage, grabbed him by his shirt, and after shaking him as if he were a small bundle—the lackey was weak with fear—shouted right in his ear.

"You wretch! Tell me this instant what happened here, for if you don't, you'll die on the spot!"

The lackey, shaking uncontrollably and scarcely able to force the words out of his throat, told him briefly what had transpired. His narration appeared to fell Adas like an axe.

"Go to sleep!" he ordered the lackeys.

After they left, he locked the door and collapsed in the armchair recently occupied by Dr. Alfons. He sat and stared at the light cast by a table lamp with a pink shade. Drowning his gaze in that pink pool of lamplight, he sat without thinking, without moving, but also without sleeping, until the pool started to fade, to fade away completely, until the summer sun rolled like a golden wheel out of the purple mist and glanced through the window into the salon.

XII

But we must now return to the mysteries and the sorcery of that night.

Flooding over the earth like a boundless sea and lighting innumerable candles in the sky just to show more clearly how deep, how dark, and how impenetrable she was, old Lady Night set about dispersing her charms. She breathed over the meadows and river deltas and covered them with thick grey billows of fog that stood motionless, like countless regiments ready to embark on a far-off campaign. With her bountiful broad palm she stroked the meadows and the fields, and the ripening fields of rye and wheat bowed with a soft murmur under that caress, and then, straightening their stalks, they raised their heads and stood quietly, as if holding their breath, waiting to see what would happen next.

Then the old Sorceress-Night took a handful of golden sand out of a small sack and cast it into the wide open spaces: the tiny golden grains scattered and began flying around, carefully, slowly, making their way through the dense shadows and the pillars of fog, swirling above marshes, rising upwards, and then pausing for a moment in one spot; these were the will-o'-the-wisps that flared so often over the Torsky swamps. Some of them, floating above the hayfields, got as far as the lord's orchard that loomed in a thick dark mass on the declivity, and the braver ones that dared to penetrate the dark thickets quickly vanished.

But all this did not satisfy Lady Night. She cupped her hands, dipped them into a large sack, and scooped out a myriad of crystal peas that she scattered over the ground. The peas fell on the grass, the leaves, the flowers, catching on their sharp points, rolling into the depths of colourful goblets, crumbling into tiny pearls on leaves adorned with fine silky hairs, dropping heavily and audibly here and there from tall trees, and glancing against the wide skirts of the broad-leaved burdock.

Having poured out her entire store of pearly dew, the old Sorceress-Night shuddered—and a silent shiver permeated all of nature. A coolness drifted over everything, a soft coolness, but one that was so penetrating that even the ancient oak and linden trees seemed to feel it, and their crowns shuddered so abruptly that thousands of pearls dropped to the ground. The nightingales fell silent in the thickets, the wind held its breath, and all that could be heard was the quiet falling of the dew—as if unseen tears were rolling evenly and endlessly from hundreds of eyes. Occasionally a black beetle flew by, buzzing dolefully and protractedly, like the distant echo of a worrisome thought. And it seemed as if all of nature had grown still, swooned momentarily in numb anticipation.

Ah! There it was! The gate that led from the yard to the orchard creaked ever so faintly, and a figure, stepping cautiously, flashed through it and, like a minnow in a swamp, sank instantly into the darkness that filled the orchard. It sank and seemed to disappear, to dissipate without a sound, without a trace, so that the gardener, who had been awoken in his hut by the creaking of the gate, strained his ears in vain to hear the slightest rustle in the orchard. He waited a good minute and then, not hearing anything except the noisy snoring of his dog that was sleeping alongside the hut, fell asleep again.

It was only after about ten minutes that the dark figure, hidden in the darkness about a dozen steps away from the hut, silently crawled farther, winding its way like a snake through the bushes and the tall burdock plants. Creeping out of the orchard, the black figure straightened up, sighed, shook off the droplets of dew that clung to its hair, face, hands, and clothes, and then set off at a trot down the path across the hayfield.

In a single breath it ran right up to the little bridge that was slung over the Torsky River and stopped there; taking out a bundle of black clothing from under its coat, it groped around near the bridge, found a large stone, placed it inside the bundle and, tightly twisting the roll, swung its arm as if to throw it into the water.

But no! It must have recalled that the water near the little bridge was shallow, and so, after thinking for a moment, it began running downwards along the river, wading through dense wet grass that reached to its waist.

After running about two hundred steps to a spot where the river curved and created a deep slough surrounded by shrubs, the nocturnal apparition abruptly heaved the bundle into the water and ran away as fast as it could. It ran for quite a while along the river, then jumped across it in a narrow spot, and turned to go past the hill, across the potato field, to the smaller manor. For a while it ran down a furrow, then it stopped, squatted, and listened.

What was that?

Was there something moving in the middle of the field? Was it a wild boar rooting for potatoes? No, a boar would be black, and this figure was white. The nocturnal apparition began to move slowly forward. And then the second apparition, the white one, straightened up for a moment—it was a woman, a peasant, holding a hoe.

"The beast!" the black apparition muttered. "Just look where she's come to steal potatoes."

But the black apparition did not attack or scare the thief, it did not shout, but, quietly stooped over and almost crawling, edged its way forward, continually glancing back over its shoulder.

Now, the white apparition once again bent over, and you could hear its laboured breathing and the hoe striking against the dry earth, and now you could hear its loud sighs—some words, either a prayer or a curse—but suddenly, what is this?

From the road nearby, new voices could be heard. Hurried footsteps thumped on the well-trodden path, and there was the sound of desperate wailing that tore at the heart, and then the words: "Daddy! My dearest daddy! Let me go! I don't want to live! I want to kill myself!"

It was a girl's high-pitched voice. And an old broken voice replied: "My dear child! God be with you! What are you saying? Have faith in God. He saw the injustice that was done to you, and He will avenge it."

The black apparition froze, listened without stirring, listened for some time yet, even though the wailing girl and her old father were now quite far away.

And the woman who was stealing the potatoes also scrunched down and waited until they had passed her. But it was not her lucky day. No sooner had those two gone by, when the gate at the manor creaked and the thumping of horses' hooves was heard, and a moment later two carriages rattled down the road. The woman once again bent down and huddled in a furrow.

But the dark apparition, hearing that noise, straightened up and, heedless of its former cautiousness, set out at a run in the direction of the road, waving its arms and shouting at the top of its lungs: "Hey! Hey!"

"Oh, my God! I'm done for!" the woman who was stealing potatoes groaned at the same moment and, dropping her sack and her hoe, fled down the field.

But the shouting of the black apparition did not stop the carriages hurtling down the road. They continued rattling towards Torky, and when the woman turned around a short while later to see if the black apparition was chasing after her, she did not see anyone in the field.

Trembling from fear and the cold—she was dressed only in a long white shirt that was soaked with dew—she stood for some time without moving, catching the sound of the carriages as they rumbled through the village, the distant barking of dogs, and the faint sighs of dreamy nature on a summer night.

Now the rumbling stopped for a minute, and in its place resounded a loud, prolonged whistle: "Fiiii! Fifififiiii!"

Silence. Then there was the rumble of carriages once again, but the sound grew ever softer, more distant, indistinct, until it melded with the vague nocturnal murmurs of slumbering nature.

The woman sighed heavily, crossed herself, and slowly, cautiously, made her way back to the spot where she had abandoned her hoe and the sack of potatoes. The black apparition had not taken anything; everything was lying where she had left it. But the woman did not dare to dig any longer.

She hastily grabbed the sack, threw it over her shoulder, picked up the hoe, and made her way as swiftly as she could down a furrow to the end of the field. Once there, she avoided the hayfield and cut across the potato fields until she reached the road, and then, looking around fearfully and breathing heavily because of the weight of the sack, she hastened to the village.

When she reached the village she left the road to avoid going right through it where the night patrol might see her. With some difficulty she crawled through the ditch and under the fence that surrounded Herder's yard, and crept down the path to a spot behind the barn.

There she stopped for a minute and peered through a crack in the fence. Herder's house was still lit, and there was an unusual ruckus in it. And then the dogs started barking, and the woman with the potatoes did not wait for them to come out on the path; crossing herself and whispering the Lord's Prayer, she trudged along as fast as she could. Now she stopped and turned onto a narrow path that led to a stile. Groaning heavily, she started clambering over it with the sack still on her back.

Just then another figure, all out of breath, as if it were being chased by a monster, sprinted towards the stile from the other direction and ran up so quickly that it rammed right into the sack of potatoes on the woman's back.

"Oh, what's this?" the startled figure cried out and stopped.

"O my God! What's this?" the woman shouted at the same moment, letting go of the sack that fell with a thud at the startled figure's feet.

"Is it you, Marta?" the startled figure asked.

"O my God! It's Tsvyakh!" the woman exclaimed. "What are you doing? Where have you been?"

"Where did you get the potatoes?" Tsvyakh asked, without answering her question, as he picked up the sack and heaved it over his shoulder.

"I dug them out at the other manor. What else was I to do? I'm not going to die of hunger. But tell me, where have you been roaming around? They said the bailiff had locked you up in jail."

"Yes, he locked me up, the double-crosser, may his mouth be locked and sealed forever. They beat me up in the tavern, and then they locked me up as well. But what do I care about their jail? I pried up a board in the floor and crawled out. But that doesn't matter. That's nothing. But as for what I saw just now—O my Lord, Marta! What I saw just now!"

He had already crawled over the stile. When he recalled what he had seen, he started shaking uncontrollably, and he cringed and huddled up to his wife like a terrified child. His voice, that had been raised almost to a shout a moment ago, was now lowered to a barely audible whisper.

"Well, what did you see? Why are you trembling?"

"Oh, Marta! It's terrible to even think about it! Let's go into the house, I can't tell you out here . . ."

"Well, what is it? Tell me!"

"No, no, no! Let's go to the house. You know, I was in the Lady's manor yard . . ."

"Something always makes you go to that manor yard. Oh, Tsvyakh, Tsvyakh! You're asking for trouble by going there!"

"No, I'm not. Just listen! Oh, you'll never believe what I saw! O my Lord, you would have died on the spot if you had seen something like that. I still have shivers running up and down my spine when I recall it. Let's go, let's go to the house! Quickly, so no one sees us."

And Tsvyakh surged ahead, and his wife hurried after him, continually crossing herself and whispering a prayer.

Tsvyakh's house stood at the end of a garden, long and narrow like a catgut cord, and all it had in it were four wide rows. The cottage was old, thatched, run-down, and had not been whitewashed for a long time. In front of it, facing the road, were two spreading and partially hollow willows that served as fence posts for the gate.

There was no light in the cottage. The children were sleeping. Tsvyakh and his wife sat down on the earthen embankment along the front wall.

"Well, tell me, what did you see?" Marta asked.

Tsvyakh bent over her, embraced her head with his left hand, pulled it towards himself, and began whispering rapidly, running out of breath and stuttering.

"O my Lord! That can't be! Oh, dear Mother of God!" Marta exclaimed from time to time as she listened to his narration. "For God's sake, Tsvyakh! That just can't be! You're drunk! You've dreamt it all up."

"May the sacred earth swallow me if I'm lying even a tiny bit!" Tsvyakh swore.

"And you saw everything? With your own eyes?"

"That's what I'm telling you: I saw it!"

"O Lord, Lord! What can it mean? What will come of it?"

"How am I to know!"

Marta wrung her hands and glanced at him.

"Oh, I know. Oh, I know what will happen, Tsvyakh! They'll blame it all on you! You'll be blamed for everything. You'll answer for everything!"

"Who? Me?" Tsvyakh cried as if he had been stabbed. "What are you talking about? How can that be, if I'm not guilty?"

"Well, you'll see! You'll remember my words! O Lord! What will I do then?"

"But Marta, why are you worried, when it couldn't be me. After all, I saw . . ."

"It would be better if your eyes crawled out of their sockets, so that you couldn't see God's world, that's what!" his wife cried. "It would be better if you had just sat in jail, where they put you. But wait! Did anyone see you run away from jail?"

"Who was to see me? If they had seen me, do you suppose they would have let me go?"

"And could you get back in there again without anyone seeing you?"

"Why not? Of course I can."

"Well, you know what? I advise you and beg you, I ask you in the name of God: go right now and crawl back into jail, and sleep there until morning. And in the morning I'll come to see you, bring you something to eat, and I want to find you still sleeping, do you understand?"

Tsvyakh thought about it for a moment, and then, leaping to his feet, said hurriedly: "I understand! You've given me good advice. Good night!"

And without saying another word, Tsvyakh bent over double and ran past the garden, going back the same way that he had come home a short time ago.

His wife, sitting a moment longer on the embankment, whispered a prayer, went into the cottage and, without changing her drenched clothing, lay down on the plank bed spread with straw and a thick blanket. But she could not fall asleep for a long time; her teeth were chattering, and she tossed and turned, sighed heavily, and kept whispering prayers.

And the old Sorceress-Night saw all that, heard all that, and she even saw and heard more than that. People's crimes, their suffering, their fears, were nothing new to her, but she still likes such scenes, and she scatters her abundant charms to enhance them with the wildest poetry, with penetrating terror. She likes to tease people, awaken their fantasies, and fill them with thousands of imagined monsters, larger and more terrifying than real life. Like a good director, she cares not only about the content of the play, but also about the stage settings and the costumes.

And so, while in this quiet dark corner of the earth, silent, terrified, and half-conscious actors play out a horrible, bloody drama and do everything required of them to ensure that the plot leads to a denouement that remains unknown to them, the old Sorceress-Night follows their every step with a thousand secret eyes, peers into their eyes, their hands, their bosoms, into the very depths of their souls, whispers secrets into their ears, secrets so incomprehensible and so horrific that their blood turns to ice, their will is rendered helpless, and their entire being, like a reed in the wind, bows before the breath of a mysterious fatalism.

It is pitch-dark.

A candle flickers like an expiring life.

Deep groans resound as if they are emanating from the bowels of the earth, and it seems that they jolt not only human souls, but the very pillars of nature.

The actors in this bloody drama dart about feverishly, search for something, carry something, whisper something, ponder something, consult and contrive, but it is all done without any cohesiveness, without a plan, as if their senses are muddled, as if they are stunned, thunderstruck.

And when they suddenly glance beyond themselves, in a direction where they should not be looking at all, they see, pressed against a dark window, the pale, terrified, familiar, odious face of an unexpected, unwanted witness.

There is a deathly moment of deathly fear. Soft whispers. One more glance—the terrifying face is not at the window.

Go outside! There is no one, no one to be heard! It was a spectre, an apparition, a joke, a frightening joke of the old Sorceress-Night.

"Tee-hee-hee! Hoo-oo-oo!" shrill laughter resounds right here, over their ears. Their hearts faint, their bodies grow cold. But a moment later their chests rise slowly, their consciousness and their resolve return. It is an owl that nests in the hollow of an old linden tree. It is another prank of the old Sorceress-Night.

"With a stick, with a stick, with a stick! Whack it! Whack it! Trrr! Tsi, tsi, tsi, tsi, kueet!"

A nightingale is chirping-chanting in a cherry tree, under the very window from which it occasionally can hear a dull groaning and rattling.

The tiny bird does not understand what these savage tones mean; it sings and trills, glorifying the wondrous summer night, and the twinkling stars, and the fragrant linden tree, and the dreaming roses and white flowers, and those delicate clouds that have flown far, ever so far away to the east and are already beginning to be flooded by a barely discernible greenish-purplish hue, the first sign that the sun is approaching the horizon.

From this moment on, all these charms of the night are powerless; it is sleep that embraces the earth and its poor, sinful children, drawing them closely to its breast and soothing their hearts with an ephemeral tranquility . . . until the morning awakens them to a new life, to new worries, to new endeavours, and to new suffering.

Part Two

I

The sun was rising grandly over the Torsky plains. On the ground and in the air there was a stillness, a solemn gravity; in all of nature something invisible, unfathomable, poignant, and overpowering was quivering, as if awaiting, in mute anxiety, the arrival of a formidable judge. Something akin to a profound, forcibly suppressed sigh could be heard; apprehension crept along the lowlands in a grey fog, appropriating ever-greater expanses, blowing coldly against the clear, cloudless sky as if seeking to find a place for itself there, as well.

And the sun was rising slowly, grandly and tranquilly, in all its majesty. Ahead of it spread a sea of purple, a crimson lake that rolled irrepressibly from the east and, rising ever higher, flooded half the sky, revealing to the apprehensive, impotent, sinful earth the face of a grim avenger, a face blazing with fury. But then the eastern edge of that blood-red lustre was gradually suffused with gold and, assuming the appearance of an immense hearth, glowed like white-hot platinum.

And suddenly, from out of this hearth the sun burst forth, and its face was blindingly bright, awe-inspiring, intolerable to the human eye.

It cast a swift, knowing look at the earth. There were no secrets on the earth for the sun; it had known the earth to its core from time immemorial—after all, the earth was bone of its bone and flesh of its flesh; it had known the earth fully, from the time when, caught up in mad, universal eddying, inflamed, and barely condensed out of the cosmic gases, it had torn away from the sun's majestic body and, frolicking and whirling like a naive young lamb, had rolled into the dark, frigid expanses of space to live for a galactic moment—a few hundred million years—in freedom, apart from its mighty progenitor, even though it remained tightly dependent on it.

From that moment, a substantial span of time had passed; the once innocent and frisky lamb had time to grow weary, cool down considerably, and cultivate a profusion of all kinds of "domestic fowl" that scour its surface as they search for something, think about something, hurry to get somewhere, scuffle and fight among themselves, are born and die like teeming bubbles on the water's surface on a rainy day.

The sun gazes grandly and majestically at this remarkable spectacle that it helped to bring forth. It likes the earth, takes an interest in it, as a child in a toy, and day after day it gazes upon its novel but age-old transformations with the same fascination with which we are apt to look at the wondrously changing patterns of a kaleidoscope.

But today the sun woke up in a bad mood. It sensed that something evil had happened on the earth, and the moment that it glanced down upon it, cast its eye on the Torsky manor yard, and peeked into the window of the annex, it felt like turning away and, like a stern but loving old mother, grumbled reproachfully at its daughter-earth: "Aha, so you're at it again!"

The earth remained gloomily silent and attempted to hide its face with a cold mist, but its ruse did not work.

The sun, seeing what the earth was trying to do, wrinkled its radiant brow and called out: "Hey there, my golden rays! Off you go! Cut through that fog! Pierce it! Plunge right through it! Do not let the earth obscure the truth with its veil! Do not allow it to assist in the concealment of this deed! Clarify everything, bring everything out into the light of day! May people not call me the righteous sun in vain. I want to be just, and I do not want injustice to rule the world from its hiding place."

And the cool mist was torn asunder and, like a ragged old veil, it dropped in shreds upon the face of the earth. A deep sigh of shame and pain heaved the earth's bosom, quivered in all of nature, made every living soul shudder. A sharp, oppressive odour, like that of warm blood, wafted through the air.

Infants cried in their cradles, horrifying nightmares weighed heavily on people who were sleeping, and those who awakened looked around in dread, not knowing what had come to pass on the earth, and they crossed themselves and whispered: "May the Holy Spirit be with us and our house!"

In the Torsky manor, everyone was still sleeping. Although the working day was beginning, no one was in a hurry to get to work. Even the tenant farmer, who woke up for a moment and saw that the sun was rising, just dropped his head wearily back on his hard, straw-packed pillow, and was out like a light. The young herdsman was also sleeping like a log; it was not up to him to rise on his own; he knew that his master, the tenant farmer, would wake him up after milking the cows, and for him every moment of lost sleep was more precious than gold. And the servants were not in a hurry to go anywhere; they could sleep until the Lady summoned them.

Nevertheless, the heavy ominous atmosphere that had settled on the Torsky manor this morning quickly communicated itself to its inhabitants. First, it took hold of the animals.

The gardener's dog that slept near his hut suddenly began to howl mournfully. The unsettling ululation cut through the somnolent stillness of the early morning like a dull rusty knife, drilled into the ears of the people who were sleeping in various nooks and corners of the manor yard, and awoke in them a foreboding of evil. The gardener, hearing the howling, leapt to his feet, poked his head out of the hut, and called out to the dog: "Hush, Bossay, hush! Come here, come!"

Bossay glanced balefully at his owner and then, raising his muzzle and turning to face the annex, let loose such a bloodcurdling howl from his powerful throat that the gardener's heart froze. He got up from his pallet and walked out of the hut.

"Hush, Bossay, hush!" he said to the dog. "What's wrong with you? Why are you howling?"

The wise animal ran up to his master and began fawning on him. He fell silent, but whenever he glanced over at the annex the hair on his back began to bristle; it was obvious that the dog was trying to stop himself from once again opening his muzzle and howling from the depths of his terror-stricken heart.

"How strange! What's wrong with him?" the gardener muttered to himself. "Can it be—God forbid!—that something evil has happened here?"

And he walked out onto the path and cast his eyes over the orchard; but then, not seeing anything out of the ordinary, and chilled by the heavy dew and the early morning coolness, he called the dog and went back to his hut.

"Now, now, Bossay!" he said to the dog, patting him on the head and trying to calm him down. "Don't be afraid! Lie still, and don't startle people out of their sleep."

The dog peered with trusting eyes into his owner's face, as if trying to understand what he was saying. And then, seeing that his master was crawling back under the sack that served as his coverlet, he found a comfortable spot on some straw in a corner, curled himself up into a ball and, after turning around a couple of times, placed his head on his hind legs and also fell asleep.

But peace did not return to the yard.

Granted, today the nightingales were not singing before sunrise, and only sparrows chirped and shrilled among the leaves in the trees, as if predicting rain.

And then the cows in the barn began to grow restive: they were surprised that their master was taking so long to come and milk them; they knew that, right over there, behind the wall of the barn, lay a pile of wilted clover that had been mown yesterday, and was to be given to them after today's milking. Its fragrance drifted in through a hole in the wall, and they stretched their heads in that direction. Finally one of them bellowed slowly, lingeringly, mournfully. No one came to the barn in response to her call, so she bellowed a second time, and the other cows followed her example and raised their voices as well.

The mooing spread through the yard, waking Hapka in the kitchen and, in an outlying room, the tenant farmer, who instantly leapt to his feet, glanced up at the sun that was starting to gild the window of his small dark room and, grumbling drowsily, began shaking the herdsman and shouting in his ear: "Well, get up, you lazybones! Get up! The cows are bellowing, and you're just lying there!"

In the kitchen, Hapka, who had been awakened by the bellowing, rubbed her eyes, whispered "Jesus, Maria," and, raising her head and seeing that it was broad daylight, muttered: "May you perish, you damned lazybones! The poor cattle are still tied up and they're bellowing, but you're lying abed, the devil knows why! And where can that disgusting tenant farmer be, may he not live to see God's world!"

And, rising from her bed, she poured some water in a bowl, washed up, and then, while combing herself, began to sing in Polish at the top of her lungs:

> "I heard the wonderful voice of Mariya
> Who turned to us:
> 'Come to me, my little children,
> I am calling you.'"

The barn started to come alive.

In the hayloft Hadyna woke up on a pile of straw. How had he come to be here, since yesterday he had fallen asleep in the storage room adjoining the kitchen? The matter remained unexplained, even though the solution to the puzzle might have been found in the fact that, next to him, deeply buried in the straw, lay Paraska, who had ended up not sleeping in the Lady's room that night. How they met up and made their way to the hayloft was also one of the night's mysteries.

Awakened by the bellowing of the cows, Hadyna rubbed his eyes, sat up, and for a moment tried to recall where he was and what was happening. Through a hole in the roof, daylight peeked in on him; it jolted him, brought him to his senses, and clarified his situation.

He jumped to his feet, glanced around and, seeing Paraska's foot sticking out of the straw, leapt to her side, dug out some straw, shook her by the shoulder, and cried out in an alarmed voice: "Paraska! May you come to no good! Paraska! The sun has risen! Everyone in the manor yard has woken up, but we're still sleeping! Get up right now and run to the Lady's quarters before she catches on why you're not there. Because if she does, we're doomed! Come on, hurry up! I'll run on ahead, so that no one sees us together!"

And, without waiting for a reply from the still sleepy Paraska, he jumped down from the hayloft to the straw on the threshing floor, and then poked his head into the yard and looked around to see if anyone could spot him. Having determined that the yard was deserted, he crouched down like a cat, sprang to the opposite door, and dashed into the storage room without anyone catching sight of him.

Once there, he set about getting ready as if nothing had happened, whistling and singing, obviously trying to ensure that Hapka, who was in the kitchen, could hear him. After a moment he walked into the kitchen and began to wash up.

Hapka, who had already finished combing herself, was busily lighting a fire in the stove. "So, you have nothing better to do than to sleep until noon, huh!" she grumbled at him.

"Until noon, indeed! Don't worry, I'll get all the work done that I'm supposed to get done, and if need be, I'll even find time to rub the small of your back if you start getting sharp pains down there."

"May you get those sharp pains yourself, so that no doctor can ever do anything to help you, you filthy heathen!" Hapka yelled angrily. "Have you ever seen the likes of it, my good people," she continued to shout, turning to the door through which no "good people" had any intention of entering, "how this bedbug dares to talk to me. Why, I'll break every bone in your body, you infidel! I'll scald your eyes with boiling water!"

"Well, well, there you go—rattling on again," Hadyna said in a milder tone as he dried himself with a towel and combed his dishevelled hair that still had blades of straw stuck in it. "I didn't say anything all that bad! And, if the truth be told, what right do you have to tell me to get to work, to order me about? Are you my overseer, or the head steward? Our gracious Lady hasn't instructed you to do that."

"But my heart aches when I see such parasites. My hands are all covered in soot from working at the stove to cook up enough food to stuff your gullets, but you don't do anything to deserve it! I don't know if you have no shame or even the slightest fear of God—I swear to God I don't know. But never fear, it will all be reckoned up to your account one day. Oh, yes, every crumb that you gobble up without earning it will be counted up double against you!"

"Well, well, she's at it again! Just give me a piece of bread, and you'll see how energetically I'll get to work. You think I'm a lie-abed looking for an easy life! But when I want to, Hapka, you miserable creature, I can do the work of two. It's true that to work for others—the devil only knows what for and why—well, I just don't want to! And who would want to? But when I set out on my own . . ."

"Oho-ho! You'll overturn a bald mountain then. I've seen workers like you before. They were big talkers, and they had big ideas, just like you, about getting out on their own. But when they were out on their own, my, oh my, they started singing a different tune. And they were ever so happy to herd chickens out to graze, yes they were!"

"Oh, I'm not like that, Hapka! I swear to God I'm not like that. At my place a chicken will have enough to eat at home. Why only yesterday our gracious Lady told me to mow the grass under the priest's window. And although I haven't eaten yet, I'll show you that I can get the job done even on an empty stomach; I'm going to get the scythe this very minute, and you'll see for yourself that before you finish boiling the potatoes, I'll have done what I set out to do."

"It's not such a big job! But I'm sure you won't get it done. Something would be sure to drop dead in the forest, if you did."

"Just you wait, you'll see!" Hadyna shouted as he ran out of the kitchen.

Lady Olimpiya was dead to the world. It was the first night for a long time that she had slept so soundly, so peacefully. It was the first time that no nightmares had tormented her, that she had felt no fear, had not awoken, had not yelled in her sleep. Lying on her back with her arms outstretched, she was breathing deeply, evenly, with her mouth half-open, but from time to time her lips moved almost imperceptibly as if she was whispering secrets, words that no one was to hear.

The locked room was stuffy, suffocatingly hot, but the sultriness did not wake her. Nor did she awaken when the dog howled, or when the cow bellowed, or when Hapka's singing resounded through the manor yard, or when Hadyna sharpened his scythe, or when the tenant-farmer rattled past her window on his cart as he drove off to Lviv with the milk, or when the herdsman, shouting and cracking his whip, herded the cows to the pasture.

Of late, even the singing of the nightingales had awakened her, as had the creaking of the gate, the crack of a whip, or any distant noise or nearby rustle; today, however, it seemed that nothing like that bothered her, nothing disturbed her. She slept soundly, deeply, tranquilly, like an infant after it is bathed, like a person who has recovered from a serious lengthy illness and, for the first time in a long while, falls into a refreshing, reinvigorating sleep.

Suddenly, a loud rattling noise resounded in the passageway that led to her bedroom door; someone who was obviously in a hurry had stumbled on the churn propped up against the door in the sunless vestibule and had kicked it so hard that it rolled off with a clatter to one side. Even this commotion did not rouse Lady Olimpiya.

Someone's hand hesitantly, slowly, pushed open the door to the bedroom; the door creaked on its rusty hinges.

Lady Olimpiya did not stir; she continued sleeping blissfully.

Paraska, deathly pale, scared out of her wits, shaking, and breathing heavily, walked into the bedroom; it was clear that some terrible news was about to issue from her colourless, widely parted lips. She came up to the Lady and took her by the hand—Lady Olimpiya kept on sleeping. Paraska did not dare to tug at the Lady's hand, so she lifted it and then dropped it, and then, once again, she lifted it and dropped it—Lady Olimpiya did not feel anything; she was lying perfectly still, as if she were dead, but she was breathing evenly and softly in a deep, tranquil, healthy sleep.

"If you please, my gracious Lady! If you please, my gracious Lady!" Paraska whispered breathlessly as she leaned over Lady Olimpiya; but it was only when she gave the Lady's arm a sturdy tug that the Lady, without budging, opened her eyes and looked at her in sleepy astonishment.

"Is that you, Paraska?" the Lady said slowly. "Is it morning already? My, but I slept wonderfully well."

"If you please, my gracious Lady! Please get up. Please! There's such a . . ."

"What is it? Has something happened?"

"Oh, if you please, my gracious Lady! There's been a misfortune! A terrible misfortune!"

"A misfortune?" the Lady said calmly as if she did not believe or understand this word. "What kind of misfortune?"

"Oh! A terrible misfortune! His Reverence has been murdered!"

"His Reverence? Which his Reverence?"

"Why, ours—the old one."

"What? Fr. Nestor?" the Lady shouted as if she had only now grasped what she was hearing and, striking her hands together, sat up in bed. "For God's sake, Paraska, what are you saying? That can't be!"

"I'm telling the truth, if you please, my gracious Lady! Please come and have a look! I only took a quick peek from a distance, and I almost died of fright. He looks so terrible lying there, all covered in blood."

"O Lord! What a misfortune! What a misfortune!" the Lady whispered, and she began shaking as if she had a fever. "What can this mean? This is terrible! It is utterly incredible!"

And mumbling under her breath, trembling and sighing, she got out of bed, washed up and, after hastily smoothing her hair and throwing on some clothes with Paraska's assistance, walked out of her room on legs that almost refused to do her bidding and hastened to the annex.

II

The entrance door to the annex where Fr. Nestor's lodgings were located was wide open, and three people could be seen standing in the vestibule: Hapka, the gardener, and Hadyna.

It was Hadyna who, on his way to mow the grass under Fr. Nestor's window, had noticed that not only was the outside door to the vestibule ajar, but that the second door leading to Fr. Nestor's room was also wide open and, after glancing inside and seeing the misfortune that had struck the priest, had raised the alarm.

Lady Olimpiya, walking with an unsteady, uncertain gait, approached the group that, not daring to go in, was standing in the doorway of Fr. Nestor's lodgings. The servants, pale and terrified, parted silently to let her through.

"What has happened here?" Lady Olimpiya cried out in a broken voice.

"Something terrible!" the gardener cried. "His Reverence has been murdered. Look, he's lying over there."

And he pointed into the half-darkened area.

From the entrance door everything in the vestibule could be seen; and through the open door leading from the vestibule to the bedroom, a dark unmoving mass was visible near the bed in the centre of the room. It was only after one's eyes became accustomed to the semidarkness that reigned in the room (the windows in the room and the vestibule were draped) that it was possible to discern the figure of a man lying stretched out on his back in a pool of blood on the floor, with his head turned towards the door.

"O Lord!" the Lady shrieked after glancing inside, and then she crossed herself: "Spare us, and save and protect us from something like that!"

Everyone remained silent, and Lady Olimpiya felt that all eyes were focussed on her with a kind of heartless curiosity, a dull suspicion, and unspoken reproaches.

Under the crossfire of these mute looks, she felt very uneasy, but in the depths of her soul something shouted: "Do not let your guard down! Show yourself to be strong, calm! Do not let your guard down!"

"The gendarmes should be sent for at once," the gardener muttered gloomily. "It's obvious that something criminal has happened here."

For Lady Olimpiya, these words were like the first shot in a battle, like a spur that goads a horse. She squared her shoulders, her eyes flashed with energy, and her anxiety vanished.

"It's obvious, you say? But were you inside, in the room?"

"Well, no, no one has been in there," Hapka responded. "It's scary, and maybe we shouldn't . . . I really don't know."

"At least the reeve should be sent for," the gardener finished her thought for her. "It is not right for us to go near someone who has been murdered."

"But who knows, perhaps he has not been murdered?" the Lady said.

They all stared at her. From the moment that they saw Fr. Nestor on the floor, stretched out in a pool of blood, such a possibility had not crossed anyone's mind. And even now, no one really thought otherwise, but still, they all gasped in surprise. The Lady did not give them any time to get over their shock.

"Let's just go in! Let's take a closer look! After all, it's just a man lying there! Who knows if there is any reason to call the reeve and the gendarmes. But if it does turn out to be necessary, then of course we will call them."

These last words, spoken calmly and decisively, rectified somewhat the unpleasant impression that Lady Olimpiya's first words had made.

Slowly, carefully, continually looking around, they all stepped forward. In the vestibule they did not see anything suspicious.

Lady Olimpiya was the first to enter, but it seemed to the gardener that she avoided looking at Fr. Nestor, kept her distance as she walked past him, and turned her attention to looking carefully around the room.

"Everything is in order," she said. "There is nothing to indicate that a thief . . ."

But just then, Hapka's loud outcry interrupted her: "If you please, my gracious Lady! His Reverence is alive! His Reverence is still breathing!"

"O Lord!" the Lady shrieked, and her voice sounded so different from the way she had been speaking a moment earlier—not really joyous, and not really mortally alarmed—that they all felt as if a knife had pierced their hearts.

After making her discovery, Hapka immediately fell on her knees beside Fr. Nestor and raised his head from the floor. Fr. Nestor's face was startingly pale, his forehead and hair were covered in blood, and his shirt was also bloody. He was breathing, but his eyes were closed, as if he was in a deep sleep. He was dressed only in a shirt and trousers, and even though the bed was mussed, there were no traces of blood on it; it was clear that the catastrophe had struck him at night, when he was not yet in bed, but dozing in his chair.

"Water, Paraska! Get me some water!" Hapka shouted; she was known in the village for "knowing how to cope" in cases of sudden and serious ailments.

"As for me," the gardener said as he looked around the room and the vestibule, "my advice would be to send for the bailiff and the gendarmes right now. That window over there in the vestibule is open, and a thief could have come in through it, may the devil take him!"

"But a sick man must be attended to," Hapka cried and, with Paraska's help, she began washing the blood off Fr. Nestor's head and tried to revive him.

The Countess was standing as if struck dumb, not daring to watch as the servants tended to Fr. Nestor. But the gardener's words once again stabbed her like an awl.

"Come, let's take a look and see if the window is actually open," she said in an obvious effort to remain calm.

The gardener came up to the window, pulled back the blind, and pushed the window to open it.

As it turned out, the window did not open. The lower latch was missing, but the upper one was in place, and it secured the window.

"As you can see, the window is locked," Lady Olimpiya said sadly, but with an unmistakable note of triumph in her voice.

At that moment, Fr. Nestor opened his eyes, and a long, deep, painful groan issued from his chest.

"O-o-o-o-oh! O-o-o-o-oh!"

"He's alive! He's alive!" Lady Olimpiya cried out.

She once again sounded alarmed. She tried to look at him, but recoiled instantly, as if she had seen a snake.

"Oh, I can't stand the sight of blood! I can't stand the sight of wounds!" she exclaimed.

"My gracious Lady need not be troubled," Hapka said as she finished washing Fr. Nestor's forehead and bald pate. "There are no serious wounds, just this one bruise that was bleeding. It's not likely that his Reverence will die from it."

"Well, what about the blood on his chest? Where did that come from?" Hadyna asked. "Look, his shirt is all bloody."

Hapka unbuttoned Fr. Nestor's shirt, but there was no wound on his chest. Clearly, the blood on his shirt must have come from the wound on his head.

Hapka's words seemed to have a calming effect on Lady Olimpiya. After the wound was cleansed, the Lady finally conquered her fear and looked more closely at Fr. Nestor.

Now he was not as terrifying as he had been a moment earlier. Pale as a corpse and still unconscious, he was, nevertheless, breathing regularly and groaning heavily, and there was no death rattle in his throat. The wound on the upper part of his forehead, just a bit to the left, was a large one, almost the size of a hand; it was swollen, a dark blue colour that verged on black, and it was only on one side of it that there was a lesion of about an inch and a half from which blood was still flowing. Hapka was doing her best to staunch the flow with a sponge and a wet towel.

After looking more closely at the wound, Lady Olimpiya said calmly and resolutely: "That's people for you! You gave me such a scare! Robbers! He's been murdered! God only knows what you came up with! But it was just a simple accident: Fr. Nestor fell out of bed at night and struck his head on something hard. It has happened to him a couple of times before, but up to now he has not hurt himself like this. But it is nothing all that terrible. He will stay in bed a few days, and he will be as good as new.

And you wanted to call the reeve right away, and the gendarmes. Tfu! A doctor—perhaps a doctor should be called, but it might not be necessary to do even that. The wound is not at all serious. He banged himself up a bit, got bloodied, but that's nothing."

"But if you please, my gracious Lady, just look how much blood he has lost. It's enough to weaken a young person, and he's an old man. A doctor is definitely needed," the gardener said. He was somewhat mollified by Lady Olimpiya's decisive words, but he still had a nagging feeling that something about the situation was not quite right.

"If you please, my gracious Lady, his Reverence has never fallen out of bed before. He sleeps very peacefully. And what could he have hit his head against?" Hadyna imprudently got involved.

"Why are you butting in?" Lady Olimpiya said in a snit. "Who needs you here? You would do better to go and do your work than to stand around here, gaping and talking nonsense."

"But I was just . . . I didn't . . ." Hadyna mumbled, taken aback not so much by Lady Olimpiya's words, as by the look that she gave him, a look that he knew all too well.

And so, having satisfied his curiosity, he did not waste any time in leaving; he walked out of the room, picked up the scythe he had left leaning against the outside wall and, going by way of the gate and the orchard to the garden under the window of the annex, vigorously began to cut down the weeds that overran the small plot, filling it with greenery, flowers, and the fragrance of fresh vegetation.

In the bedroom, they were still fussing over Fr. Nestor. Lady Olimpiya, having seized upon the idea that Fr. Nestor, because of a troubled dream or a moment of weakness, had fallen and struck his head against something hard like the foot of the bed or the bootjack, stuck firmly to it and kept repeating it over and over again, as if trying to convince herself and everyone around her that it must have happened exactly like that, and that there was no other possibility.

And if that was the case, then the incident lost all its sensational, criminal character and became an ordinary, unfortunate accident, for which no one could be held responsible, and about which there was no need to carry on.

Through the power of suggestion, this view was quickly espoused not only by Hapka and Paraska, but even by the doubting gardener, who for some time had kept on muttering—as he looked carefully at the corners of the legs on the bed and the bootjack that Fr. Nestor used when he took off his boots without anyone's help—but who now, finally half-convinced, shrugged his shoulders and shook his head.

"Hmm . . . hmm . . . maybe that is what happened. There's no way I can know. If my gracious Lady says that it is not the first time he has fallen out of bed . . ."

"Of course, of course! I know that better than anyone, because I am the one who usually comes to see him in the morning. He told me about it more than once!" the Lady said hastily.

"Well, yes. It's not hard to have such an accident, especially for an old man like that. And my gracious Lady says that there is nothing missing in the room? There is no sign of someone having been hard at work here?"

"Well, you can see for yourselves that everything is in order. The cupboards are locked, the wardrobe is closed. If thieves had been here, they most certainly would have left a much bigger mess. They would have been looking for money, and you know that when strangers look for money, especially at night, they really do not care about leaving things neat and tidy."

"That's true," the gardener said, growing ever more convinced of the veracity of Lady Olimpiya's statements. "But if you please, my gracious Lady, there is just one thing. When we came here, the doors were all open."

"What? They were open?" Lady Olimpiya asked in surprise.

"Hadyna said," Paraska got involved in the conversation, "that when he went to mow the grass and weeds in the garden plot, he glanced at the entrance door. He just happened to look at it—the door was ajar. He pushed it open, glanced inside the passageway, and saw that the door to his Reverence's room was wide open. 'I was instantly alarmed,' he said, 'because Fr. Nestor usually locks himself up very carefully for the night.'"

"Now, now, now!" Lady Olimpiya interjected. "He locks himself up! That's a lie! Fr. Nestor did usually lock himself up, that is true. But there were times—he is, of course, an old, feeble, forgetful man—that he forgot to lock the doors. More than once

I found the door to his vestibule unlocked in the morning, even though he was still sleeping."

"I also found the door unlocked a couple of times," Hapka confirmed the Lady's words; she was still fussing over Fr. Nestor, who continued to moan and breathe heavily, but who, despite all her efforts, had not regained consciousness.

"Well, girls," Lady Olimpiya said, "We must do something with him. Hey there, old man! Help us lift him and put him back in bed! We cannot leave a sick man lying on the floor."

"But if you please, my gracious Lady, wouldn't it be a good idea to wash his chest and back with cold water? Maybe he'll come to sooner if we do that," Hapka said.

"Fine, fine! Well then, hold him up! Take off that shirt. That's good! Here is the water."

And all four of them, including Lady Olimpiya, began to wash and massage Fr. Nestor.

The fresh, cool water truly did revive him. He raised his head, and a flame of consciousness flickered in his eyes. His moans grew louder, more expressive, and among them indistinct, broken words began to come through.

"O-o-o-oh! It hurts! O-o-o-oh . . . it's awful! My head! Where's my head? Who took away my head? O-o-o-oh!"

"He is delirious! The poor man! He must have a terrible pain in his head. Come on, Paraska! Quickly now, make up the bed! We'll carry him over to it."

"What about his shirt? Will we put the same one on him?" Hapka wanted to know.

"Of course not! I'll get a fresh one from the wardrobe. After all, would it be proper to put him in bed in such a bloodied shirt? The doctor will come, people will come—it just would not be right for Father to be lying in bed in such a state."

And, without wasting any time, she took a white shirt out of the wardrobe and put it on Fr. Nestor.

Then the three women, with the help of the gardener, lifted him into bed. Lady Olimpiya adjusted the pillow and tucked little cushions under it, so that the sick man would be more comfortable.

"I think some alcohol should be applied to his head," the gardener said. "It's very helpful for wounds like that."

"You needn't worry, we know that without being told," Hapka responded as she began to attend to Fr. Nestor's wounded head, rinsing out the bloody towel and the sponge.

At the slightest touch to his head, Fr. Nestor groaned terribly, convulsively clutched at the pillow, at his chest, at whatever he could, and then passed out. The pain was clearly intolerable.

After Hapka rinsed everything, Lady Olimpiya brought a bottle of brandy from her living quarters; the alcohol was applied to a sponge that was then placed on the wound, and the priest quickly calmed down and seemed to fall asleep.

"We must not trouble him too much. We should go away and leave him in peace. He will sleep for a while, and that will help restore his strength," Lady Olimpiya said gently, like a mother caring for an ailing child.

The gardener was the first to heed her words and, after bowing to her, left to get on with his work.

"As for you, Paraska, fetch some water and wash the floor," the Lady said in the same controlled voice. "It isn't right to leave a pool of blood here. Wash the floor well, and sprinkle it with sand. It is summer, so it will dry quickly, and doing this will not hurt the patient."

"Certainly, my gracious Lady," Paraska said and, grabbing a bucket, she ran to fetch some water.

Having attended to everything, the Lady breathed more easily.

"O my Lord!" she said, turning to Hapka. "What a scare you all gave me! I thought perhaps a murder had truly been committed here. I was numb with fear! Because just think, what if, God forbid, something like that had actually happened here, at my place, and especially to his Reverence! O Lord! I simply would not be able to live down the shame of it all, the gossip of the people. But, thank God, this time He spared me such a misfortune!

"What do you think, Hapka, will he regain consciousness soon?" she suddenly interrupted her heartfelt flow of words and, coming up close to Hapka, gazed fearfully at the pale, old face of Fr. Nestor, a face that looked half-dead.

"I don't know, if it please my gracious Lady," Hapka said, also looking intently at Fr. Nestor. "For some reason his wound doesn't look all that good to me. It may be worse than I thought it was at first glance."

"Worse? What do you mean, worse?"

"I'm afraid that it's not only the skin that's torn, but that the bone beneath it is broken."

"What are you saying, Hapka! How can that be?"

"I'm not sure. But when I touched the bruised spot, it seemed to me that the bone gave way under my finger."

"But Hapka! If the bone was broken—after all, the brain is under it—he would no longer be alive!"

"No, if it please my Lady. He would be alive. It doesn't necessarily mean that he would die right away. But it seems to me that his brain has been injured. Why else would he be lying unconscious for such a long time? And when the brain is injured, then God only knows if he'll recover."

"Well, Hapka, do not even think about anything like that!" the Lady said as if she were reproaching her, but with such a note of cheerfulness in her voice that a listener who was swifter than Hapka would have detected an ill-concealed joy at such a prediction.

Just then Paraska came back with the water, and the Lady changed the theme of the conversation.

"Well, Hapka, we should go and prepare some breakfast. As for you, Paraska, stay here, and if the patient wakes up, call either me or Hapka."

"It's absolutely necessary that someone be with the patient at all times. And it should be someone who knows what to do," Hapka said.

"Well, there's . . . O my Lord! I was so stunned that I forgot the most important thing. But when I was on my way over here earlier on, I thought about him. Hapka! What can it possibly mean that Demenyuk is not here? Where is Demenyuk?"

"I don't know, if it please my Lady. I haven't seen him since yesterday evening."

"How can that be—did he not spend the night at home?"

"I don't know; I didn't see him last night, or this morning."

Still talking, they walked out of the annex into the yard. Lady Olimpiya glanced at the small garden under the window, where Hadyna was almost finished cutting down the weeds.

"Listen, Hadyna," the Lady said, "have you seen Demenyuk? Someone has to sit and watch over his Reverence. I do not always have the time, Paraska has even less time, and Demenyuk would be the person best suited to watch over him."

"I saw Demenyuk last night, but not today," Hadyna said.

"Last night? At what time?"

"I don't know. It was dark already. Aha, it was just before my gracious Lady bumped into me in the yard."

"Where did you see him?"

"Here."

"Where, here?"

"In the living quarters of his Reverence. They talked for a long time, and then Demenyuk left. He said he was going over to Herder's place."

"How did you see that? How did you hear it?"

"I was walking in the orchard . . . the gardener asked me to walk around the orchard to see if anyone had sneaked into it. I looked over here and saw a light in Fr. Nestor's window. I walked up to the window and saw . . ."

"What did you see? What?" the Lady asked hurriedly. Chills ran up and down her spine, the colour drained from her face, and a cold sweat broke out on her forehead.

Hadyna did not notice that. Standing with the scythe in his hand, he had lowered he head; he realized that he had spoken out of turn, and that his words could get him into trouble.

"Well, go on, go on—what did you see?" the Lady insisted.

"Well, nothing special!" Hadyna lied. "I told you what I saw. Demenyuk knocked on the door; Fr. Nestor asked: 'Who is it?' And he replied: 'It's me, Demenyuk.' Fr. Nestor opened the door, Demenyuk walked in, and they started to talk . . ."

"About what?"

"How should I know about what? I couldn't hear. I only heard Demenyuk say: 'I'm going to Herder's place.'"

"And he left?"

"Yes, he did."

"Did you see him leave?"

"I didn't see him leave, but I heard Fr. Nestor lock the door after he left."

"He locked it?"

"Yes, he did."
"With the lock?"
"I think so. I heard the key turn in the lock."
"Well, and what happened next?"
"I don't know. I left . . . I left and went to sleep."
"And where did you sleep/"
"Why, right here, in the little storage room."

Lady Olimpiya conducted this initial interrogation face to face with Hadyna as she leaned on the garden fence. Hadyna, holding the scythe, was standing on the other side of the fence, and a few steps back of it. Hapka had gone directly to the kitchen after leaving Fr. Nestor's room, and Paraska was left washing the floor. The Lady and Hadyna were talking rapidly, in hushed voices, even though there was no one around who could have heard them, as the gardener had gone off with his dog to make his rounds on the far side of the orchard.

"Well," the Lady said, feeling somewhat comforted by Hadyna's words, "I hope that Demenyuk will come soon. Finish mowing the weeds and take them to the barn, and then come to see me, and I'll tell you what to do next."

She walked across the yard to her living quarters, but something seemed to stop her on the doorstep. An uneasy feeling took hold of her heart. Her chest grew so constricted that she actually dreaded the thought of being enclosed by the four walls of her uninviting suite.

And so she kept on walking past the ruins of the old manor, through the pasture, and out onto the street, and all the while a single thought was swirling in her head: "That Hadyna is a beast! He knows something, but he will not say what it is! He saw something, he heard more than he is letting on. But I'll ferret it out of him. He has to tell me everything that he knows. But I must do it slowly, adroitly, cautiously, without tripping up. O my Lord! How this half hour has exhausted me! But this is nothing, as yet. What will happen next?"

At that moment, her lowered eyes inadvertently glanced up and looked out at the street. And all at once her legs went numb, her breath caught in her chest, and her heart seemed to stop beating; she broke out in a cold sweat, turned pale, and grew stiff; she stood stock-still, and everything went dark in her eyes.

The most terrible spectre would not have terrified her as greatly as what she now saw, even though it was the most mundane, commonplace, natural thing.

A gendarme was walking down the village street, an ordinary, patrolling gendarme, dressed in a uniform and a cap topped by a rooster feather, and carrying a carbine. Catching sight of the mistress of the manor, he saluted her and then, quite unexpectedly—and this is what struck Lady Olimpiya most forcibly—instead of going past the yard, he turned off the road and began making his way directly towards her.

III

Lady Olimpiya knew the gendarme Sheremeta only by sight. Up to now, because of her social position, she had felt so far removed from people of that ilk that even though she had often seen him, and even though he had even been in her yard a number of times for a variety of reasons, she had paid little attention to him. A gendarme was a gendarme, but as to what kind of a man he was—whether he was good or bad, competent or incompetent, and exactly in what way he may have been competent or incompetent—that did not interest her in the slightest.

It was not at all surprising, therefore, that when Sheremeta approached her, and when she instinctively felt in her heart that she would have to endure her first and probably critical battle with this man, she looked at him as if she were seeing him for the first time in her life; and she concentrated in her eyes all the strength of her will, all her perspicacity and her sagacity shaped by her upbringing, education, experience, and the world view inherent in her social status in order to decipher, to penetrate the soul, the thoughts, and the intent of this plebe, attired in a uniform, on whom she could smell the denatured alcohol that he used to clean the buttons of that uniform.

Gendarme Sheremeta was a tall, stately man, with a drooping black moustache, a long aquiline nose, gleaming black eyes, and ruddy cheeks on a healthy, suntanned face. His figure radiated health, strength, and energy, and his eyes shone with common sense honed by experience. It was only now that Lady Olimpiya noticed that this gendarme was an extraordinarily handsome man, and that if he were wearing, instead of a gendarme's uniform, a batiste shirt and a fine, expensive suit, and that if he were not a gendarme, but some grand count or baron, then he would be a sensation, ladies would be dying for him, and he would be the "star," the "lion" of society. This observation flashed through her head from God knows where, probably from her habit of making such "aesthetic" evaluations of everyone who caught her attention for the first time.

But she was not in the mood for aesthetics just now, and that is why, in the very next moment, she began to watch his face more intently in order to assess, to estimate the power of his intellect, for at any given moment it could become either her very worst enemy if it should prove to be too great, or her greatest ally if it turned out to be feeble and limited.

First of all, however, it was important for her to determine why he was turning into her yard. Did he know what had happened? From whom and how could he have found out about it? What tactics should she use against him? The street in front of her yard was wide, and the pasture that led past the ruins of the old mansion to the manor yard was also quite long, and therefore, before the gendarme, who was walking with broad, measured steps drew near her, she had time to regain her composure after her first sudden rush of fear.

She had stopped at the very end of the pasture, where it adjoined the manor yard, so that the gendarme, when he conversed here with her, could see the yard, but did not have a good view of the annex where the "misfortune" had taken place, and, generally speaking, could not figure out what was going on in its depths.

Lady Olimpiya thought, quite logically, that if the gendarme already knew what had happened here, he would go directly to that spot, and if he did not know, then it would be best not to let him come too close, so that he would not needlessly find out about anything.

The instinct of self-preservation told her that, at all costs, she had to try to gain some time, to delay the disclosure and the spreading of the news regarding the "terrible misfortune" that had happened in her yard.

As he drew nearer, the gendarme saluted her once again and came to a stop at a distance that showed the respect due a countess.

"I truly beg your gracious Ladyship's pardon," he said smoothly, evenly, as he placed his left hand on the barrel of his carbine, "for being so bold as to disturb you by taking advantage of this fortunate timing. I only did so because I happened to see your gracious Ladyship in the yard."

"That means he does not know anything! He has come here on another matter," Lady Olimpiya thought, and she took courage in that fact. She did not say anything to the gendarme; she just looked at him directly with an expression that was partially severe and partially politely questioning.

"Yesterday there were guests from Lviv at your gracious Ladyship's manor and at the young Lord's manor as well," the gendarme said.

"Yes, there were."

"And could your gracious Ladyship tell me: have they all left, or are some of them still here?"

"I am not sure. There is no one at my place, but there may still be someone at Adas's manor. Do you need anything from them, sir?"

"No, no!" the gendarme said hastily.

"You can go to the other manor and find out there," the Lady added with a hint of sarcasm in her voice.

"Oh, no! Why would I? I only . . . and this, of course, is a mere formality . . . Perhaps your gracious Ladyship would be so kind as to tell me . . . Among the guests there was a certain lord that the other lords referred to as Kaytsya. Do you know his Christian name and his real surname?"

"Kaytsya . . . Kaytsya . . ." Lady Olimpiya repeated, as if trying to recall who it could be, but in actual fact she was thinking: "What does this mean? What does he want? It is clear that he is a clever beast—he is getting to the point of his visit in a roundabout way, and there is no way of knowing where he is heading with his questions. Why is he interested in this Kaytsya? I do not think that he actually needs him for any reason at all. I think he wants to trip me up. Well, just you wait, it is not as easy to get the better of me as you might think it is."

And then she added out loud: "Excuse me, Constable, but I have such a poor memory . . . Of course, Kaytsya—that must be Lord Kalyasanty . . . he is an acquaintance of my son, a wonderful man . . . yes, yes, he was here yesterday—but as for his real family name, I swear I do not remember it. I rarely am out in society, and I see those lords only when they are good enough to come and visit me, so how would I know all their names and titles?"

The Lady was speaking freely, trying to make it seem that her words were flowing from her heart.

The gendarme stood before her, listened humbly to her words, nodded his head in agreement, and when the Lady finished speaking, said once again in his customarily calm and firm voice. "I sincerely beg your gracious Ladyship's pardon, but I am going to take the liberty of asking you one more question. It would be very important for me—that is, it would not be so important, as necessary, for me to know: where might I find this Lord Kalyasanty? Is he a lord from a neighbouring district, or from a village, or from Lviv?"

"I really can't say. I think he came here yesterday from Lviv, with Adas. But it is to be understood that he must have an estate. My Adas does not associate with just anyone at all."

"I understand! I understand! And I would not presume to think otherwise. Count Adam is known throughout the entire district as a shining example of an upright young lord. But as for this Lord Kalyasanty . . . what did your gracious Ladyship say his real family name was?"

"I did not say what it was," the Lady said sternly, and she assumed an expression that made it clear that she was growing bored with the conversation. "I told you that I do not know his real family name."

"Oh, that's right, that's right! I beg your pardon, I truly beg your pardon! So, your gracious Ladyship says that Lord Kalyasanty is a landowner."

"Yes, I think so. I cannot be sure about that, but judging by how extremely knowledgeable he is about horses, about hunting, about property, about forests and all kinds of husbandry, I assume that he is. Oh, he is a very well-informed man. And such pleasant company!"

As she was speaking, Lady Olimpiya felt anger stir in her soul and creep up to her heart. Why was this gendarme badgering her, vexing her with this Kalyasanty? Was she some sort of an information bureau?

But she was even angrier with herself than with the gendarme. Instead of retorting harshly and curtly so that he would stop bothering her, she was standing here, being polite, and talking to him as if it were her duty to do so, and getting into such intimate details with him—something that it was not at all proper for her to talk about with a man who was so markedly her social inferior.

And what was even worse, all her efforts to appear as a proud, angry, and unapproachable Lady before this gendarme were crashing to the ground like birds without wings, and her anger at the gendarme was fruitless—she could not, she physically could not help but assume a friendly mien, and talk gently and in detail about things that he did not even ask her and that he did not need to know.

Her heart was filled with an excruciatingly unpleasant and shameful feeling arising from her helplessness, her inability to control the situation, just like a wagon that, propelled by its own weight, rolls unstoppably downwards on an inclined surface.

"I suppose that's so, I suppose it is," the gendarme said, "but still . . . It may well be that it is only human malice . . . In fact, I would be glad to be convinced of that . . . But, if it please your gracious Ladyship, we have received a complaint about that Lord Kalyasanty. It is a rather unpleasant matter . . . "

"What is it? A complaint about Lord Kalyasanty?"

"Yes. It was very unpleasant for me to hear it, and mainly because the complaint touched the sometime guest of your gracious Ladyship and the young Count."

"But what is it all about? What happened?"

"Nothing that unusual!" the gendarme said. "I think that it is either just gossip, or a minor matter that should be looked into. Your gracious Ladyship will have to forgive me for not being able to speak more precisely, but my position does not permit me to do so. If the young Count was here, I have no doubt that he would explain the entire matter to us in a flash, and no further measures would be necessary."

"I am very sorry that Adas is not here. He is probably at his manor, because I do not think that he went to Lviv last night with his guests."

"Why is that? Had he, perhaps, intended to leave with them?" the gendarme asked in alarm.

"Yes, he had intended to, but I do not think that he did. He was very tired after all that he had to do yesterday."

At that moment Hadyna came up from the depths of the yard holding up a pair of trousers and calling out with a frightened expression on his face: "If you please, my gracious Lady! If you please, my gracious Lady!"

Lady Olimpiya looked over her shoulder and shot a thunderbolt at him with her eyes.

"Leave me alone!" she exclaimed angrily. "You can see that I am busy."

Upon seeing the gendarme, Hadyna was at a loss for words, but he still found it necessary to call out to the Lady once more: "I just wanted to say . . ."

"Oh, you blithering blockhead!" the Lady shouted, turning to face him, and she could feel cold fear flooding her body.

Something was whispering to her that what Hadyna was about to say could instantly turn the matter in an entirely different direction and cause her a lot of trouble.

And so, making a supreme effort to control herself, she said to Hadyna, trying to speak as calmly and as unconcernedly as possible: "I'll be ready in just a moment. If you have something to say to me, go to my vestibule and wait for me there, but do not bother me here!"

Hadyna turned around and left.

"You see, sir," she said, with a hint of regret in her voice, "this is what I have to cope with time and again! They are all such blockheads, and they come to me with the most trifling matters. Something got torn here, something is missing there, something needs to be done here, and something else over there—they can never figure out anything on their own, they all come to me! They come to me with everything!"

"It is clear that your gracious Ladyship has trained them like that, and so they all turn to your Ladyship like to their mother. It is clear that they trust your gracious Ladyship, they know that your gracious Ladyship truly cares about everything, gets involved in everything."

Lady Olimpiya accepted this compliment with a smile.

"It may well be that I trained them to do that—to my own detriment. But I would still prefer it if they used their own heads at least occasionally before running to me with every little trifle. Because there are times, you know—our estate is quite small, but still, my head spins when they come at me from all sides, one about this, another about that, and the third one about yet something else. And you have to give everyone something, advise everyone, talk to everyone, explain, clarify, and yet, bear in mind—more often than not, it is all in vain! Despite it all, they do things their own way, get things muddled, bungle them, and make an utter mess of everything. Oh, what a fate is ours with these people!"

The gendarme listened to these complaints with obvious pleasure. It was hard to say whether he felt flattered that such a grand lady, a countess, was talking to him as to an equal, or if he desired the information for some other reason; but in any case, he listened and did not seem to be in any hurry to leave.

"Well, I have really gone on and on," Lady Olimpiya finally said, "but you, sir, are probably in a hurry."

"No, not at all! I am very grateful. I wanted to ask your gracious Ladyship one more thing."

"Well, please do," Lady Olimpiya said, speaking a lot more pleasantly than she had at the outset, even though she would have been glad to see the last of this potentially dangerous witness on her property.

"I sincerely beg your pardon for returning once more to yesterday's events, but could your gracious Ladyship tell me who else was here yesterday with the young Count?"

"Who else was here? I swear to God that it is hard for me to remember names. Hmm . . . oh yes! Dr. Vasong was here, a lawyer from Lviv, and the . . ."

"Thank you, your gracious Ladyship!" the gendarme said as he bowed to her. "That is enough! All I needed was one name. Dr. Vasong—oh, he is a renowned lawyer, an excellent lawyer. That's wonderful! Thank you, your gracious Ladyship! I kiss your hands in farewell."

And saluting, he wheeled about smartly in a crisp military manner and walked away.

Lady Olimpiya remained standing where she was for a minute or more, following him with her eyes.

She found it hard to believe that the gendarme was truly gone, that for the time being a threatening cloud had passed over her home. It was almost as if she expected the gendarme to halt, come back, and begin talking about other matters. As much as she had focussed, at the beginning of their conversation, on the thought that he did not know anything, now that he was gone, their long conversation and the eagerness with which he had listened to what she had to say gave rise in her heart to a new suspicion that there was something more behind it, that he knew something, that he was guessing at something.

But no, the gendarme walked down the road, through the village, without stopping and without looking back. The Lady continued watching him until he almost disappeared from view. Then she sighed deeply and, turning around, slowly walked to her living quarters. Hadyna was sitting in the vestibule.

"Now, what do you want? Why did you come flying at me with your tongue hanging out? What was so important that you came running up to me as if a pack of dogs was after you?" the Lady attacked Hadyna with a string of reproaches.

"Well, maybe it's nothing, if you please, my gracious Lady," Hadyna replied, still holding the trousers in his hand, "but I thought . . ."

"That's just it—you're always brooding about things, but you never do anything worthwhile. And when you do come up with an idea, it is the kind that needs to be shovelled out!"

"But it was just because of these trousers," Hadyna babbled, completely disconcerted. "It seemed to me . . ."

"Well, blockhead, what was it that seemed to you? What do I care about some trousers? You could see that I was conversing with a stranger, and you come crawling to me with some kind of trousers! Tfu! Oh, the things that you do to me—others would be hard put to even think of them."

"But if you please, my gracious Lady—please hear me out. These trousers are the ones that his Reverence was wearing yesterday." Hadyna said.

"Well, so what?"

"I found them in the barn, under a pile of straw; they were pushed right down to the bottom."

"What? In the barn? How did they get there?"

"That's just it—I don't know. There's something strange going on here!"

"Tfu! A body can't have any peace for even a moment! Have you told anyone about this?"

"Well, no, I haven't told anyone."

"Well, that's good! Take those trousers and return them to his Reverence's room, and do not say anything about them to anyone. Perhaps there truly is something strange going on here, but we must proceed cautiously. There is no need to spread the news around, to start any rumours. And what about his Reverence? How is he?"

"I think he's better. He's awake. Hapka's with him."

"Fine, fine, and I am on my way there as well. So, you know what," the Lady said, as if she had just thought of something, "give me the trousers, and I'll take them back myself. And you run to the other manor right now to see the young Lord. Go that way, along the meadow, and tell the young Lord . . . Or better yet, do not tell him anything, just give him this card!"

And the Lady quickly took a visiting card out of her night table, hastily wrote a few words on it, sealed it in a small envelope, and gave it to Hadyna, who took off at once for the farmstead by way of the meadow.

"Quickly, now!" the Lady shouted after him, and she herself hastened to Father Nestor's room.

But before she arrived at the annex, the gardener came running out of the orchard with a vest in his hand.

"If you please, my gracious Lady," he said as he drew nearer, "please have a look at what I found in the orchard!"

"Oh . . . a vest," the Lady uttered slowly, looking at it reluctantly, "so what?"

"Doesn't my gracious Lady know whose it is?"

"What is this? How am I to know?" the Lady was indignant.

"I think it belongs to his Reverence."

"His Reverence! Where was it?"

"I found it in the orchard . . . in those bushes by the fence."

"What the deuce is going on! How did it get there?" the Lady exclaimed.

"I don't know, if you please, my gracious Lady. But it seems to me that something terrible has happened here. It didn't get there on its own; someone must have thrown it there."

"But who would have done that, and why?"

"Well, it's a sure thing that his Reverence didn't throw it there himself. Just look, it's a new vest, a very good one. It seems to me that he was wearing it yesterday."

"Perhaps your dog grabbed it, dragged it into the bushes?"

This conjecture bothered the gardener more than anything.

"My dog never goes to his Reverence's room; he stays with me. He does not make a habit of dragging clothes into the bushes."

"Well then, I am at a loss to understand what could have happened," the Lady said rather harshly, and turning away, she continued walking to the annex.

The gardener followed her with the vest.

"But if you please, my gracious Lady, I think there's something amiss here. There's some evil afoot. God forbid, but it would not take much to have us all land in trouble. Here is my advice: summon the reeve without any further delay, call the people together, and report the matter to the gendarmes. Let them conduct a thorough search . . . The vest did not run into the bushes all by itself, someone had to carry it there. And you can be sure that he did not break in just to get the vest; he must have taken something bigger, more valuable, and then he threw the vest away. This is a very dangerous business, if you please, my gracious Lady. It reeks of a criminal offence."

He was speaking slowly, in an even, garrulous tone, and it awoke in Lady Olimpiya's heart annoyance, disgust, almost a shivery feeling, like a cold, heavy, and unending autumn rain.

"Well, fine, fine!" she said, trying to stop herself from shouting irritably. "We will do everything that is necessary right away. In fact, I just sent a note to my son, the young Lord. He is better informed about matters like these than the rest of us. And then we will see what should be done."

As she was speaking, they entered the vestibule in which Paraska was still busily spreading sand over the freshly washed floor. Then they walked into the bedroom, and what they saw was something that they least expected to see.

Fr. Nestor, holding on to the sideboard, was sitting up by himself on the bed, and next to him stood Hapka, feeding him, as one would feed a child, with white bread soaked in boiled milk. The deathly pallor that had been on Fr. Nestor's face an hour earlier had vanished. Towels were wound around his head, but other than that, Fr. Nestor looked the same as ever, and it was clear that the terrible nocturnal misadventure had not left a serious mark on him.

Lady Olimpiya struck her hands together in amazement when she saw the sudden and wondrous change.

IV

"Well, how are you feeling, your Reverence?" Lady Olimpiya cried. "O my Lord, what a scare you gave us. Everyone was thinking that you had been robbed, murdered, and God knows what! . . . And I kept saying: wait, he will come to right away! Don't I know you? After all, this has happened to you many times before. Well, tell me, tell me, and let this man hear it as well . . . Do you see, gardener? What did I just tell you? You see, Father, you must have drunk some tea that was a bit too strong yesterday. A little too much rum in it, right? . . . But did I not tell you that it might hurt you? Oh, Lord, to hit your head so hard! You could very well have killed yourself! Oh my goodness! You must have struck your head against the corner of the bed, right? I've sent for the blood-letter from Zvoryna—he should be here any minute. Although I do not really think he is needed. Well, how do you feel? A trifle weak? Well, who wouldn't be! You have lost ever so much blood! But Hapka and I will take you under our wing! In a few days you will be as good as new."

She was speaking animatedly, going on and on, jumping from one topic to another as if she wanted to tire Fr. Nestor with her flow of words, to prevent him from saying anything. At the same time, she kept turning rapidly first to Fr. Nestor, then to Hapka, and then to the gardener, as if the unexpected joy had moved her greatly.

But her chattering had a completely different effect on Fr. Nestor. Upon seeing Lady Olimpiya, he fell silent. The fiery glow in his eyes began to die down. The feverish blush vanished from his old face, and it once again became pale and greenish, like that of a corpse. His whole body began shaking, and a moment later he grew enervated, his head sagged, and Hapka had to lie him back down on the pillow. His bony hand lying on the quilt clenched convulsively. And then it began to jerk uncontrollably, and he looked as if he wanted to say something. But his strength gave out, and only a sigh escaped his bloodless blue lips.

"It might be better if my gracious Lady left him alone. All of this is tiring him out. He shouldn't be talking yet," Hapka said almost in a whisper.

"What do you mean, he shouldn't be talking?" the Lady asked, sounding as if she was offended by Hapka's observation. "After all, he was talking to you just a moment ago."

"It was . . . only a few words . . ."

"What did he say to you?"

At that moment, Fr. Nestor groaned sharply, and he began tossing on his bed so violently, and his hand jerked so spasmodically, that Hapka could not respond to the question.

"You see, my gracious Lady! He has taken a turn for the worse again. Please leave! Please leave!"

"A doctor must be called," the gardener said decisively.

"What is this nonsense all about?" the Lady shouted with a stubbornness born of despair. "He is sick, he is dying—tfu! But I am telling you that in two or three days he will be up and about. After all, I know him. He has had attacks like this a couple of times before. He needs to be stirred up, to begin talking. Fr. Nestor! Come now, pull yourself together! Raise your head! Tell me, how do you feel?"

And walking up to the bed, she took him by the hand. Fr. Nestor groaned once more, and then he slowly closed his eyes, turned blue, and took on a lifeless appearance.

"My Lady! You're trying to finish him off!" the gardener shouted. "Get away from here! You can see he's dying!"

Lady Olimpiya wanted to vent her fury at the impertinence of this insolent peasant, but the sight of the unconscious Fr. Nestor was so terrible, and his hand turned so cold and wooden, that she involuntarily stepped aside. Nevertheless, she did not want to walk out of the room ahead of the gardener.

"He looks just the same," she said as if talking to herself, but loud enough for the gardener to hear. "He has attacks of *that illness*. And before the attack he walks about as if demented and hides his things in every corner. But later, no matter what —he can't remember what happened to him. One time he took off his cassock and stuffed it in the hollow of a tree. We had such a time looking for it—but we did not find it until a few months later —all rotted. And it was a brand new cassock!" Talking in this manner, Lady Olimpiya turned to go into the empty kitchen.

The gardener stopped her with a question: "Did your gracious Lady truly send for a blood-letter from Zvoryna?"

"That is my business!" the Lady responded curtly as she turned her back on him. "I truly do not understand why you are meddling in this affair to such an extent. Go and tend to your orchard, and do not stick your nose into what is of no concern to you. Do you understand?"

And without waiting for a reply, the Lady walked into the kitchen, slamming the door behind her.

"So that's how it is? Fine, then," the gardener said and, scratching his head, he walked slowly to the orchard.

He sat down in his hut and tried not to think about the Lady, about Fr. Nestor, about his illness, and his vest. But he did not succeed. He felt that something was wrong, something that made his heart burn as if it were being stung by nettles. He simply could not sit still. He got up and walked around the orchard; after looking once more into every dark and overgrown nook, but not noticing anything unusual, he returned to his hut. He once again tried to sit quietly, without thinking, but his inner disquiet began to choke him anew.

Finally, having thought of something, he got up, crossed himself, took his walking stick, and went through the orchard to the meadow, across the little bridge over the river, past the other manor, and from there to the district road that led to the little town of Zvoryna, where the gendarmes, the lower court, and the blood-letter, who took the place of a doctor, were all located.

About two kilometres past the other manor, he met up with Demenyuk and Malanka who were coming back from town.

"Where in the world have you been, Demenyuk?" he shouted.

"Oh, it's nothing but trouble that's hounding me," the old man replied.

It was only now that the gardener looked at him more closely. "O Lord! What is wrong with you?" he exclaimed. "You look half-dead, as if you'd been taken down from a cross! Your hair has turned grey overnight! Come on, speak up, Demenyuk!"

In a few brief words, Demenyuk, interrupted by Malanka's sobs, told him what had happened. Taking Herder's advice, at daybreak he went with Malanka to see the gendarmes and the blood-letter, and then reported the entire matter to the court. What would be would be, but he would not forgive the injustice that had been perpetrated against his daughter.

"And back at the manor, Demenyuk, there is an even more terrible misfortune!" the gardener interrupted him. "His Reverence was assaulted and nearly killed."

"What? His Reverence? Who did it?"

The gardener told him briefly what he knew and what he had seen. Demenyuk struck his forehead in horror, and Malanka stopped sobbing and turned ashen with fear as she listened to the gardener's story.

And then something happened that the gardener thought that he would never live to see. Demenyuk wrung his hands, clenched them over his head, and roared as if he had been seared by a hot iron bar.

"Oh woe is me! Oh, I'll lose my mind! I'm the guilty one! I'm accursed! Oh, strike me down! Oh, flog me, it's all my fault!"

And without looking at anyone, without hearing anything more, without thinking about the gardener, or his daughter, or even his own grief, he tore off to Torky as fast as his feet could carry him.

For a moment, the gardener and Malanka stood stunned, unable to comprehend what Demenyuk's sudden outcry could possibly mean.

Then Malanka ran after him, calling out: "Daddy! Daddy! Wait! Wait!"

Perplexed, the gardener watched them go; he stood there for quite a while longer, trying hard to make sense of the tangled matter. But then he gestured hopelessly: "God only knows what is going on! It's not up to me to figure them out. It's not my millet, and they're not my sparrows. They have made their beds, and they will have to lie in them. But I had better go and inform the gendarmes about what has happened."

And, pulling his hat down over his forehead and sweating profusely, he walked at a quickened pace to Zvoryna.

V

By ten in the morning, the news about a horrifying incident at the manor had flashed like a thunderbolt through the village.

No one could say for certain from whom he had heard it first, because whenever two people met up, it came out that both of them already knew that something had happened at the manor. Some said it was a robbery, others that there had been looting, and still others that there had been a murder.

The women ran from house to house telling everyone about the horribly mutilated corpses of the Lady, the young Lord, and all of the lords who had been guests at the manor and had spent the night there.

There was talk about robbers who had attacked the manor at night in search of money, about some Jews, and finally about a band of gypsies that had passed through the village a couple of days ago and, after not being given anything at the manor, had threatened to wreak revenge on the Lady.

Three neighbourhood women hastened to tell the reeve's wife the news—of course, each had her own version of what had happened—and to ask her to tell her husband the whole story.

At first the reeve did not believe them, but when the women started to swear by all that was holy that it was true, that they had heard about it from others, and that the entire village was talking about it, he spat angrily, put on his heavy wool coat, draped his seal of office over it, picked up his walking stick, and set out for the manor.

As he was walking along the road, men and women came up to him from all sides, greeting him and saying hesitantly: "Well, Mr. Reeve, sir, is it true?"

"Is what true?"

"Well, it's like this . . . they say that . . . uh . . . something is going on at the manor . . ."

"It's like this, and it's like that!" the reeve responded angrily. "I do not know anything at all. Where did you hear about it?"

"Well, there is talk. The entire village is talking. I can't remember who told me about it first."

"Humph, who told you first?" a garrulous woman added. "We all heard it first. It's as if a bell had rung over the village; there has to be something to it."

"Well, come with me to the manor, and we will find out for ourselves."

"That's right! That's the smartest thing to do, the devil take it! Because it isn't likely that anyone was caught in the act."

It was quite far from the reeve's house to the manor, and along the way more and more people joined the crowd.

Among them was Tsvyakh—he had been released from jail by the gendarme that morning. He was talking the loudest and running from house to house like a madman, telling everyone that something terrible had happened at the manor and adding that he had just heard it from this or that neighbour, whereas in actual fact he was the one who had told them about it only a moment earlier.

"Well, my good people," the reeve said, when they were near the manor, "we can't all go into the yard."

"Why not?" shouts came from within the crowd. "Who is to stop us? Let's go!"

"But we can't!" the reeve said resolutely. "What if it isn't true? What if nothing has happened there? The Lady could very well complain to the courts that we attacked her manor."

His statement that a complaint might be lodged about what could be construed as an attack pacified the crowd. They toned down their demands, all the more so because in their hearts they felt that none of them actually knew if and what kind of misfortune had occurred.

"It will be best if we do it like this," the reeve said. "You wait here, and I will go to the manor with three householders. We will find out what is going on. And if it is truly necessary, we will call you."

"Fine, fine, let it be as you say," the people chorused.

After selecting three householders, the reeve led them toward the manor yard. As he approached the gate, he cleared his throat to boost his courage, adjusted first the hat on his head and then his belt and his bag with the government seal, crossed himself, opened the gate, and walked in. He was an older man who still remembered the late Count and the feudal system very well, and therefore he never liked to have anything to do with the manor.

The new constitution had not succeeded in erasing the peasants' old feudal memories, and the division of the village into the community and the manor alienated the villagers, heaped up mounds of new, mutual irritations, suspicions, and arguments, all the more grievous because they were supposedly dealt with fairly, on a legal basis, but usually turned out to be bad news for the community, even when they did not bring the manor any visible benefits.

The reeve had scarcely opened the gate and walked into the narrow pasture that led to the manor yard, when he abruptly drew back as if he had seen something terrifying. As he tried to back up into the street, he bumped into the man behind him, who was just coming through the gate.

"What is it, Mr. Reeve, sir?" the man asked as he halted.

"Damn it!" the reeve said unwillingly. "Some old woman has spread a lot of nonsense about everyone here having been slaughtered, robbed, burglarized. But just look, the Lady is over there, in the yard—completely healthy. And the young Lord is with her."

"Well, that's true," the man said. "It appears that there was no slaughter here. But it still would be worthwhile to ask about the robbery or burglary."

"It's fine for you to say that it would be worthwhile! That's easy for you to say, because you do not know the law. But as a reeve I do not have the right to get involved with what goes on at the manor, not unless the Lady herself asks me to do so. And if she had been robbed, or burglarized, then, never fear, she would have raised a ruckus by now not only in the village, but in the entire district. Let's get away from here!"

"Oh, Mr. Reeve, sir," the two men who were last to walk through the gate remonstrated. "It doesn't seem right to come here and then turn around and flee without saying anything. The Lady and the young Lord will think that we're afraid of them."

"Well, if you want to, go ahead and ask," the reeve said. "As an official it is not proper for me to do so, but you can."

"Well yes, we can! But why should we? You have the most authority in the village, so it would be best if you did the asking," the peasants argued.

They were all curious to know what had happened at the manor, but no one had the nerve to approach the Lady whom they all disliked for her aristocratic arrogance and her implacable aggressiveness with respect to the peasants, especially if there was even the slightest justification for it.

And who knows how long they would have argued among themselves, if Adas had not seen them and approached them from the yard where, up to now, he had been engaged in an animated conversation with his mother.

"What do you folks want?" he asked sternly, coming up to them and not even responding with a nod to their bows.

The peasants stood there, bowing and looking at one another. No one dared to be the first to speak.

Finally, it was the reeve who said: "If it please your gracious Lordship, there are rumours flying through the village that something at the manor is not right . . ."

"What's not right?"

"That something has happened."

"What is supposed to have happened at the manor?"

"How am I to know? The people are buzzing, but they do not really know anything. Some say that there was a robbery, others say there was a burglary, and still others, that there was a murder. So we came . . ."

"Have you people gone mad, or what?" Adas shouted, and his face flushed with anger. "There has been no robbery, and no burglary! Nothing has happened here that would require your assistance. If we need you, we will call you, but now, please leave!" And, without waiting for a response, the young Lord turned around and was about to leave them.

"So, you see! Didn't I tell you?" the reeve said, shoving his hat down on his ears and turning around to go back into the street.

The householders who had come with him also appeared completely confused, at a loss as to what to do next.

At that moment Tsvyakh's carroty-red tousled head appeared in the half-open gate. Turning his bloated alcoholic face to the reeve, he said something in a whisper to him, but he whispered so loudly that not only the departing householders heard him, but also the young Lord.

"Don't believe him, Mr. Reeve, sir. I'm telling you that something terrible has happened here."

"Well, what is it?" the irritated reeve shouted. "Speak up if you know something, and do not tease us as you would tease a cat with a blade of grass."

"Ask the young Lord," Tsvyakh said in the same loud whisper, "what is going on with his Reverence."

"Aha! Aha!" the householders seized upon his words. "We had forgotten about that. They're saying that something happened to his Reverence. Let's go and look in on him."

"That's another matter altogether," the reeve said. "We do have the right to go and see him."

Even though Adas heard this entire conversation and was almost bursting with anger, he pretended that he had not heard anything. He wanted to play out the role that he had assumed as long as possible.

"What is it?" he asked severely once again, turning to the men. "Are you still waiting for something?"

"Well, no, your gracious Lordship," the reeve said a bit more boldly now. "Heaven forbid, we are not at all interested in your gracious Lordship and Ladyship."

"Then why are you still standing here?"

"Well, we are already on our way."

And all four of them started walking, but instead of going back out the gate they headed for the pasture that led to the manor yard.

"Where do you think you're going?" Adas asked, and his face turned ashen.

'We want to look in on our old priest, his Reverence," the reeve said as he bowed to him with an exaggerated politeness.

But now, seeing that the young Lord first flushed and then grew pale, that his expression changed, and that he was clamping his teeth as if he was seething with anxiety, the reeve began to suspect that something terrible had actually happened, something so terrible that the Lord and Lady would be happy to conceal it from the villagers' eyes.

No longer timid and indecisive as he had been only a moment ago, he now stepped forward boldly, confidently, feeling that he was in the right and on firm ground.

Even though Fr. Nestor lived in the manor yard, he did not belong to the manor household; he was only a lodger, and the community had every right to be concerned about him. The young Lord could not send them away, he could not forbid them to see their priest, and it was from him that the reeve and the other householders hoped to find out what had actually happened in the manor yard that night.

But Adas was not about to give up so easily. "You can't see his Reverence just now," he said in a slightly milder tone.

"And why is that?" the reeve asked in a slightly sharper tone, seeing that "his gracious Lordship" was becoming more amenable.

"His Reverence is sleeping."

"Sleeping? How can that be? We've known his Reverence for a long time. His Reverence never sleeps at this hour, before dinner."

"I'm telling you that he's sleeping now. You can come a little later," Adas once again shot off irritably.

But the men did not listen to him. They kept on walking; holding their caps in their hands and bowing to the young Lord, they had no thought of retreating.

Adas was shaking with fury; it looked as if he was about to pounce on the stubborn peasants with his teeth and nails.

"Mother dear," he finally shouted, "say something to these men! They are pushing their way in like swine and insisting upon seeing his Reverence. Someone has fed them a lot of nonsense, and they've come here . . ."

But he could not finish what he was saying. The reeve appeared before him, drew himself up full height, and showed him his badge of authority.

"Sir," he said slowly, but emphatically. "I am the reeve of the community. I heard that something untoward has happened to his Reverence. We have the right to see him, and you are not in a position to stop us from seeing him. And you should not be so bold as to call us swine, for we live under the same laws of the Kaiser that you do."

As he spoke, the gate opened once again. The people gathered out in the street could hear their envoys talking at length with the young Lord who was raising his voice and so, singly and in pairs, they slowly started coming into the pasture where they congregated around the reeve. The group was already quite large, and it was growing bigger by the minute.

The word "swine" that the young Lord had flung at the peasants infuriated them to the depths of their souls. They began to mutter, and then to grumble ever more loudly. Those who were at the back spoke more boldly.

"What? We're swine? Just look at him! What a snotty-nosed bastard! If we're swine, then you can be sure you won't be our swineherd! Let's go and see his Reverence, Don't pay any attention to this young whippersnapper! That's all he is!"

And the throng pushed its way forward into the manor yard. But at that moment, Lady Olimpiya blocked their path.

"Really, Adas!" she said, wringing her hands and shaking her head. "How can you say such things about such respectable householders! Mr. Reeve, sir, please forgive him! He is so worried, so upset—there has been so much unpleasantness over there . . . O Lord, and here as well! His Reverence has fallen a bit ill. He had an attack at night you know, *that illness* sometimes strikes him at night. Yesterday, along with the guests, he drank some strong tea mixed with rum, and there you have it! And at night the poor man was tossing about, fell out of bed, and banged his head. He is better now. In the morning he had a fever, but now he has had his breakfast, and he is sleeping. There is no need to worry. I give you my word that there is nothing wrong with him, but he needs to be left in peace for a couple of days. So please, go home now.

"Adas will go to Lviv today and bring back a doctor, just to be on the safe side. And in the meantime, you can be sure that nothing untoward will happen to him in my home. After all, you know that I have not mistreated him in any way in the past, and I certainly will not mistreat him now."

She spoke with an unusual gentleness, sincerity, and geniality. Her words stopped the people dead in their tracks, calmed them, disarmed them.

It was true that none of them had ever heard of Fr. Nestor having attacks of *that illness*, i.e. epilepsy, but at this moment no one stopped to think about that, and the Lady was speaking so unaffectedly and with such certainty that it never occurred to anyone to doubt the veracity of her words.

As they all turned around, ready to leave, Lady Olimpiya rejoiced in her heart that she had saved her home from this latest threat.

Adas had already winked at her with his usual cynical smile as if to say: "You spoke splendidly, mother," when suddenly, from the annex where Fr. Nestor lived, there came the sound of loud shouts, heartrending wails, and women's "ritual laments," as if they were mourning a deceased person.

Those loud, mournful cries pierced the villagers' hearts like thorny prickles.

Lady Olimpiya blanched and clutched her head; Adas jumped with a start and spun around as if he had stepped on a snake with his bare foot; and all the peasants involuntarily craned their necks as if catching with their ears something that was new, unheard-of, and terrifying.

"What is that?" the reeve asked.

"Someone is lamenting over there!" the people shouted.

"Let's go and see for ourselves what's going on," others added.

Lady Olimpiya and Adas stood dumbstruck. It did not occur to either of them to try to stop the people who, in mute silence—either simply turning away from them or casting angry and even contemptuous looks at them—rushed like a lava flow to the annex where Fr. Nestor lived.

And the crying, shouting, and wailing were spreading from the annex with an ever-growing intensity, grief, and despair. Even at a distance, two voices could be distinguished: a deep, slightly hoarse male voice and the shrill and strident voice of a girl, the voices of Demenyuk and his daughter Malanka, who were wailing over the unconscious priest.

VI

Lady Olimpiya did not follow the people to the annex. She felt that she did not have the strength, and that it would be to no avail to try and convince this crowd that nothing untoward had happened.

But what frightened her most was the sudden appearance of Demenyuk, whose voice she had instantly recognized. This man had been with Fr. Nestor until late last night and had left in such a way that she had not seen him. But had he actually left? Had he gone away? Did he know something about the events that had transpired last night, and what exactly did he know?

She racked her brains in vain, wrestling with these questions that raised a storm of anxiety in her heart, a storm that did not show any sign of abating.

If she were alone with him, she might have dared to interrogate the old man, to find out everything that he knew, to reach the point of being completely sure of herself, but she would never dream of doing that in the presence of all those other people, those suspicious and hostile people. She would not be able to withstand even one of his penetrating, questioning looks, nor would she find it within herself to ask him even the most mundane question.

Adas was no less, and perhaps even a great deal more terrified, confused, and disconcerted when he heard Malanka's voice coming from the annex.

This girl, who only yesterday he had viewed as a cute little "birdie" with whom he could pleasantly amuse himself and then, having plucked and disgraced her, cast her aside without a second thought, had now become a terrifying enemy, a powerful threat. Why? He simply could not figure that out.

After all, nothing had happened between them, she could not accuse him of anything, and what she had done for him she had done of her own free will, without being forced to do so. But nevertheless, her mournful wails and groans drilled his heart as if they were harrowing reproaches, and he was seized by an unutterable dread.

This young Lord, who had been so proud and arrogant before the peasants only a moment ago, such an apparent knight, now that he was alone with his mother turned into a small, helpless, timorous child that, having groped its way into a dark corner, is frightened by the beating of its own heart. He was on the verge of tears, his hands were shaking, every feeling within him died except for the purely animal instinct of self-preservation.

"Mummy, I can't stay here any longer!" he said in a distraught, almost tearful voice.

"Do not be afraid, my son!" Lady Olimpiya said, taking his hand. "Be strong. Do not give up."

"No, no, no, I can't stay here! Among these savage, coarse people . . . In these surroundings . . . I'll go mad, mummy, I'll go mad!"

"God help you, my dear Adas! What are you saying? We must present a united front. We must not give up! We must fight! Remember, if we do not stand strong—we are doomed."

"I can't! I just can't!" Adas clutched his head and moaned in helpless confusion. "I have to get away from here! I have to breathe freely, recoup my strength . . ."

"Well, fine, fine," the Lady said. "You know what, sonny? Get into the hansom and go to Lviv."

"To Lviv?" Adas cried joyfully.

"Yes. After all, you do have business to look after in the casino, right?"

"Aha, aha! In the casino! I had forgotten about that!" Adas said brokenly, gasping raggedly for air like a man who is choking.

"Well, that is one matter. And secondly—you must meet with your fiancée."

"What? What are you saying, mother?" Adas gaped at her and asked in astonishment.

"You must, my dear son, you must!" the Lady said firmly. "Now, after what has happened here, it is crucial that you maintain normal relations with your fiancée's family. It is critically important! You will realize this yourself when you give the matter more thought. And Edzo told me yesterday that they—the mother and daughter—are going to be in Lviv either today or tomorrow."

"But mother!" Adas exclaimed in horror, his face reflecting his agony. "Now, after what has happened here, I can't face her! I can't say a single word to her."

"What are you saying, my son? Unless she does not want you to speak to her. But that is impossible. No one knows anything as yet. And so you should go about your business as usual, with no constraints, and you should speak freely, as if nothing has happened. And in passing you can mention to Edzo that the priest whom he saw at our place has become slightly ill, but do this quite casually, by the by! Mention it as a trifling detail that is not worth talking about. And I am telling you once again, my dear Adas—you must do this. A great deal depends on it."

Her voice, her intonation, her gestures, her deliberateness and decisiveness—all served to restore the courage of the enervated young Lord. That old woman, withered, grey-haired, and stooped with age, gained stature in his eyes, and he sensed that she was strong, healthy, and brave enough for the two of them.

He felt that it was not she who would lean on him, but that he could lean on her. He recognized that the resources of her will were proving so considerable that they would suffice for the two of them.

"Fine, my dear mummy, I'll try to do everything!" he said, kissing her hand. "But just let me catch my breath for a moment in the fresh air. Let me pull myself together, calm down a bit."

"Go ahead, pull yourself together! Calm yourself! But do not forget for a moment that hard times and a formidable struggle lie ahead of us, and that we must prepare for that wisely and thoroughly. We must safeguard all our avenues of escape."

"You have superhuman strength, mother, a superhuman mind!" Adas whispered in awe.

"No, my dear son, I have only peace," Lady Olimpiya said simply. "Just imagine, last night was the first night that I slept like a rock. It is as if my nervous disorder just vanished—my nerves are perfectly calm. My head is clear, the incessant roaring is gone. I feel that my former strength has returned. And so, my son, do not forget. Go at once to Lviv, and you know what? After you have done everything that I have told you to do, come back home, if not today, tomorrow at the latest."

"Come home?" the young Lord once again looked glum.

"It is imperative! Imperative!" the Lady was speaking in the same decisive voice. "And do not come alone. Bring a doctor with you. We must do absolutely everything possible to keep up appearances."

"Fine, I'll do that," Adas said.

"Do you have money?"

"Yes. I think that what I have will be enough."

"Take care! Do not go around spending money foolishly! Be cautious and careful, and come back, if possible, today, and if not, then tomorrow, with a doctor."

The young Lord, tearing away from his mother, headed for the coach-house.

"Hey, Hadyna! Hey there, Hadyna!" he shouted. "Are the horses ready?"

"Yes, they are!" Hadyna answered from the stable.

"Hitch them to the hansom!"

"Yes, your gracious Lordship!"

"Adas! Come here a minute!" Lady Olimpiya called out.

While Hadyna led the horses out of the stable and hitched them to the small hansom, Adas once again approached his mother.

"Listen, my dear son," she said, leaning in close to him. "It is a good thing that I remembered! As soon as you get to Lviv, find Mendel."

"Mendel? The moneylender?"

"Yes, that's the one. Beg him to give you some money for a promissory note. Promise to pay any rate of interest that he asks for, and borrow at least a thousand guldens."

"But why?"

"You must, my son. When you think about it, you will see that it must be done. It is absolutely necessary to borrow that money. Or at least make sure that a promissory note is signed, or even better—a few promissory notes, two or three for smaller sums. And it would be to your advantage if you talked with several Jews, and not just one, so that the rumour spreads among them that the young Torsky lord borrowed money on such and such a day."

"Well, for them it won't be anything new!" Adas said glumly.

"So much the better, so much the better! But today it is absolutely necessary that you do that. Do you hear me, my son, absolutely necessary!"

"Well, if it's necessary, then I'll do it. That much I can do."

The hansom was ready.

"Well then, good-bye, my dear mummy!" Adas said and, kissing her hand, he jumped into the carriage.

Grabbing the reins in his left hand and the whip in his right one, he clacked at the horses and cracked his whip. The horses moved forward, and Hadyna ran up ahead to open the gate.

"My mother is a strange woman!" Adas thought, as the horses galloped down the road towards Lviv. "I can't think straight, I'm an absolute wreck, and I feel as if I am tied up in a sack, but it's only now that she has regained her peace of mind. She has even laid out a formal plan of action for me. Oh, a woman like that will not lay down her arms very quickly! There are not many people who could engage in a fight with her and win."

The horses were flying like the wind. The expansive fields of the nobles and the narrow plots of the peasants flowed by like a mottled river on both sides of the road; tall poplars, curly-leafed mountain ashes, and cherry trees that had long since been stripped of their berries flashed by above the ditches.

Far away in the distance, at the horizon's edge, glimmered *Vysoky Zamok and the rounded mound commemorating the *Lublin Union that glistened like snow in the sun.

The air was calm, warm, clear. From nearby meadows drifted the fragrance of freshly mown grass. Here and there, the sweet scent of honey wafted from broad fields of clover. Heavy-laden freight wagons and peasant ladder-wagons pulled by small, scrawny ponies rolled down the road.

The occasional pedestrian walked along a path on the other side of the ditch. And all these people, covered with sweat and dust, were headed to Lviv: some to strike a bargain at the market, some to earn a bit of money, some to engage in speculative ventures. Hundreds of thoughts, dreams, and hopes flew to the large city with its barely visible tall spires at the foot of the mountain.

Adas raced past everybody. With a cigar in his teeth and his whip at his side, he held the reins in both hands and, urging the horses on by clacking at them, he flew past the sluggish carriages and peasant wagons like a shiny apparition, leaving behind the envious looks and the unfulfilled dreams vainly straining to catch up to him.

"Now there's someone who has a good life in this world!" the dusty and weary pedestrians think.

The poor wretches do not know that the external brilliance conceals a far from brilliant interior, that in the heart of this dazzling darling of *Fortune there is incredible filth and a fiendish inferno, the likes of which they could not have conjured up even in their most terrifying dreams. They do not know that he is being chased to that distant, mysterious city by *Furies the sight of which would freeze their souls with a deathly terror.

But how are they to know this! In their souls everyday worries buzz like bumblebees that nest in the ground; and with all that buzzing, how are they to hear the droning of the stinging hornets that nest in towering oaks?

Glossary

Glossary

This glossary of terms, events, and the names of people and places, is provided for the convenience of the reader who wishes to gain a fuller appreciation of the cultural nuances and the historical, social, and political contexts of the stories.

Adas	diminutive form of Adam used by relatives and friends; also referred to as Lord Adam Torsky
akaphist	[also akathist] a laudatory service in honour of Jesus Christ, the Virgin Mary, a saint, or a revered religious personage; includes prayers of veneration, petition, and thanksgiving
Baba-Yaha	[also Baba-Yaga] the goddess of death and the progenitor of all witches in Ukrainian folklore; often depicted as a giver of gifts to deserving heroes; she knows what transpires in this world and the next, and symbolically, her hut stands on the boundary between these two worlds
Belial	the spirit of evil personified; the devil; Satan
Boykos	culturally and linguistically distinctive Ukrainian highlanders; inhabitants of the middle Carpathian Mountains in southwestern Ukraine
Catherine II	(1729-96); wife of Russian Czar Peter III whose death she is said to have orchestrated in 1762; Empress of Russia, 1762-96
Chernivtsi	historical capital and the political, cultural, and religious centre of the region of Bukovyna in Western Ukraine; near the border of Rumania
chervinets	[pl. chervintsi]; gold coin; approximate value: ten roubles/dollars
Chloe	Class. Myth.: another name for Demeter, goddess of fertility; now, a beautiful girl in pastoral literature
Church of St. Yura	now, a Ukrainian (Greek) Catholic Cathedral in Lviv; [English: St. George's Cathedral]
Constantinople	the former name of Istanbul from 330 to the capture of the city by the Turks in 1453

Glossary

Constitution	the 1867 Constitution adopted when the Austro-Hungarian Monarchy was formed granted the part of Poland under Austrian control a measure of autonomy, with its own national assembly and administrative and educational systems
Cracow	[Polish: Kraków] city in southern Poland; capital from 1320-1609
Damocles	a legendary courtier (4th c. BC) forced to sit under a sword suspended on a single hair to demonstrate the perilous nature of happiness; now, impending danger
Daphne	Class. Myth.: a beautiful nymph; was turned into a laurel tree to save her from the amorous pursuit of Appollo, the sun god
Dr. Alfons	also referred to as Lord Alfons Dzyerzhykray, and as Fonso by relatives and friends
Drohobych	industrial city in the sub-Carpathian region in Western Ukraine; until 1939, national, cultural, and educational centre
Dublyanchyk	nickname of Edzo Chapsky's younger brother who had studied in a school in Dublyany
ducat	historical gold or silver coin used widely in Europe
endorsement	a priest's assignment to a parish in Halychyna had to be confirmed by the local lord who was deemed to be the protector of the church and the parishioners
Eparchial News	a periodical publication for the clergy; included information about clerical vacanices and assignments
Fata Morgana	a mirage often visible in the Straits of Messina
Fonso	diminutive form of Alfons; also referred to as Lord Alfons Dzyerzhykray and Dr. Alfons
Fortune	the personification of chance or luck as a force in human affairs
Furies	Class. Myth.: merciless goddesses of vengeance who wreaked eternal punishment on criminals, especially those who neglected filial duty; often represented as three goddesses with hair composed of snakes
Goethe	Jonathan Wofgang von Goethe (1749-1832); German poet, dramatist, novelist, and eminent scholar
gulden	Austrian florin, roughly equivalent to a dollar
Halychyna	[also Galicia] historical region in southwest Ukraine

Glossary | 410

Heine	Christian Johann Heinrich Heine (1797-1856); German poet and essayist
Herder	Johann Gottfried von Herder (1744-1803); German critic and poet; court preacher; friend of Goethe
Kaytsya	nickname of Lord Kalyasanty
Kolomyya	historically important commercial and administrative centre in southeast Halychyna
kozak	Ukrainian equivalent of "cossack"
kreutzer	former copper coin of Austria; a penny
Lord Alfons Dzyerzhykray	also referred to as Dr. Alfons and Fonso
Lord Emil Dolenga	also referred to as Milko
Lord Kalyasanty	also referred to by his nickname: Kaytsya
Lord Tadey Rozvadynsky	also referred to as Tadzo and Tadyk
Lublin Union	a treaty signed by Poland and Lithuania in 1569 to form the Polish-Lithuanian Commonwealth, giving Poland control over a large part of Western Ukraine
Lviv	historical capital of Halychyna (Galicia) and Western Ukraine; cultural intermediary between Western and Eastern Europe
mammon	wealth regarded as an idol, or as an evil influence; Matt. 6:24; Luke 16: 9.11,13
Mephistopheles	one of seven chief devils in medieval demonology
Milko	diminutive form of Emil; also referred to as Lord Emil Dolenga
Modzrejewska	Helena Modrzejewska (1840-1909); a Polish actress; famous in England and America under the abridged name of Modjeska
officer's bond	money posted as security for an officer's fulfillment of his contract; redeemable upon completion of service, but forfeited in case of a breach of trust; also, money posted in the form of a bond at the time of an officer's marriage to protect his honour, i.e., to ensure a lifestyle commensurate with his rank
penates	Roman gods who watched over the home or the community to which they belonged
Peremyshl	[Polish: Peremy l] oldest city in Halychyna; now a Polish city near the border of Ukraine; historically, a Ukrainian political, cultural, educational, and religious centre

Glossary

Peter III	(1728-62); czar of Russia; husband of Catherine II, Empress of Russia from 1762-96; allegedly murdered by Catherine's supporters
Pharisee	a member of a Jewish sect (1st c. BC - 1st c. AD) that had pretensions to superior sanctity and was strict in its religious observances; now, a sanctimonious, self-righteous, or hypocritical person
Philippopolis	founded by Philip II of Macedonia in 342 BC; now Plovdiv, a wealthy commercial city in southern Bulgaria; in the late nineteenth century it was on one of the routes of the Orient Express (est. in 1883) from Paris to Istanbul
Prinzipienreiter	a highly rigid person; a stickler for details in matters of principle
Rus	historical name of Ukraine; see next entry: Rusyn
Rusyn	historical name, corresponding to the term Ruthenian, of a Ukrainian inhabitant of the western provinces of Ukraine that were part of the Austro-Hungarian Empire: Halychnyna, Bukovyna, and Transcarpathia
rynsky	[pl. rynski] Austrian gold coin roughly equivalent to one dollar
Samson	11th c. BC Israelite leader Judges 13-16; famous for his strength; tricked and blinded by the Philistines
Seret	town on the Seret River in southern Bukovyna in Western Ukraine until 1918; now in Rumania
Shevchenko	Taras Shevchenko (1814-1861); born a serf, his inspired visionary poetry championing liberty and justice led to exile and military penal servitude; revered both as the historical bard and the castigating prophet of Ukraine, his profound influence on its national and cultural life continues to this day
Smyrna	ancient city on the west coast of Asia Minor; the site of the Turkish city of Izmir
Stanislav	[now: Ivano-Frankivsk] a city in Subcarpathia, Western Ukraine; historically important religious, educational, and cultural centre
Stryy	a regional centre in the province of Lviv in Western Ukraine; one of the first centres of the Ukrainian national and women's movements in the late 1800s

Swabian	inhabitant of a district in Bavaria now divided among Germany, Switzerland, and France
Tadyk/Tadzo	diminutive forms of Tadey; also referred to as Lord Tadey Rozvadynsky
talyar	[pl. talyary] a thaler, a German silver coin; a dollar
Tarhovychany	members of a confederation of Polish magnates formed in 1792; their cooperation with foreign powers led to the Second and Third Partitions of Poland in the 1790s that wiped the name of Poland from the map of Europe for more than a century
Theresianum Institute	a military school for nobles founded in Vienna by Empress Maria-Theresa (1740-80)
Thomas	the apostle known as doubting Thomas would not believe that Christ had risen until he saw and touched his wounds; John 20: 24-29; now, a person who refuses to believe without proof
Torsky/Torska	in Ukrainian usage, the masculine form of this surname is Torsky; the feminine form is Torska
Towarystwo Demokratyczne	a republican-democratic political organization formed by Polish émigrés in France in the 1830s; aspired to bring the principles of the French Revolution to Poland
Vysoky Zamok	[English: High Castle] a high chalk ridge towering over Lviv; site of original fortifications going back roughly a thousand years; site of a 37-hectare park built in 1835 and a mound erected in 1869 by the Poles to commemorate the Lublin Union of 1569
Wallenrod	Lithuanian hero of the narrative poem "Konrad Wallenrod" by the Polish poet Adam Mickiewicz (1798-1855); was captured and raised in Poland by the Knights of the Teutonic Order and became their Commander-in-Chief; after discovering his roots, he leads them on a military expedition that destroys them; the poem is a thinly-veiled portrayal of the hostility of the Poles towards the Russians who occupied part of Poland from the partitions of the 1790s to 1918
year of 1848	serfdom was abolished in Halychyna in 1848

Other books available from

LANGUAGE LANTERNS PUBLICATIONS
www.languagelanterns.com

WOMEN'S VOICES IN UKRAINIAN LITERATURE

English translations of selected short fiction
by Ukrainian women authors

Translator: *Roma Franko*   Editor: *Sonia Morris*

Volume 1: The Spirit of the Times
Olena Pchilka (1861-1930), ***Nataliya Kobrynska*** (1855-1920)
Soft cover, 480 pp.; ISBN 0-9683899-0-2 (v.1) 1998

Volume II: In the Dark of the Night
Dniprova Chayka (1861-1927), ***Lyubov Yanovska*** (1861-1933)
Soft cover, 480 pp.; ISBN 0-9683899-1-0 (v.2) 1998

Volume III: But . . . The Lord Is Silent
Olha Kobylianska (1863-1942), ***Yevheniya Yaroshynska*** (1868-1904)
Soft cover, 480 pp.; ISBN 0-9683899-2-9 (v.3) 1999

Volume IV: From Heart to Heart
Hrytsko Hryhorenko (1867-1924), ***Lesya Ukrainka*** (1871-1913)
Soft cover, 480 pp.; ISBN 0-9683899-3-7 (v.4) 1999

Volume V: Warm the Children, O Sun
Stories about childhood and adolescence by several of the authors
Soft cover, 480 pp.; ISBN 0-9683899-4-5 (v.5) 2000

Volume VI: For a Crust of Bread
Stories about social values and marriage by several of the authors
Soft cover, 480 pp.; ISBN 0-9683899-5-3 (v.6) 2000

Ukrainian Children's Literature in English Translation

Translator: *Roma Franko* **Editor:** *Sonia Morris*

Once in a Strange, Faraway Forest
Yaroslav Stelmakh

Colour illustrations by
Anatoliy Vasylenko

A whimsical tale for children and their favourite adults

Soft cover, 96 pp.; ISBN 0-9683899-8-8   2001

Ukrainian Short Fiction in English

Translator: *Roma Franko* **Editor:** *Sonia Morris*

Broken Wings
Anatoliy Dimarov

Transitions, choices, and turning points: coming of age in Soviet Ukraine.

Soft cover, 320 pp.; ISBN 0-9683899-6-1   2001

Ukrainian Short Fiction in English

Translator: *Roma Franko* **Editor:** *Sonia Morris*

A Hunger Most Cruel
Anatoliy Dimarov
Y evhen Hutsalo
Olena Zvychayna

The Human Face of the 1932-1933 Terror-Famine in Soviet Ukraine

Soft cover, 288 pp.; ISBN 0-9683899-7-X   2002

Ukrainian Short Fiction in English

Translator: *Roma Franko*   Editor: *Sonia Morris*

Passion's Bitter Cup

Selected Prose Fiction by

Mykola Chernyavsky
Ivan Franko
Hnat Khotkevych
Yevhen Mandychevsky
Mykhaylo Mohylyansky
Stepan Vasylchenko
Volodymyr Vynnychenko
Sylvester Yarychevsky
Mykhaylo Zhuk

Soft cover, 352 pp.; ISBN 0-9735982-0-4   2004

Ukrainian Short Fiction in English

Translator: *Roma Franko*   Editor: *Sonia Morris*

Riddles of the Heart

Selected Prose Fiction by

Mykola Chernyavsky
Ivan Franko
Hnat Khotkevych
Mykhaylo Kotsyubynsky
Osyp Makovey
Mykhaylo Mohylyansky
Panas Myrny
Leonid Pakharenko
Valeriyan Pidmohylny
Stepan Vasylchenko
Volodymyr Vynnychenko

Soft cover, 352 pp.; ISBN 0-9735982-1-2   2004